GILDED TEARS

A RUSSIAN MAFIA ROMANCE

NICOLE FOX

Copyright © 2021 by Nicole Fox

All rights reserved.

No part of this book may be reproduced in any form or by any electronic or mechanical means, including information storage and retrieval systems, without written permission from the author, except for the use of brief quotations in a book review.

❀ Created with Vellum

MAILING LIST

Sign up to my mailing list!
New subscribers receive a FREE steamy bad boy romance novel.

Click the link below to join.
https://sendfox.com/nicolefox

ALSO BY NICOLE FOX

Kovalyov Bratva Duet

Gilded Cage (Book 1)

Gilded Tears (Book 2)

Princes of Ravenlake Academy (Bully Romance)

Can be read as standalones!

Cruel Prep

Cruel Academy

Cruel Elite

Bratva Crime Syndicate

Can be read in any order!

Lies He Told Me

Scars He Gave Me

Sins He Taught Me

Belluci Mafia Trilogy

Corrupted Angel (Book 1)

Corrupted Queen (Book 2)

Corrupted Empire (Book 3)

De Maggio Mafia Duet

Devil in a Suit (Book 1)

Devil at the Altar (Book 2)

Kornilov Bratva Duet

Married to the Don (Book 1)

Til Death Do Us Part (Book 2)

Heirs to the Bratva Empire

Can be read in any order!

Kostya

Maksim

Andrei

Tsezar Bratva

Nightfall (Book 1)

Daybreak (Book 2)

Russian Crime Brotherhood

Can be read in any order!

Owned by the Mob Boss

Unprotected with the Mob Boss

Knocked Up by the Mob Boss

Sold to the Mob Boss

Stolen by the Mob Boss

Trapped with the Mob Boss

Volkov Bratva

Broken Vows (Book 1)

Broken Hope (Book 2)

Broken Sins *(standalone)*

Other Standalones

Vin: A Mafia Romance

Box Sets

Bratva Mob Bosses (Russian Crime Brotherhood Books 1-6)

Tsezar Bratva (Tsezar Bratva Duet Books 1-2)

Heirs to the Bratva Empire

The Mafia Dons Collection

The Don's Corruption

GILDED TEARS
BOOK TWO OF THE KOVALYOV BRATVA DUET

I'LL MAKE HER CRY GILDED TEARS IF SHE EVER RUNS AGAIN.

Esme was just a girl in a nightclub.

Until I made her the center of my world.

The queen to my kingdom.

The mother to my child.

We had the future in our hands.

And then she left me on that mountain to die.

Little by little, I clawed my way back.

Back to life.

Back to strength.

Back to where I belong.

And now, the time has come to reclaim what belongs to me.

Once upon a time, Esme thought I was her savior.

She thought wrong.

Because by the time I find her again…

I'll be her worst nightmare.

GILDED TEARS is the second book in the Kovalyov Bratva duet. Make sure you've started with Artem and Esme's story from the beginning in Book 1, GILDED CAGE.

1

ESME

THE MOUNTAIN LODGE, PICACHO DEL DIABLO, MEXICO

Everything has gone wrong at once.

The seconds after Artem leaves stretch out into endless eternity. Minutes slither past, mocking me.

Don't just sit there.

Don't just panic.

But I don't know what else to do. I can barely form a coherent thought.

The cabin is quiet and moonlight splices in through the tiny little cracks in the blinds that Artem pulled down before he left.

How long since he walked out that door? I know it's been a minute, maybe two, but it feels like so much longer.

My heart drums hard against my chest. I know it's warning me, but I don't know what it's warning me against.

I feel my baby turn inside me and I cry out in shock, in pain. I place a hand over my stomach and try to infuse as much calm as I can into my voice.

"Hush, little bird," I whisper. "We're going to be all right. Papa's gonna come right back."

Why does that sound like a lie?

Images of dead men and circling birds of prey fill my head. I see blood and violence and my hand clinging onto a gun I don't want to hold.

The panic took root in my soul the day I saw the dead man down the ravine. It's been dormant until now, just biding its time and waiting for an excuse to come out and torture me.

But it's more than just my own head creating monsters.

It's also the look on Artem's face before he had left.

That was the look of a man with blood on his mind.

The look of a man who had faced violence so many times that he had become immune to its hold.

In other words… the look of a man who lied to me when he said he was ready to give it all up.

I can't bring myself to relax or lie still. So I abandon my search for calm and head out of the room.

"Cillian."

"Heyo, there she is," he mumbles cheerily.

But I can tell that that his unruffled façade is forced.

He gives me a tight, unconvincing smile. "It's late. You should be in bed."

"You should be with Artem."

I hadn't meant it to sound so accusing, but Cillian flinches back slightly. It's the first chink in his armor. I wonder how long it'll take him to be honest with me.

He shrugs nonchalantly. "That old grouch? I have more fun with you."

I narrow my eyes at him and join him on the couch. One glance tells me that there's a gun placed surreptitiously under the cushion beside him. I pretend that I don't notice.

"You mean, Artem forced you to stay back to protect me," I say.

Cillian's smile is my answer.

"You're the most important thing in the world to him, Esme. You and that baby you're carrying."

"He doesn't know what's out there."

"He can handle himself."

I sigh uncomfortably and lean back against the sofa.

"I don't know how you do it," I tell him. "Isn't your stomach in knots for at least twenty-three hours of the day?"

Cillian considers that question for a moment. "I suppose it used to be. At the beginning, when I was a green boy with no experience and little confidence. But it's like anything else in life—you get used to it."

"I don't want to get used to it."

"I know," Cillian says softly.

"Can I ask you something?" I venture.

He raises his eyebrows just a little. "Shoot."

I frown.

He laughs softly. "Sorry, wrong choice of word," he corrects. "Let's stick with, 'Go ahead.'"

"What was Marisha like?" I ask as delicately as I can.

Cillian's expression doesn't change, but I can tell he's surprised that I'm asking him at all.

"You're better off asking Artem," he says evasively.

"I'm asking you."

"Marisha was… She was lovely," he admits. "I liked her a lot."

"Was she cut out for this life?" I ask, feeling my throat constrict just a little.

"No one's really cut out for this life," he says. "It chooses most of us. After that, there's no going back."

"How did the life choose her?" I'm stroking my belly again and again. I don't dare to meet his eyes.

"Well, she fell in love with Artem," Cillian replies. "She had no choice after that. If she wanted him, she had to accept the baggage he came with. She knew she couldn't have one without the other."

"Like I'm trying to, you mean."

Cillian's eyes soften. "That's not what I mean, Esme."

"I know," I sigh. "Did he tell you?"

"That you want him to walk away from the Bratva?" Cillian asks. "Yeah. He told me."

I can't tell what he's thinking. I can't decipher if he resents me for trying to pull Artem away from a life that they've shared together for so long.

So I just ask him.

"Do you hate me for that?" I ask directly.

Cillian does a double-take. He stares at me in surprise. "Of course not," he says with all apparent sincerity. "Why would you even think that?"

"If Artem walks away from the Bratva, that would change a lot between the two of you," I reason.

Cillian shakes his head. "We wouldn't be brothers-in-arms any longer," he concedes. "But we would still be friends. That wouldn't change."

"So you don't think I'm crazy for wanting a life that's separate from all this?"

"No, I don't," he answers. "It makes sense, really. Happy endings don't exactly go hand in hand with life in the Bratva. You want more for yourself and your child. I can hardly blame you for that."

"Thank you."

There's a moment of silence. Then, without looking at me, Cillian murmurs, "If Saoirse showed up at my doorstep and asked me to walk away from everything, I would."

It's my turn to do a double-take. "Really?"

"Really."

"Even after all this time?"

Cillian looks up at me. "Is that pathetic?"

I feel emotion well up inside me as I look at his face. All I want to do is hug him. For someone who always looks so happy-go-lucky, right now, his expression is haunted.

I settle for moving a little closer to him on the sofa, and I place my hand over his.

"No," I say as strongly as I can muster. "It isn't."

"That's nice of you," he says. He tries to smile. "But I know it is. She's long since moved on. She doesn't spend her days thinking about me."

"You don't know that."

"I do."

"You just need to find the right girl," I argue.

I don't even know if I'm right. I just want to be able to tell him something remotely hopeful.

"Maybe that's it," Cillian laughs. "Maybe I need to find my Esme."

I blush a little and sit back, trying not to peer out into the night searching for Artem. It's probably been about fifteen minutes since he left, but it feels like an hour has passed on this sofa.

"He'll be all right, Esme," Cillian says, sensing my worry. "Have you ever seen him fight?"

"A few times actually," I admit. "It's terrifying."

He nods knowingly. "Artem is an instinctive fighter. He was always a force to be reckoned with in combat. I wouldn't want to go up against him."

"He could be outnumbered."

"Sure, by bears," Cillian fires back, though I don't quite believe that he believes that. "We don't know that a human being triggered the perimeter traps."

"Do I need to remind you about the man I saw down the ravine?"

"Artem can handle it," Cillian says again.

But this time, it sounds like he's trying to convince himself.

2

ESME

I get to my feet and groan with frustration. With nothing else to do, I start pacing.

Cillian just sits on the sofa and watches me. But his body is tense and his eyes are alert.

"Esme."

"We haven't heard anything, Cillian."

"That's a good thing."

I run my fingers through my hair, feeling as though I'm going insane. "Maybe we should go out there and see if Artem needs some help."

Cillian frowns. "We are not going anywhere. You're staying right here."

"Cillian!"

I'm about to argue harder when a gunshot blasts through the night.

I gasp. My heart is thundering so loudly that I almost miss the second gunshot.

"Cillian!" I scream again. I rush over to him just as he gets to his feet.

I need him to say something. Anything. Lie to me if he has to.

It was just rocks falling.

A car backfiring.

A bird calling.

But please, for the love of God, tell me *something*.

Cillian says nothing.

"We have to help him!" I beg desperately.

I keep looking out through the window, hoping for a sign.

Only darkness stares back.

But that doesn't scare me. Not anymore.

At long last, Cillian turns his gaze to me. With a grim set to his mouth, he says, "No."

"No?" I repeat, staring at him in shock. "We just heard two gunshots!"

"Artem told me to stay here with you, no matter what. Two gunshots falls in the 'no matter what' category."

"I don't think he assumed he was going to be facing a fucking firing squad!" I snap in near-tears—just as another gunshot tears through the silence.

"My don gave me an order," Cillian says tonelessly.

"Your don!?" I repeat furiously. "Your fucking don gave you an order? Cillian, he's not your don, he's your friend!"

"Esme, you don't understand—"

"I *do* understand!" I yell.

"No, you don't," Cillian interrupts. "Because if you did, you would understand that Artem can survive a firing squad if he has to. But he won't be able to survive losing you."

"I'll be fine—"

"He barely survived losing Marisha, Esme," he says, raising his voice this time. "He's not going to survive losing you. And he'll never forgive me for leaving you, either."

I feel desperate tears slip down my cheeks. My voice falters.

I turn away from Cillian as a new round of gunshots pelts the silence. I lunge for the cupboard under the sink and pull out one of the guns that Artem has stashed when he thought I wasn't looking.

It feels heavy and ungainly in my hand. I hate it instantly.

But I'm determined to use it if I need to.

I rush to the door, ready to go out.

Only for Cillian to block my path.

He shakes his head sadly. Those mirthful blue eyes are brimming with sorrow.

"Esme, you know I can't let you walk out of here."

"Too bad you won't be able to stop me."

For some reason, I didn't really believe Cillian would go this far.

But as I tried to walk around him, he blocks me again.

"I can't just leave him out there," I say desperately, my eyes looking past Cillian into the darkness of the mountains.

"You're right."

Relief floods through me. I see the panic and fear in Cillian's eyes, too.

We're both aware that the gunfire has ceased.

Now there's nothing but silence—dark, taunting silence that could mean absolutely anything.

"Let's go," I say fiercely. "I'm ready."

To my surprise, he shakes his head again. "No. You're staying. I'll go."

"Cillian, I—"

He moves so fast I don't even have time to react. He rips the gun suddenly from my hands and pushes me down onto one of the chairs on the table.

"What the fuck are you doing?" I demand once I've processed what the hell just happened.

"Making sure you can't leave."

Acting quickly, he grabs the sheet I gave him earlier that night and uses it to tie me to the chair.

I try to struggle, try to thrash, but my movements are sluggish with shock and his knots are swift and secure.

By the time he's done, I can barely budge.

"Are you fucking serious, Cillian?" I hiss at him.

"I'm sorry," he says, voice drenched in apology. "I'm sorry, Esme. But I'm not taking you with me."

"Fuck!" I scream.

I tug as hard as I can.

The knots don't move at all.

Cillian takes the gun, as well as one of his own, and heads out the door. He glances back at me from the threshold, his blue eyes catching the moonlight for a moment.

Then he disappears into the darkness.

3

ESME

I scream Cillian's name again and again until my throat is hoarse and my voice is gone.

But I know that he's not coming back to untie me.

I can't hear a thing. The weight in my chest just keeps getting heavier and heavier until I feel that familiar shooting pain lancing through my stomach.

The last time I felt it was weeks ago.

Right after Stanislav's funeral.

When I'd first discovered that Artem was responsible for Cesar's death.

My baby kicks hard. I know that my rising heart beat and intense panic can't be good for him.

"It's okay, little bird," I say, falling back to my brother's old nickname for me. "It's okay. We're going to be all right."

I'm on the verge of saying that his Papa is gonna be all right, too, but I stop short at the last moment.

I don't know if that's true.

For the moment, I don't even know if I'll ever see him again.

The thought races through me like poison. "Oh, God," I gasp as claustrophobia grips my throat and tightens its cold fingers around my heart. "I can't breathe… I can't…"

But there is no one to help me.

Another shooting pain courses through me, worse than the first.

My stomach feels suddenly twice as large and twice as heavy and I try to breathe and I try to calm down, both for myself and for the child inside me, but my thoughts are chaotic and uncontrollable and they're rising up in me like a dark swirling tide and I can't get my heart to ease and the blood is pounding so hard in my temples and the night outside is so horrifyingly silent and why won't anyone come to help me and where is Artem and where is Cillian and who is out there in the darkness and what do they want and where did they come from and oh, God, oh, God, oh, God, if something doesn't happen soon then I feel like I'm going to—

"Breathe, Esme," I whisper out loud.

∼

MANY YEARS EARLIER

"Breathe, Esme."

"Cesar?"

My eyes fly open to find my brother kneeling in front of me, his gaze fixed on me with concern.

I don't know how he managed to get so close to me without me noticing.

But then again, my head had been buried in my hands while I cried.

"What's wrong, little bird?" Cesar asks.

"Papa hit me."

Cesar's eyes flare with anger. "He did what?"

I nod as another tear slips down my cheek. "He asked me to play piano for his friends and I said I didn't want to. I don't like his friends. They look at me weird."

"So he slapped you?"

"He said that he was my father and I was to do whatever he asked of me."

I place my hand against the cheek Papa slapped. It still stings, but I don't know if the pain is real or imagined. Perhaps it's a bit of both.

Cesar sits down beside me on the grass and takes my hand. "I remember the first time Papa hit me."

I look at him in shock. "Papa's hit you?"

Cesar nods. "I was younger than you are now," he tells me. "Probably about seven."

"What happened?" I ask. I'm still sobbing but not as hard anymore. My breath comes a little easier as I lean into my brother's warmth.

"I can't remember," Cesar replies. "I know that sounds strange, but I honestly can't remember. I was doing something he didn't want me doing. Or maybe I said something he didn't like. Either way, he punched me in the face. My nose started bleeding, I thought it was broken."

"Was it?"

"No," Cesar shakes his head. "But his ring left a mark."

I gasp, noticing the tiny white scar on the bridge of his nose. "That's how you got it?"

"That's how I got it," he says. "But Papa never hit me again after that. You know why?"

I shake my head and wait for the massive revelation that I think is going to come.

"I never gave him a reason to," Cesar tells me. "I do whatever Papa wants, and I do it however he wants. And you must learn to do the same."

For some reason, I shudder. "What if I can't?"

"Does your cheek hurt, little bird?" Cesar asks.

I nod. "A lot."

"It will get a lot worse if you continue to defy him. I know you're growing up, but that's only going to make him harder on you."

"I'd rather take the pain than do everything I'm told to do," I snap defiantly.

Cesar smiles. "You're braver than I am. But you're also young. Pain takes all sorts of different forms, and it stays with you, little sister. It works its way into your skin and never leaves. You and I have been born to a don. Our life will never be easy. We will always be bound by the expectations of the Moreno cartel."

"Then maybe I don't want to be a Moreno anymore."

Cesar raises his eyebrows and looks me dead in the eye. "If you're not a Moreno, who will you be?" he asks.

I shrug. "Someone else."

He ruffles my hair. "That's a good plan."

"Are you making fun of me?" I demand.

"No, I'm not," Cesar says softly. I believe him. "You're not just braver than I am, little bird. You're smarter, too. I don't have the option of not being a Moreno. But you might."

"How?"

"You might have to disappear one day," he tells me. "Find a quiet corner of the world to call your own and just… live."

"Why would I have to disappear?" I ask, alarmed by the notion of disappearing at all.

"Because if you don't, Papa will look for you," Cesar tells me. "And if he finds you…"

"I'll be back to being a Moreno," I finish.

Cesar's eyes are dark with grief. I notice that his fingers tremble slightly. I reach out and take his hand, massaging it gently between mine.

"I can't disappear, Cesar," I say at last.

"Why not?"

"Because I can't leave you."

He smiles at that, but he's still sad—I can see it in his eyes. "And I can't leave you," he replies.

"Then I'll just do what you do. I'll listen to Papa and I won't give him a reason to hit me again."

Cesar nods, but he doesn't look proud like I'd hoped he would.

He looks… broken.

"You could disappear with me," I say softly. "We could disappear together."

Cesar raises his eyes to my face, but it's like he's looking right through me. "I shouldn't have mentioned it at all. There is no escape, Esme," he replies. "Not from this life. It consumes you whole until there's nothing left. The real world won't accept you after you've been spit out by this one."

The look in his eyes scares me. "Cesar..."

"Let's not talk about disappearing anymore, okay?" he says abruptly.

I have no choice but to nod.

∼

I open my eyes once more.

Fresh tears slip free. I had long since forgotten about that memory. The fact that I've remembered it now feels ominous and revelatory in equal measure.

I take a deep breath. It comes easy this time. Easier, at least.

I strain against my bindings. Suddenly, I feel one of the knots give.

Just a little bit. Just a tiny sliver of hope.

But that's enough.

I suck in another inhale, regroup, and push harder. With each shove, the sheet slackens a tiny bit more. And more. And more.

Until, with one final push, I manage to get one hand free.

From there, it's easy enough to disentangle myself from the sheet. I wriggle out of it and rush to the bedroom.

Crouching down on all fours, I pull out the gun that Artem's stowed under the bed. Once I'm armed, I turn off all the lights in the cabin and slip outside, into the shadows and the moonlight.

The night outside is dewy and crisp. Bright stars overhead, and the trees standing tall and silent like soldiers.

My hand is weak and sweaty with anxiety as I hold the weapon and move forward into the trees. I don't know what difference I can hope to make, but I'm resolved to try.

Maybe one bullet in this gun will mean the difference between life and death for Artem.

I don't hear any noise to guide me. Ten minutes in, I realize that I don't even know which direction to walk. I'm walking in circles for all I know. Trapped in my own head. Held back by my lack of instincts, my lack of experience.

And then I hear something.

A sharp noise that has me freezing in place.

It snaps me out of my daze. Suddenly, I'm acutely and painfully aware of the position I've put myself in.

I've walked into the forest without any notion of what I'm going to face.

I have no protection, except for the gun in my hand, which isn't much, seeing as how I'm barely confident in which end to aim where.

I should have listened to Artem.

I should have listened to Cillian.

I should've never left the lodge.

I hear the sound again, and this time, I'm certain of what it is—footsteps, coming right towards me.

The night air turns cold against my skin. I hear the trill of frightened birdsong, the chirp of crickets, the whistling and crunching and motion in the brush that surrounds me.

And underneath it all, those footsteps, like thunder behind the storm clouds.

Please, dear God, let it be Artem. Let it be Cillian.

The owner of the footsteps appears from between two tall trees.

It's not a friend.

I don't know who it is beyond that. But he sure seems to know me.

"Well, well, well," the man says. "I thought I got stuck with the grunt work, scanning the area for Artem's men. And I stumble across Artem's woman instead. Lucky me, huh?"

I take a step back and keep my arm sheathed behind my hip. I don't want him to see that I have a gun until the last possible second. The element of surprise is all I have at this point.

"Budimir will be thrilled," the man continues in slightly accented English. "He assumed you'd escaped us. A smart woman wouldn't have chosen to stay with Artem. He's a dead man walking."

I flinch back at his words, but I can't move. I can see the gun in his hand, too. He's probably a hell of a lot more skilled with it than I am.

"He's going to kill you all," I snap.

"Can I ask you a question?"

"No."

"Why *did* you stay with him?" he asks.

The way he speaks to me strikes me as odd. It's as though we're old friends and he's resuming a conversation we left half completed.

"He's my husband," I reply, chin held high.

He raises his eyebrows. "Is it possible that you actually care for him? That he cares for you?"

The shock is evident in his tone, but I bite down on my tongue. He's going to use me as leverage, as bait... and I've just offered myself up on a silver fucking platter.

He takes my silence as an answer. Whistles softly in surprise.

"Well, that's going to make this a lot harder for him, isn't it?"

That gets my attention. "What are you talking about?" I demand, unable to keep the fear from my voice.

He drops the "old friends" voice and lets the real underlying venom glisten through.

"I'm talking about the fact that I'm claiming you for my own," he hisses, a dark smile playing across his face. "Then I'm going to drag you to Artem and he can watch as my seed slips out of you."

A shiver of fear runs down my spine, but I'll be damned if I let him see that.

This son of a bitch is confident he can overpower me. Like it or not, the odds are definitely in his favor.

But I'm not about to go down without a fight.

I'm stronger than I look, motherfucker.

4

ARTEM

I stare at the man I used to think of as a second father.

Budimir's face is familiar, and yet completely unrecognizable to me. Is it possible I used to think of him as kindly? Is it possible I used to think of him as loyal?

Everything I thought I knew about him confronts me as he stares me down, his beady eyes gleeful and triumphant.

"I must admit," Budimir remarks, "this is the last place I expected to find you."

"That's why I'm here," I retort.

I look around at the men that surround me. I recognize only two of them. What happened to the other men of the Bratva, the men I served and bled with, the men who were once loyal to me?

Did they turn their backs on the true don?

Or did Budimir have them killed?

"I can see the wheels in your head spinning, nephew," Budimir says, taking a step forward. "Do you have nothing you want to say to me?"

"I have many fucking things I would like to say to you," I snarl.

Budimir chuckles as he looks around at his men. "What did I tell you, boys?" he asks. "My nephew is nothing more than a wild animal without discipline or intelligence."

"Is that what you think of me?" I ask evenly.

"Come now, Artem," he says. "It's not an insult if it's true."

I take a step forward, but at the slightest motion, half a dozen guns cock in my direction.

Gritting my teeth, I freeze. Attacking now would not only be stupid and short sighted—it would also be proving the bastard right.

"Really, Artem," Budimir sighs, "I had hoped to have a long-awaited chat with you. I can't do that if you look so damn aggressive."

"The time for conversation is done," I snap.

Budimir glances at the man to his right and nods once. Five soldiers begin to creep toward me from different angles.

I don't bother with my gun. The moment I open fire, they would cut me down in a hail of bullets.

But they've all holstered their weapons, too. They're closing down the distance to where I stand in the middle of the clearing one slow step at a time. Hands empty.

Let us fucking brawl, then.

The moment the first man comes within punching distance of me, I clench my fist and send my knuckles straight to his face.

He tries to block at the last minute, but he's too late and he ends up with a mouthful of blood and dirt.

I turn fast, ready with my second punch. But then I feel something snake around my legs.

Is that a fucking lasso?

Before I can do anything else, my ankles are yanked from under me. I hit the ground hard, facedown in the muck. The wind whooshes painfully out of my lungs.

The rest of them are on me instantly. A flurry of kicks and nightsticks to the ribs, the back, the legs.

It's over as soon as it starts. I'm tugged upright onto my knees and someone secures my hands behind my back and lashes my ankles together.

I spit blood onto the earth in front of me. I can't move unless I want to topple over. Trussed up like a fucking pig.

"Ah," Budimir says approvingly, as he moves closer, "you've finally learned your place, nephew. On your knees in front of me."

I snarl up at him. "The man you force on his knees will rise again, stronger and more vicious than before."

It's something Father used to say. Something I never paid much mind to when he was still alive.

Budimir just laughs. "If he can get up at all. Which you definitely won't be able to do when I'm done with you."

"So then do it," I growl. "Kill me and be done with it."

Budimir's eyes flash for a moment and I detect a note of surprise. "Oh, I will," Budimir nods. "But not just yet."

I roll my eyes. "You always had a flare for drama, didn't you?"

"This coming from the man who drank his weight in alcohol for months after losing his whore."

"She was my fucking *wife*."

Budimir shakes his head at me like I'm a stupid child who isn't understanding. "I've had wives, Artem. Several, in fact," he muses.

"And I have not mourned for a single one. That's something I've never understood about you."

He eyes me strangely, as though he's genuinely curious about the answer.

"I've never understood the attachments you've formed with these women. They should be merely distractions, a place to put your cock for the night. But you… you seem to care."

"You're right," I nod. "You wouldn't understand. It's beyond your capacity."

Annoyance zips across his eyes. There's so much pride there that it's a wonder I never noticed it before.

"It must have burned you," I guess softly. "Taking orders from my father, doing his bidding, and deferring to him at every turn. Must've fucking chewed away at your soul every goddamn time. Is that why you did this?"

"I've been planning this little takeover for the last few years, yes," Budimir agrees. "Which is right around the time I started poisoning your father."

I freeze, my blood going cold as I repeat Budimir's words in my head.

"What the fuck did you just say?"

"That got your attention… Hmm, yes," Budimir nods. "I've been poisoning him for years now. Old bastard wouldn't go down easy, though."

My heartbeat thunders in my chest, loud and insistent and pumping with anger so strong that I bite down on my tongue and taste blood almost immediately.

It takes a moment to focus my attention back on Budimir.

When I do, I see red.

"You fucking bastard," I spit. "Traitor. Coward. Murderer."

"You really didn't know?"

The red haze of my fury intensifies, but I can't bring myself to respond.

There is no excuse for my inattention. I should've seen. I should've stopped it.

I should've saved my father.

"Of course you didn't know," Budimir tuts smugly. He's obviously trying to goad me. "You were so wrapped up in your own anger, your pain, your grief, that you never saw what was right under your nose."

I feel sick with shame, but I can't dwell on that right now.

"Your father was a sharp man," my uncle continues. "And he was dedicated to the Bratva. He knew I had ambitions, he knew I wasn't always content with being his second, but he also assumed my loyalty would trump the rest."

I say nothing. I just kneel in the dirt and think about how I could've been so blind.

"His assumption was not the only thing that worked against him however," Budimir continues. "I was careful and smart and above all, I was patient. I started poisoning him in doses so small it was nearly impossible to detect. As his condition deteriorated and doctors got involved, I made sure to find the right doctors, the ones that would tell him what I wanted them to, rather than the truth of what was happening to him."

Each new revelation feels like a hot brand being pushed into my flesh. My restraints are tight and I can barely move in them, but I push them against the ropes anyway, leaving gnashes against my wrists as I apply more and more pressure.

"The two of you have run the Bratva together for four decades," I point out. "Four fucking decades. He was your *brother*!"

"True enough," Budimir admits. "And I regret the lengths I was forced to go to. But he was not fit to lead the Bratva."

"Are you out of your fucking mind?" I demand, taking that statement personally. "His name struck fear into everyone who heard it."

"He built his reputation well. But he was not as ambitious or as ruthless as he should have been. Age and illness was making him weak. And the sicker he got, the more he spoke about you."

I raise my eyebrows and hold my breath, unsure if I want to hear what was coming next.

"He was nervous of you," Budimir says. "He was uncertain of how you might lead, but he was still convinced that you would rise to the challenge."

His words slap me right across the face. I feel a strange sense of loss pass through me.

It makes me realize how little time I spent with Stanislav. How little I really knew about the man.

All our conversations inevitably turned into arguments. After a point, I had tried to avoid them altogether.

Perhaps if I'd put my pride aside, I might have been better able to know the man I was forced to bury.

"I knew I couldn't hand the Bratva over to you," Budimir goes on, darkness edging back into his tone. "You're not fit to lead us. You're not fit to lead *me*."

I raise my eyes to his, wiping them of emotion first. "So that's it, then?" I ask. "You didn't want to take orders from your nephew."

"I was insulted that Stanislav didn't even consider the possibility that I might have more to offer than you," he continues. "I have no sons, which means you would have inherited the Bratva in time."

"After you."

Budimir nods. "After me. I floated the suggestion one morning some years ago when you were still in the throes of grief over your woman. You had been a boundless disappointment and I felt sure that Stanislav would see the wisdom in my suggestion."

"He denied you," I guess.

"Denying me would have been one thing," Budimir grits. "He treated it as a joke. Practically laughed in my face."

I grind my teeth. Mistake after mistake after mistake that I made. It cost my father his life.

It's about to cost me mine.

"You still hear his laughter, don't you?" I ask. Goading him is the only real weapon I have at my disposal at this point. I might as well go down swinging.

"Every single fucking day," Budimir seethes.

My muscles clamp tight with fury, but I remain on my knees as adrenaline courses through my body.

My uncle blinks and looks around like he's waking up out of a trance. "Enough. Where's the girl?"

I don't flinch. Don't so much as blink as I glance up at him, my eyebrows knitting together.

"What?"

"The girl," Budimir fills in impatiently. "Moreno's daughter."

"Oh," I say like I'm just now understanding. "So you don't have her?"

Budimir frowns. "You're saying you don't either?"

"The last time I saw her was in the clinic right before your men stormed the place," I tell him. "I came back but you had already taken the clinic and she had disappeared."

"Ah, yes," Budimir recalls. "I do believe you left me a message."

I remember the blood message carved into the traitor's skin.

Tvoi dni sochteny.

Your days are numbered.

"You never did come for me, though," Budimir muses, almost as an afterthought. He sounds almost disappointed. "I really expected more from you. I expected you to want revenge."

"I do."

"Really?" Budimir asks. "As far as I can see, you've been hiding up here in the mountains all by yourself."

"You didn't give me much of a choice."

Budimir smiles. "As I said to Stanislav enough times, you are nothing more than a disappointment. The girl should have been married to me. I would have used her to full advantage."

"Another request that my father obviously denied?" I ask.

I try to hide how my blood boils at the thought of Esme in Budimir's bed. His nasty fingers over her skin, threading through her hair…

Over my dead fucking body.

"Stanislav was blind when it came to you," Budimir goes on. He's feeling very fucking long-winded tonight, it seems. "You always thought he was hard on you. And he was, to an extent, but mostly to your face. Behind closed doors, he fought for you. Why, I don't know. I think he was trying to preserve his legacy. And I suppose he wanted to see you happy."

It feels like a knife, shiny and cold, is being plunged into my ribcage. I can feel the chafing around my wrists where the skin has started to tear down against the rope.

But I welcome the pain.

I need the distraction.

"Don't you worry. You won't have to bear the weight of the Bratva any longer," Budimir reassures me. "Once I've dealt with you, I will find your pretty little wife and make her mine. And in doing so, I will solidify whatever connections her father maintained. The Bratva will live on under a true leader."

"You will never be don," I snarl at him. "Not truly."

The wrinkles on Budimir's face deepen as he turns on me, black hatred etched across his face. His eyes are dark and beady, but bright with assumed victory.

"In case you haven't noticed, nephew," Budimir drawls, "I am already don. The powerful take what they want. And I took the Bratva."

"Then you're a fool," I fire back. "You're right about me. I was unfit to lead the Bratva, but that was then. I am a different man now. I have grown up, I have matured, and most of all, I have learnt. And the most important lesson I have learnt is that some things can never be taken by force. Loyalty, for instance. And trust. Your men follow you not because they are loyal, but because they've been made promises. And when a better offer comes along, they will stab you in the back the same way you stabbed my father in the back."

Budimir considers my words carefully.

I can see that I've got under his skin just a little. That makes me bear down, unwilling to let go of the miniscule edge I've gained.

"You want to prove you're the rightful don?" I go on. "You want your men to die for you if need be? Well, then prove to them that you're willing to die for them."

Budimir's eyes glimmer. "And how would I do that?"

"Fight me," I say instantly. "Just you and me. Hand-to-hand combat. No weapons."

Budimir's eyes narrow. I anticipate his refusal. I don't truly believe he will entertain the thought for a moment, but I do want to humiliate him in front of his men.

If nothing else, it will eat at him like my father's laughter still does.

"A fight for the Bratva?" Budimir asks mildly. "An archaic tradition."

"But simple," I retort, "and straightforward. Unless, of course, you're scared, uncle."

His eyes flare with anger. I know I've already bruised his wounded ego. It doesn't take much, apparently.

There is so much I should have been before now. I have been blind.

"Very well."

The words are flat and dark. I can only stare back at Budimir.

"What?"

"You want a fight?" he asks. "You've got one. You and me, hand to hand combat, no weapons."

He's got something up his sleeve.

I know enough about Budimir to know that he never enters into a fight he can't win. Which means he's confident he's going to kill me.

But he's never come up against me before. If this is the only chance I'll get, then I swear to see him on his knees before me before the night is done.

"Cut his restraints," Budimir orders.

There's slight hesitation amongst the ranks that forces Budimir to issue the order again.

"Cut his restraints," he barks. "Now!"

I don't know what the old man is playing at, but I'm certainly not going to waste this opportunity.

He thinks he can fuck with me?

I'll just have to fuck him over first.

The moment I'm cut loose, I get to my feet, stretching slowly so that my muscles loosen up again. Blood flows to my hands and my ankles as I try and shake off the unsteadiness.

Budimir looks at me through eyes that have narrowed into slits, but he looks remarkably calm for a seventy-year-old man who's about to take on someone less than half his age.

"You don't mind a quick pat-down first, do you nephew?" Budimir asks politely.

I grunt in response. Immediately, two of his men come forward and pat me down quickly. They remove the knife in my boot and the one in the waistband of my pants.

I am left bare, completely unprotected. The only weapons at my disposal now are my fists and my mind.

My uncle steps forward and shrugs off his dark jacket. His white shirt is impeccably crisp and taut against his torso.

I have to admit—for an older man, Budimir is in good shape.

"I may be old, nephew," Budimir says, as his hands roll into fists. "But that doesn't mean you're going to win."

"Give me a good fight, old man," I snarl at him. "I'm aching for blood tonight."

5

ARTEM

We circle each other. Budimir's men form a tight ring around us.

I'm no fool. I know there's no way I can walk out of this ring, whether or not I win.

But hopefully, if I can get Budimir at my mercy, I can use him as leverage to get myself out from under their fire. That's the murky plan forming in my head as we size each other up.

I try and read the intention in Budimir's face, I try and predict his next move, but his eyes are black pits of determination.

"I thought of you as a second father," I hear myself say in a low voice.

"I know you did," Budimir says. "You were meant to. I worked carefully to maintain my relationship with you. I didn't want you getting suspicious. Of course, I didn't have anything to worry about once your head was turned by that woman."

Marisha.

"You should have known, Artem. Women exploit your weaknesses, and if they don't, they make you weak."

"The time for talking is done, old man," I snap. I've had enough of his preaching. "Let's get this over with."

Budimir laughs. "The impatience of youth. That's where we differ. See, I like to take my time."

Then he lunges.

I bolt to the side, grab his outstretched arm, and twist it back.

He manages to slip out of my grasp, taking advantage of the fact that my wrists are stiff and vulnerable from the restraints.

The moment he's free, he swings at me, decking me square in the jaw before I can get out of the way.

The punch was badly placed. It only succeeds in pissing me off.

I move forward with a vengeance and hit him once in the stomach. When he keels over, I strike him in the face.

Blood blossoms around his nose, but I know I haven't yet broken it.

I grab his neck viciously and force him to double over. One well-placed blow to the back of the head will send him to his knees. I cock back, ready to end this right fucking now.

But it's all too easy. Too quick.

Budimir's men are quiet as they watch us. Even in the face of their supposed don's approaching defeat, they remain damn near impassive.

My instincts warn me a second before I see the glint of a steel blade.

Budimir's arm lashes out and buries the blade in the side of my stomach.

Pain bursts in me like fireworks. I grunt and stumble backward as it radiates through my torso. My hands scrabble at my side and find the blade still buried to the hilt in me. Blood gushes endlessly.

Gritting my teeth and refusing to drop to my knees again, I grip the hilt of the dagger and draw it out. It's pure agony.

Budimir stands where I left him, still hunched over, a trickle of blood running from his nose into his beard.

I raise my hand, ready to fling the dagger right into Budimir's heart.

He nods at someone behind me.

And a gunshot pierces straight through the hand that's holding the dagger.

The knife clatters to the forest floor. A sensation like a red-hot poker drills through my bicep. The hand on that arm goes limp and useless.

I don't bother turning to the man who shot me.

Instead, I keep my eyes on Budimir. I have to channel all my remaining strength into staying on my feet. Even then, I barely manage it. I'm swaying back and forth like a drunken sailor.

"I shouldn't be surprised," I spit. The pain is clouding all my senses, pressing in around me from all sides. "How could a man like you know anything about an honorable fight?"

"This is exactly why you would never make a good Don, nephew," Budimir sighs. He wipes the blood off his face. His men move closer, flanking him on either side. "It's not about honor or loyalty. It's about power and the men ruthless enough to wield it. I will do what I have to, to get what I want. And those who cross me will die. Just like you are about to do."

Budimir reaches out his hand. A gun is placed against his palm. His fingers curl around the grip and he raises it to my forehead.

"Say hello to your father for me, will you?" He grins triumphantly.

I close my eyes and picture my wife. My child. My best friend.

I'm leaving them all behind. I wasn't good enough.

Forgive me.

6

ARTEM

"What the fuck is that?"

I open my eyes.

Budimir is still holding the gun to my forehead. He hasn't pulled the trigger. The pain of the stab wound and the gunshot are overwhelming. I strain against my thundering heartbeat.

That's when I hear the noise that stopped him.

Running footsteps and the crunch of leaves underneath heavy boots.

A gunshot blasts through the air. Instantly, one of the masked soldiers crumples to the forest floor, blood spurting from his neck.

Budimir ducks, falling behind his men who converge around him. I duck away too, but his men surround me, their guns jabbing into my blood-soaked ribs.

In the darkness surrounding the clearing, a flash of yellow-gold.

Then another bullet slices through the air.

One of the men standing in front of Budimir drops to the ground, his eyes wide even in death.

The soldiers jump into action. Guns clack as they are racked and aimed. The nearest troops pour into the shadows.

I hear the sound of a fist meeting flesh. A grunt—so achingly familiar.

No.

No, no, no.

"Bring him to me!" Budimir commands. His tone is black with anger.

From the trees, a pair of soldiers re-emerge into the moonlit clearing.

They're holding Cillian's limp, bloodied frame between them.

My shoulders sag at the sight of him.

He's going to die with me here. All because he cared enough to try and save me.

Against all odds. Against all reason…

He tried.

"Ah, the Irishman," my uncle groans in exasperation. "I should have known he was up here with you."

Cillian looks like shit. There's a nasty gash in his arm and an appalling lack of color in his face. If he loses much more blood, no amount of medical attention will save him.

"Leave him out of this," I call out, even though I know that bargaining was pointless now.

"Leave him out of this?" Budimir says in amusement. "He's a part of this, just as much as you. I assume this is the loyalty that you hold in such high regard?"

Budimir raises his gun again.

This time, he's pointing it at Cillian.

My best friend glances up at me and I can see the apology written all over his face.

He knew that intervening would mean his death.

And he attacked anyway.

"Here's another lesson, my dear nephew," Budimir continues as I stand there, frozen in place, with the butt of a gun pressed to the back of my head. "Loyalty and stupidity aren't so far apart. These men that surround you were smart enough to recognize power when they saw it. That is why they answer to me."

Then he turns his gaze to Cillian, who is now chalk-white and weakening by the second.

"Where's the girl?" he asks.

"What girl?" Cillian asks, so convincingly even I almost believe him for a moment.

"Artem's fucking *wife*," Budimir snarls.

"She abandoned him the first chance she got," Cillian replies. "We haven't seen her since the clinic."

Cillian, you fucking legend. I will forever be in your debt.

"Well, then," Budimir sighs, "you're of no more use to me."

He cocks the gun and fires.

Once.

Twice.

Three bullets emptied into my best friend's chest.

I roar wordlessly at the top of my lungs. It's a primal, haunting sound, ripped straight out of my soul.

I don't even realize I'm moving forward towards Cillian until something hard and blunt clocks me at the back of my head.

I drop to the ground, soft dirt squishing between my fingers as I stare at the body that's just dropped limp at Budimir's feet.

"Cillian," I whisper. "Fuck... Cillian..."

I try to keep crawling forward, but I'm hit again, right on my spine. I fall flat against the fallen leaves. They scratch at my face and I suck in my breath as their rotting smell fills my nostrils.

Cillian...

I hear footsteps moving closer. Someone puts a boot toe under my ribs and rolls me over. Every motion is agony.

As I peer up, I catch a glimpse of the crescent moon hanging over me, just before it's blocked out by Budimir's face.

"You see, Artem?" Budimir lectures. "You see how much more satisfying it is to be patient? Now, I get to walk away and you get to lie here in the dirt where you belong. You get to lie here with your dead friend and bleed out slowly while you go over all your mistakes."

He spits on my face. Cocks his gun one more time and unloads it into my stomach.

Then he turns and pads away.

The forest slowly empties. Silence takes over once more.

My head spins with memories, past and present, but none of them feel real. None of them feel like they belong to me anymore.

I see a tan woman with haunting hazel eyes, a mangled body and a bloody baby in her arms.

I see an old man with heavy brows and a wizened sorrow on his face.

And last of all, I see a blonde Irishman, with a smile on his lips and an apology in his too-blue eyes.

7

ESME

There's a moment when everything feels like it's going in slow motion.

As though my only coping mechanism is to compound everything down into milliseconds so that I don't have to deal with the inevitable threat walking towards me.

I'm going to drag you to Artem and he can watch as my seed slips out of you.

The man's words hang in the crisp mountain air.

They're too ugly for my little paradise. Too filthy. Too cruel.

His face is contorted with lust and anger and a desire to inflict pain. He licks his lips slowly and for the first time, I truly understand what it means to have your skin crawl.

Nausea bubbles up inside me like a volcano, but I tamp it down and try to focus.

I bring my hand up. He sees the gun in my violently shaking hand.

His eyes go wide.

Before I either give into the urge to puke or lose my only opportunity at this, I pull the trigger.

It's harder than I think it will be. Or maybe I'm just weak and afraid.

The force of the recoil sends me stumbling backwards, but I manage to keep my feet.

He bellows and jumps to the side. A piece of tree bark behind him splinters on impact.

I missed.

A foot or more wide.

"You fucking bitch!" he growls, his jaw clenched with anger.

Then he makes a run in my direction.

I raise the gun again, but I'm too slow. He's on me.

His body crashes into mine. Drives the wind from my lungs as we land in a tangled heap in the dirt. When my hand comes swinging down, it hits a rock embedded in the forest floor.

The gun goes clattering from my grasp.

I don't have time even to scream, because he's swatting my thrashing limbs aside as he struggles for control. I put up a fight—as best as I can.

But I never had a chance.

He tucks each of my wrists beneath his knees as he straddles me. Two quick slaps across the face knock me silly. I taste blood.

"You're going to pay for that, you cunt," he snarls.

"No... no, please..."

"Yeah, that's right. Beg me to let you go. It won't help, but I'll let you beg me anyway."

My head is pounding with the weight of my fear as he spreads my legs with one of his knees. He releases one of my hands so that he can fumble with my clothes.

I bring it up hard, slapping him clean across the face. My nails tear skin, leaving streaks of glistening blood on his cheek.

He recovers almost instantly and slaps me back just as hard.

My eyes un-focus for a moment. All I can see is blinding white light.

But I keep struggling.

I will not simply lie in the muck and grime of the forest and accept that I'm going to be raped.

"Lie fucking still, you bitch!" he screams at me thunderously.

A smarter woman might have listened. And maybe I might have, if it hadn't been for the child inside me.

I couldn't let this happen—for my baby's sake. He manages to rip at the front of my nightgown. The thin fabric gives way easily. He pulls again, harder, and the tear widens until it's reached my stomach.

"No... no!"

"I told you to shut the fuck up," he barks. "Unless you want this to go…"

His threat trails off as his eyes fall to my swollen belly. "You're pregnant?" he asks in amazement.

His shock is the distraction I need. My free hand grabs a handful of the dark, gritty soil and I fling it hard into his wide-open eyes.

He yells back in shock. Cocking back, I swing my fist straight into his nose as hard as I can.

Something gives way beneath my knuckles. Bone or flesh, I don't know, but I feel his blood slicking the back of my hand.

The bastard falls back into the dirt, cupping two hands to where I struck him and cursing rapid-fire.

I scramble onto my knees as I root around in the dirt, desperately looking for the gun I'd dropped.

I can feel him at my back, inching closer as he tries to coax his vision clear once more.

Where is it? Where the fuck is it?

And then I see the butt of the weapon glinting out at me from under a ragged leaf.

I lunge for it. My fingers close around the grip just as the man's hand closes around my ankle.

"I might have gone easy on you, bitch," I say. "But now I'm gonna fuck that baby right out of you."

He tugs hard. I lose my position and my head slams against another half-buried rock.

In that moment of disorientation, I see a flash of a woman behind my eyelids.

I've never met or seen her before.

But I feel like I know her.

She's pregnant. She's terrified. She's staring death in the face…

She's staring my brother in the face.

And I feel a kinship with this Marisha I've never known and never will know. This woman who was married to my husband, who was carrying his child, just as I am now.

A woman whose last view of the world was my brother's stormy eyes —just before he murdered her.

And suddenly, I'm furious.

I'm determined.

But most of all, I'm tired.

I'm tired of being a plaything in a world ruled by powerful men who think they can just take what they want.

I'm tired of having to fight them off, shout to be heard, beg to be left alone.

I whip around fast. My hands don't shake anymore. The gun is steady in my grasp as I turn it on him.

I have the satisfaction of seeing his eyes bulge with fear.

And then I shoot.

This time, pulling the trigger feels like the easiest thing in the world. My hands are steady. My aim is true.

And when the bullet reduces his face to a mess of blood and bone, it's not disgust or guilt or anger than I feel.

It's power.

The man's body hits the ground with a dull, lifeless thump. I sit up a little straighter, the gun still clutched between my hands.

I take a deep breath, staring at the body in front of me, savoring the way he lies there, unmoving.

I remember the way I felt after my first kill. *Mischa*—the man in Tamara's apartment I'd stabbed again and again.

That guilt nearly ripped me in half.

This time is different.

I don't know what that means just yet.

8
ESME

When my legs feel strong enough again, I rise off the ground, taking the gun with me. I turn and walk away from the body, venturing deeper into the woods.

I find my way back to the cabin and then, using that as my starting point, I head off in a different direction.

The moon hangs low in the sky, illuminating my path as I hear the scurrying of forest creatures all around me.

Minutes later, I come across a clearing. This is it. This is the place.

It's bloody carnage everywhere I look. Crimson stains the ground, but I don't shy away from it. Instead, I leap right over the sticky puddles and keep moving forward.

Because I see him.

Artem.

He's lying on his back in the middle of the clearing. Nothing else moves. Nothing makes a sound.

I rush forward and sink to my knees at my husband's side.

"Oh, God," I whimper. A sob breaks through my façade of calm. I squeeze his hand between mine and say it again—I don't know what the hell else to do. "Oh, please, God, no."

I need him to move. To say something. Just fucking *blink,* goddammit.

But nothing.

Nothing.

Until…

His finger twitches in my grasp.

"Artem?" I say. "Artem?"

Suddenly, the tiniest of motions—his chest rising and falling slowly. It's so faint I can barely tell.

But it's there.

It's fucking there.

He's alive.

Gratitude floods back into my body. "Thank God," I breathe. "Thank fucking God." I bend forward and kiss his forehead, his cheek, his lips.

"Artem," I whisper, "can you hear me? Stay with me. Please, just stay with me."

I shake his shoulders, rubbing my hands against his face and slapping him gently, trying to bring him back to consciousness.

His clothes are absolutely soaked in blood. I look for the wounds. A bullet hole in the bicep, a jagged stab wound just above his hip, and a nasty shot buried in the center of his stomach. Each one worse than the last.

I don't know much about emergency medicine, but it doesn't take much to realize the obvious: it doesn't look good.

I rip a long strip off the raggedy end of my nightgown. That one gets knotted around his bicep. The flow of blood staunches at once.

I repeat the process twice more and press the torn, balled-up fabric into his stomach and ribs. He groans each time. His eyelids flutter, but they don't open.

I stand up, still clinging to his hand, and look around. It's cold. My skin is raised in goosebumps over every inch of my body.

But I know what I have to do.

I have to get him to town.

Up on this godforsaken mountain, he's as good as dead. We have no medicine, nothing to operate with, and no one who knows how to do that shit anyways.

And even though I haven't seen any more signs of the men who did this, there's no telling if they'll come back. All that's left of them is the blood on the earth and stomped tracks leading away.

So we have to move. That's the only option. Every other route leads to death.

The question is… how?

I try to pick Artem up, but he groans again, louder. He's too heavy anyways.

Which means my only hope is to bring the car to him.

I kneel back down and lean forward so that my lips are at Artem's ear. "Hold on. I'm coming back. I'm coming back for you."

I don't know if he hears me or not. It doesn't matter. I'll keep trying until he's cold in my arms.

I turn and run through the forest with moonlight guiding my way. I run fast despite my shaky legs and my fast beating heart. It feels like I'm burning up on the inside, but cold air hits my skin from all directions. I'm tired, but I refuse to give in to the fatigue. I can break down later.

For now, I have to run.

As I go, I search the forest for any sign of Cillian. Did he chase the attackers? Did they take him? Did he go for help?

I can't wait around for him to get back, though. I just have to keep going forward.

It's what Artem would do.

I get back to the cabin in record time and head straight for the car.

I'm aware that traversing through parts of the forest in the car will be difficult and quite possibly dangerous, but what fucking choice do I have?

I get into the car and turn it around slowly, inching into the woods with the headlights on. They only highlight how treacherous the path is. Huge boulders rear up on every side with barely enough room to squeeze between them. Unstable gravel could send the car sliding into the ravine at any moment.

I navigate through it carefully, but my pace enrages me. I'm moving at snail speed. It's not fast enough. Artem is bleeding to death and Cillian is who the fuck knows where.

"Faster, faster, dammit!" I cry to the empty car. I smack the steering wheel like that'll help.

I inch through the forest. Every scrape of rock on the car doors makes me wince, but it doesn't matter.

At long last, by some fucking miracle, I make it. My headlights pick out Artem lying in the middle of the clearing.

Dying a little at a time.

I'm as close as I can get, but the trees still keep me from getting any nearer. There's still a good fifteen or twenty yards to traverse with a comatose man who weighs double what I do.

I throw the back doors open and then sprint over to him.

"Artem," I gasp. I'm praying that I'm not too late.

I nearly keel over with relief when I realize he's still breathing. But his breaths are even shallower than they were before, dwindling down to almost nothing. I grab the collar of his bloodstained shirt and try to pull him up.

He doesn't budge.

"Artem," I beg, frantic. "Please, you have to help me. Please… just get up."

The panic ratchets up to my throat when he stirs. His eyelids flicker open for a moment—one beautiful, heart-wrenching moment—before sealing shut again.

"Artem!" I slap his cheek several times, hard. "Artem, please. I can't get you into that car by myself."

Where the fuck is Cillian? He'd know what to do. He'd be able to help.

The dying man in my arms is well over six feet. I try again to slip my arm under his shoulders and tug, but all my might amounts to about three inches of progress. When his groans turn into agonized whimpers unlike any noise I've ever heard him make, I stop and collapse to the ground again.

I'm tired. I'm freezing. I'm pregnant.

And as strong as I think I am, I'm just not strong enough.

All of that means my husband is going to die out here. He's going to bleed away, wither to a cold corpse, and I'm just going to have to sit here and watch that happen because I'm too fucking weak.

No.

No.

No.

Something lights up in my chest. Like a fire within. It's not just desperation. Not just determination.

It's *anger*.

Suddenly, out of nowhere, I'm mad. Mad at him and at the guns that did this to him and the world that keeps doing this to me, again and again.

"Fuck you, Artem!" I half-cry, half-scream. "Fuck you for bringing me here and leaving me like this!"

I'm so angry I can barely form words. I pound my fists against the cold, hard-packed dirt of the forest floor.

"I didn't ask for any of this, but you came out of nowhere and you gave me this baby! You gave me your name! You married me. So fuck you—get the *fuck up!*"

I'm mad at him.

I hate him.

I love him.

I can't possibly lose him.

I start beating my hands against his chest over and over again like a woman possessed. The forest echoes with my cries.

And then by some miracle, my madness breaks through his catatonia.

His head lurches forward, but it falls back onto the forest just as quickly.

But his eyes remain open.

I grab his face with both my hands and meet his eyes. He looks through me at first, but I don't care.

"Artem, listen," I start to say. "Get up now. You're not dying here. Not like this. I know it's hard, but you need to get up. Now."

I can't bring myself to be gentle or patient. I can't bring myself to be kind.

I just need to get him in the car and then I can concentrate on my bedside manner another time.

He just stares at me blankly.

My hands tighten around his face. "You are *not* fucking dying on me, you bastard," I snarl at him. "I don't care that you're bleeding. I don't care that you're in pain. You get the fuck up and you get in that car."

He looks at me again, not saying anything. His lips tremble.

Then he tries to get up. It's painstaking and horrible to watch. Two steps forward, one step back, again and again as he tries to overcome the pain, loses, redoubles his effort, tries again.

As he wins another inch. And another. And another.

I'm doing everything I can to help. I'm pulling his shoulders from the front and pushing against them from the back. I'm whispering under my breath, "Yes, yes, a little more, a little more," like a goddamn lunatic.

And eventually, somehow, he gets to all fours. From there, he uses me like a crutch to push up to half-kneeling. And then two feet on the ground.

And then he rises, still leaning almost all his weight on me, but that's fine, that's okay, we're going to make it.

I almost stumble over, but the adrenaline is coursing through me.

Somehow, I manage to support his weight as we stumble to the car together.

His blood soaks my clothes. The strips of my nightgown are flapping in the night breeze, crusted red. Artem's groan in my ear is low and constant. He's muttering nonsense syllables and his eyes keep falling closed.

But we move forward.

One step at a time.

Until at last we make it to the car. Artem falls against the side of the vehicle, his head knocking the roof. He crumples listlessly into the back seat. I have to heave his legs inside.

Once the door is closed, I let myself breathe for a moment. But only a moment. I don't have any longer than that.

I open the front door and start to climb inside. Just before I'm all the way in, though, something catches my eye.

Something sparkling golden in the moonlight.

Frowning, I go look at it. It's something caught on the spiked leaf of one of the bushes. My heart starts pounding as I get closer and closer.

Until I'm close enough to see and my chest seizes up entirely.

It's a lock of blond hair.

One end stained red with blood.

My body aches like I've been punched in the gut. Cillian is somewhere out there. With the bad men or alone, I can't be sure.

But he's hurt, it seems. Maybe dead.

I look around and scan the forest one more time, hoping against hope for another sign that he's okay.

"Where are you, Cillian?" I whisper into the night.

No response.

I can't wait around for him. Artem is dying too fast for that. We have to go, now.

I offer up a silent prayer for the sad-eyed Irishman. Then I get back in the car and start the long journey into town.

I hope to God we make it in time.

9

ESME

The tires crunch over rocks and dirt. The car breathes exhaust into the night. And little by little, we wind down the mountain.

I feel like I'm sleepwalking. As if this is all just another night terror.

But this time, Artem can't save me from it.

Who can?

I don't make the conscious decision to go to Aracelia's house. I don't even realize that's where I'm going until I'm parked outside her home, staring up at it as though it has all the answers.

Bringing Artem here might be a mistake. But it's the only option I have.

I run up to her front door and pound the door as hard as I can. I keep ringing until she opens the door.

She looks calm. Serene. Not sleep-addled in the least—as if she'd been awake and expecting me.

I shake that thought aside. I'm just panicked, that's all.

"Hola, Esmeralda," she murmurs in that weird, whimsical way of hers.

Not that it even matters, but relief floods through me when she remembers my name. Her eyes run along my body as she takes in the bloodstains on my ripped nightgown.

"What the fuck happened?"

The calm aura that had engulfed her the first time we'd met is still there, but as she takes stock of the situation, it changes somehow. Intensifies. Sharpens.

"I'm sorry," I say desperately. "I couldn't go anywhere else."

"Someone is hurt," she guesses.

"My husband. Please, Aracelia, I need your help. He's dying."

She glances towards the car that's parked behind me. "He's in the car?"

I nod. "Will you help me?" I ask. "I have no one else to go to."

For a moment, I think she's going to turn me away. But then I see her jaw set with determination.

"Venga," she says. "I'll help you."

I'm so overwhelmed with gratitude that I almost hug her. But she pushes past me and hurries toward the car.

It's dark now. A cloud over the moon blots out all the light from the sky, and her house is far from any other building.

Still, there's no telling who might be out in the night. Watching. Waiting to finish what they started.

We go to the car and I throw open the back door.

Aracelia takes one look at Artem and purses her lips up with a professionalism that ER doctors would envy. "He's a big man," she says. "How did you manage to get him in here on your own?"

"He helped."

He doesn't look like he'll be repeating that, though. The back seat is soaked with blood and Artem is groaning softly. His eyes are pinwheeling wildly beneath his eyelids.

"Stay there," Aracelia orders. Before I can answer, she turns and strides behind the house.

While she's gone, I lean forward and mop the cold sweat from Artem's forehead.

"Stay with me," I whisper to him. "We came this far. I can't lose you now."

A tinny squeak invades the night. A moment later, Aracelia rounds the corner of the house again—this time, pushing a wheelbarrow.

She brings it over and parks it as close to the car as she can manage.

"You grab his head," Aracelia tells me. "I'll take his legs. We need to move fast."

It takes several minutes and a lot of effort to move Artem into the wheelbarrow. When he's finally in, I'm not sure whether to laugh or cry.

He looks absurd in there. Far too big for it, so that his limbs are dangling over the edges. Like a big, goofy scarecrow.

But all it takes is the sound of one *plink* of blood against the rusted metal to bring me back to reality.

Aracelia grabs the handles with a grunt. I race alongside her, keeping the wheelbarrow steady over the uneven ground.

We go around back and wheel Artem right up to the back door. Then Aracelia and I each throw our shoulders into one of the handles to stand the cart upright.

As soon as the balance shifts, I run around to the other side and stop Artem from falling out onto his face.

He weighs as much as the mountains do, but Aracelia tosses the wheelbarrow aside and comes to help me. We each loop one of his arms around us and get him indoors.

It feels like an hour has passed since I arrive. Aracelia and I set Artem down on the red rug that adorns the entrance to her home. She locks the door quickly.

I'm drenched in sweat, dirt and blood, my limbs are strung out with fatigue, but I feel wide awake.

Aracelia looks disheveled, too, but there's a calm about her that forces me to focus.

"Take a breath," Aracelia tells me. "And then we'll move him to the dining table. I can work on him there."

I breathe in and out as I gaze down at Artem's pale form, while Aracelia heads into the next room and clears the dining table of its candles and ornaments.

Once it's empty, she gets a thick sheet and covers it over before walking towards me again.

"Ready?" she asks.

I nod as I bend, shifting my hands beneath his underarms to pick Artem up. Shooting pain races through my body but I ignore it and heave him up as Aracelia grabs his legs. The last few feet to the dining table are a struggle, but we manage to heave him up onto the wooden surface.

He falls onto his side, but I gently maneuver him onto his back.

I feel nausea surface and I clamp my hand down over my mouth.

"The bathroom is right behind you," Aracelia says, pointing it out to me.

I run inside and throw up violently into the commode. Nothing but bile and stomach juices comes up.

The nausea recedes for a moment, but when it comes back, it does so with a vengeance. I dry heave for several minutes until I taste blood.

Once I'm done, I fall limply against the bathroom floor and sob until my tears run dry.

I support my head in my palms and try to breathe past the pain. My head is bursting, but it's the weight on my chest that I want to get rid of.

Then I feel a kick. A strong, powerful kick. Almost like the little baby inside me is trying to reassure me.

"I'm sorry, little bird," I whisper, running my hand along my stomach. "I'm supposed to be reassuring you."

Cesar was right. This life is nothing but violence and pain.

The odd thought sends a shiver of fear coursing through me. Is this a sick preview of the rest of my life? If Artem didn't leave the Bratva behind, then it most certainly would be.

Forever stitching wounds. Staunching blood flow and plugging bullet holes. Living in fear, night in and night out, for as long as we both manage to survive.

Artem told you he was done with it all. That he was choosing his family over the Bratva.

Even as I think that, though, I don't believe it. No matter how hard to hope, I know it isn't true.

He was lying to me. I knew it then—deep down, at least, even if I was afraid to say it out loud—and I know it now.

I just wasn't ready to face the truth.

He'll never walk away from his birthright.

My husband was not made for a quiet life on a remote mountain.

He was not made for the life I craved.

I'm parched and weary and I can feel dehydration set its claws into my starving body, but I can't bring myself to get up.

For right now, this cool bathroom floor is comfort in a cruel world. I plan on staying here, at least until I feel like I can stand without falling right back down.

I'm so drained, emotionally and physically, that death feels like it would be a relief.

Cesar, is this what you felt at the end?

Did you kill Artem's wife because you knew it was the easiest way to commit suicide?

Did you hate this life as much as I do?

10

ESME

Sometime later, the bathroom door opens.

Aracelia peers down at me. "Esme," she says softly.

I look up from where I'm curled in the tiled corner. "Is he okay?"

Her tone is neutral. "I managed to stop the bleeding and bandage him up. His color has improved a little."

I bite my lip to stop from crying. "I... I... thank you," I stammer. "How long have I been in here for?"

Aracelia steps the rest of the way into the bathroom with me. "Almost an hour and a half."

"Oh."

She kneels down in front of me, her eyes alight with sympathy. "Come on," she says. "Let's get you cleaned up."

She takes my hand and leads me out of the bathroom. As I emerge, I see Artem lying flat on the dining room table. I break away from Aracelia and float towards him.

She has done an amazing job. She's stripped away his clothes, wiped him down, and washed away all the blood and grime. His body looks clean, almost pristine, except for the bandages that cover his arms and stomach and the soft blue towel she's drawn over his waist.

I smell a strong, peppery scent coming from the bandage around Artem's stomach and I notice that a rub has been applied to the wound before the bandages were put on.

"It's a special poultice," Aracelia tells me before I can ask. "All-natural, but they have amazing healing properties."

I nod, unwilling to question her. In any case, he looks much better than he did when I first found him. That awful, rattling groan has quieted to a gentle inhale and exhale.

"I know I've put you in a compromising situation," I tell her. "I'm sorry for that."

She sighs. "I was hoping what I saw in your tea leaves was wrong."

I blink back fresh tears. "Apparently, I'm not that lucky."

"No, but you are strong," Aracelia tells me. "Strong enough to live through this."

You are strong.

Cesar had told me the same thing a lifetime ago, before I had believed in my own strength.

"Come now," Aracelia prods gently. "You need a good soak in the tub and after you're done, it's important you eat something."

"I'm not hungry."

"You need to eat, Esme. For your child."

I nod slowly, reluctantly, and follow her into her bedroom. The floral patterns are overwhelming but they help soothe me somehow.

They're simple. Pretty. Innocent.

A stark contrast to the world I've been incapsulated in for far too long.

"Go on," she encourages me. "I'll set some fresh clothes for you on the bed."

I walk into the bathroom, dazed, to find that the tub is filled with steaming water. After I strip down, I get into the tub and let the water soothe my aching body. I run my hands over my stomach and watch as my baby moves inside me.

It's just you and me, little bird.

Something about that idle thought catches. It snags on the corner of a harsh realization. A growing realization.

The realization that I made a choice about what happens next. One I couldn't fully process until right now.

It's just you and me, little bird.

A single tear slips down my cheek.

The only one who has the power to give me the life I want is me.

If I want a different life, I have to take it.

And I can't make Artem come with me.

I can't bring him with me at all.

My muscles cry out for me to stay in the bath forever. But now that I've made my choice and acknowledged it to myself, I feel like the clock is already ticking. Ticking down to what, I'm not sure—until I lose heart or lose the opportunity, maybe.

I just know I have to do it now.

I have to leave forever.

I get out, dry off in a hurry as panic flows through me faster and faster, and go into the bedroom.

There's a pair of faded blue jeans on the bed next to a flowing floral shirt and a dusty pink sweater.

I dress hurriedly with fumbling hands. Then I head back towards the dining table where Artem lies.

I can hear Aracelia in the kitchen, but before I speak to her, I slip outside to the car. I rummage through the trunk and the center console until I find what I'm looking for.

When I walk back into the house, Aracelia is standing by the dining table checking on Artem. She looks up and catches sight of me.

"Don't you look better?" she says with a smile.

I return the smile shakily and step forward.

"I want you to have this," I say, holding out the bundle of money in my hand.

She arches an eyebrow. Not quite surprised, but not quite expecting this, either. "Esme..."

"It's the least I can do," I insist. "After all you've done for me."

"What about you?"

"I kept some for myself," I say. "But I want you to have this."

Aracelia hesitates but then she takes the money with careful fingers and sets it down on the table beside Artem.

Turning my gaze from her to him, I move a little closer and put my hand on Artem's arm.

"I'm leaving, Aracelia," I say softly without looking at her.

"Where?" I notice that she doesn't sound in the least bit surprised.

"I don't know yet. But I have the car and enough money to hold me over for the next few months. I'll figure it out."

In the corner of my vision, Aracelia nods. "What would you like me to tell him when he wakes up?" she asks.

I gnaw at my lower lip. "Tell him…"

I trail off, wondering what message I can possibly leave him with.

I'm sorry?

I couldn't do it anymore?

I have to protect myself and my child?

I can't trust you to walk away?

I can't trust anyone but myself?

Nothing feels right. Nothing seems enough. "Don't tell him anything," I say finally. "He'll know why I left."

"But will he understand?"

No, he probably won't.

"It doesn't matter," I reply. "Our lives are on different paths now."

Aracelia nods again. "When do you want to leave?"

"Now," I reply. "As soon as possible. If I stay any longer, I'm afraid… I'm afraid I won't be able to go."

"I'll pack some food for you."

She disappears into the kitchen, leaving me with my husband. I raise his hand to my lips and kiss his bruised knuckles. Then I bend my head down and kiss his closed eyes, his forehead, his cheeks.

I save his lips for last.

"I loved you," I whisper in his ear. "Remember that I loved you."

I let go of his hand and step back. The final goodbye sticks in my throat, refusing to come out.

So I leave it unsaid. I blink away my tears and turn.

And then, one step at a time, I walk away from Artem. From the man who saved me and ruined me and saved me again.

Doubt threads through my thoughts. But that is just fear trying to confuse me.

I made my decision and now it's time to see it through.

I loved you.

I used the past tense, but that's just self-preservation.

I still love him. I always will. I don't know how to stop.

11

ARTEM
ONE WEEK LATER

Old memories tether me to the darkness.

They set their hooks in my soul and pull me in a thousand directions at once.

I'm vaguely aware of the real world somewhere far in the distance. I can hear voices. Feel the light pressure of gentle hands on my body. And the pain, of course. So much goddamn pain, searing through every inch of me.

But I'm not there. Not really.

I'm too lost in this torture. Consumed by it. Torn to pieces by hook after hook after hook of memories I thought were long since gone.

Budimir's face. Sneering at me. Taunting me.

My father's grizzled brow. Arched in a disappointed downwards V.

Cillian's blue eyes. Fading away into the darkness. That ever-present glow extinguished.

Last of all, there's Esme. That molten gold spark in her irises that only flashes when she's fiery with emotion. The tumble of her dark hair. Her scent, her skin, her laughter, her moan…

I force my eyes open.

The overhead light stabs in like an ice pick, but I refuse to close them again.

I've had enough of the darkness. It's my turn to fight back.

There's a burning pain in my side, but I ignore it and sit up slowly. When I manage to get mostly upright, I take stock of my surroundings.

I'm lying on a dining room table in a house that's been decorated with a few too many floral patterns. Pinks and blues and greens in various pastel shades.

There's a grumpy-looking cat staring at me from a chair in the corner of the room. But no people. No Esme, no Budimir. Just me.

I'm not waiting around to see who this house belongs to, or figure out how I got here. If Budimir's behind this—more of his fucked-up torture—then I want to escape while the route out is unguarded.

I look to my side and notice that the table faces a set of sliding doors that open out into a pristine garden. Looks as good as any other direction.

I inch off the table. The moment I land on my feet, pain rips through my body like an earthquake.

I almost collapse. I have to grip the edge of the table to stop from crumpling down in a heap. It takes a long minute of breathing and steeling myself against the pain yet to come.

But when I'm good enough to move, I wince and start to limp towards the sliding doors.

Where is Esme?

Where is Cillian?

Are they...?

I can't bring myself to say it. Can't even think it, actually. The thought is too much.

"You're up."

I whip around—hissing in pain when I realize what a mistake that sudden motion was—and find myself faced with a tall, willowy woman in a long grey kaftan. She has a mess of curly hair that frames her thin face.

And she's looking at me as though she knows exactly who I am.

"Who are you?" I growl.

"Aracelia," she replies coolly. "My name is Aracelia. And you're Artem. Esme told me."

I flinch at the sound of her name, but I can't see any sign that Esme might be in this house.

"Where is she?" I ask. I can't figure out why this woman's name feels familiar to me.

"How about I check your wounds first?" she suggests. "Would you mind sitting down for me?"

"Yes, I would mind," I seethe. I'm about to totter over if I'm not careful, but I refuse to show weakness. I ball my hands into fists and focus on staying upright.

"There's no need to be churlish," she says with a mild sigh. "I am the one who saved your life. Well, Esme and I."

She moves towards me, but I growl at her and she freezes. Just then, I pick up a bitter, rancid smell that fills my nostrils and threatens to make me retch.

"What the fuck is that smell?" I demand.

"My poultice," Aracelia explains. She extends a long finger towards the mass of bandages covering my abdomen. "It's meant to help you heal."

"*Heal*?" I repeat. "It fucking reeks."

God, everything hurts so badly. I can barely think straight.

She scrunches her face up and I can see that I've offended her.

"Where are my clothes?" I ask, realizing suddenly that I'm butt-naked in the middle of what I assume is this woman's living room.

"On the clothesline. I had to wash them because they were covered in blood. If you'd like, I can get them."

She disappears into a door around the corner before I answer.

I turn on the spot, trying to figure out why this place strikes a familiar chord with me. Flowers in vases and jars and perched on windowsills, incense burning in every nook and cranny, a small table with Tarot cards spread out across the top…

And then it hits me.

When Aracelia reappears, I limp back around to face her once more.

"You're the woman who gave Esme a reading," I say. It sounds like an accusation.

"I did," Aracelia agrees. "I also dabble in midwifery and natural cures."

I glance down at the green goo that seems to be oozing out from under my bandages. "I need to get this shit off me."

She shakes her head. "I wouldn't. It needs time to do its' job. And you need to rest."

"I can't fucking rest," I bite back. "I need to get Esme and—"

"Esme is gone."

I freeze. My eyes fly to her face, searching for signs that she might be lying. She stares back at me, unblinking.

"What did you say?" I grit.

"She left a week ago," Aracelia replies. "She took the car and drove off."

She didn't say it, but I can hear the underlying message nonetheless: *She's not coming back, either.*

She left me here. She ran.

For good.

I snatch my clothes from her hands and start getting dressed. I can feel her watching me, judging me, probably glad that Esme left me as unceremoniously as she has. I don't stop until I'm fully dressed. My clothes feel as if they don't belong to me, like I've donned a second skin that's not my own.

Everything feels strange, wrong. Like my world has been shifted off its axis.

I straighten up and look at the woman. *Aracelia*. Even when I say her name in my head, it comes out in a snarl. Something about her just pisses me the fuck off.

Did she tell Esme to run?

I know that this woman has nothing to do with the weight on my chest. That she's not responsible for my pain. That she just happens to be the only one here right now with any semblance of answers.

But she's in my way and I'm unable to keep my fury from unfurling.

"Where is she going?" I demand.

She blinks at me. Either too stupid or too fearless to pay much attention to my tone.

"Somewhere else."

My hands clench into fists. Even that tiny action sends pain rushing up and down my arms. I have a high threshold for physical pain, though.

It's the emotional shit I could never deal with.

But I don't have a choice anymore. Pain of all kinds is here to stay.

Matter of fact, pain is all I have left.

I shove past the woman and head out of the house. I've just limped through the door when I hear her call my name.

"Artem!"

Despite myself, I freeze.

"For what it's worth… I think leaving was incredibly hard on her," she tells me. Her tone is sorrowful, sympathetic.

But I am too black with loss to accept it.

I spit on the ground and keep stomping away.

Aracelia doesn't pursue me. But when I glance back twenty minutes later, just before I round the hill and her hovel disappears from sight, she's still there. Still standing in the lit rectangle of her back door. Watching me go.

I spit once more and keep walking into the mountains.

～

I must've left sometime around midnight, if I had to guess. And yet the sun is high overhead by the time I reach the top of the mountain trail.

My bandages are red at the edges with blood. Everything hurts. More pain than I've ever experienced at once.

The cabin comes into view. It looks the same way it always has. Quiet. Peaceful.

It's painful to even glance at it.

Too many memories of happy days with Esme, waiting to taunt me like ghosts.

I don't go inside. I'm not ready for that. There are things that need to be dealt with first.

I only stop at the shed, long enough to pull out a shovel.

Then I keep going, delving into the woods with single-minded purpose. One bloody, painful step at a time.

The smell hits me before I reach the clearing. It turns my stomach and I have to slow my pace just a little. The pungent odor smells distractingly like rotting meat.

I feel a crackle of pain as I realize that that's exactly what Cillian is now. Nothing more than a heap of rotting meat.

When I turn the corner, that's what I'm going to see.

Just a few more steps.

Just one more.

Then I break through the brush and prepare myself to look upon the body of my best friend, who died trying to save me.

It's not there.

I do a double-take. I must be dreaming, hallucinating. Maybe my injuries have wrecked my brain.

I stomp around the edge of the clearing, looking for signs. When I reach the spot where he fell after Budimir shot him, I see the blood on the ground. But no body to be found.

Wincing in agony, I sink to one knee and look closer.

The blood is mostly mud now. Caked into the dirt and darkened by the days and nights since everything happened here.

This close, I can see that there's a faint trail leading off into the brush. Like something heavy was dragged from this spot and away.

The shovel falls from my hand.

Did Cillian escape?

Or did Budimir drag him off and leave me to die alone?

I close my eyes and sigh.

"Cillian," I whisper to nobody at all.

I wish I believed in heaven or hell. I wish I could close my eyes and picture him free of pain. Reunited with his love.

But I don't. There is nothing after death. Just darkness.

So, wherever my best friend is, he's either Budimir's newest pincushion, or he's worm food. I'm not sure which fate is worse.

"Thank you, brother," I whisper. "I'm sorry. You put your faith in me and I let you down. I should have been a better don. A better friend."

It's killing me inside that I don't even have anything to remember him by.

I can't live with that. I need something. Call me stupid or sentimental, I don't care. I just can't let him disappear into the ether.

I look around me and see a huge mound of rocks off to one side. I rise to my feet and limp over there.

And then I start to work.

I find a nice spot underneath the largest tree I can find. I shuffle back and forth from the rock pile to the spot I've chosen. One by one, I pile the stones up.

It's slow-going, and hard. But I welcome the pain that claws at my body. It feels like penance. Like I owe this much to Cillian.

I work until the sun it burning hot in the sky. Sweat drips down my face, pools in my bandages, and soaks through my clothes. But I don't allow myself a chance to rest. Not until it's done.

With every stone added to the construction, I keep seeing another mistake. Another way I let down my father, my best friend, the men in my command.

What makes it worse is that I've done all this before. I had been so blinded by grief over Marisha that I missed all the ways in which Budimir was undermining my father and plotting his death.

One mistake leading to the next.

And now years later, it appears that I've learned absolutely fucking nothing. I've been so consumed with Esme that I had ignored my duty to the Bratva.

I hid up in the mountains while Budimir hunted us.

And now, Cillian is dead because I ignored my instincts.

Not again. I will not let it happen again.

Eventually, I get the rocks piled up into a stable pyramid of smooth white mountain granite. Then, I fashion a small cross from some thick branches, lash it together with strips of bark, and wiggle it between the stones.

When I'm finished, I step back to evaluate my handiwork.

It's a pitiful tribute to the memory of a good man. A few twigs and some pebbles in this fucking shithole of a world.

But it's all I have to offer.

The pain in my chest has now dulled to a hollowness that swallows emotion. I think about Esme, about her beautiful dark hair, her hazel-gold eyes, and her easy, open smile.

I still feel love when I think of her. But I have to try and let go of the possessiveness. Her hold on me is what caused me to lose my way.

She left. So let her be gone.

If I want to focus on what I have to do next, it's my only option.

She's probably driving as far from this nightmare as she can. She's carrying my baby, and in a few months, I will have a child.

But I no longer assume that I will see or even know that child.

The baby is lost to me. Just like she is.

I look again at the makeshift remembrance in front of me and feel the hollowness in my chest grow.

I always assumed that Cillian would be my right-hand man when I became don. Now, I'm looking at a different reality.

He won't be my second, but rather the ghost on my shoulder, reminding me never to lose focus again.

I have lost everything now. I have lost my father, my best friend, my wife and my child. Budimir has picked away at me, bite by bite by bite, like a vulture plucking a carcass down to the bone.

I have nothing left anymore.

Nothing but revenge.

I turn and look out over the ravine and towards the snow-capped mountains beyond.

I take a deep breath. And then I roar out, "I'm coming for you, uncle. Do you recognize me? No, how can you—when I barely recognize myself? My name is not Artem Kovalyov. Not anymore. My name is death. And I'm coming for you."

12

ESME

THREE MONTHS LATER—A SMALL TOWN NEAR TIJUANA, MEXICO

"Emily?"

I balance the tray on my huge belly and try to sidestep Sara, the other waitress, as she rushes past me to the kitchen. There's a mess at table three I need to sort out and a couple at table four who've been trying to flag me down for the last ten minutes.

"Emily?"

I can see the annoyance on the couple's faces but I really need to get table one their dinner. Jose got their order wrong the first time, so they've had to wait an extra half hour for the right meals. Which of course means they're snippy and hungry.

And since they can't see Jose, I'm the outlet for their annoyance.

"Emily!"

Fuck.

I'm still not used to the name I go by now. My reaction time is slower than I'd like to admit.

I turn to find Ruby, my manager, staring daggers at me. My arms are already screaming from holding three plates each.

"I've been trying to get your attention for, like, ever," she snaps.

Her bright red lips are pursed with irritation and a lock of strawberry blonde hair has come loose from its usually pristine topknot.

"Sorry," I mumble. "I'm a little backed-up here." I fidget back and forth to readjust my weight on my feet.

Ruby's eyes fall to my stomach and then back up to my face. "When are you due by the way?"

Fuck, again.

"I've got a month to go," I lie smoothly.

"Are you sure?" Ruby asks. "You look huge."

"Gee, thanks," I say, trying to make light of my discomfort. "Just what every girl dreams of hearing."

I *had* a month to go—a whole damn month ago. According to my doctor, as of this morning, my due date is five days in the rearview mirror. I should be resting at home, swollen feet propped up.

But I need the paycheck from the diner, shitty as it is.

"You know what I mean," Ruby sighs, rolling her eyes.

"Um, Ruby, hold that thought for a sec, will ya?" I plead. I'm on the verge of dropping all the plates in my hand. That would really piss off the angry couple. "Let me get this order to table one and I'll be right back. Pinky promise."

"Fine," she says. "Be quick about it."

I nod and waddle to table one, intentionally steering clear of table three so that I can avoid the mess a little longer.

"Hey, guys," I apologize. "Really sorry about the wait."

The couple just clucks their teeth in irritation. At least they look happy to see me.

"Did you bring my curly fries?" the boy chirps.

"Right here, little man," I say, giving him my best smile.

He blushes a little as he accepts the fries. His sister doesn't look as happy with her sloppy joe, but she lights up when I put down a side of potato wedges.

"Some complimentary wedges," I say. "For the delay."

That seems to appease the dad, who nods in acknowledgement, but his dark-haired wife looks at me with a pinched expression.

"How far along are you?" she asks.

"Got a month to go," I say brightly.

"You shouldn't be working."

I don't know if she means to show concern, but her tone implies otherwise.

"I don't have that option," I sigh before I can stop myself.

She narrows her eyes. "Single mother?"

I bristle a little at the question, but the reality of my life these days is hard to deny. "Yes," I admit. "I am."

She looks like she's about to say something else. But I'm not sticking around to be insulted—or worse, pitied.

So I pivot around to table four and pull out my notepad.

"I'm really sorry about the wait, guys," I say to them.

Both their expressions soften when they take in my huge belly. They don't give me any attitude as they relay their orders. When we're done, I walk away and let loose a heavy sigh.

Ruby's waiting for me back at the counter with her arms crossed. I used to be concerned by that particular stance, until I realized that it was Ruby's resting pose. Same for the bitch face she wears around the clock.

I start to say, "I still have one more table to—"

"It can wait," she says, cutting me off. "I want to talk to you about something."

Fear rises up inside me like bile.

I can't lose this job. I can't lose this job. I can't lose this job.

"Maternity leave," Ruby says.

I hesitate. "What about it?"

"You need to go on maternity leave," Ruby repeats grimly. She's eyeing my stomach.

Sometimes, it feels like my pregnancy is the only thing that defines me anymore. That's all people see. It's the first question they ask.

"I will," I say. "But not yet."

"When, then?" Ruby asks. "When the kid pops out between table three and table four?"

"I'm fine," I argue. "I feel strong and fit and capable."

"Do you know what you look like?" she asks.

"Umm..."

"You're the skinniest pregnant woman I've ever seen," Ruby continues impatiently. "You're skin and bones and the biggest fucking stomach on the West Coast."

Ouch.

"You're making customers uncomfortable."

My eyebrows knit together. "Excuse me?"

"Oh, don't get all bent out of shape," she sighs. "You always sound like you're two seconds away from completely breaking down. And it doesn't help that you look twelve."

"Are you not happy with my work?" I ask bluntly.

Ruby meets my gaze. "You're a hard worker, Emily," she says. "And I hired you because you were determined, confident and honestly, a little desperate. But you need to take a fucking break."

I bite down on my bottom lip. "If I do, will I have a job here when I get back?"

Ruby hesitates. "You'll have a baby."

"I can still work."

"And who's gonna take care of your baby?"

It's a really good question. One that I can't answer just yet.

But that won't stop me from trying my best to salvage this situation.

"I have family," I blurt out in desperation. "They'll take care of the baby while I'm at work."

"Oh, yeah?" Ruby says, with raised eyebrows. "Who?"

"My… uh… great aunt and uncle," I say. "Tío Charlie."

"You've never mentioned them before."

I shrug. "Don't bring your personal life into the workplace, right?" It's a lame lie but it's the best I've got.

Ruby sighs, obviously onto the fact that I'm just blatantly making shit up. "I won't tolerate a baby at work, Emily," she says. "Got it?"

"Got it," I note. "But if it's all the same to you, I'd still like to keep working."

Ruby groans. "Jesus! Fine. Just go deal with the mess on table three."

Sighing with relief, I head over to table three just as Sara, the other waitress working today, swings by.

"You okay?" she mutters to me over her shoulder.

She has beautiful blue eyes that remind me of someone I knew in my old life. The life I ran from. I have to focus hard every day not to be distracted by them.

"Fine." I brush a flyaway bang out of my face. "Ruby's just trying to get rid of me."

"She's brusque," Sara acknowledges. "But her heart's in the right place."

"I know, and I get it. But I really need this job."

Before Sara can respond, the door to the diner opens. A small group of four men walks in.

I'm immediately on high alert.

They are dressed in dark sunglasses and dark coats. All of them are stony-faced, tattooed, and intimidating as hell.

Please don't pick my section, I pray silently. *Anywhere but my section.*

Which means that they of course head directly for my section.

I sigh with frustration as they take the table I've just cleaned up. Shitty luck.

I put my game face on and walk over to them. There's no point putting it off.

Their eyes fall on me wordlessly and nerves claw at my throat. I've known men like this my whole life. I've learned the hard way not to stick around for a second longer than I have to.

"Good evening," I say politely. "What can I get you guys?"

"I want a steak."

I turn to the burly man who spoke. He removes his shades to reveal dark, piercing eyes that might be considered attractive if the rest of his face weren't so… threatening. My eyes flicker down to the massive eagle tattoo that takes up the entire left side of his thick neck. It looks shitty, blotchy, amateurish.

A prison tat, if I've ever seen one.

"Rare," he tells me. "I like my meat bloody."

I have to resist the urge to cringe at the salacious way he gives me his order. His gaze roams down to my stomach and he licks his lips. Goosebumps prickle my skin, but I manage to hold it together.

"I'm sorry, sir," I say, keeping my tone professional. "We don't have steak."

He raises his eyebrows while his friends snicker. Clearly, he's the ringleader and he's so predictably menacing that I almost want to roll my eyes.

If only he knew the kind of life I've had.

"I want steak," he says. "So do my men."

So do my men. Those words aren't lost on me.

They're definitely mafia, probably small-time drug runners operating out of nearby Tijuana.

But I've had enough of the mafia for one lifetime.

"I'm sorry—"

"Let me put it to you in a way you can understand," he interrupts. He leans forward a little, scanning me from head to toe, though his eyes linger on my stomach and breasts. "I want fresh meat. One way or the other. You know, I've always had a thing for pregnant women."

My forced smile turns sour. I take a step back. "I'll see what I can do."

I back away and head straight for the kitchen. Once I'm in the safety of the kitchen, I can breathe a little easier, but the thought of going back out there turns my stomach.

"Emily, you okay?" asks Jose, the line cook.

I nod and force a smile back onto my face. "I'm fine," I reply. "I just... you know, difficult customers."

"What else is new?" Jose asks, rolling his eyes.

"Not shit. Anyway, can you whip up four steaks... rare?" I ask desperately.

"Steaks?" he repeats. "We don't have steak. Tell them to pick something off the fucking menu. That's what it's there for."

"I can't tell these customers that," I groan.

He walks past me and peers through the little partition that looks over into the restaurant area. "Table three?" he asks.

"That's the one."

"Fuck, those dudes look scary."

"My point exactly."

"I've got some pork ribs though. Go ask them if they'll have those?"

"Jose, *please*," I beg. "Men like them don't like hearing the word 'no.'"

"Just ask," he snaps. "I've got three other orders to fill."

Gritting my teeth, I turn, ready to go back into the lion's den to ask them a question I already know the answer to, when Sara almost runs right into me.

"Whoa!" I exclaim.

"Sorry," she says. "Sorry. Listen, Emily, why don't you let me take that table?"

"Really?" I ask, relief surging through me.

I do feel a little bad palming the table off on her. But I'm just so tired and my spine feels like it's on fire.

"Sure thing." She smiles brightly. I just want to hug her. "You hide out here for a bit and I'll go handle the table. I'll ask them about the pork ribs."

I sag in thanks as Sara disappears back into the restaurant. Turning, I take a seat on one of the little stools in the hallway that the staff uses to steal a quick break from time to time.

My legs cry with relief.

But I haven't even been sitting five minutes before Sara returns with a grim look on her face.

"Oh, God, what happened?"

"I'm sorry, Em," Sara sighs. "They want you."

"What?"

"They told me... um... They're horrible," she admits. "I tried to tell them that you'd clocked out for the night but—"

"It's okay," I say quickly. "I can do it. Thanks anyway."

"And Jose... they want steaks," she calls over to him.

I glare at him. "Told you."

"Fuck," he mutters. "Fine, I'll send Larry out to buy a few steaks. They'll have to wait."

I know that means I'll have to deal with them for longer.

This is so not my night. Sara gives me a reassuring look and pats me on the shoulder as I move back into the dining area.

The moment I appear, a round of hooting and wolf whistles rise up from table three. I grit my teeth and approach them.

"We'll get your steaks," I say, brusquer than I should be with any customer. "But it might take a little longer than usual."

"Oh, that's okay," the man with the eagle tattoo remarks. "We have you here to keep us entertained."

"What's your name?" the man closest to me asks. He's got bloodshot eyes and a nose so sharp it looks cartoonish.

"Emily." Even after three months of my new identity, it still sounds clunky coming out of my mouth.

"You don't look like an Emily."

I just shrug. What am I supposed to say?

Good call—you got me! I'm actually Esmeralda Kovalyov, neé Moreno, daughter of one of Mexico's most powerful cartel bosses and the estranged wife of the don of the Kovalyov Bratva. But really, the pleasure is all mine.

As fun as it would be to see these assholes shit themselves, I can't imagine that ending well for me.

"How old are you?" another one asks me while I fantasize about stabbing them.

"Why does that matter?"

They laugh as though my irritation is exactly what they're going for.

"Damn, kitty has claws!"

I bite back the retort on my tongue. "I'll bring over the steaks as soon as they're ready."

"Are you hungry?" Eagle Tattoo asks me.

I stop reluctantly and pivot to face them again. "What?"

"I asked, are you hungry?" he repeats, enunciating each word like I'm an idiot. "Because I've got a delicious piece of meat that I'm sure you'll love."

This fucking asshole.

My skin prickles with heat. I can't help wondering how a certain tall, dark Russian would react to these men.

I chase that thought away as soon as it comes.

You're on your own, Esme. There's no tall, dark Russian to come to your rescue anymore. There's no point thinking about him now.

"I'm vegetarian," I reply smoothly. "Can I get you anything else?"

"Beer," Eagle Tattoo says. "Lots of it."

I bring four huge pitchers of beer to their table and then scuttle back to the kitchen the moment I can. I feel their eyes on me the whole time.

It makes me want to scream.

I need just one fucking minute away from their awful stares. Anywhere is fine, as long as it's *away*. I don't even think about where I'm going until I end up in the walk-in refrigerator.

The cold feels good against my fevered skin. I try and breathe, rubbing one hand against the crest of my stomach.

The baby is kicking furiously. I wonder if that's because he can sense how agitated I am.

Then the door to the walk-in freezer opens. I turn to find Sara, looking at me with concern.

"Are you all right?" she asks.

She's a sweetheart and a good friend, but it pains me that I can't tell her everything. Not even my real name. Not even that one little, insignificant fact about who I really am.

"Sorry. I just needed to catch my breath," I say. "I'll be out to help in just a second."

"There's no need," Sara tells me. "Michael arrived early for his shift and there are only a couple of tables left. We can manage. You take your time."

I smile gratefully. "Oh, you don't need to..."

"You can go home if you want," she suggests.

"What about the assholes at table three?" I ask.

"Michael can handle them," she says with a shrug. "He's plenty scary himself."

That's definitely true. Michael is ex-military and doesn't tolerate bullshit in any forms. Especially not the "I've got a delicious piece of meat you'll love" variety.

He's a teddy bear on the inside, but you have to get to know him to see that side of him.

"Thanks, Sara."

I expect her to leave, but she takes a step towards me.

"How are you, Emily?" she asks.

I flinch. Not because of her proximity, but because she really believes my name is Emily. The more I get to know her, the more it feels like a betrayal to keep certain things from her.

"Fine," I reply vaguely. Details are what get you every time. Better to stay distant, abstract.

"I'm worried about you."

I raise my eyebrows. "Why?"

She sighs. "Because you're over-worked and very pregnant," she says. "If you need money, I have some saved up."

My eyes fill with tears of gratitude. It's been a hard three months. Maybe harder than I even realize.

"Thank you. I really appreciate the offer," I say. "But you're saving up for college. I can't take that in good conscience."

"You can pay me back when you're able to," she says. "I know you're good for it."

I've been closeted from the world for so long, distrust ingrained into me from such a young age, that sometimes it still shocked me that there are such genuinely kind and generous people out there.

People like Sara.

"I can't, Sara," I say. "I love you for offering, but I'm good."

The stash of money I'd taken with me from Aracelia's has dwindled fast. No matter how sparing I am, it doesn't seem to make much of a difference. This job helps slow the flow somewhat, but even then, my tattered envelope filled with bills has been getting thinner and thinner.

I never realized how expensive the simple act of living could be.

After leaving Aracelia's house in the nameless village near Picacho del Diablo, I'd ditched the car on the side of the road and taken a bus into this grimy Mexican border town outside of Tijuana.

It checked all my boxes: anonymous, transient, and out of the way.

Perfect.

Not exactly paradise. But it's the best place I could find to have my baby. It had taken me a day to find a cheap place to stay, a one-room apartment that cost me first and last months' rate plus a hefty security deposit and an uncomfortable brusque conversation with the chain-smoking landlord to secure.

It isn't anything to write home about. The bed is pushed to one side of the wall next to the kitchen and the shower is separated from the rest of the space by a plastic curtain.

To make matters worse, the toilet is located outside my apartment and I share it with the tenants in the two apartments down from mine.

But for the price—and more importantly, for not having to divulge a single piece of personal information—I've been willing to put up with all that.

It took me a little longer to find a job. No one was willing to hire a pregnant girl. Ruby at the diner was the only one who took a chance on me.

Even with my job, though, I've been just scraping by, hanging on to the last couple of hundred dollar bills from Artem's stash.

How much longer can I live like this, I wonder?

"Emily?"

"Yes?" I say, looking up at Sara's big blue eyes.

"I know there's something you're not telling me," she murmurs, much to my surprise. "I know there's something you're running from. But I just want you to know: you can trust me."

My heart thrums chaotically for a moment.

"Esme," I whisper.

"What?"

"My real name is Esme."

Sara's eyes go wide. "Oh."

"You're right about what you said, too," I continue. It's like a gushing flow. Now that I've started sharing my truth, I can't stop. "I *am* running from something: a life I didn't want."

"And... the father of your baby?" she asks.

I shake my head. "Not exactly. We wanted different things," I answer sadly. "I couldn't compromise. If it was just me, maybe I could have. But I have my child to think of."

Sara nods. "Was he a dangerous man? Like the men out there?"

Either Sara is incredibly perceptive or I'm just that transparent. I take a deep breath and try to explain.

"He is more dangerous than all of them put together," I tell her. "But not to me. He was good to me. I believe he maybe even loved me."

She reaches out to touch my hand reassuringly. "Then...?"

"There is no separating work from your personal life," I say. "Not when it comes to the mafia."

"Mafia?" Sara breathes. "He's in the mafia?"

"Something like that," I confirm with a nod. "And he wasn't going to leave that way of life. So I did."

She squeezes my fingers between hers. "Thank you for telling me, Esme."

I smile. "I'm sorry I lied to you for so long."

"I understand why you did," she says simply. "Why don't you go back home? I'll hold down the fort here."

"You don't have to do that."

"It's okay to accept help every now and again, Esme," she says.

It feels better than I can express to hear her use my real name.

The weariness hits me all at once. Three months of running and hiding and scrapping and looking over my shoulder all the goddamn time. To have someone offering me simple help, with such an honest, trusting smile...

It's overwhelming.

"Thank you."

I give her a tight hug before we exit the walk-in fridge together. Then she offers me a parting wave and heads down the narrow corridor towards the dining area, while I turn into the bathroom.

I'm parched and tired, but I've gotten so used to the discomfort that I barely even notice it anymore. I splash some cold water on my face and stare at my reflection in the mirror.

Ruby is more accurate than I've given her credit for. I look scarily thin, a fact that's only highlighted by my massive belly.

My rent is due in a week and I'm counting on my tips to get me over the edge. Otherwise, I'll have to dip into my emergency cash reserve, which I've been hoping to save for the baby.

I have no plan once the baby arrives. I know that's as reckless as it is stupid.

But really, what are my options?

I can't afford to hire a nanny or a babysitter and Ruby has made it abundantly clear that she won't have me waiting tables with a baby on my hip.

What are you gonna do, Esme?

"Excuse me, sir!"

My head darts in the direction of the sound.

That was Sara's voice.

She speaks up again. "You can't be in here. The diner's restrooms are on the other side of the restaurant."

"Well, I'm already here, so don't be a bitch about it."

I recognize the gruff voice instantly and I freeze.

The burly man with the eagle tattoo.

Is it possible that these men are on Artem's payroll? Or worse, are they on Budimir's?

Are they intentionally hunting me down or is this just a cruel coincidence?

"I'm sorry, sir—"

But before I hear an end to Sara's sentence, I hear her gasp.

A second later, there's a low thud and a shocked cry.

The son of a bitch hit her. He put his hands on her.

I rush to the door and inch it open to peer out so I can figure out what's happening.

I can see the eagle-tattooed man. He's pushed Sara up against the corridor wall that serves as a gateway between the staff quarters and the main restaurant. It doesn't get much traffic, which is probably why he's followed her here in the first place.

I catch a glimpse of Sara's face. Her head is craned back in an awkward position, held in place by Eagle Tattoo's meaty paw clamped around her neck.

"You want my cock, don't you, you little slut? Just like your whore friend who ran away," he growls at her, licking her neck as she whimpers in terror underneath his clutches. "Don't look so scared, baby. You're gonna love it."

I back away from the door, frozen with horror.

No matter how far I run, it seems violence is destined to plague me. And I am in no position to confront it, either.

Not in my current condition.

But Sara... Sara needs help.

Your friend needs you.

What are you gonna do, Esme?

13

ARTEM
PICACHO DEL DIABLO, MEXICO

You wake up.

It's before dawn and the air is frigid and every inch of your body hurts.

But you wake up anyway.

You get out of bed. Shoes on. You run a ten-mile trail throughout the mountains. The cold makes your lungs scream, but the altitude no longer affects you the way it once did.

When your legs refuse to go any farther, return to the cabin.

Get the gun.

Creep into the woods. Find animal tracks. Follow them.

A doe and her two fawns, camped in the underbrush. The mother and one of her children get away.

The other is not so lucky.

Bring the carcass back to the cabin. Sharpen the knife.

Skin the deer, dress it, hang it to dry.

Go down to the ravine to rinse the blood and sweat from your body.

Morning light now illuminates the mountains.

At the riverside, you shadow box and lift boulders. No weights to be found out here. The rocks serve that purpose.

Pick up the heaviest one you can find. Carry it up the hill. Again. Again.

Your muscles cry out for rest. For a moment's respite.

No.

Another rep. Another.

Sun is high overhead now.

Then—target practice. Lying in the dirt. Plinking the rock targets a hundred yards away, two hundred yards away, three hundred yards away.

Don't miss. Don't you dare fucking miss, you son of a bitch.

You don't.

Sun beginning to set. You run again until you can't anymore.

You return to the cabin.

You drink whiskey until you black out.

And when the morning comes, you do it all over again.

14

ARTEM

The water's cold this morning. Colder than usual. Snowmelt coming down from the top of the mountain range, I bet. Winter is thawing.

I force myself to stay in for a minute longer than I want. To plunge my head beneath the surface of the water and stay there, stay there, stay there until my lungs are crying out for oxygen.

And then just a moment longer.

To prove a point to—fuck, to someone, though I don't know who the hell cares. There's no one out here but me.

I get out of the water about fifteen minutes after I've gotten in. Ice cold droplets sink into my skin, but I shiver and air dry as I walk over to the rock where my clothes are laid out.

I glance down at my body as I dress again.

I have three new scars glistening with the river water. Two from the bullet wounds and one from the stab wound that's left a long, thin lightning bolt down the side of my torso.

My stomach is a mess of callused tissue. That one took the longest to heal.

Beneath the scar is new muscle. Fresh muscle. Lean and taut and powerful.

My body is a weapon in and of itself. The way it is meant to be.

I plan on using it to its full advantage.

I will not be left lying in the dirt again.

I head up the steep pathway that leads away from the ravine. The climb used to be difficult for me, but with time and day after day of running and hefting rocks, it's become laughably easy.

Once I'm back on relatively flat surface, I walk fast towards the cabin. These trails are as familiar to me now as the back of my hand. Little by little, I've made this land my own.

Traps lurk throughout the woods. Some to catch forest creatures for food. Some to catch any fools who dare wander too close.

The trunks bear markings that point the way to this trail or that one. Others are scarred with bullet holes.

Some from me.

Some from the night everything changed.

I pick up the trail that leads directly to the cabin. As I mount the highest point of the ridge, I hear a whine.

Sighing, I glance to the side to see big brown eyes staring at me from behind a large boulder.

"Fuck," I growl. "Not you again."

The dog limps towards me. He looks like shit. A paw that's twisted inward and fur matted all to hell.

"Fuck off," I say, walking past him.

The dog whines again like he's saying something back to me.

I sigh with exasperation. "Is it too fucking much to ask to be left alone?"

The dog blinks up at me, apparently shocked by my reaction. Or maybe he's just trying to figure out how crazy I was.

According to the people in town, I crossed over into wild, insane mountain man about two and a half months ago.

They're not wrong.

I ignore the mangy fleabag and keep walking. But I can hear the mutt trailing behind me.

When I get to the cabin, I head inside and check my alcohol supply.

I have five or six bottles of the strongest shit I could find in this fucking hick town. That'll probably only hold me over for two days. Three at the max.

Another whine. The mutt has snuck into the cabin. He's sniffing around the pasta that's stuck all over the floor.

Apparently, I upended the table last night. Both chairs still lay on their sides. The table, too. And pasta everywhere.

"Fuck," I mutter.

The smell in here is mostly booze and sweat. Underneath it all, though, is a stink that set in weeks ago.

I need to fucking clean up.

I pick up one of the fresh bottles of whiskey, set one of the chairs upright, and sink into it. I crack the top and take a burning swig.

I don't usually start drinking so early, but I'm feeling restless today. Worse than usual.

The mutt eagerly laps up the pasta.

I take another drink and set the bottle down on the floor. When it clinks, the mutt looks up with a startled little flinch and fixes his sad eyes on me.

"Don't fucking judge me," I snarl. "At least I don't look like you do."

The dog starts wagging his tail and pads over to me. I don't touch. I don't want the mongrel to get too comfortable with me.

I don't mind him eating shit off the floor, but I'm in no position to look after anything.

The whiskey settles my nerves. I get out of the chair and survey the cabin.

It looks like a fucking shithole. Mostly because it is. I know where all the important shit is—the whiskey and the weapons—but the rest of it is a haphazard mess.

Sighing, I right the table and the other chair back to their normal positions. One of the table's legs is crooked, but I'm in no hurry to fix it.

Then I move around the cabin and straighten what I can.

The place is nowhere near clean, but it's the most I can bring myself to accomplish right now.

When I'm sick of trying to fix this unfixable chaos, I grab my jacket.

The dog perks his head up.

"Don't even fucking thinking about it," I tell him. "You're not coming with me."

He actually lets out a little whine, as though he's understood me perfectly.

"Too fucking bad," I reply. "I'm not your damn owner." I glare down at him. "Nobody would want you anyway."

The dog just blinks at me.

"Yeah, *now* you decide not to understand me."

I wonder if I should be concerned that I'm talking to a fucking animal. It feels inconsequential, though, given everything I've lost.

I've had three months to think on all those losses. And what I've decided is that they were all necessary.

I needed the bullshit to be stripped away. For my vision to be cleared.

I needed a reminder of who I am and what my purpose in life is.

Had I really been prepared to give up my claim to the Bratva?

Yes, I had been.

And for what?

A *woman.*

A woman with dark hair and hazel-gold eyes and a smile that was so pure that it made me aware of just how tainted my own soul was.

She was not for me.

She was never been meant for me.

A wife? A child? A family.

These are things that belonged to other men. Normal men.

But I am no normal man.

I am Artem Kovalyov.

I am Don of the Kovalyov Bratva.

That is my only purpose in life.

Until death absolves me of my responsibility.

∼

I head out of the cabin. There's a black Jeep parked right outside the porch. I'd nabbed it about a month ago, a few miles outside of Devil's Peak.

I have grown unreasonably attached to the vehicle, but that won't stop me from changing it in a few weeks.

I'm not going to let sentiment rule me any longer. I have made too many weak decisions to repeat them.

So as soon as I feel myself longing for something, fitting in with something… it gets tossed.

I climb into the Jeep. The dog watches me from the porch, chin on his paws. He already looks too fucking comfortable.

If he's still here when I get back, I'll fire a few warning shots to scare him off for good.

I'm not interested in company. Not even the four-legged variety.

I drive fast down the trail to the village. I take the turns recklessly, but I'm confident I can drive this path blindfolded now. It's so damn familiar to me.

My time here is ending soon.

I needed these few months to recover. I was too wrecked from Budimir's attack to do anything else.

But now, after months of intense training, my body is at its peak physical shape. My mind is in a stronger place, too.

I'm focused. I'm determined. And I'm thirsty for blood again.

I park in a tight space outside the bookstore that Esme used to frequent. I catch a glimpse of myself in my rearview mirror and I pause for a moment.

My beard is now my dominant feature, swallowing the bottom half of my face and casting attention to the dark circles under my eyes.

I barely recognize myself. But maybe that's a good thing.

I get out of the car and head straight to the grocery store. I'm running low on supplies and I need to replenish.

I hunt regularly, so I'm good with food.

But alcohol is something I can't forage for in the forests around the cabin.

And God fucking knows I need that. It's the only thing that gets me through the nights.

I can feel eyes lock on me as I stride around the grocery store, throwing things into my cart. Anyone in my path clears away instantly, before they even meet my gaze.

I like it this way.

I'm standing in front of the liquor section when I feel someone walk up to me. My body clenches in response to the unwelcome attention.

People have started calling me *El Ruso Loco*. The Crazy Russian.

I like that, too.

But apparently, word hasn't gotten to quite everyone just yet. Either that or there are still people in this town who are fucking clueless.

"Hello, Artem."

I smell her before I look up at her. That thick, floral scent laces the air around her like an aura.

Aracelia.

I groan inwardly, but I keep my eyes dark and my expression impassive as I drop a bottle of whiskey into my cart without acknowledging her.

"You're not planning on saying hello?" Aracelia asks.

"Hadn't planned on it, no."

"Having a party tonight?" she asks with interest.

I pivot in place, turning the full force of my black eyes on her. "You're in my way."

"I think you're in your own way."

I roll my eyes. "Where'd that come from?" I demand. "Your self-help book of the month?"

"Just a personal observation," she replies with a shrug.

The woman has absolutely no sense of self-preservation. She's annoying enough to kill, but it really wouldn't be worth the effort. I'd have to bury her body afterwards and it would just mess with my evening of drinking.

A man can fantasize, though.

"How've you been?" she persists.

"Are you fucking serious right now?" I groan. "You're making small talk?"

"You could use a friendly conversation—"

"We are not fucking friends," I snarl.

I lean in so that my nose is inches away from hers. She stares back at me without any reaction. She doesn't even take a step back.

She shrugs. "That's a matter of opinion."

"It's my fucking opinion."

"Meaning what?" she asks. "Mine doesn't count?"

Fucking hell. The shit I have to put up with.

"No," I reply blackly.

"Why?" she demands. "Because I'm a woman?"

Her eyes flare with indignation. I notice a couple of people gawking at us from the aisles. That does remarkably little to help my mood.

"No," I retort. "Because you're fucking nuts."

"You should look in the mirror before you go around throwing insults like that," she says placidly.

One well-placed hit and she'd be out cold. It'd be so easy and the silence that follows would be so fucking welcome…

I try to walk around her, but she moves right in front of me, putting her body between me and the exit.

"Why don't you come around to my place for dinner?" she suggests brightly. "You look like you could use a real meal."

"I have food."

"Alcohol doesn't count as food."

"Why the fuck do you even care?" I ask.

She shrugs. "I think Esme would want me to make sure you're alright," she says.

I freeze. My eyes narrow. Icy, flinty, furious.

"Fuck off, you crazy bitch," I rasp.

Then I push past her so hard that she stumbles into the long shelves and upends several racks of beans.

Leaving the chaos in my wake, I head straight for the checkout counter and push my cart through.

"Hurry the fuck up," I tell the pimple-faced youth who looks about ready to piss himself. I'm not sure how good his English is, but some messages are universal. He gets the gist of it.

He grabs the items from my cart, trying to be as fast as he can, but he's so nervous he keeps stumbling, making silly mistakes and sweating through his green grocery store shirt.

"You have five seconds to finish up or else I'm gonna walk out of here with my alcohol and you're gonna have to pay for it."

His eyes go wide and the amount of sweat on his brow seems to double instantly.

"Do you have to terrorize the boy just because you're mad at the world?" comes a sickeningly familiar voice.

Fucking Aracelia.

"Don't you have a séance to go perform somewhere?" I ask. "A Ouija board that needs a friend?"

"Not today," she replies seriously. "But if you're interested in communicating with someone, I can find the time for you."

"*Ti durak!*" I groan in Russian. *Shut the fuck up.*

The boy almost drops one of my bottles of whiskey while he tries to run it under the scanner.

But my anger is directed at Aracelia right now. She's standing behind me with a bunch of bananas in her arms. Cradling it like a fucking baby.

"You know where I live if you change your mind about dinner," she says. As though we'd been having a perfectly civil conversation.

Then she pivots around and moves to the empty check-out counter next to the one I'm at.

I turn my attention back to the pimply boy in front of me.

"Didn't I tell you to hurry the fuck up?"

He actually lets out a little whimper that reminds me of the mutt up in my cabin right now.

But before I can threaten his life, a tall woman emerges out of thin air. Clearly, she's been watching the entire exchange.

She's wearing a white shirt whose top two buttons have been opened out just enough to display the impressive cleavage she's toting around. Her hair is dark and so are her eyes. She's just the kind of woman I used to gravitate to back when I was still a fool who thought chasing pussy was a worthy use of my time.

"Let me handle this, Jorge," she says smoothly. "Sorry about him, señor. He's new."

I just growl.

She looks at me through dark, interested eyes.

I know immediately why she's taken over at all. This bitch is sniffing around for cock. Some women are just self-destructive like that.

"I can offer you a discount," she says, ringing up the alcohol with impressive speed. "For the wait."

"Fine."

"If you're in a hurry, you can give me your address and I'll drive everything over in an hour when I'm done with my shift."

Fuck, she's bold. And it should have been sexy as fuck. But my cock has barely twitched.

"Is that part of the job description?" I ask.

"No," she replies, meeting my gaze and offering me a seductive smile. "But I like to go the extra mile for customers I like."

"You don't like me," I sigh. "Your pussy is wet for me. There's a difference."

She blinks at me for a moment in stunned horror.

I nod, satisfied with how that went. "Keep the change," I tell her as I hand over a wad of pesos.

Aracelia is standing by my car when I re-emerge into the parking lot. She stares at me as I load the groceries into the back seat and send the emptied cart flying into the curb with a shove.

"Move," I bark. She's blocking the driver's seat.

"Artem, I'm worried—"

My hand whips out instinctively. Finds that throat I fantasized about snapping.

I squeeze hard. Maybe too hard.

Aracelia tries not to make a noise, but I can see the fear in her eyes. She drops the two bags of goods she was holding. One of the bananas tumbles out onto the dirty asphalt.

I pull her towards me, real fucking close, and look her right in the eye when I speak.

"Leave me the fuck alone, Aracelia. I won't tell you again."

Then I let my hand drop.

Aracelia is silent. Her eyes glaze over for a moment. Finally, she says, "Esme was right to leave you."

Then she steps aside. I get in my truck and pull out. As I drive past, she's standing there on the curb.

Watching me with those huge, unblinking eyes.

I feel nothing. Just an empty hollowness that sucks away my capacity for compassion, for regret, for doubt.

It's the best fucking feeling in the world.

I drive up to the cabin fast. The wind in my hair, the sound of the car engine roaring on the climbs... it's good. It's right. *Action. Motion. Decision.* It's what's been missing from the moment I first stepped into the white-tiled bathroom and found Esme cowered in the corner.

When I pull up outside the cabin, the mutt is missing.

"At least someone in this fucking town can take a hint," I grumble.

I swing open the car door and drop down to the ground.

The moment I'm out of the Jeep, however, something feels off.

I can't see anything obvious. It's just a feeling, warning me that someone has been here.

Someone has been fucking around in my space.

I grab the gun I brought with me and walk straight into the cabin. I kick the door open and walk in, but whoever was here has left some time ago.

One thing's for certain: someone's definitely been here.

I move around the cabin, trying to sniff out what the fuckers wanted. I throw the bedroom door open and walk in.

Then I see it: my alcohol is gone. Whatever remained, that is. And the pistol I left on the kitchen counter.

Someone's gonna die for this.

I stride right back out to the wrangler and pull out a bottle of whiskey. I open it fast and take a long swig. When I lower the bottle, sensing eyes on me, I turn my head to the side and see two large brown eyes staring dolefully at me from behind a huge, thorned bush.

The mutt.

He's shivering. It's clear he was here when the intruders came by.

I take another swig and put the bottle down. The loss of one gun is irritating but not a tragedy. I never keep all my weapons in one place. They're stashed around the cabin grounds and the woods at large.

I stomp over to the shed, fuming, to retrieve a rifle tucked in the ceiling in there.

The mutt follows behind me, shivering the whole fucking time.

"You better fucking learn now," I tell him. "If you stick around, there's gonna be a fuck ton more of this shit."

The dog whines a little, as though refuting the fact.

"You want a peaceful life?" I continue. "You want safety? That's not gonna happen with me."

The dog doesn't move. I duck into the shed. I find the rifle I'm looking for and sigh gratefully.

Then I step back out into the cold air and cock it.

Whoever you are, you picked the wrong fucking man to fuck with.

15

ESME

My heart is beating so hard. For a few moments, it's all I can hear.

I try and block out the sound, but there's an internal conflict raging in my head.

I can't help her. I'm nine months pregnant.

But she's your friend.

I have no friends. I have only my child. And my child always comes first.

You told her who you are. You trust her.

He's too big, too strong, too powerful, too dangerous.

You've handled men like him before. You've killed men like him before.

Exactly. And I left that life behind. I don't want to be a murderer.

Even if the man out there deserves to be murdered?

But my baby...

Can you live with yourself if you stand here silent while Sara gets raped out there?

...

No. No, I wouldn't be able to live with myself.

I open my eyes. My hands have fallen over my belly protectively. I hear Sara's muffled scream and I know without having to look that he's clamped his hand down over her mouth.

I look around the bathroom desperately, searching for something I can use as a weapon. There's nothing that immediately jumps out at me, but I know I have to move fast.

I notice the ugly blue weight next to the bathroom door. Marni uses it prop the door open after she cleans the bathroom and wants some ventilation. I grab it, slightly comforted by its weight in my palm. I slip out of the bathroom without making a sound.

Noise from dining area spills down the cramped hallway even through the shut door. I can hear Eagle Tattoo's goons laughing and throwing their weight around. The clink and clack of silverware. The low pop music that plays all day long.

I ignore it all as I tiptoe close to where Eagle Tattoo has Sara pushed up against the wall. His face is buried in her neck, snuffling like a wild animal.

Her skirt is pushed up around her hips, his hand wedged between her thighs. The sight turns my stomach and strengthens my resolve.

I'm scared.

But I have to do something. I have to fight.

I'm stronger than I look, you know.

I lift the weight up over my head with both hands. Sara turns and sees me over the bastard's shoulder at the last second. Her cheeks are tearstained, her expression terrified, but hope flickers across her face.

I bring the weight down hard, as hard as I can. The edge of it cracks against the back of Eagle Tattoo's head with a wet, nasty noise. His hands slacken at once around Sara's wrists.

But I can't see his face.

Have I struck a fatal blow or have I just succeeded in pissing him off?

I'm not gonna be able to fight him in my condition.

Oh, God, what have I done, little bird...?

Just as I'm contemplating my next move—run, scream, beg—he stumbles backwards and bumps into the opposite wall.

He slides to a seat, legs akimbo in front of him.

And the first trickle of blood drips down past his ear.

More comes soon. The trickle becomes a torrent. Blood, hot and sticky, marring his face like warpaint.

He looks at me in shock and fury. Still not quite processing what happened, where all his pain is coming from.

I rush to Sara, who wraps her arms around me. She's shaking violently. Her body feels small and vulnerable against the swell of my belly.

I glance towards Eagle Tattoo, whose eyes are glazed over in shock, awareness fading in and out as he tries to cling to consciousness.

His eyes are trained on me, not Sara. It sends a chill straight through my spine. Then he loses the fight to stay awake, and his head lolls forward. Behind him on the bare concrete wall is a smear of blood.

"Oh, my God," Sara gasps over and over again. "Oh, my God. Oh, my God..."

I steer her further down the corridor, towards the door that leads to the back alley of the restaurant.

As we stumble out into the cool night air, I feel my lungs expand to take in as much oxygen as I can. But it still doesn't relieve me.

"I... Is he... dead?" Sara asks.

"Fuck," I say. I'm still in disbelief at everything that just happened. "Fuck... what have I done?"

"You saved me," Sara says, looking at me with gratitude. "You could have been seriously hurt, Em... I mean, Esme."

I look down at my hands, expecting to see blood. But there's none. I'm untainted by the assault. So is Sara. Physically, at least.

Of course, emotionally and mentally, we will carry the scars of this night for years to come.

I try to shake off my panic. "Are you okay?"

She looks down at her body as though she expects to see her evidence of her fear and trauma. "I... I don't know... he... touched me..."

Her resolve breaks. She sobs, her words dissolving into something strangled and inarticulate.

I move forward and grab both her hands in mine. "It's okay," I reassure her. "It's gonna be okay."

"That's never happened to me before... I feel so—"

"Violated? Stripped bare? Emotionally raw?" I offer.

She meets my gaze as tears pool in her too-blue eyes.

Fuck, her eyes are so much like his.

"Yes," she says emphatically. "That's exactly how I feel."

"I know how that is," I tell her. "It's happened to me. A long time ago, but I still remember."

I can feel the trauma of that night at The Siren float to the surface, but I tamp it back down. If I give in to the emotion now, I'm not so sure I'll be able to remove myself from its clutches.

I need to keep a clear mind. Especially now. I can break down later. When I am safe.

If I'm ever safe again.

"I have to go," I say.

Sara squeezes my hands. "No."

I shake my head. "I can't stay, Sara," I say. "I just assaulted a man. He might be dead for all we know and it's only a matter of time before he's discovered in that hallway."

"I'll tell them why you did it," Sara says instantly. "We can call the police. I'll tell them he tried to rape me and you were only defending me."

I stare at her, wondering if there was ever a time when I was that naïve.

"No, Sara," I say as gently as I can. "They'll never believe us. It's our word against his and no one ever believes women."

"But—"

"Did he get inside you?" I ask bluntly.

"What?" Sara gasps. She recoils from the words.

"Did he put his penis inside you?"

She shudders. "No."

"Then there's no evidence of a rape," I finish. "And even if there was, he can easily claim that it was consensual."

"Esme—"

"There are no cameras on this side of the restaurant," I point out. "Even if the police press charges, they'll be dropped. Mafia guys like that have strings they can and *will* pull."

"No. No. Esme, there has to be another way."

"He could be dead, Sara," I repeat. "It might be our word against a dead man. And not just any dead man. A mafia boss. Some kind of higher up at least. He might be the head honcho; he might be one of the under bosses. It doesn't really matter."

Translation: we're fucked.

I don't say it quite like that, but the implication still stands between us.

"What are you gonna do?" Sara asks desperately. "Where are you gonna go?"

"I'll be fine," I reply, mostly to stave off her questions.

They're questions I don't have answers for.

"Go back in there," I tell her. "Pretend like you've just discovered his body. You're shaky and panicked, so that'll work in your favor."

"Esme," Sara begs, squeezing my hand. "Don't leave."

I don't want to leave, but I have to.

"This is your home!"

I laugh bitterly. I was a fool to think I could settle anywhere for long.

I have no home.

I grab Sara's shoulders and force her to look at me. "Go on," I order her. "I'll be fine."

"But—"

"Now."

I push her back towards the door. She moves forward even as she looks back over her shoulder at me.

"Esme…" She begins as if she wants to say something. Then she trails off, at a loss for words.

I give her a reassuring smile and shoo her inside. But the moment she disappears through the door, my smile drops.

Oh God, what have I done?

I've blown up my life—again. And now, I don't have the luxury of time to plan my escape.

I walk out of the alleyway, trying to maintain a calm pace, but I speed up instinctively the moment I clear the restaurant. I head down the street.

But instead of hailing a cab, I just keep walking.

The motion helps with my flustered thoughts. I'm hoping I can have a plan put together by the time I reach my apartment.

I thought I left this kind of life, these kind of worries in my rearview mirror. But somehow, it always manages to catch up with me.

And I've killed someone else. Another dangerous man.

He deserved it. That is my only solace.

My footsteps make sharp sounds against the sidewalk. People look at me pass as they always do. Men in cars, men walking by me. They all look at my stomach, every time.

I feel that familiar sharp shooting pain. But it's mild and honestly, I've gotten used to it. I've had pain through my entire pregnancy. The stress has followed me from the mountains. It doesn't seem like it's looking to abandon me any time soon.

When I get to my apartment, I walk up the three flights of stairs, stopping to rest on each landing, before I finally make it to my unit.

I've got the key in the door when I hear running footsteps. A second later, Juanita and Eva round the corner with their mother, Gabrielle, right behind them. She's pregnant, too, with a stomach that's almost as large as mine.

"Emily!" Gabrielle croons when she sees me.

She's got a load of laundry attached to her hip and a thin sheen of sweat that clings to her brow. I will myself to smile back, hoping that my face won't betray me.

"Hola, Gabby," I greet.

The little girls, Juanita and Eva, race towards me and encircle me from either side.

"Hola, Emily," Eva says, flashing me a huge smile that reveals her lack of front teeth.

"Hola, princesa," I reply, tweaking her nose. "Where have you troublemakers been?"

Eva tattles on her sister immediately. "Juanita made a mess on my bedsheet," she says. "So we went to do the laundry."

"I didn't make the mess—you did!" Juanita cries out.

"Chicas!" Gabby says tiredly. "Here's the key. Please, go inside."

"We wanna talk to Emily," Juanita whines.

"Tomorrow," I tell her, knowing full well there will be no tomorrow. "Do as your mother says."

Gabby shoots me a grateful smile as both girls skip to their door. I've been in their apartment twice before. It's a tiny studio. The girls share a single queen mattress with their parents. A new baby on the way will only make things harder.

"Are you okay, Emily?" Gabby asks.

"Me?"

She nods. "You looked a little worried."

I hadn't even realized I was being so obvious. Or maybe I wasn't. Maybe Gabby is just that good at sussing out when something was wrong. After all, she is the mother to two young girls.

"I'm not," I reply—a little too fast.

"Is it that baby?" she asks. "It's past time you popped that little guy out, huh?"

She's circling her own stomach with soft hands. I wonder if she even realizes she's doing it. "Way past time," I agree. "But apparently, he's comfortable in here."

Gabby gives me a little wink. "Don't make it too comfortable for him," she says. "You want to meet him at some point. Or her."

"Or her." I still haven't found out what the sex of the baby is. I've had chances, but every time, I decline.

"Oh, that reminds me," Gabby says with a snap of her fingers. "I have an extra baby blanket you can have if you want."

"An extra one?" I ask. "Won't you need it for your little guy?"

"I'm stitching a new one for her," Gabby tells me.

"Her?"

Gabby nods and rings. "We found out yesterday. Another girl."

"Wow!" I smile. "Congratulations."

"I hate saying it, but it does make things easier in terms of hand-me-downs," she admits.

"Are you sure? You could probably still use it," I point out, knowing that there is no way Gabby would ever just discard a perfectly good blanket.

"I'd rather you have it."

I feel my heart swell as she gives me a kind smile. It's amazing how many little kindnesses have gotten me through the last few months.

"Thank you, Gabby."

"Of course. Stay right there. I'll go grab it."

"Oh, you don't have to—"

But she's already gone, shuffling through the cracked-open door of her apartment a few units down.

I sigh and lean against the wall. She's back a moment later, sans laundry basket but with the blanket in her hands.

It's a soft yellow fabric that would have been a bright, sunshiny yellow in its heyday. The years have robbed it of its thickness and most of its color, but the worn-down love spots just make me smile. There's even a little bee embroidered into one corner.

"Aw, Gabby, it's beautiful," I purr. "Did you stitch it yourself?"

She nods. "When Juanita was born. So it's over eight years old now. I wish I could give you something a little more fresh."

I put my hand on her arm. "I love it," I insist. "It's beautiful and sentimental. I'll always keep it."

She beams. I have to resist the urge to give her a hug. I don't want this to seem like a goodbye. Gabby is already plenty suspicious.

And the fewer people who know I'm leaving, the better.

"See you tomorrow," I say. Then I slip into my apartment.

The moment I'm inside, I start making a list of what few possessions I have to my name. It's depressingly short.

First, I grab the large duffel bag that I've stored underneath the sofa. I wrench it open and move around the apartment, assessing what I can take with me and what needs to be left behind.

I had been preparing to bring my baby back to this apartment, so I've been buying little things over the last couple of months whenever I had a little cash to spare.

A travel basinet, a load of diapers, a few onesies that I'd brought from a secondhand store.

The baby's stuff takes up most of the space in the duffel bag. I pack my things on top. A few threadbare dresses, a tiny bag of makeup. And a small velvet pouch containing the wedding ring that Artem gave me.

Once the contents of my life have been packed away into a single bag, I hoist it onto my shoulder and look around the space.

Water-stained walls and a rickety table look back at me.

At least there won't be anything about this place to miss.

But the moment I think it, I realize that it's not the place I'll miss, but the people.

Gabby and her daughters.

Cranky old Ruby, surly Jose, kind Marti.

And Sara, with sapphire eyes like Cillian's.

I'll never see any of them again.

16
ESME

I turn off the lights and head downstairs. My only plan is to get out of this town as fast as possible. I don't even know where I'm headed.

I start walking towards the bus stop. It's about a twenty-minute walk and in my condition, I know it'll take me longer.

But it doesn't matter. I don't want to waste money on a cab.

The streets have emptied out. Only a handful people walking around, a few already drunk after a long day of work.

This town is filled with sad outcasts like me. Day drinking and desperation follows them around like homeless animals.

I try not to judge. After all, I'm a homeless animal myself at the moment.

I start cramping halfway to the bus station, so I'm forced to stop and sit at a park bench to wince and stretch out my legs as best as I can.

But the second I sink onto the bench, the voice starts up.

You're weak.

You're pathetic.

You're naïve. Can't even save your own baby.

Lately, my head is filled with thoughts like these. Always in Papa's voice. Like he lives in my head and lurks. A parasite. A virus. A taunting spirit that chimes in whenever I find a moment of silence.

I force myself to stand. The cramps start up again with a vengeance, but this time, I ignore them.

Fuck that voice. Fuck those thoughts.

I limp down the street with a scowl on my face and my hand white-knuckling the straps of the duffel bag to get through the pain.

When I finally turn into the bus station, I'm panting and sweating, but I push myself forward.

The man sitting behind the clerk counter is an older African-American man with an impressive white mustache.

"Good evening, sir," I say quietly. "Can I have one of the bus schedules please?"

His eyes rake over me through the Plexi-glass. I wait patiently for him to finish his once-over.

"Where you headed, hon?" he asks.

"Um, I don't know," I admit. "That's why I need the bus schedule."

His expression doesn't change so much as it softens. Then he pulls out a leaflet and hands it to me.

It's a maze of weaving colored lines. There are so many bus routes that I know I won't be able to decide where I'm going by just picking blindly.

"Excuse me a minute," I tell him, moving to one of the benches a few yards away.

I sit down, relieved to be off my feet even for a few minutes. Then I comb through the bus schedules.

It takes me a minute, especially with the adrenaline still pumping in my system, but eventually I figure out that there are three different buses heading to three different towns in the next hour.

I've heard of none of these towns. Somehow, that leaves me feeling deflated. I realize how ill-equipped I am to make this choice at all.

The first bus leaving is in twenty minutes, but its destination is too close for my liking. I cross it off and move on to the second bus. Its destination is two hours away, a little better but it still doesn't sit right with me for reasons I can't explain.

But then, none of this does.

"Need some help?"

I look up to see the man who'd handed me the bus schedule. He sits down next to me, glancing at my duffel bag.

"There's only one reason a young girl such as yourself would leave town in the night without a plan," he tells me. I freeze instantly as he finishes, "You've run into a spot of trouble."

I glance at his face, searching for a threat. But I can see only concern and perhaps a desire to help.

I give him a nervous smile and look back down at the bus schedule.

"It's more like trouble seems to run into me," I tell him.

He chuckles and sighs. "That's true for some people," he agrees. "Forgive me for saying this, but you're in no condition to be travelling."

I rest my hands on my huge belly and I feel an answering kick. A strong kick.

I bite down on my tongue to keep the emotion at bay.

"I'd rather not be traveling at all," I concede. "But I don't really have a choice."

"I thought as much. Are you running from the father?" he asks bluntly.

I glance at him, my jaw tight. But I say nothing.

"You don't have to tell me anything," he tells me. "I know this isn't my place and you probably don't want an old man's advice anyhow. But I tried running once. It's no way to live."

His words are hitting a little too close to home. I really don't need to doubt my next move, but I can't stop him, either.

Or maybe I just don't want to.

"You gotta stand your ground and fight back," he continues. "That's the only way to do it."

I sigh bitterly. "My situation is complicated."

"It always seems that way," he says. "Especially when you're young. How old are you—nineteen, twenty?"

"Almost twenty-three."

He waves a hand. "Too young to run."

"You don't know what I'm running from."

"Perhaps." He falls silent.

"Can you help me?" I ask, once the silence has stretched out long enough for me to know that staying is really not an option. "I need a quiet town. Somewhere I can have my baby."

"How long are you planning on staying?" he asks.

"I don't know. A few months, maybe longer," I answer. "I just need somewhere quiet and safe."

"There aren't many places like that for a young single mother," he tells me. "But if that's what you're looking for, take this bus."

He points to the red line bus that leaves in an hour and ten minutes.

"It is not the most glamorous place in the world," he admits. "But there are a few women's shelters there. They'll take you in, baby and all."

"Women's shelters," I repeat.

"It's the only place I can think of that doesn't require paying rent."

"Thank you," I whisper.

I wish desperately that I could just stay here. It isn't perfect in this town by any means. But I've grown comfortable here, I have friends, and there's a comfort that comes with familiarity.

I won't have any of that if I leave.

"What's your name?" I ask, because for some reason, I don't want to stop talking.

Or rather, I don't want to be alone.

"Geoffrey," he replies. "And yours?"

My real name slips out before I can stop myself. "Esme."

"It's lovely to meet you, Esme," he says genuinely. "You know, no matter how bad life gets, there's always a way out of it."

"I wish I had your kind of faith," I sigh. "But my life has changed so much in less than a year. It feels surreal, and not in a good way."

He nods. "I know what you mean. I was living on the streets when I was fifteen. A year later, I was dealing drugs. Soon after, I was using. It took years before I was strong and brave enough to get sober. And even then, I can't take all the credit."

"You fell in love?" I guess.

"Yes, I did," he replies with a distant smile. "She was the most beautiful girl in the world. She still is."

"What's her name?"

"Olive," Geoffrey tells me. "She's thirty-three years old now. Has two boys of her own, too."

I frown. Geoffrey must be at least sixty, if not older.

He sees my confusion and smiles. "She's my daughter," he explains.

"Oh!"

"I was in my twenties when she was born, and I was too fucked up to be her dad," he tells me. "When her mother stopped me from seeing her, I was angry, but I understood."

He rubs the back of his neck like he's going through the emotions all over again.

"I vowed to get clean. It wasn't easy. I fell off the wagon a few times. But when Olive was about eleven, I finally managed to make it stick. It took a while longer to make her trust me again. To make her mother trust me again. But it was worth it."

Someone shuffles into the bus station and heads towards the booth. Geoffrey stands with a muted groan and pats me on the shoulder in a fatherly way.

Then he goes back to the ticket office. He has a small limp and a hunched back, but his shadow stretches on for miles beneath the lone fluorescent light high overhead.

I look down at my map, at the new town that I'm to make my home.

I feel resigned to the decision. It's not perfect, but this isn't about things being perfect. It's about survival.

I stand up, steadying myself on the armrest of the bench, and take one step towards the ticket booth. The shooting pain is there, but I ignore it.

Until, one step later, it doubles.

Triples.

Suddenly, it's all I can feel, sharp and insistent and glaring. Then— moisture between my legs. A trickle of something that catches me off guard.

For one horrible second, I think it's blood. Like all the stress my body has been through in the last few hours is finally taking its toll.

But when I look down at the concrete floor, it's not blood I see.

It's water.

My water just broke.

Oh God.

I'm having this baby.

I'm having this baby now.

"Esme?"

The other passenger has moved off to a far corner. Geoffrey is looking at me from behind the glass of the ticket office with his eyebrows knitted together in concern.

I meet his gaze. The world spins. I feel my knees shake a little but I will myself to keep standing.

"I... need to get... hospital," I choke out. Another wave of pain has me wincing.

I hear footsteps, fast, but with a discernable limp. Then I feel a hand on my arm, strong and firm.

I lean into his weight at my side to stop from falling over. I have to trust him. I don't have any other choice.

"Hold on, girl," Geoffrey orders. His voice is so deep and soothing that for a moment, it actually succeeds in calming me.

"I... I can't," I gasp. White light streaks across my eyes like shooting stars. "This baby is coming..."

And then, one by one, the stars snuff out.

All that's left is darkness.

17

ARTEM

A SMALL FARM OUTSIDE OF PICACHO DEL DIABLO, MEXICO

"Señor!" Guillermo greets, giving me a smile that I'm sure he thinks is convincing. "Nice to see you."

I don't bother with the fucking small talk.

Or with any talk.

I just punch him square in the face.

The weapons dealer stumbles back with a yell of pain. Blood spout from his nostrils.

"Keep in mind—the next punch *will* break your nose," I tell him calmly.

"What the fuck?" Guillermo stammers as he tries to get his bearings. The blood is thick in his hands now.

He's stumbled right into a murky puddle of mud and horse shit. His black rubber boots are mired in it.

"That was a warning," I tell him. "A taster of what I will do to you if you don't give me the information I need."

"I... information?" Guillermo stammers. "I have no information. Just guns."

"I have enough of your fucking guns," I remind him. "I've kept your fucking side business going for the past few months. Which is why you owe me."

Guillermo's wipes the blood off his upper lip and spits on the earth.

"Fuck, it hurts," he complains. "I think it's broken."

I narrow my eyes. "If I wanted to break your nose, trust me, it would be fucking broken right now. You're fine. Be a fucking man and shake it off."

He looks up at me, new fear tainting his expression.

"Mira, cabrón," he says, straightening up. "I'm just the gun supplier around these parts okay? I'm not involved in the politics."

"Like fuck you're not," I say. I feint closer.

He lunges backwards like I'd shocked him with a cattle prod. Ends up even deeper in the pile of shit.

Good. That's where trash like him belongs anyway.

"Now, you're gonna answer my questions," I tell him, with a meaningful glance over his shoulder. In the distance behind him, two young boys are playing in the field. His sons, I presume. "Or Papa won't be joining the boys for dinner."

He gulps visibly and nods. "Sí, sí, sí. What do you wanna know?"

"My cabin was ransacked. No more than a few hours ago," I say. "What do you know about that?"

"Nothing."

I sigh and take a casual half-pivot, as if I'm going to walk away. Which is probably why he doesn't see my fist coming.

He hits the ground hard, with a squelch. Shit flies everywhere. The blood is pouring even faster now. His lip is busted, too.

I stand over him, one foot planted on either side of his fat legs like sausages encased in denim.

"You wanna try that again?" I ask conversationally.

"Now it's broken!" he cries out.

"I did promise that," I tell him. "And I'm a man of my word. The next time you piss me off, I'm gonna have to break a leg."

"What...?"

"Or a hand," I say with a shrug. "I'll let you pick. Start thinking now about which way you're leaning."

"All right, all right!" Guillermo protests. He's glaring up at me, mud and shit and blood streaking his face. "I may know something. But I'm just mostly guessing here. Keep that in mind."

"Noted." I squat down so that I'm at eye level with the farmer. "Go on."

"A few months ago, Lobo came around here asking to buy weapons," he sighs. "He seemed pretty fucking upset because his father has been missing for a while."

"Lobo?" I repeat. "Am I supposed to know who the fuck that is?"

"Razor's boy."

The name sounds familiar, but I can't figure out why.

"Razor?"

"He is—was—a narcotraficante," Guillermo replies. *A drug dealer.* "He controls the trade routes on this side of town."

That connects the dots for me. The memory resurfaces like an unwelcome ghost from my past.

Razor is the motherfucker who thought he could come for me.

The one who's bones are still rotting somewhere in the ravine by the cabin.

I see his face in my mind's eye. That stupid snarling expression that had quickly turned to fear once he'd realized that he was no match for me.

"As far as crime lords go, he wasn't a very good one," I say flippantly.

Guillermo's eyes go wide. "The kid thinks you killed his old man."

"Then he'd be right."

"Fuck," Guillermo mutters. "Fuck."

"I killed his father and his goons months ago," I point out. "Why's the kid all riled up now? Is he as slow as his fucking father or just scared?"

"He's young," Guillermo tells me. "Nineteen, I think."

"Won't stop me from killing him, too."

"He bought new guns from me just last week," Guillermo tells me. "It was like he was preparing for something."

"How many men does he have?"

"I'm not sure. Ten, maybe fifteen. I recognized only two of them," he says. "The others were new."

"Which means he's hired them," I conclude. "So he is scared. At least he's not stupid."

"Amigo, no offense, but are you?"

I laugh. "No, I'm not stupid. I am Bratva."

Guillermo's face goes bone-white with fear.

He knows that word. Enough to be afraid of it. He's smarter than I gave him credit for, it seems.

I straighten up and look out towards the farmhouse where both boys are now jumping off the porch in turns.

Innocent and fearless. Too young to be as scarred as I am.

There was a time when I'd entertained the notion of a quiet life like theirs somewhere peaceful.

But that was only a fever dream.

I was a fool to think I could leave the Bratva behind.

It is part of me.

Sutured into my skin, as necessary to me as air.

"Where can I find the little bastard?" I ask.

Guillermo stays on the ground at my feet. "They work out of a small farm to the southwest of the mountain range. Right off the highway. You can't miss it."

I nod. "You've been useful, Guillermo."

It's the closest he'll get to a thank you.

∽

I leave Guillermo lying in the shit and jump into my Jeep. Then I start the drive to the farm he described.

With every mile that passes under my tires, I get angrier.

This fucking kid thought he could fuck with me by ransacking my cabin like some a goddamn cat burglar.

He and his men are about a get a lesson in the art of fear mongering.

You don't fuck with Artem Kovalyov.

The adrenaline is pumping through me as I drive fast down the rural highway. I see the house rear up in the distance. I stop half a mile away and pull my truck out of sight behind a pyramid of hay bales.

Then I sit and wait for nightfall.

∽

When darkness comes, I tuck a pistol into the back of my jeans and grab my rifle. It takes me half an hour to get within range of the house. I move slowly, stopping and starting often, and always watching for signs of life.

When I come up on the structure, I can see only a few men outside.

They're smoking cigarettes and laughing. I see a mound of beer cans littering the ground at their feet.

Fucking perfect.

I screw the silencer onto the pistol as I take stock of the situation. I know I have to be fast. There are three men out front, and I have to hit all three before any of them can warn the other men inside the cabin house.

My hands are steady as I take aim. It helps that all three men are sitting close together.

So considerate of them.

Then I shoot.

One. Head shot.

Two. Head shot.

Three. Head shot.

When I lower my gun, I see their bodies lying next to their beer bottles. I might have thought it was poetic, if I were the poetic type.

The silencer has done its job. My bullets barely made a sound. No one inside seems to have heard.

I leave the corpses cooling in the night and set back off down the path I took to get here.

The boy will get my message soon enough. And when he does, I have no doubt he will rally his men and bring them down to the cabin… to my neck of the woods.

And then…

Well, then we're gonna have some fun.

18

ARTEM

The walk to the car and the drive home that follows both go quickly. I can move much faster under cover of night.

The moment I park outside the lodge, I jump into action, setting traps in the surrounding area and getting all my guns in order.

I pick the spot I'm planning on luring them to and start setting up traps around the perimeter. I work quickly and quietly with a flashlight clenched between my teeth to illuminate my hands.

With some old car parts filched from the junkyard on the outer rim of town, I fashion jagged-toothed traps that will snap shut on anyone who wanders too close. I pity the poor fucker who gets caught here.

When I hear the crunch of leaves in the underbrush, I get up fast and snatch the gun resting at my side.

They're here sooner than I expected…

Or not.

It's just the mutt from before.

"Fucking hell," I mutter. I set the rifle down and return to finishing my traps.

The dog pads over to me. Instinctively, I put my hand out and push him away from the sharpened sticks.

"Unless you want to lose a leg," I tell him, "I would clear away from this general area."

The dog cocks his head to the side as though he's really listening to me. I finish setting up and make sure each trap has been expertly hidden by leaves.

Once that's done, I head back to the cabin to check on a few things. I probably don't have very long. They could arrive in a matter of minutes, but I'm counting on my traps to tip me off.

The dog follows behind me. I realize that the annoyance I usually feel has lessened somewhat.

When we get back to the cabin, I put some water down in a bowl for him.

Motherfucker has the audacity to look surprised.

"Don't get too excited," I growl at him. "This is a one-time thing."

He laps up the water, finishing it in seconds. I fill it up for a second time and then go back to cleaning my guns.

When I start towards the door, the dog follows behind me.

I put my foot in the way. The dog does that curious head-tilt shit he loves doing.

"Just for today," I grumble, "you can hang out in the cabin. Don't make yourself too comfortable. And stay off my goddamn bed."

Then I shut the door on him, trapping him inside. I hear whimpering on the other side and pawing at the door, but I ignore it and keep walking.

It's for your own good. You don't want to get caught in the crossfire.

I head back to the location I've marked in the woods, settle down amongst the leaves, and lie in wait.

I should probably feel like a man who's been backed into a tight corner.

But I feel more like a hunter stalking his prey.

※

It takes them longer than I'd anticipate to get here. Long enough, anyway, to make me second guess whether they'll come at all.

But then I hear the crunch of boots on gravel and a smile stretches across my face. I have a fight on my hands.

Fucking finally.

I double-check my position against the new arrivals. From the direction they're coming in, I know they'll fan out, but they won't be able to circle around me. So I don't have to worry about defending my back. Not just yet anyway.

I see movement and I keep my gun cocked. It's obvious from the clumsy, careless movements that they're not expecting me to be lying in wait.

Amateurs.

The moment their figures approach, I assess the situation. I can see four of them but I know there are more at their backs.

All the men I can see are armed, which means the rest will be as well. None of them are yet aware that I'm here, watching them.

Two of the poor souls wander within range of my bullets. The other two in the lead party are still weaving between trees, making a clean shot difficult.

I decide to hedge my bets and wait a little longer. This will all be over soon enough. Might as well enjoy it while it lasts.

Snippets of their hushed conversation carries over to where I'm hidden.

"... we need to be fucking careful..."

"... are you fucking serious? He's one man. There's nine of us."

Well, thank you for that morsel of information.

"He's not just one fucking man. He killed three of ours today."

"From a distance, under cover. That's not a fucking accomplishment. That's the coward's way out."

I laugh silently. I'd give the braggart a brave man's fight if that's what he's after, but it will end exactly the same way.

This is much cleaner and easier for the both of us.

I peer around the corner and catch a glimpse of the fucker who just spoke. He looks young, but definitely older than twenty. He should fucking know better.

He was not meant to be my first target, but he's just changed my mind.

I take aim with the rifle.

Don't blink. Don't hesitate.

This is just more target practice.

Without a silencer, the gunshot blasts through the air, careening through the silence like an avalanche.

Before the first bullet has even met its target, I've shot a second time. Two bodies drop to the forest floor.

The remaining men scatter in a frenzy of panicked limbs.

Two down. Seven to go.

I back away quickly, moving towards the cabin and making more noise than necessary. I want them to hear me—they need to follow me in order for my plan to work.

"He's trying to run!" someone shouts.

Assuming they've gotten me on the defensive, they rush out at me with their guns raised. The trees provide plenty of protection and all the bullets bury themselves harmlessly in the thick trunks.

They charge forward in search of a better line of fire.

And then a blood-curdling scream penetrates the air.

Two more follow on its heels. I smirk with satisfaction, knowing that the steel traps have done their work.

Rapid-fire Spanish wails out into the night. I don't have to speak the language to know that the trapped bastards aren't exactly offering their thanks to me.

I circle back around, making sure to keep a good distance between me and the remaining men.

Three of them are caught. One poor son of a bitch has already fainted. Blood pools around his nearly severed leg. He'll be dead in minutes.

The other two have been caught at safer angles. There's still blood, but not nearly so much.

They're all still in shock. So in shock in fact, that no one really even notices me until my bullet buries itself in one of their skulls.

Three down. Six to go.

Of course, that gets their attention. The remaining able-bodied men open fire immediately.

I pivot to the side and unload a clip on these motherfuckers.

Dead.

Dead.

Five down. Four to go.

My eyes zero in on the last remaining youth, the only member of this misguided little gang whose leg is not stuck in one of my steel traps.

His arm is raised, his gun pointed at me, but I know already that he no longer has the confidence or the ability to shoot me.

Even if he does, I'm confident he'll miss.

"Drop your gun," I command.

"You'll kill me if I do," he says, his voice shaky.

Now that I'm looking at him, I realize his features strike me as familiar.

"You Razor's kid?" I ask.

The boy flinches. Guillermo had mentioned he was nineteen, but he looks even younger to me. Nowhere near a man.

Not that that changes anything. He came for me. This is the price he'll pay for that transgression.

"You killed him," he says, but the accusation sounds weak.

"He messed with the wrong fucking don," I reply unfeelingly. "I assume you found his body."

"What was left of it," the kid spat at me. "And there wasn't much after the ravine spit him out."

"At least you got to bury him in peace. That was a luxury I wasn't afforded, and my father was a fuck ton more important than yours."

"I'm going to kill you," the boy says. His voice is shivering so pitifully that I have to resist the urge to laugh.

I glance over at his three men in my steel traps. Their unseeing eyes look up at the star-lit heavens.

"Is that so?" I ask. "Because you came at me with nine men and yet, here we are, mano e mano."

"Fuck you."

"Drop the gun," I say calmly. "Now."

His arm trembles but he refuses to lower it. I sigh with exasperation and jerk my head towards his comrades.

"They can't save you, you know. It's just you and me now, kid."

"I'm not a kid," he barks.

"No?" I ask. "Then shoot me."

"I… what?"

"Shoot me," I enunciate clearly.

He gulps like he thinks this is a trap. I spread my arms wide and smile.

It's a tense standoff for a second, though I don't understand why. I'm giving him the chance to avenge his father. Pull the goddamn trigger.

And then, he does.

The gunshot rips out.

But Lobo's hand is trembling so badly that, even though I don't move at all, the bullet only grazes across my left arm. It's nothing more than a flesh wound.

Pity.

I stoop low and throw my body against his. His eyes go wide but he's too slow or shocked to get out of my way.

We hit the ground in a heap.

The moment I've got him pinned underneath me, I rip the gun out of his hand and fling it into the dirt several feet away from us.

He struggles like a fish out of water until I punch him in the face. Then he goes limp immediately.

Just like that, the fight leaves him. Lobo looks up at me with defeat and hopelessness.

"Are you going to kill me?" he asks.

It's a child's question. Not a man's.

I sigh. "Yes."

I clamber off him, leaving him stunned and shivering on the earth.

He sits up a little on his elbows and looks around. He's trying to determine what his odds are of getting out of this forest alive.

I pick up my gun and check the clip for my remaining ammo before returning to face the boy.

"Don't even think about running," I say. "It's pointless. You're not gonna get away. Not from me."

"You killed all of my men," he says. There's an awestruck note in his tone.

I shrug. "I've been training since I was a boy. I was told I'd be in charge one day. Unlike you, I was prepared for that inevitability."

"I *am* prepared. I... I... *was* prepared," he stammers. But as he glances around at the bodies of his friends and followers, the last of his confidence snuffs out.

"I think the evidence speaks for itself."

I take a step forward. He flinches and seems to huddle lower into the ground.

"I know what it means to inherit your father's legacy," I tell him. "It's all worthless in the end."

His eyes go wide. "Then why do you do it?"

"Because I have no choice."

I raise my hand. The boy seems to understand that the conversation is over. His lower lip starts to tremble and I can see the desperation flit across his eyes.

"It won't hurt," I reassure him. "You won't feel a thing."

"I feel it now," he replies. "I can feel it already."

A tear slips down his cheek.

I still feel nothing.

My finger is poised over the trigger. I'm ready to pull.

Do it.

End him.

But I can't.

I sigh in frustration and let my hand fall down to my side.

"Get out of my sight before I change my mind."

His eyes go wide with disbelief.

"I said, *go.*"

The kid scrambles off, tripping several times before he manages to gain enough wind to disappear into the woods.

I stomp back to the cabin in the blackest mood I can remember. I'll let the night foragers take care of the bastards' bodies.

At the lodge, I kick in the door, drop my guns on the kitchen table, and collapse into a chair, head buried in my hands.

"What the fuck?" I mutter under my breath again and again. "What the fuck, what the fuck, what the fuck…"

A whine answers me.

I raise my head to see the mutt lying between my feet. He's gazing up at me with those big, emotional eyes.

"I actually pity you too much to kill you," I grumble.

He flicks his ears as though my threat is hollow and he knows it.

The worst part is, he's right.

"What the fuck am I supposed to be doing?" I ask him.

I've been training like a madman for months. But I haven't left the mountain. I could've gone at any time once my injuries healed. Just get in the Jeep and make for Los Angeles.

And if tonight hasn't proved that I'm as good as ever—better, even—then I don't know what will.

So what am I waiting for?

I should be retaking what's mine. Hunting down Budimir and slaughtering him the way he deserves.

Instead, I'm freezing my ass off on this fucking mountain.

To prove some unknown point.

To some unknown person.

And I don't even have an answer as to why.

The mutt nuzzles at my hand.

"Get away from me, you idiot," I sigh. I push his nose away from me.

He doesn't take it personally. His tail wags, thumping against the floor. Those eyes haven't changed. No matter how much I shove him aside or curse at him, he still looks at me like his savior.

It makes me sick. I'm no one's savior.

Not anymore.

I get up abruptly. The chair screeches back on the floor.

"I'm going to bed," I announce. To the dog or the empty room or no one at all—I'm not entirely sure who the intended audience is.

Thump-thump-thump.

The mutt chases after me.

"No, you're not coming," I snap. I point back to the living room.

He doesn't move.

Thump-thump-thump. His tail thwacking against the wooden floorboards. His tongue is lolling out now eagerly. And those eyes. Still liquid amber and hopeful.

With an angry growl, I charge back into the kitchen.

I fill a bowl with water and another with some leftover deer meat, then set both down on the floor where the mutt can get to them.

"Eat," I instruct.

I point at the bowls.

He just stares at me.

"Eat, you fleabag."

When he still doesn't move, I growl and clench my fists.

"Fine!" I shout. "You don't wanna eat? Then don't eat! I don't fucking care."

I stomp into the bedroom and slam the door shut.

He watches me the whole way.

Thump.

Thump.

Thump.

19

ARTEM
THE NEXT EVENING

I've been running on the trail for almost three hours and I'm fucking exhausted. Sweat drips off my body despite the sunset chill. I stripped my shirt ages ago. It hangs over my shoulder, completely drenched.

The mutt won't leave me alone.

He bounds way off in front, and then once he's put enough distance between the two of us, he bounds right back, nipping at my heels affectionately.

"Next time you do that, I'm gonna fucking kick you."

He gives me a look that clearly tells me he doesn't believe a word I'm saying.

Fuck, even *I* don't believe a word I'm saying.

It's my last loop of the trail for the morning. We climb the final rise and soon I can see the patchy cabin roof come into view.

A little higher and I can see that the front door is open.

That's not right.

I'm a thousand percent sure I closed it before I left.

"Fuck," I growl under my breath.

I circle around and retrieve a gun from the shed. Then I go back to the front and carefully, slowly mount the steps.

I crane my neck into the house to peer through the half-open door. I'm expecting Lobo to be back, seeking the vengeance he wasn't man enough to claim yesterday.

And then I hear a sing-song voice that makes my stomach turn.

Before I can react, the mutt races through the door with his tail wagging. I sigh in disgust and follow him inside, gun dangling at my hip.

"Oh, hello!" Aracelia says, bending to pet the animal. "Where've you been?"

I step into the cabin and glare at her. "What the fuck do you think you're doing here?" I demand. "I was about to shoot you."

She shrugs. "Well, I'm glad you didn't," she replies. "Sit down. I made dinner."

"What?" I look at her with a dumbfounded expression.

"Dinner," she replies pointedly, setting down a pot of something that smells pretty good. "Pozole. And fresh tortillas."

"What I want right now is a nice, cold beer."

Aracelia rolls her eyes. "Don't you think you drink a little too much?"

"Fuck off, Aracelia," I say, sitting down and reaching for a bowl despite myself.

She smirks a little as I spoon a generous heaping of pozole into my bowl. The mutt whines at my feet but I shake my head.

"Don't you fucking look at me," I curse at him.

"Venga, perrito," Aracelia coos. She plucks a juicy piece of pork from the broth with her skinny fingers and feeds it to the dog.

I watch the steam rise off my bowl and my stomach churns with hunger. But before I pop the first spoonful into my mouth, I glance at Aracelia as she takes the seat in front of me.

"It's not poisoned, is it?"

"Please," she says, rolling her eyes. "If I'd wanted you dead, you'd be dead."

I narrow my eyes at her, but mostly to cover up the fact that I'm actually starting to like the crazy old bat. I assume she's old at least, she's got the kind of face that keeps you guessing.

"So—"

"*Piz-dets*, can I at least eat in peace?"

"No," she replies tersely. "You need to face certain things. The denial is not helping."

"Not this again."

"Esme—"

"Is gone," I finish abruptly. "She doesn't fucking need me."

"I didn't say she did," Aracelia replies calmly. "But you need her."

"I don't need anyone."

"We all need someone."

"And who do you have, eh?"

"Oso," she replies, without hesitation.

"Who the fuck is that?" I demand. "Boyfriend?"

"My cat," she replies. As though it's a serious fucking answer.

I just stare at her for a moment. "Your cat?" I repeat.

She smiles. "And you."

I shake my head at that. "No. You do not have me. I am not your fucking friend."

"So you keep telling me. But the truth is we're bonded now, Artem," she tells me. "Whether you like it or not."

"We're bonded? What the fuck have you been smoking?"

"I saved your life," she says with a nonchalant shrug. "That creates a bond between two people. You're just not willing to admit it. You know, denial will only get you so far, boy."

"Who're you calling a boy?" I ask, glaring at her.

That word brings up bad memories. Memories of my father, the night at The Siren when everything in my life changed forever.

"A man would face the things he's afraid of. You won't. Por lo tanto, that means you are a boy."

"I'm not fucking afraid of anything. Not anymore."

"That's because you've pushed away everything you care about." She taps her forehead like she sees something I'm still too slow to get.

I don't appreciate the gesture.

"I didn't push anything away," I argue. "Esme left of her own free will. Goddammit, why are we even having this conversation?"

"Esme left because she felt like she had no choice," Aracelia retorts. "She was afraid for the baby. Have you even thought about the baby?"

"I think about the baby every single fucking second of every single fucking day," I rasp. It hurts to say. But it's true.

Even if this is the first time I've ever admitted that out loud.

"And?"

"And…" I hesitate. "Maybe Esme was right to leave. The baby deserves better."

"Better than what?" Aracelia demands. "A father who loves him?"

"My world is no place for a baby."

Aracelia sits back and sighs. The mutt licks her hands and she fondles him behind the ear absentmindedly. Her own bowl of pozole remains untouched.

If this old bitch really has poisoned me, I'm gonna be fucking pissed.

"Let me perform a séance for you," she says abruptly.

"What? Fuck no."

"Why not?"

"Because I don't believe in that kooky shit."

"You don't believe in it?" she asks pointedly. "Or you're afraid of what it might bring forth?"

I roll my eyes. "Seriously?"

"If you don't believe in it, then what's the big deal?" Aracelia asks. "It won't cost you a thing."

I glare at her. "I don't have the patience for that shit. I'm this close to kicking you the fuck out of here."

"Fine," she sighs. "Then let me tell you what I'd read off your aura so far."

"Jesus."

"You're a broken man who's searching for purpose in all the wrong places. You're lost and getting revenge is not going to fix you."

I pause for a moment. "You don't know anything about this."

"I know that someone close has betrayed you," Aracelia continues. "Someone you used to trust."

"That's very vague," I tell her, acting as though her awareness of the situation isn't completely unsettling.

She ignores me. "You feel as though you've let your father down," Aracelia continues. "A father you lost very recently. You had a difficult relationship with him, am I right?"

"Most people have difficult relationships with their father."

"But you still crave his approval and you know he wouldn't have approved of you walking away from your duties," she says. "Which is why you chose to push Esme away in favor of… this life." She gestures broadly to encompass the lodge, the mountain, the solitude.

I shift uncomfortably in my seat.

"Is there a point to this?" I ask impatiently.

"The point is that you don't have to choose, Artem."

"Esme expected me to."

"So your solution is to abandon her and your child?"

I bring my fists down on the table so fast and so hard that the whole room seems to rattle with my rage. Even Aracelia flinches.

It's the first time I've gotten a fearful reaction from the woman.

It's oddly satisfactory.

"Don't you fucking dare," I roar at her. "Don't you *fucking* dare."

Aracelia looks up at me with wide eyes as I stand up from the table.

"It's time you leave. Now."

The mutt whimpers in the corner. Aracelia remains frozen in place for a moment as if contemplating something.

And then she rises.

"Okay," she agrees. "I'll go."

She heads for the door while the mutt watches as though his best friend is walking out on him, but he makes no move to follow her.

At the threshold, Aracelia turns around and glances at me.

"You can scare everyone away, Artem," she tells me. "But at the end of the day, you'll be alone. And trust me: no one—*no one*—can live alone forever. Certainly no one can fight alone."

With that bullshit parting speech, she walks out, keeping her back straight and proud.

I close my eyes and sink down into my seat once more when she's gone.

Fuck.

I hate to admit it, but the woman got to me. Her words keep rolling around in my head, getting harder and harder to ignore.

No one can live alone.

No one can fight alone.

I think about the resources I have available to fight Budimir. My forces are limited at best, and as determined as I am, I know I can't take Budimir and his forces like that.

I have been up in these mountains for months now. It was only ever meant to be a temporary respite, and yet it has burgeoned into a far longer stint than I ever predicted.

Yes, I had to wait for my wounds to heal, but I've been healed for at least two months now.

I've been training my body hard, trying to train my mind as well.

But at what point had it gone from preparation to procrastination?

I can't hide out in these mountains anymore.

I have to act. I have to move.

I have to take control of the Bratva once more.

And in order to do that, I need to destroy them first.

But Aracelia was right about one thing: I cannot do that alone.

I leave my bowl of pozole to cool as I grab a handgun and storm out of the cabin. The mutt follows close behind me.

For once, I don't mind the company.

I make a beeline straight for Cillian's memorial. The path is familiar now and well-marked by my daily visits.

I sink to my knees in the dirt and stare at the pyramid of flat white stones, with that pitiful cross of sticks on top.

The mutt starts exploring the area, sniffing around and wagging his tail with contentment.

It's a nice evening, but I've lost the ability to appreciate beauty anymore.

"Brother," I say, looking at the trees in front of me rather than the grave. "You should have been here for this. We should be going into this side by side."

Silence greets me with brutal familiarity. Some days, I have trouble recalling that shit-eating smile of his.

"I might be a father now," I continue. "Esme will be past nine months at this point. She's most certainly had the baby." I run a hand through my hair. "And I don't even know if I have a son or a daughter."

I can hear the anguish in my own words. Like seeing my reflection for the first time in months.

The mutt moves closer and butts my hand with his head. Without thinking, I start stroking his head.

He looks at me with shocked eyes. I realize this is the first time I've interacted with him in any real way.

"Aracelia is a crazy bitch. But she thinks I need to find Esme," I muse. "Ending Budimir is more important, though. Isn't it? If you were here, you'd know what to do."

A wind rustles through the trees. I'd like to believe it's a sign, but I know it's not. It's just wind.

There are no signs. Only fools stupid enough to look for them.

"Maybe you'd tell me to forget the Bratva and go find Esme," I guess bitterly. "Maybe you'd tell me to take back the Bratva and then go in search of Esme."

But I can only guess.

I remember the time he'd told me about the girl he'd left behind in Ireland.

The girl he'd sacrificed everything for.

Would he give it all up to be with her?

It kills me that I don't have the answer.

The mutt settles down next to me and places his head on my knee. I rest my hand on his head and take a deep breath.

"It's time to be honest with myself," I say out loud. Like I'm testing the possibility before I commit to it.

The mutt looks up at me. I feel the truth that I've been hiding behind all these months. The truth I've pushed back behind a rigorous training regimen, bottles of whiskey, and a lot of pent-up anger.

"I have to take back the Bratva," I announce. "And I have to find Esme."

It feels right. Both of them.

One can't exist without the other.

The mutt looks at me with big clear eyes. Ignorant to what is to come. Thankfully, he won't be around for any of it.

The wind fades away and silence takes over again.

I turn my attention to the creature next to me. "I know I've been an asshole since the moment we met," I tell the dog. "But thanks for sticking around anyway."

Fuck, I'm actually gonna miss the mangy fucker.

I pet his head slowly and then I get to my feet.

It's time to stop planning.

It's time to stop pretending.

It's time to do what I was meant to do.

I have a mission, and I intend to see it through.

But first…

I need back up.

20
ESME

The first thing I'm aware of is a constellation of stars.

They blaze across my eyelids, illuminating the murky darkness that's enshrouded me.

The second thing I'm aware of is the feeling of emptiness.

Not a raw, biting emotional emptiness, but a physical ache that makes me want to reach for something.

I'm missing something.

Or I'm not remembering something, because the more aware I become of new state of consciousness, the more I realize that something is not right.

Where am I?

Who's with me?

What am I missing?

The questions keep tearing around in my head and I can't seem to clear the fog long enough to answer them.

But I can see the answers on the periphery, right behind the confusion.

I hear a strange beeping sound. I feel something connected to my arm. An IV drip? But I can't be sure. I could just be hallucinating.

After all... I'm at home in my bed, aren't I?

And at any moment, Cesar's going to walk through my door and pull me back to reality.

I try opening my eyes but they're heavy and I don't know why but a vague feeling of fear grips me.

Cesar...

Cesar?

There's another name floating around in the ether, just out of my reach. I want to say it, its form etched on my lips, but for some reason I can't quite grab at it. It feels too far away.

I shouldn't worry so much. I'm just in bed at home like always. Sleeping in on a lazy Sunday, perhaps.

Maybe Tamara visited this weekend? That would make sense. She always manages to find liquor when she comes to stay with us. Sometimes, she convinces me to indulge with her.

I only do it when Papa is away.

But still... I don't want to be caught. And Papa could come home at any minute.

I try and say Tamara's name but I'm distracted by the sound of footsteps, the hush of voices carrying through to me as though from a distance. Perhaps from another room?

The maids never enter my bedroom when I'm in here. Certainly never when I'm sleeping.

But am I sleeping? This position feels a little foreign. And forced.

I sleep on my side with a pillow between my arms. So why am I on my back?

Then I hear a cry. A sharp wail that sends an electric bolt of realization straight through me, shocking me back to reality.

I am not a child anymore.

My home was destroyed months ago.

I don't know where Tamara is.

Cesar is dead.

Artem is gone.

And my baby… my baby is…

Where is my baby?

The shock forces my eyes open but I have to squint against the bright light that assaults my irises. I struggle to sit up, reminding myself to breathe before a panic attack sets in.

I've been living on the edge of a panic attack for months now.

Once my vision starts getting clearer, I look around at the small, run-down hospital room I'm lying in. I don't recognize it at all, but then again, why would I? I've never been here before.

This is not my city.

This is not my home.

I can see the profile of a nurse. Her hair is dirty blonde and tied into a tight knot at the back of her head. She's talking to someone just out of my line of vision.

"My baby!" I gasp, breaking free of the parched hoarseness that grips my throat. "My baby…"

She doesn't hear me. She's so engrossed in her conversation that she doesn't even glance in my direction. The panic builds as bits and pieces of memory resurface.

I don't remember much, apart from the fact that I'd been preparing to run.

No, wait—I'd assaulted a man. Possibly even killed him. I needed to get out of town.

And then my water broke in the middle of a bus depot.

I remember being in pain.

I remember feeling scared and helpless.

I remember worrying about the future.

But not once did I ever envision waking up alone. Hollow. Terrified beyond reckoning and drowning in fears and nightmares and long-buried memories.

The emptiness I feel now makes sense.

I glance down at my stomach. There's only a small bump left. There's certainly no baby inside me anymore.

My body craves the fluttering kicks I've gotten used to over the last few months. Without them, I feel lost. Unmoored.

"Where's my baby?" I demand, raising my voice to anyone who will listen.

The blonde nurse gives a start of surprise and turns to me. "Oh, my," she says. "You gave me a fright! Well, I'm glad you're awake."

She comes forward and begins examining the IV drip attached to my hand. I flinch away from her as my eyes flit across the room.

There's a baby bassinet in the corner, but there is no baby in it.

Oh, God, did I lose...

Him?

Her?

I don't even know what I was having.

All that stress, all that anxiety, all that panic… has it finally caught up with me?

Did it cost me my child?

"My baby," I beg desperately. Tears are pouring unchecked down my face. "Where is my baby?"

She looks at me finally. For the first time, she looks me right in the eye and sees the panic on my face.

"Oh, honey," she says. Her eyes soften. "Don't worry."

I try to breathe, but nothing helps. Nothing will help but the knowledge that my child is okay.

"We'll bring him up momentarily," she tells me. "He's just fine. He's beautiful."

I feel relief rest over me like a warm blanket on a freezing cold day. I fall back against my pillow and breathe deeply, taking in as much oxygen as I can.

He's okay.

Oh, God. Thank you. He's okay.

Wait.

"He?" I ask, looking up at the nurse again.

She smiles. "You didn't know you were having a boy?" she asks.

"No," I admit, almost embarrassed for some reason. "I wanted it to be a surprise."

A second later, another nurse walks into the room, but I don't register her at all. My eyes are focused on the blue bundle in her arms.

I sit up immediately, ignoring the slicing pain in my stomach.

"Easy there, honey," the blonde nurse cautions me. "You're fresh out of surgery. You need to go slow."

I nod impatiently, but I lift my hands up and out, waiting for my baby to be placed in my arms.

The second nurse walks forward and puts the little blue bundle in my arms.

I see a flash of dark hair—a mess of it, really—and then I see his eyes.

"Hello, little bird," I murmur.

I stare down at my son, unblinking. He's gorgeous. More beautiful than my imagination could have ever concocted.

And he looks like Artem.

The resemblance is indisputably obvious. He has Artem's coloring, lighter than mine. He has Artem's square jaw, his angular nose, his straight and direct gaze.

The only thing that I recognize that has come from me, are the eyes.

My son has large hazel eyes, framed by dark eyelashes. I can see my own reflection as he stares up at me, as though he's trying to figure out who I am.

"Hello, little bird," I say again. "It's me. Your mama."

It's the first time I've said the words out loud. Raw emotion wells up inside me. My vision blurs behinds tears, but I force them back, unwilling to lose sight of my son for even a moment.

He gurgles in my arms. I cradle him tenderly as I press a delicate kiss on his forehead.

"You are beautiful, mijo," I whisper.

"He really is," the blonde nurse agrees. She smiles down at the both of us. "Pure beauty. And trust me, I don't say that about every baby."

Laughter bubbles up to my lips.

For the first time in a long time, I feel truly and freely happy.

"Is there someone we can call for you, dear?" the blonde nurse asks.

And just like that, my happiness deflates just a little, reminding me of all the problems that still exist. All the trials I have yet to overcome.

"No," I answer swiftly. "There's no one."

The second nurse moves forward just a little. The two of them exchange a glance. I can see pity in their eyes, but it doesn't affect me anymore.

"What about the father?" the second one suggests gently.

I open my mouth, but snap it shut a moment later. How do I answer that question?

I left the father.

We wanted different lives.

I had to save my child from the world I was born into.

"There is no father," I say simply. "It's just me and him." I leave it at that.

The blonde nurse moves forward and puts her hand on my shoulder. "Sometimes, that's all you need."

I smile gratefully at her. "Thank you."

"He's going to need a name."

A name.

It's strikes me that in all the months I had to plan and prepare for his birth, I've never once thought about names.

At least, not since those early days in the cabin, when it was just Artem and me. When we'd still been wrapped up in the glow of new love and fragile hope.

Thinking about it now, I realize how idealistic those conversations were.

We were just pretending.

Pretending that happiness was possible.

Pretending that we could make it as a family—against all the odds.

My son gurgles loudly and I wrench my attention back to him.

"Are you hungry, my angel?" I ask.

He raises his little fists before settling into my arms.

"You wanna try feeding him, honey?" the blonde nurse asks.

I nod as the nerves set in a little. I grew accustomed to carrying a baby while I was pregnant. But now that he's out, a fully-fledged human being in his own right.

It terrifies me.

I am solely responsible for him.

In all the world, I am the only one he has.

I am the only one he can count on.

"It's okay," the blonde nurse reassures me. "Breast-feeding can be a little tricky the first time around, but you'll get the hang of it."

I smile, finding comfort in her soothing words. "What's your name?" I ask her.

"Nurse Sedley," she replies. "But you can call me Maria. And this is Annette."

For the first time, I focus on the nurse that brought my son in to meet me for the first time. She's dark-haired, like me, but her eyes are dark and husky, her lips full and blushing with color.

"I don't remember anything about the labor," I say.

"It was a C-section," Annette tells me. "You were in no fit state to undergo a natural labor. But Dr. Farrow did a fantastic job. He stitched you up well. You will have pain for a few days, but you'll heal."

I nod hesitantly as I try to process all of that. "You were there?"

"I was," she says. "I was the one who washed your little boy up and swaddled him. He has an amazing set of lungs on him."

I smile, realizing I haven't heard him cry yet. He's been quiet in my arms for the longest time. I sit up a little straighter and shimmy down my hospital robe on one side.

Maria moves forward and holds my boy for a moment so I can get my right breast out. I'm aware suddenly how different my breasts feel at the moment. Heavier than I would have expected and larger than I'm used to.

"Your milk has come in nicely," Maria comments.

I hold my son up to my breast and gently guide his mouth towards my nipple. He seems uncertain at first but Maria helps me wheedle his mouth open.

When he finally clamps down on me, I give a little yelp and cringe as the pain shoots through my nipple.

"It's okay," Maria coaxes. "Easy does it."

It takes several minutes for me to get accustomed to the strange sensation. "This is... weird," I admit.

Maria smiles. "It takes some getting used to," she agrees. "I've had four babies and breast-feeding was a new experience each time."

"Really?"

"Mhmm. People don't talk enough about how hard it is," she tells me. "Everyone assumes it's this natural art that just comes to you."

I wince a little as the baby bites down on my nipple a little. "Wow, and he only has soft little gums."

Annette rests a reassuring hand on my leg. "Trust me, darling: it'll get easier."

I brush the back of my knuckle against his velvety soft cheek. "He's so beautiful."

"He really is," Annette agrees. "And those features! So different."

"His father is Russian," I say without thinking.

"Oh?" Maria blurts.

I look down at the baby to cover over my awkwardness. I probably shouldn't have shared that with them, but it had just slipped out.

I sigh inwardly. Maybe I don't have to be so nervous. After all, if Artem wanted to find me, he would have done so by now.

Why hasn't he even tried?

I try not to let that thought consume me. But it hurts more than I'm willing to admit.

It hurts so bad some nights I can barely sleep.

He didn't even try to fight for me.

I disappeared and he just... let me go.

"You wanna tell us about his father?" Maria questions, putting a hand on my arm. "Because you can. You can trust us."

Can I trust anyone?

I look between the two women in front of me, and I'm struck by how much I want to tell them, how much I want to share my story with them. With someone. With anyone.

Because, honestly, I'm sick of being alone.

I'm sick of keeping people—good, kind, generous people—at arm's length because I'm so scared of being found, of being betrayed.

"Don't cry, honey," Maria says. Only then do I realize I've got tears running down my cheeks.

"I'm sorry," I mutter, trying to wipe away my tears.

"Did… did he do that to you?" Maria asks.

I stare at her with confusion. "What do you mean?"

I follow her gaze and notice that she's staring at the bruise on my arm. I have no idea how I'd gotten it in the first place. Maybe from the fall in the bus depot? I can't be sure.

I look up at her concerned eyes and I realize what she's thinking. I'm about to correct her but I stop before I can find the words.

After all, what is the point?

I can't give her details.

I can't explain specifics. At least, not without also giving up my identity in the process.

The idea of Artem finding me is… confusing.

But the idea of Budimir finding me is downright terrifying.

Especially now that I have my little Phoenix.

"It's complicated," I tell Maria in the end.

"It's okay, sweetheart," she tells me. "You don't have to talk about it."

She helps me switch my son to my left breast, so he can feed evenly. Immediately, the tension that was mounting in my chest eases a little.

"Any thoughts on names?" Annette asks eagerly.

It takes me a second, but when the idea comes, it's so perfect and fully formed that it's a wonder I didn't think of it months ago.

"Phoenix," I say. "His name is Phoenix."

My little bird.

Rising from the ashes of the house that Artem burned to the ground.

"Aw, honey," Maria says, running her hand over Phoenix's downy hair. "That's perfect."

"Love it," Annette agrees.

I don't even know if they're just saying so for my benefit, but I appreciate their enthusiasm. For a moment, it makes me feel less alone.

Then the doctor walks in, a tall, mustached man with feather-white hair and hooded eyes. Annette and Maria move aside so that he can examine me.

"Good afternoon," he says, nodding towards me without a smile. "You're looking well."

"You're the doctor who performed my C-section?"

"Your emergency C section," he clarifies. "You were unconscious when you arrived. You were brought in by an older African American man."

Geoffrey.

"We asked him a few questions when we needed some of your personal information," the doctor continues. "But he couldn't give us any. He claimed that you two were not related."

"That's true," I reply. "We're not related. I met him a half hour before my water broke."

"I see," the doctor tuts. "Well, I'm going to need you to fill out some forms for us."

"Forms?" I ask, panic rising inside me like bile.

"Yes, we need your name, age, nation ID number. Things of that nature," he says. "We need to know who to contact."

I can feel my breaths come in again, sharp and painful.

When will I be rid of this feeling, this weight on my chest?

"There's no one to contact," I say. "It's just me."

The doctor cocks his head to the side. "No husband, boyfriend? No mother or father?" he presses.

"No," I repeat firmly. "No one."

I stare down at my son and the weight of my words settles over both of us. The path I have chosen is going to be a lonely one.

Did I do the right thing by leaving Artem?

Or have I just deprived my son of a good father?

No. No second-guessing. I did this for Phoenix's safety. For my own.

There was no other choice.

"Uh, doctor?" Maria says, but I don't look up to watch the exchange. "She just woke up mere minutes ago. She's still disoriented and very tired. Perhaps we should give her a few hours?"

"I can give her one," the doctor says, looking at me with his leering, hooded eyes. "But I'm going to need you to fill out those forms."

He gives me a curt nod and strides back out the door.

If I fill out those forms, someone will find me. Budimir, Artem, my father's allies—*someone*. That much is guaranteed.

I've managed to stay under the radar this long. But now I'm trapped here, I'm physically incapacitated, and I have no one to ask for help.

I try to control the panic I feel, but my body hurts, my breasts hurt, and I'm so fucking scared that I can't keep the sobs at bay.

They burst from me the moment the doctor has cleared the room.

"Oh, darling!" Maria cries out.

Annette moves forward, too. "Honey," she murmurs. "What's wrong?"

I look up at both of them, wondering how much to say, whether or not I should say anything at all.

"Childbirth is a difficult and emotional journey, honey," Maria assures me.

"No," I say, shaking my head. "I... I can't fill out those forms," I admit at last.

Both nurses exchange a glance. "Why not?" Maria asks.

I shake my head and Annette sighs. "Honey, you were admitted to this hospital. We're gonna need you to sign a few things."

"I can't," I reply desperately. "I can't sign anything. I can't pay for anything and I can't put my name on anything."

"Esme..."

"I shouldn't have told you my name," I whimper. "I'm such a fool."

"Shh," Annette consoles me. "Hush now, darling. Your son needs you to be strong."

I know. I know I need to be strong.

I just don't want to have to be all the time.

I want Artem.

I want my husband.

The moment the thought let loose inside my head, I felt it deep down inside my heart. The truth of it. The desperate, powerful longing for him that's never stopped.

That never will stop.

No matter what he does, I love Artem Kovalyov.

"I need to stand up," I say, at last. "I need to stand. Can you get the IV out? Please… please?"

Annette and Maria exchange a worried glance. But then Maria nods.

I cover myself up and hand Phoenix over to Maria, while Annette moves forward and starts releasing me from the drip.

The moment I'm free, I get out of bed, frustrated by how little my body wants to co-operate. Another bolt of pain courses through my body and strikes at my stomach.

But I don't have the option of a slow recovery.

"Honey, you sure you wanna stand right now?" Maria asks.

"Yes," I insist. "I need to walk. To breathe."

I can feel my anxiety levels spike and I hear a siren in the distance.

Are they coming for me?

I killed a man in the diner. They're no doubt looking for me.

I should have been out of the town by now.

"Honey. Esme!" Maria grabs my shoulders and pulls me around to face her, forcing me to meet her gaze. "You're in real trouble, aren't you?"

I nod, feeling another sob scratch at my throat. "Yes. Yes, I am."

"All right," Maria says with finality, looking towards Annette. "Annette and I are gonna go do our rounds now. We'll be gone for ten minutes. Understand?"

I pull her to me and hug her as tight as I can.

"Thank you," I whisper in her ear as I look towards Annette. "Thank you both."

"Your clothes are on that chair over there," Annette says. "Next to the duffel bag you had with you when you were brought in."

Anette comes forward and puts Phoenix back in my arms. Then she and Maria head out the door, glancing back at me the whole time.

The moment the door shuts on me, I set Phoenix down on the bed and pull off my hospital robe.

I dress fast, wincing every now and again at the pain. But it's secondary, a mild irritant to the stress of escape.

Lingering above it all is a vague sense of déjà vu.

I realize I've been here once before.

I've woken up in a hospital room and fled it towards an uncertain future.

Of course, I found Artem in the end.

But I'm not sure it will be that simple this time around.

Once I'm dressed, I make sure that Phoenix's swaddle is nice and tight before I pick him up and settle him in the crook of my arm.

Then I hoist my duffel bag onto my shoulder. It's heavier than I remember, but that's probably only because I'm weak from the operation.

I slip out of the hospital room and walk through the hospital, keeping my head low so that I don't have to meet anyone's eyes.

I walk calmly out of the hospital with my heart beating fast.

Only once I've cleared the area do I allow myself to pick up the pace.

Phoenix stirs in my arms. His eyes flutter open and then he lets out a loud and angry wail.

A harsh wind tears at our faces. I tuck my son as close to my body as I can, but I'm still clumsy after the surgery and I can barely balance him and the duffel bag at the same time.

I've only walked about a block when I feel someone tailing me. I glance behind and see a shitty black car trailing behind me.

Oh, God. Oh, God. Who has come for me?

Who did that doctor tell? I knew I shouldn't have trusted him. Shouldn't have trusted anyone. They know my name, my real *name…*

I try to tell myself that I'm paranoid, my fear is getting away from me.

But then I hear the window roll down.

"Esme."

I freeze.

They've come for me.

"Esme."

I turn slowly to face my pursuer.

And then relief floods me with warmth.

"Geoffrey."

He parks and steps out of his car. He limps around to me slowly, his eyes glancing down at Phoenix.

"Congratulations."

"How did you find me?" I ask. It's embarrassing how the sight of a friendly face has me near tears.

"I was driving by to see you," he explains. "I wanted to make sure you were okay. And then I saw you walking away from the hospital like you had ghosts on your tail."

I give him a forced smile. "That's kind of you," I reply. "But I was just discharged."

"Discharged?" he asks. "So soon."

"I, um… I insisted," I stammer. "I have to leave town."

I hear another police siren in the distance. My head turns in its direction before I can stop myself.

It feels as though the walls are closing in on me.

"Esme?"

I force my eyes to turn back to Geoffrey. "I have to…"

"You have to leave," he nods. "I know."

I just stare at him.

"Get in the car," he tells me. "I'll drive you to the bus station."

Some days, it feels like I'm living on kindness.

21

ARTEM
DUBLIN, IRELAND

The moment the plane touches ground in Dublin, I grab my duffel bag, hoist it over my shoulder and prepare to disembark. The curvy Irish stewardess who's been sniffing around me the whole flight gives me a smile.

"Hope you enjoyed your flight, sir," she says, honey coating her tone.

I nod brusquely and keep it moving.

I'm on edge. Have been since I boarded this flight.

Some might call it a suicide mission or a fool's errand. Whatever fits, I guess. True, it's a fucking long shot.

But it's the only shot I've got left.

It takes me an hour to clear customs. When I step out of the airport, the fresh Irish wind hits me smack in the face. Green hills roll in the distance beneath a cerulean sky.

I feel Cillian's absence more keenly than I've ever felt it before.

He should be here with me.

But even as I think it, I know that Cillian would never have stepped foot back in this country. It wasn't a refutation of the land itself.

It was a refutation of the family that exiled him from it.

I bite back the anger for my best friend's sake and unclench my fists. This is not the time for doubts. It's not the time for old grudges, either.

It's time for war.

I didn't bother with booking myself into a hotel ahead of time. For all I know, I'll be dead by nightfall.

Besides, my purpose is clear. Things must be done in their proper order.

I take a cab from the airport and drive out about an hour from the main city to an address that I've picked out from one of my old portfolios.

I feel strangely naked. Since I'd taken a commercial flight out here, I couldn't travel with the usual arsenal of weapons that I would usually have with me. I was already flying under a fake identity I purchased in Mexico City, so the added scrutiny of a gun in my luggage would've been unnerving.

But it does mean that I'd be showing up on the devil's doorstep without so much as a pocketknife to defend myself.

That won't do.

I need to rectify the situation.

The cab stops outside an old warehouse-like building in the middle of nowhere.

"This is the place?"

"Aye," the cabbie replies. He looks back at me. "You sure you know what you're doing, son?"

I hand him the cash and get out without saying a word.

At the front entrance of the warehouse, I find two men smoking by the front façade. They straighten up when they see me. One stamps out his cigarette.

"You lost?" the older man asks. He's got blue eyes that reminds me of Cillian and a sports cap that supports some team I'm not familiar with.

"I hear you sell quality caviar," I enunciate clearly.

At the code phrase, both men raise their eyebrows. Their faces shift from suspicious to courteous at once.

"Come right on in, sir," the younger man welcomes, jumping to his feet.

I follow him into the warehouse, which carries a distinct and unpleasant scent. The other men walks behind me. Together in that single file line, we go to the very back of the building.

The younger man fiddles with a lock. When the bolt slides free, he pulls it open and steps aside to usher me in.

I nod my thanks and enter.

The moment I walk in, the smell of oil and metal fills my nostrils.

Sleek, shiny guns stare back at me from every nook and cranny. I'm spoiled for choice.

"We've got a variety of caviar for you," the older man says pridefully as he slips in the room behind me. "Only the finest."

"I can see that," I rumble. "Good thing I came hungry."

~

By the time I walk out of the warehouse, I'm armed and most definitely dangerous. My duffel bag rattles with fresh weaponry as I walk a few miles down the road and catch a cab back into the city.

Now that I have guns on me, I feel much, much better.

I have the taxi drop me off at a bar that Cillian mentioned a few times over the years.

The pub is typically Irish in façade. It's got a distinctive sign out front that says "O'Malley's" in a swirling Gaelic script. The paint job looks a little old.

But other than that, the place looks relatively well kept. Completely innocuous.

I walk in, bag and all, and sit myself down at the bar directly in front of the bartender. The man has an impressive ginger beard, but his hair is dark brown, the exact same color as his eyes.

He casts an appraising glance over me. His eyes linger on my tattoos as though he's looking for signs.

"What can I get you, friend?" he asks, though his tone doesn't suggest we're friends at all.

"Beer," I reply. "Guinness is fine."

"Coming right up."

As he fills my beer mug up to the brim, I survey the barroom. There are three men occupying one booth and a few lone customers hunched over their alcohol at single tables. Drunks, by the looks of them.

The men sitting at the booth are eyeing me curiously. I get the sense that if I ask them the right questions, I might get the answers I need.

"New in town?" the bartender asks.

"Brand new."

"Ever been to Dublin before?"

"I haven't even been to Ireland before," I reply.

He drums his fingers on the beer tap. "Business or pleasure?"

He's trying to be casual, but I can sense the underlying interest in my answers. "For some, business is pleasure."

"Talking about yourself there, lad?"

I have no trouble understanding his thick Irish accent. Probably because Cillian had the same one when he first landed in the States.

Of course, he'd worked hard to lose his accent over time, but it brought back old memories.

Memories that make me very fucking angry.

"I am." Underneath the bar counter, I crack my knuckles and ready myself for a fight.

I haven't drawn a gun yet. But the moment where that might become necessary is fast approaching.

The men at the booth are still staring daggers into my back. This is definitely the right place.

I just have to figure out where to poke.

"What's your business then, friend?" the bartender pries. His tone is growing icier with each exchange.

I shrug nonchalantly. "This and that. But the reason I'm in Dublin at all is to do a favor for a friend."

"Oh?" the bartender says, raising his eyebrows.

"Cillian O'Sullivan," I say, raising my voice slightly to make sure the boys in the back can hear me. "Ever heard of him?"

The bartender stills instantly.

Jackpot.

"Can't say I have," he says. "Close friend of yours?"

"Very."

"You haven't touched your beer," he remarks, pointing down at the full mug in front of me.

I look down at it as if I'm considering taking a swig.

But the truth is that I left my taste for alcohol back in Mexico. If I never drink again, it'll be too soon.

That was the old Artem who drank until he didn't have to face his demons anymore.

The new Artem looks his demons in the face when he buries a knife in their chest.

I raise my gaze back up to lock eyes with the bartender. Here we are—the moment where the violence starts.

I'm fucking ready.

"I'm Russian, *friend,*" I spit, purposefully emphasizing the term of not-so-endearment. "I don't drink this Irish piss."

The bartender's fake smile drops at once. "What the fuck did you just say to me?"

I smile coolly. "I think you heard me just fine."

More to the point, the boys in the back heard me.

The bartender's eyes flick over my shoulder. But I'm way ahead of him.

I already feel them coming, and I act before any of them have even realized that I'm far more than they bargained for.

Grabbing the hilt of the dagger I've had hidden against my thigh since I sat down, I turn and hurl it through the air.

The blade buries itself in the neck of the man closest to reaching me. His face freezes in shock.

He wasn't ready to die.

To which I say—then he shouldn't have come anywhere near Artem Kovalyov.

I don't let any of his mates recover. I swing around, grab the hilt that's protruding from the dying man's neck, and step behind him in the process.

I use him as a deadweight human shield, just before the three men still standing reach for their guns.

That's my window of opportunity.

I cock back and throw my knife a second time. The moment it leaves my hand, I grab the gun tucked in the back of my waistband.

The knife finds its home in a second man's beefy neck. Struck an artery, by the looks of the blood spatter. He falls to the ground, gurgling. I let my human shield go and he hits the deck like a sack of potatoes.

Boom. Boom. Boom.

The third sound is the man I've shot thudding onto his knees. He has just enough time left in his life to look down at the bloody mess where his beer gut once was and then back up to me.

Horror is etched in his eyes. Disbelief, really.

He looks like he wants to say something to me. Ask me who I am or how I managed to do this. His fat lips sputter with the word.

But then the clock of his life ticks down to zero and he collapses on top of his friend.

Goodnight, friend.

Satisfied with my handiwork, I turn slowly and turn my attention to the bartender.

His eyes are wide with fear as he realizes just how out of his depth he is.

"Drop your gun," I order.

He was dumb enough to pick up a pistol from somewhere behind the bar, but not brave enough or fast enough to use it on me in the fight.

He does as I say immediately. The moment the gun is down, I saunter back over to the bar.

The other lone drinkers are nowhere in sight, clearly having raced out of here the moment shit got real. Smart thinking.

I sit down on the same barstool I'd been occupying only minutes earlier and pick up my beer mug. Raising it to my nose, I take an inhale.

"Smells as bad as it tastes, I bet," I drawl. I hurl it against the mirrored wall behind the bartender. He flinches as it streaks past his ear and shatters into a million glistening pieces. The mirror goes with it, huge shards collapsing to the ground.

The man's hands are still raised. I can see his fingertips trembling.

"Can we dispense with the pretense now?" I ask conversationally.

The bartender looks at me with fearful calculation. I know exactly what he's thinking. He's wondering if he's going to live to see another day.

"Who the fuck are you?" he asks in a hushed voice.

I remember the words I roared over the ravine after I built Cillian's makeshift grave.

I am death.

But I want this poor sap to be cooperative, not to piss his pants in terror. So I save the theatrics for another time.

"Does it matter?" I ask instead.

"Well, what do you want?"

"A better question," I agree. "But first, you need to answer me."

"You didn't ask a question."

I raise an eyebrow. "Yes, I did. And you lied to me, which better men than you have lost their lives for. So, do you wanna try this again?"

He nods. I note the panicked swallow of his Adam's apple.

"Excellent. Did you know Cillian O'Sullivan?"

"Not personally," the bartender stammers. "But I know… of him."

"Fair enough." The gun in my hand is still aimed at the bartender. "I assume you know his father."

The bartender stills and his pale deepens. Then he nods.

"Also excellent. Where do I find him?" I ask.

"Listen—"

"Just so you know, I don't take kindly to excuses," I tell him. I tap the butt of the gun on the countertop to remind him who's still in charge here.

"He'll gut you. Ronan O'Sullivan is not a man to be trifled with."

"Clearly, neither am I."

The bartender looks past me at the bodies of the thugs littering his pub floor. "I know where you can find him," he sighs, with resignation and defeat in his tone.

"There's a good man." I tuck the gun back into my waistband. The man droops with audible relief.

"I'm reaching for a pen and paper," he calls to me as I stand up from the barstool. "I'll give you the address."

I laugh and shake my head. "Oh, no, friend. I'd rather you just took me yourself."

"You... you want me to take you?" His pallor is back and sicklier than ever. I just killed three men in the blink of an eye, right in front of this sorry bastard, and yet he's still almost as scared of Ronan O'Sullivan than he is of me.

The Irishman's reputation is impressive.

A lesser man might be afraid of that, of him.

But not me.

I'm the most dangerous man on the planet, and I have nothing left to lose.

~

The bartender closes up and we head out onto the street. He leads me to a pretty nice car, certainly one that's above the pay grade of a simple bartender in a podunk pub on the outskirts of Dublin.

But I don't question him as I fold myself into the passenger seat of his car.

We drive through the town, but I can't seem to concentrate on anything. My mind is racing.

This was Cillian's home. He grew up on these streets. He got into fist fights and chased girls down these streets. He loved these streets up —until the day they spat him out on a one-way flight to America.

And yet, I can't picture him anywhere.

I can't see him fitting in here.

His family's betrayal had forced some quintessential Irishness out of him. Like a part of his soul never left his home country.

"I've got my blonde hair and blue eyes," Cillian would always tell me as we stumbled drunk from one club to the next in our younger and more reckless teenage years. "Gifts from Mother Ireland. And they're the only things I'll keep."

The memory stings worse than I expected.

"Do you have a name?" I ask the bartender. Anything to distract myself from the storm raging inside my head.

"Does it matter?" he snarls.

I laugh darkly. "You're right. It doesn't."

He pulls to a stop outside the gates of a fancy compound. It's sprawling, but nowhere near as luxurious as the one Stanislav owned.

I can see the smirk pulling at the corners of his mouth. He obviously thinks he's got me cornered. *Tables are turned, motherfucker,* he's no doubt laughing to himself. There are probably several dozen armed men on the inside, which will leave me indisputably outnumbered. Security cameras, armored doors, weapons hidden in every corner…

Big fucking deal.

The bartender looks at me out of the corner of his eye from the driver's seat, probably wondering why I look so fucking calm right now.

"You're going to just walk in there with me?" he asks as he rolls down his window and waits for the guard on duty to step out of his little hut.

I shrug. "This is what I came here for."

"An audience with Ronan O'Sullivan?"

"That's right."

"Even if it costs you your life?"

I shrug again. "My life is not as important to me as you might think," I reply. "Perhaps that's a necessary part of being a good fighter. You can't win if you're scared of being killed."

"Is that how you killed three men in a matter of seconds?" he asks.

"That," I agree, "and I'm very fucking good at killing."

I can see the grudging respect in his eyes as the uniformed security guard emerges from the outpost and saunters over.

The two men converse quickly. I can't hear what they're saying, but I'm not really paying attention anyway. I'll end up inside one way or another.

The bartender turns to me. "He wants your name."

"Tell him it's Cillian O'Sullivan."

The bartender's eyes bulge, but when I don't break my stony expression, he sighs and repeats the name to the guard.

I'm just hoping that the cameras won't catch my image behind the sports car's tinted windows. Any idiot would be able to tell I'm not who I just claimed to be.

I'll never know for certain. But a minute later, the gates swing inward. We move inside, park, and get out of the car.

"Stop."

An armed guard blocks my path, his eyes narrowed on me. He clutches his gun threateningly.

I yawn pointedly and wait.

Then the front doors of the mansion swing inwards on silent hinges. A small group of armed men pour out, but I know they're just lackeys.

Did he come? I wonder. *Did the sound of his son's name call him out here?*

For a second, I think I fucked up. That my plan has failed and I'm about to take a bullet to the skull courtesy of some underpaid stooge with a twitchy trigger finger.

And then he emerges.

A tall, grizzled man. Blond hair faded to snowy white.

But it's the shock of his bright blue eyes that has me reeling for a second.

If Cillian had lived into his fifties, this is what he would have looked like.

The thought twists in my gut like a serrated knife.

Ronan O'Sullivan's eyes fall on me. Despite the startling blue, they darken with anger.

He moves his gaze over my shoulder to skewer the idiot who'd let me in.

"Any fool can see that this man is not my son," he says, his native brogue booming out like rolling thunder.

Then he sighs and waves a dismissive hand.

"Kill him."

22

ESME

ON A BUS SOMEWHERE SOUTH OF CARLSBAD, CALIFORNIA

Geoffrey leaves us at the bus depot with a warm hug and all the cash in his wallet, even when I insist that I can't take it.

"You need that, hon," he says, closing my hand back over the money. "Pay it forward."

Then he's gone, and I'm on my own again.

The ride is long, made even longer by the headache of crossing the border. I don't get much sleep because Phoenix keeps fussing from the second we pulled out of the station.

All the way through San Diego and Encinitas, he fusses. We stop and start and stop and start and passengers come and passengers go. And through it all, Phoenix fusses.

The other riders glare. Some complain, both under their breath and to my face.

But there's not much I can do to quiet him.

Except of course for feeding him. Then he settles for a few minutes, but I'm aware that my milk isn't coming in as fast anymore.

Probably because I haven't had a real meal in more than twenty-four hours.

I'm feeling the effects of the IV drip fading, too. Whatever magic juice was in that stuff is disappearing faster and faster, and without it, I'm left feeling weak. My body aches everywhere too.

What I really need is rest. Food, safety, a warm place to lie down.

I'm not asking for much. But I don't know where I'll find even those meager comforts.

I no longer have the luxury of worrying about my own needs, either. Phoenix needs me and I need to get out of town.

I look down at him in my arms. In the last few hours, he's finally fallen asleep. Nuzzled up against the sunshine yellow blanket that Gabby gave me and drifted off, though he still twitches from time to time.

For a little thing, he requires a lot.

I've already used and discarded five diapers. That fact alone is starting to panic me.

If he's going to go through diapers at this rate, I'm going to run out far sooner than I expected. I have some cash left on me but I need to make this last couple of hundred dollars last at least a month or two.

I'm pretty sure that no one will be willing to hire a new mom.

And even if they would, what can I do with Phoenix?

My life feels like it's collapsing slowly. Burning to the ground just like Papa's compound did.

But I have no choice but to kick away the debris and move forward.

At last, the bus driver calls out the name of the town Geoffrey circled on a map for me. It's nowhere I've ever heard of, which is perfect as far as I'm concerned. It'd be best if no one else ever heard of it, either.

The town is about an hour from the ocean. I wish it were closer, but beggars—which I think it's safe to say I am at this point—can't be choosers, right?

Still, my body itches for the ocean I grew up near. For the peace and calm that comes from being near salt water and ocean breeze.

But I can't give in to those urges anymore.

Only one thing matters: keeping Phoenix safe. What I want is no longer important.

We descend to a squealing stop. I gather my things and shuffle my way off the bus.

It's a relief to be off. But as the bus roars away, leaving me alone at the station with nothing but cockroaches for company, the old fears set in.

Am I making a mistake?

Should I just go back to Artem?

"No," I say out loud firmly. I stamp my foot for emphasis.

A rat picking through a garbage can a few yards away looks up at me in alarm. He eyes me as if to say, *What's wrong with you, woman?*

In my arms, Phoenix is still sleeping. Well, thank heavens for small favors, I suppose.

I fish through my pocket and retrieve the little piece of paper with the shelter's address on it. It's meant to be a women's home, but I have no idea what to expect.

Geoffrey was kind to me. So were Gabby and Ruby and Sara.

But I've lived on kindness for too long. I need to try and forge a path for myself that doesn't require pinning all my faith on other people.

I start walking, with Phoenix strapped to my chest. I've wound the blanket around my body so that he's nestled against my breasts without me having to hold him in place.

The duffel bag is heavy on my shoulder, and I keep having to switch sides so that I don't throw my back out.

My Caesarean stitches have started to throb in the last few hours. I grit my teeth against it, hoping the pain will fade once I've gotten some rest.

The sidewalk is filled with trash and dirt. Cars whizz by on the road every now and then, kicking up old burger wrappers and cigarette butts.

Eventually, the town proper springs up around me. Though that's not saying much. It's mostly fast food joints and strip malls with graffitied windows.

I have to stop a jogger to ask for directions to the shelter. She's a blonde woman with an amazing physique, and the way she looks at me tells me how different I must look than the Esme Moreno I used to be.

Pure pity in her eyes.

I try not to let it bother me. I'd pity me, too.

"Women's shelter?" she says, her eyes falling to the sleeping baby slung to my chest. "It's about a block from here. Keep walking straight, make a sharp right, and you'll find it. You can't miss it."

"Thank you so much."

I watch her jog away. As she goes, I feel a tug of longing, a sense of loss for the life I used to have.

I was nothing more than a trapped bird in a gilded cage in those days, of course. But there were moments now when I actually missed it.

No more gilded cage seems like an improvement. Like progress.

But how can it be, when all I have left now is gilded tears?

Maybe it's better to be trapped and happy, rather than free and miserable.

The last stretch to the shelter really wears on me. One block that feels like miles.

But when I see its rusting sign and cheap paint job, I feel nothing but pure relief.

At least, until I walk inside. I was willing to put up with a hell of a lot up to this point.

But this... this is bad.

The building looks like it's falling apart slowly. A decaying carcass rotting slowly in the SoCal sun.

A crumbling staircase hugs one side, its banisters faded and the paintjob chipped in so many places that I can see the dark rotting wood underneath.

The floors look like they've been clawed at and the ceiling is heavy with water leakage.

I notice a few women at the far end of the broad corridor that reaches back into the guts of the building. But when they see me looking, they avert their eyes.

No one is working behind the desk up front. I walk over anyway and stand there helplessly.

Minutes tick past. I hear muffled thumps and muted conversation every now and then from way in the back, but no one shows their face.

My ankles are burning from standing. I look around for a chair, but there's none around except for the lone chair behind the desk I'm standing at.

Desperate to get off my feet, I drag the chair from around the desk and sit down, feeling my feet sigh with relief.

I close my eyes and exhale. Then I look down at Phoenix, sucking on his pacifier, which has turned out to be a godsend.

I pray that leaving hasn't screwed up his life more than if we'd stayed put.

I know I've made mistakes.

I just don't want them to hurt my son.

"Who are you?"

I look up with a start and see an older woman with round, rimmed glasses staring down at me.

This must be her seat I'm sitting in.

She was wearing brown corduroy pants and a white shirt that almost comes down to her knees. Her hair is curly and piled high on top of her head, and even from behind her glasses, her eyes are dark and piercing.

I try to stand but I can't push myself off the chair just yet. "I'm sorry," I say. "I'm so tired."

She cocks her head to the side and looks at me sympathetically. "You need a place to stay."

It's not a question but I nod anyway. "I have nowhere else to go."

It physically hurts to say those words out loud. I actually wince from the effort of forcing them out. I knew how angry Artem would be if he knew where I have brought his son.

"Your daughter?" she asks.

"Son," I reply. "His name is Phoenix."

She nods. "We don't have any women with children at the moment," she cautions. "I have to warn you that some of them might not be so... welcoming."

I frown, wondering just how nervous I should be about that warning. Phoenix has turned into my chest so I can only see the apple of his cheek. He looks so precious, so innocent.

"Okay. Will I be able to stay?" I ask.

"We do have a bed you can have," she says. "But all areas are common. You won't get much in the way of privacy."

That is definitely not what I want to hear, but I'm aware that I'm not exactly rich with bargaining power here.

"That's not a problem."

"We don't have cribs either," she informs me.

"That's okay," I reply. "I have a bassinet."

"You do?" the woman asks, raising an eyebrow.

"It's cloth."

She nods. "How nice is it?"

I don't like the sound of that at all. "Um... what?"

"How nice is it?" she repeats. "Is it expensive?"

Again, the question unsettles me. I suddenly wonder if coming here was the right choice. But again, what options do I have left?

"It's not too expensive," I say carefully. "But it's new."

"Well, let's hope no one decides they want it."

"I... what do you mean?" I ask.

The woman looks at me with a pitying expression. "You're new to this, aren't you?" she asks bluntly.

I hesitate. Apparently, that's all the answer she needs, because she just nods and continues.

"You're lucky that none of the women in there have babies," she informs me. "So the likelihood of them stealing your son's items is minimal. But if it's nice stuff they can sell… Well, just watch out for your things."

I flinch a little, but nod. "Okay."

"Come on," she says. "Follow me. My name is Maisie, by the way."

I glance at her as we go, thinking that Maisie is not a name that suits her in the slightest. She holds herself confidently, but there's a no-nonsense vibe about her that is probably very necessary when it comes to running this shelter.

The broad corridor has doors on either side. Some are open and I can see bunk beds stacked high, one on top of the other.

Other rooms are emptier, filled with old sofas and a few board games have certainly seen better days.

We round the corner and Maisie ushers me into a large room with five bunk beds arranged in an awkward formation. There are two windows set at opposite ends of the space but somehow, they don't bring in much light.

Or maybe that is just a matter of perspective.

There are about six or seven women in the room when we walk in. I'm struck by how worn and tired each one looks.

But when I look close, I see that they're not that old at all. Most are my age at most, if not younger.

Is that what I'll look like in a few months?

Maisie leads me to a bunk in the farthest corner of the room. There's a woman lying on the bottom mattress.

She's got a shaved head, which highlights the bruises and scrapes that line her scalp. In some places, it actually looks like she's pulled her hair right out.

Her eyes are beautiful—a deep, chocolate brown—but they're filled with pure malice as she looks me up and down.

"Who's she?" she asks. Her question is directed at Maisie, as if I'm not even here.

"Tonya," Maisie sighs, "this is…"

She turns to me, realizing that she doesn't actually know my name.

"Oh… uh, Emily," I offer quickly.

"Emily," Maisie repeats. She turns back to Tonya. "She's our newest addition."

"Fuck," Tonya scowls, her face twisted with instant dislike. "What a princess this bitch is."

I flinch as if she'd slapped me.

The last few months have humbled me, pulled me down to earth, and reminded me of how bad most people had it.

I always thought my father's gilded cage was hell on earth.

But maybe I was just naïve.

Even still, I thought that had been stomped out of me. That I looked ordinary now.

It took Tonya all of three seconds to sniff me out.

She knows who I really am.

"She's got a baby," Maisie notes pointedly, ignoring Tonya's previous comment.

"I can smell the little shitter from here," Tonya snaps.

Only then do I realize that Phoenix needs another diaper change.

Fuck me. That's six diapers down.

"Anyway," Tonya continues, looking up at Maisie again, "what's that got to do with me?"

Maisie hesitates for a moment before plowing ahead. "I know you like the bottom bunk—"

"Fuck no!"

"Tonya..." Maisie sighs.

"The bottom bunk is mine!"

"She's got a baby," Maisie points out. She sounds exhausted. "A young baby, by the looks of it. She's not going to be able to climb up and down every time she wants to get some rest."

"That's not my fucking problem," the woman snaps with a vicious glare in my direction. "I'm not giving up my bunk."

"It's not your bunk," Maisie says, her tone growing cold. "It's the property of the state. And since I've been tasked with managing this shelter, I get to decide—"

"It's okay," I say quickly, stepping in. "It's fine. I'll take the top bunk."

Maisie raises her eyebrows and stares at me. "You will?"

I glance at the top bunk with trepidation, knowing that it will be difficult to maneuver with my wound still fresh from the C-section.

"I... um... sure," I say lamely. "I don't want to cause any problems."

"Then maybe you should find another shelter." Tonya drawls. "That brat of yours is certainly gonna cause problems and I like to sleep peacefully at night."

"Enough!" Maisie snaps. "Emily, if you can manage the top bunk, then fine. We serve three meals a day in the dining area. The meal times are taped to the door next to the front desk. That's all."

Then she turns on her heel and walks out, leaving me with a group of women who don't look at all happy to be sharing a room with an infant and—in Tonya's words—a "princess."

"You better keep that brat quiet," one wild-eyed woman yaps at me before turning in her bunk and pulling a blanket over her head.

A few just give me dark glances and go back to whatever they were doing. But others keep their eyes trained on me, warning me with bared teeth and angry eyes not to fuck with their corner of the world.

There's only one other woman in the room looking at me with something that comes close to sympathy.

She looks older, about fifty or so, and she's so thin that the skin around her eyes and mouth is worn down like tissue paper.

As she approaches me, I see the line of silver scars on both her arms. They're so perfectly aligned that they can only be self-inflicted.

"My name's Nancy," she says in a voice just one notch above a whisper. "If you want, I can look after your baby."

The way she speaks, the way she looks me right in the eye without blinking, is deeply unsettling. I don't want to be judgmental, but the slightly manic glint in her eyes makes me take a step back.

But at least it's not outright hostile.

Though that's really splitting hairs.

"That's okay," I say as politely as I can. "I need to feed him anyway."

Her face drops immediately. I feel a chill snake through my body as she turns away and stomps out of the room with aggressive steps.

Tonya smirks and shakes her head. "You better watch out for that one," she tells me. "She gets real mean after she's shot up."

"She was high?" I ask.

"Nah, that was just her in a good mood."

Emotion is churning inside me like a volcano waiting to blow. My immediate instinct is to get as far from this place as possible.

But where would I go? What would I do? Who would I seek?

Artem would have answers.

You should be here with me.

I need you.

Our son needs you.

My pride tries to bury the need, but my resilience is fading fast. It has been months of lone survival. All that time is starting to take a toll on my resolve to strike out on my own.

Why did I think I could do this?

I lived a sheltered life. Everything was done for me. I had always believed I was strong.

But maybe I'm not nearly strong enough.

"Jesus, are you gonna start crying?"

I blink hard. Tonya comes back into focus. I shudder and try to pull myself together as I move towards the bunk's ladder.

"How old is the brat anyway?" Tonya asks. Her initial anger has softened somewhat, although she still isn't exactly what I'd call "friendly."

I glance at her, shocked that she's actually trying to make conversation. "Um… a day," I reply with a joyless chuckle. "And a half."

"Fuck," she says, her eyes going wide. "Seriously?"

"Yeah." I nod. "His name is Phoenix."

She rolls her eyes. "You couldn't have come up with anything better?"

She looks so cartoonishly annoyed that I can't help but smile. "Look at him and tell me I was wrong," I challenge her.

She eyes the bundle strapped to my chest but she doesn't make an attempt to come closer. "I can see that pink cheek from here," she says dismissively. "Looks more like a fat little cardinal."

I look away from her and attempt to climb up onto the bunk so that I can feed Phoenix. I get up on the first rung just fine, but then it becomes hard to hoist myself onto the second.

I pant for a moment, deciding to take it slow when I hear Tonya cursing violently behind me.

"Fucking hell," she says. "Are you gonna make this much noise every time you climb up there?"

I sigh and ease myself back down onto the ground. "Give me a break okay?" I say as the fatigue catches up to me. "I had to have an emergency C-section."

She rolls her eyes again, but I notice her expression has changed. "Just fucking take the bottom bunk," she snarls. "I can't deal with you creaking up onto the top every fucking day."

"Really?" I ask.

"I just said, didn't I?" Tonya replies impatiently. "Don't piss me off. Just take the bunk."

"Thank you."

"Now don't go and start crying, okay?" she says. "It's bad enough that I'll have to deal with your brat crying. I don't need that shit from you, too. You're a damn little girl that thinks she's a grown ass woman, goddamn..." She trails off into mutters I can't quite decipher, still cursing up a storm.

I suppress a smile. She's more bark than bite, I think.

Then she clears her stuff away, which is limited to blanket and a small cloth bag, and throws everything onto the top bunk.

I sit down on the hard bottom mattress. My body oozes with gratitude for the respite.

But it doesn't last long.

Phoenix stirs in the blanket and I slowly unwind it from around my body. I lay him down on the bed while I prepare to feed him.

By the time I look up again, Tonya has disappeared.

I breathe a sigh of relief, grateful to find myself alone.

Well, not alone exactly, because there are still at least four other women in the room.

But at least they're minding their own business.

Phoenix starts mewling impatiently. I know he's hungry, but I want to change him first. I grab my duffel bag and pull out a new diaper.

I change him quickly and dispose of the dirty diaper in an old paper bag that I keep in my duffel for just such an occasion.

I want to get rid of the bag immediately, but Phoenix's starting to fuss. If I don't feed him soon, he's going to start screaming his lungs out.

So I put the paper bag in a corner next to the bed and then I sit down and put him to my breast just before he starts wailing. He quiets down and suckles greedily.

I stroke his cheek and watch him for a long time, trying to think about my next move. The shelter is not what I expected. I sure as hell don't want to stay here long term.

My only option is to find a job as fast as possible. With money coming in, I'd have options. A little more autonomy.

I let Phoenix feed for twenty minutes and then I burp him and switch him over to my second breast. I make sure to keep a blanket folded over my shoulder so that no one can see him nursing.

At some point, I notice Nancy edge back into the room. Her attention falls on me instantly, but she looks away just as quickly and goes to her bunk on the opposite end of the room.

Once Phoenix has had his fill, I burp him again and secure the contents of my duffel. I'd love to take a shower and change my clothes, but I don't know how I'm supposed to manage that with Phoenix in tow.

Shit, I don't know how I'm supposed to manage *anything* with Phoenix in tow.

The thought almost makes me cry, or maybe scream and rip my hair out until I look like Tonya. I'm not sure which would feel better.

I have to stop for a second and breathe so I don't lose it.

One thing at a time, Esme.

I push my bag under the bunk bed, secure Phoenix to my chest once more with his blanket, grab the paper bag with his dirty diaper in it, and head out of the room.

To my relief, I find Maisie at the front desk looking through a long list of names.

"Excuse me, Maisie?" I interrupt.

"Hmm?"

"Where can I get rid of Phoenix's dirty diapers?"

"Oh," I she says, looking up at me for the first time. "The bathroom has closed trash cans that are emptied out regularly. You can use those."

"Thanks." I turn to leave, but before I get far, she stops me.

"Just one thing before you go…" Maisie says.

"Yes?"

"I need a couple of your personal details."

The blood starts pounding in my ears. "Oh, right… um, my name is Emily," I say casually.

She smiles sardonically. "I already know that," she says. "But everyone has a last name."

"Yeah, of course, silly me. It's, uh, Emily… Kovalyov."

"Kovalyov," she repeats. "Can you spell that for me?"

Idiot. Fucking idiot. Why did you have to use his last name!

I nod, hands trembling, and spell it out for her.

"Great," she nods. "And some type of identification. A driver's license, passport, or social security number?"

I bite my lip. "I don't have anything."

"Nothing at all?" she asks with raised eyebrows.

I shake my head and stare pointedly at the ground between my feet.

Maisie just sighs. "All right then. Lunch has already been laid out. You look like you could use some nourishment."

I scurry away as fast as I can.

Once I've disposed of Phoenix's diaper, I go to the dining room, which is basically a large rectangular room set up like a poorly conceived cafeteria.

There are narrow tables arranged across the room, with two long benches flanking each table. There's already a long line for food and I join the line.

It takes nearly ten minutes to get up to the front where the food is being served by volunteers. They're all men and women with kindly faces who still manage to avoid everyone's eyes.

Lunch comes down to two options: a vegetable stew and a chicken pasta. I get a ladle full of both, a cup of water, and a plastic fork, and head to an empty table to eat.

The educated part of my brain is aware that the food is not good. It's lacking in flavor and body.

But it's hot and it fills my belly and that's enough for me to believe that's the most delicious thing I've ever put in my mouth.

It's also the only real meal I've had in two days, so that probably factors in, too. Either that or Gordon Ramsey is now working at this grimy women's shelter south of Carlsbad.

I clean my entire plate in a minute flat. With a full stomach, I can start to visualize a plan for the future.

Staying here can only be a temporary solution. I will not allow my son to grow up in a place like this.

I take a deep breath.

I want to live near the ocean. I want Phoenix to grow up near the beach.

I know the ocean is only an hour or so away. I could take a bus, but I'd rather drive. I feel a pang of regret as I think about the car I had abandoned a few days after I'd left Devil's Peak.

I'd only been thinking about covering up my footprints, and I knew that Artem had the license plate number.

What I should have done was find a shady dealership somewhere and sell the car. They would have stripped it for parts and I might have gotten a few hundred bucks from the sale.

Instead I'd walked away with nothing, and I'd regretted the decision ever since.

I think about the ways I might go about getting another car. The choice I'm left with twists in my stomach like a knife.

There's only one way to get yourself a car at this point.

I left that life behind for a reason.

It doesn't happen all at once. This is about survival.

It would be theft. That's a crime.

Life is not black or white. It's grey. It always has been.

Artem said something similar to me what felt like eons ago. I try to sort through the internal dialogue waging in my head, but it just makes me hurt all over.

I need sleep. One night of sleep and I'll decide tomorrow.

Phoenix turns a little, trying to stretch his little hands. I leave the dining area and head back to my assigned bunk. When I approach the bed, I noticed that one of my duffel straps is peeking out from underneath the bed.

I frown and pull it out. It definitely looks like it's been tampered with. I pull the zip open and look through the contents.

Most of Phoenix's stuff is still there, and so is my supply of diapers, but a few of my clothes are missing. I had a beige sweater I loved that's now gone, and a long-sleeved black shirt that is definitely not here anymore.

"Fuck."

"Left your shit unchecked huh?" Tonya's voice comes from just behind me. "Rookie mistake."

"They stole my clothes," I say in disbelief.

"You had some fancy shit in there. That black sweater was nice."

I turn and glare at her. "You took my clothes?"

She glares right back at me. "I'm no fucking thief," she bites back. "A few of the other bitches stormed through here and went through your shit when you left with the brat."

"Why didn't you stop them?" I demand.

She raises her eyebrows at me. "You fucking serious?" she asks. "Those bitches would have skinned me alive. And you're no one to me. It's every woman for herself in here."

I shudder, realizing how entitled I must sound to her. "Sorry," I murmur. "You're right."

"At least they left all the baby's shit," Tonya tells me. "That was pretty kind."

"Right. Yeah. Kind."

"Did you have money in there?" Tonya asks.

"No."

"Good, so you're not that fucking stupid."

I'd taken to carrying my money around in my bra since I'd left the hospital. It was one of the smartest moves I'd made in a while.

But it's not enough.

I've got to be smarter now that I'm on my own.

I've got to be tougher, too.

For myself.

For Phoenix.

For the future I gave up everything for.

23

ARTEM
DUBLIN, IRELAND

Ronan's darkened blue eyes flicker over the men that surround him.

"Kill him," he says again with finality.

I don't budge. Don't so much as take my eyes off the cold bastard.

"Before you kill me," I say calmly. "Do you at least want to hear how your son died?"

He stops. Freezes, really.

And yet, his face remains unchanged. It's as though I've given him the weather report.

But I know better than to assume he feels nothing.

Men like him have curated their image to perfection. If I can't tell what's he's feeling, it's because he doesn't want me to know what he's feeling.

But I'm not looking for emotion. I'm looking for hesitation.

And when I see it, I seize my opportunity.

"He died four months ago," I say. "He took the bullet that was meant for me."

Ronan turns to me slowly, his eyes boring into mine. He really looks at me this time. He gives a small nod.

His men lower their weapons.

"Get in the car," he tells me. "We'll finish this discussion inside."

I glance back at the bartender who'd brought me here. He's staring at me open-mouthed, clearly shocked at how I'd managed to get myself out of what he clearly thought would be a short and fatal confrontation.

Fucking idiot. He's too dumb to last long in this world.

I turn my back on him and walk to the foot of the mansion's marble staircase. Before I ascend, I'm stopped, frisked and unburdened of all my weapons by a pair of suited goons.

Ronan stands at the top of the stairs, looking up at the ornate gargoyles looming above the entryway. Waiting for me, no doubt, but his back is turned so I can't see his face.

Does he feel the loss?

He clearly feels something—otherwise, why invite me back to the house?

It gives me a small glimmer of hope, but I'm still cautious. I knew next to nothing about the O'Sullivan clan. Nothing real, in any case.

Cillian had spoken about them in brief, bitter anecdotes. And only when he was very drunk or really pissed. The family portrait he painted was less than flattering.

The goons push me up the stairs. I mount slowly, wary of everything around me.

When Ronan hears me coming, he slips inside without a word.

I follow him in.

The house is surprisingly modern inside, made of clean lines and a lot of glass. Everything is sleek and jaw-droppingly expensive.

Fuck me. The O'Sullivan's are doing better than anyone realized.

"Follow me," Ronan throws back over his shoulder at me. He walks fast.

We cross a massive foyer, go through a great room with three fireplaces all burning. Libraries, lounges, a cinema, a sprawling office. I get glimpses of each room as we pass.

My admiration grows with every step.

On the far side of the house, we emerge back into the sunlight.

There's a table set out on the deck, made of bulky wood that clashes horribly with the sleek modernity of the rest of the house. It's the most Irish piece I have seen so far.

"Sit," Ronan instructs me.

I see him nod to one of his guards posted at the doorway. The man disappears into the house. The rest of them seem to disappear as well, but I can still sense them around us. Watchful and waiting for their don's next command.

"Can I offer you something to drink?" Ronan asks.

"I don't drink anymore."

He sighs like I'm an idiot and holds up three fingers to another of the guards lingering around the perimeter of the garden.

"Today, you do."

Shortly afterwards, one of his men appears with a bottle of whiskey and three glasses.

Ronan grabs the green neck of the Jameson Irish whiskey that Cillian used to favor and fills up all three glasses.

"Is someone else joining us?" I ask.

As if in answer, I clear the click of heels on wood. Then, an older blonde woman steps out onto the deck.

She's striking. Beautiful, really. She wears a gray turtleneck and black pants with silver diagonal zips that mark each pocket. Her blonde hair is piled high on her head and her makeup is expertly applied to hide the age lines around her mouth and eyes.

I hadn't expected Cillian's mother to be quite so... glamorous. She must have been in her fifties, but youth still clung to her delicate features.

Cillian hadn't inherited much from her in the way of looks. He had his dad's masculine, rough-hewn features.

But there was still a resemblance to his mother, however subtle. A sort of kindness in the eyes, maybe.

She zones in on me.

Her mouth is relaxed, her lips turned up as though she's about to smile, but I can see that her eyes are tense.

Then she looks at her husband and moves to sit down beside him. She doesn't say a word as she reaches for the third class of whiskey on the table. She takes it and gulps it down in a matter of seconds.

Her mannerisms remind me so much of Cillian that I can't take my eyes off her. She puts down the empty glance and looks at me while she addresses her husband.

"Another."

He pours more whiskey into her glass, but this time she doesn't move to take it. She just keeps looking at me.

"I was told you were with my son when he died," she says.

I can hear the tenor of emotion running like a fine edge underneath her tone. She is desperate for information.

But she's terrified of what she's about to hear, too.

"I was with him when he was shot," I clarify. "As I told your husband, he put himself in front of the bullet that was meant for me."

"And why would he do that?" Ronan asks before she can.

"Because I was his family."

Ronan's frown deepens at my reply. "Cillian has a family."

"He did," I agree. "And then you disowned him and cast him aside."

They might not like the blunt truth being dropped on them like a stranger. But I didn't cross the ocean to mince words with these people.

I continue, "You betrayed him and ran him out of his homeland. Is it any wonder he found a home somewhere else?"

Ronan is radiating raw anger now. It's the first time I've chipped through his icy exterior. Apparently, I've touched a nerve.

If I had to guess, it was a nerve that his wife has been pulling for many years.

I glance at her, trying to read her expression. She's looking down at her whiskey glass as though it's the answer to curing her misery.

I've been there.

Fuck, I might be there right now.

"Cillian betrayed me first," Ronan says, drawing my attention back to him. "Or did he leave that part out?"

"He left nothing out," I reply. "He told me about what he did to a politician's son. A man you chose above him."

Ronan doesn't move. Neither does his wife.

"What's your name?" she asks slowly.

"Artem Kovalyov," I reply.

Ronan frowns. "Kovalyov?" he says. "You're Bratva."

"Yes."

"We knew Cillian was running in mafia circles in L.A.," Ronan says. "We just didn't realize which circles."

"He's been by my side for almost ten years."

"Which is where he got shot, no?" Ronan drawls.

"You really want to trade accusations?" I demand. "Because trust me, I've got a few myself."

"You realize you're in my house now, yes?" the man rasps quietly. "You're outnumbered and unarmed."

I shrug. "I'm not afraid of death."

"The only reason that's true is because you have nothing left to lose," he says shrewdly. "Which is also, I'm assuming, why you're here in the first place."

I look the man right in the eye, trying to size him up the way he's sizing me up. But before either one of us can say a word, Cillian's mother interrupts.

"You say you were his family."

Ronan starts to cut her off. "Sinead—"

"I have a right to know about my son," she snaps, her voice strong.

I'm surprised to see Ronan back down immediately.

"You prevented me from seeing my child for the last decade," she adds. "Do not deny me this now."

Ronan hesitates, then nods.

Sinead turns back to me.

"Tell me about his life in L.A.," she says. "Tell me what he was like. What kind of man he was."

I take a moment to arrange my thoughts.

How am I supposed to explain the last ten years?

How am I supposed to condense down a good man's lifetime into a few short sentences?

"He was… the most optimistic man I've ever met," I start. "He was quick to laugh about everything, including himself. He was unfailingly honest, he was loyal to a fault, and he missed Ireland far more than he claimed he did."

Sinead looks at me with her powder-blue eyes. Like Cillian's, but softer, hazier.

"Did he hate us?" she asks.

"I don't think he hated you," I say, addressing her directly. "He resented what was done to him. He was hurt. Sometimes he didn't understand—"

"Didn't understand?" Ronan barks. "What didn't he fucking understand? He knew what he was doing. He knew who he was fucking with."

"Does it matter?" I shoot back calmly. "He was defending his woman."

Ronan grunts with anger. "That bitch was beneath him. He insisted on entangling himself with her, and then he became sloppy and irresponsible. He prioritized her over the family. He should have known better. Nothing comes above family."

"Maybe he considered her family," I point out.

Ronan narrows his eyes. "Is that what he told you?"

"He didn't have to," I answer. "I knew Cillian better than anyone."

"You say that to me?" Ronan challenges. "His father?"

"You knew the boy he was," I say. "Not the man he became."

I glance back at Sinead, who hasn't taken her eyes off me.

I sigh. My chest aches like a bruise. "He fought by my side for almost a decade. He was with me through the worst times of my life and the best. He was my conscience and my toughest critic. And he was talented. If you'd only chosen differently, he would have made an amazing don in his own right."

That brings about a spark of regret in Ronan's stubborn eyes. The idea that his legacy might have had a stronger chance of success is the only thing that really rattles him.

"He chose wrong," he replies tensely.

"He was young."

"Artem," Sinead says, her voice shaking just a little. "Did he… was he happy? Did he leave behind anyone? A woman, a child perhaps?"

I want to be able to give her something. She so badly wants it. Some hope to cling to.

But I know that lying to them now will only undo all the headway I've made since coming here.

"No," I say. "There was no one in his life. He wasn't looking to settle down."

"Was it still her—all this time?" Sinead asks.

I'm pretty sure I know the answer, but I shake my head. "I don't know. He kept his feelings pretty close to heart."

"Tell me how he died," she asks.

"Sinead…" Ronan warns, glancing at her pointedly.

"I want to know," she insists. "Please tell me."

Those eyes are so blue. So desperate.

"It was an ambush," I explain. "I was surrounded. A dozen men against me, maybe more. I was about to die and Cillian jumped into the fray."

"He knew he would die," Sinead guesses.

"Yes. As I said, he was loyal to a fault."

"The only question is: were you worth his loyalty? Were you worth his life?" Ronan asks.

I shake my head. "I'm not," I reply without hesitation. "Cillian was a better man than I am. But he was a man without a country, without a woman, and without children. His only family was me. That is why he did what he did."

I can see unshed tears in Sinead's eyes, but she blinks them back and gets a hold of herself in a matter of seconds.

I see clearly why a man like Ronan would choose a wife like her.

More to the point, I see how a man like Cillian came from a woman like her.

She doesn't fear her feelings. They make her strong.

Cillian understood that better than I ever have.

"That's all very well," Ronan says. "But it doesn't explain why you're here."

This is it.

Time to plead my case.

I take a slow breath. Then I tell them the truth, unvarnished and bare.

"I'm here to avenge your son's death."

"And you took a flight to Ireland just to tell us that?" Ronan scowls.

"I need resources."

Ronan throws up his hands in dismay. "As I suspected. You're just a fucking beggar."

He turns to Sinead and I see the silent conversation the two are having.

When he turns back to me, his eyes are wiped clean of emotion once more.

"Who is the man who pulled the trigger?" Ronan asks.

"Budimir Kovalyov." I can't put off the revelation any longer.

"What?" Sinead says in alarm, leaning into her seat.

"My uncle."

"Your uncle killed my son?" Sinead asks slowly.

"He also killed my father," I tell them. "He took control of the Bratva, robbed me of my birthright, and tried to kill me and everyone loyal to me."

"And yet here you sit," Ronan says.

He leaves the rest unsaid, but I hear him loud and clear.

Here you sit—while my son is dead.

"Budimir left me lying in the dirt beside Cillian," I tell him. "He left me to bleed out slowly. He believes I'm dead just like your boy."

"So you're nothing but a ghost."

"I am precisely that," I admit. "One that is soon going to be unleashed."

"With my resources?" Ronan says sardonically.

"That is why I'm here," I say, looking between the handsome couple, wondering how good my chances are.

"This is not about avenging Cillian," Ronan comments. "This is about taking back what you think is yours."

"It's about both."

"And if I say no?" Ronan asks.

"I'll walk out of here and find another way," I say firmly. "And I *will* find another way. I will be don of the Bratva once more. And Budimir will pay for what he did to your son."

I stare him in the face. Ronan understands the subtext here. It's politics at the end of the day, after all.

Wouldn't you rather make an ally of a Bratva don?

Ronan sighs and steeples his fingers on the table.

"I will consider your request," he says. "You'll have an answer tomorrow."

"I appreciate that, Don O'Sullivan." I stand, leaving my whiskey untouched, and get ready to depart.

"We have a room you can use tonight," Sinead says suddenly. She lurches up with me and rests a kind hand on my forearm.

Ronan growls deep in his chest but says nothing. I'm sure he doesn't like the display of softness.

But Sinead doesn't give a damn.

I hadn't expected an invitation to stay. I incline my head with gratitude.

"Thank you," I say. "But I'll decline. I have a place in mind for the rest of my trip in Ireland. You can find me at The Free Canary when you've made up your mind."

My mind flashes back to an ancient memory.

"Byrne's again?" I ask. "We went there twice already this month. That pub is fucking rank."

"I know," Cillian laughs.

"So the fuck do you love it so much?" I demand.

"Reminds me of The Free Canary," he says softly.

"An Irish institution, huh?"

Cillian snorts. "More like an Irish travesty. It was a shitty little bar wedged in between a better pub and a porn shop. But fuck... that bar was my whole fucking adolescence."

"Pity I missed it," I drawl sarcastically.

He ignores me. "Had my first drink in that bar. Fucked my first woman in one of the rooms upstairs. Had my first fight by the cash register. Fell in love in that pub."

His eyes are dreamy. Distant.

He's remembering a place he might not see again in this life.

"You think you'll ever go back there?" I ask.

"Maybe one day," Cillian says with a shrug. "When I'm old and grey and I've lived so fucking much that I ache all over. Then I'll go back and order a pint of Guinness. I'll sit at the bar and sip my beer and fall asleep to old Irish songs."

I laugh. "Jesus, that's sad. And by sad, I mean pathetic."

"Fuck you."

Our laughter fills the empty streets as we head to the next bar.

The memory fades away. I wish I had more of it. More of him.

"The Free Canary," Sinead echoes. The clench in her jaw melts under a wave of grief. "He loved that damn pub."

"He loved a lot of the things he left behind," I say. I turn once more to leave. Before I do, something else occurs to me. I pivot again and say to Ronan, "Oh, and I should apologize."

"For what?" the grizzled man asks.

"I believe I killed three of your men at O'Malley's."

His expression is blank. "If the three of them couldn't handle one fucking Russian, then they deserved to die." He laughs scornfully and waves me off.

Ronan remains seated, sipping the whiskey straight from the bottle and staring out into the lush garden.

But Sinead gets up and walks with me back towards the entrance of the house. She's quiet—weighed down with memories, no doubt.

I wish I had the ability to comfort her, but I've never been good with grief.

I can barely handle my own.

"He must have loved you," Sinead says just before I cross through the front doors once again. "To have died for you, I mean."

I turn to face her. The sunlight hits her blue eyes and makes them sparkle like the ocean.

"He would have died for any one of you, too," I tell her solemnly. "If he'd only been given a chance."

24

ARTEM

One of Ronan's men is waiting out front with a car to take me anywhere I want to go.

I tell him, "The Free Canary," then settle back into my seat.

The bartender is nowhere to be found. He must've left while I was inside.

Smart man. If I ever see that bastard again, I'll kill him.

The ride is swift and silent. We stop outside the tavern, which looks just as run down and neglected as Cillian had always described.

True to his word, there's a foul-looking porn shop on the right side and another pub on the left that looks warmer, brighter, livelier.

The Free Canary squats in the middle. Dank and unloved. The sign overhead shows a yellow bird flapping its way out of a shattered iron cage. Looks like a six-year-old fingerpainted it, to be honest.

I sigh and shake my head.

Of course Cillian would love a shithole like this.

I step out of the car. It speeds off the moment I'm clear of the wheels. The weather outside has gotten colder and greyer since we left Ronan's mansion.

I pull my jacket closer around me and step through the front doors.

The moment I walk inside, I feel like I've walked into a time capsule. Old posters and maps of Ireland from centuries ago dot the walls. The music is Irish through and through, which means it's equal parts cheerful and mournful.

I go to the bar and flag down the bartender, a skinny blonde with smudged racoon eyes and tits pressed up damn near to her neck.

She eyes me like she's not sure whether she wants to fuck me or rob me.

As long as she doesn't pull a gun on me like the last bartender I met, I don't give a damn.

"What can I get you, handsome?" she asks in a rolling brogue.

"Water."

"That's it?"

"That's it."

She starts trying to tempt me into barbeque wings. But she falls silent when I hold up a hand to cut her off.

I shake my head. "Just water," I tell her. "And silence."

She bites her lip and nods. "Aye, understood."

A few moments later, she places a glass of water in front of me and disappears down to the opposite end of the bar.

Satisfied, I take the chance to look at the walls of the bar that had built Cillian.

His words, not mine.

"That fucking pub built me."

"You sound like a country Western song."

"And you sound like a sourpuss bitch."

I hear his voice in my head, but the words are all recycled. Ancient history. Ghosts from the past.

Another one occurs to me. One I haven't thought about in a long time. Curious, I slide off my stool, grab my duffel bag, and walk outside again.

A light drizzle has started up. To my surprise, it's warm. Each drop like a soft kiss on my skin.

I take a few steps away from the building and turn around to face it again. Cillian's voice is playing in my head like he's guiding me.

"There was a little alleyway on the side, hardly big enough to fit through. Always left my fat friends behind here, the poor bastards."

My gaze tracks down. Sure enough, wedged between the porn shop and The Free Canary is a little sliver of an alley. If I turn sideways, I'll be able to shuffle down.

"So we'd go on down that way. Suck in your gut. You'll pop out soon enough. A rusty-ass ladder hung off the building. Riddled with tetanus, no doubt, but I never gave a damn."

I hold my duffel bag overhead and start the creep-walk between the buildings. The stone walls are slick with the rainwater, with moss, with years of grime and sweat.

I keep moving.

At the end, there's a ladder. It's rusted to shit and I'm wary that it can support my weight.

But I just sigh, loop the duffel bag over my shoulder, and start the climb up.

And then I emerge onto the rooftop of The Free Canary.

It's mostly empty. Scant gravel across the top. A few crushed beer cans here and there, cigarette butts, the shit left behind by the drunken kids who made the journey I just made.

"The fuck's so special about this, Cillian?" I mutter under my breath.

Then I turn and face the south, and I get it.

The city opens out in the distance. Sprawling. Lights sparkle against the oncoming darkness of night.

The last rays of the sun sneak out from under the bank of gray clouds.

Dublin looks like a place worth remembering.

I sink to a seat with my back against the low wall, duffel bag at my side. Part of me is racking through my conversation with the O'Sullivans. Wondering what they'll decide.

I ought to set that aside. Take this moment to remember my best friend.

I decided on the flight to Ireland that he must be dead by now for certain. Maybe I'll never know for sure. I don't have a body to bury, after all.

But all the blood on the ground in the forest left little room for doubt.

He's gone. I feel it in my bones.

All that's left of Cillian O'Sullivan are my memories.

I'll keep those until the day I join him.

I think for a while about the man. Growing up with him at my side. The trouble we caused and the trouble we found alike. The past is full of things that make me laugh.

But it's the future I can't stop running through again and again.

If Ronan turns me down, what will I do?

I had contacted the men still loyal to me just before I'd left the States. They swore they're behind me and I was assured of their loyalty, but we're still too few to take back the Bratva.

We need a show of force and power in order to gain the upper hand from Budimir. I know that with money, I could buy the men I needed.

But I've never been a fan of that method. It was the one of the few matters on which Stanislav and I had agreed.

Win a man with money, and he will stab you in the back the moment another offers him more.

Loyalty is in the blood, not in the wallet.

A man who fights for money fights for himself alone.

Stanislav had a dozen more sayings like that. He had drilled each of them into me over the years from the time I was old enough to listen.

The lessons had stuck.

Apparently, Budimir wasn't paying attention.

All the better. You have a few lessons still to learn before you die, motherfucker.

I can only hope that he's made just enough mistakes to undo him. Maybe he did, maybe he didn't. Truth is, I'm living on a sliver of hope and the dirty fuel of revenge.

But that'll be enough.

It has to be.

∼

I don't know when I fell asleep. I dreamed all night of strangling Budimir until he spluttered and choked and turned blue under my fingers.

But the sun wakes me up.

A little rudely, to be honest.

Yesterday's clouds are gone and the dawn this morning is bright as fuck. I open my eyes and wince against it.

And then I realize there's someone else on the roof with me.

Adrenaline surges through me at once. I leap to my feet, halfway to drawing a knife from my boot to gut the motherfucker…

When I see who it actually is.

I sigh and sheathe the knife again.

"Good morning, Sinead."

She sinks gracefully to a seat on the ground across from me. Removes her dark sunglasses and stows them in her purse.

She's wearing black checkered pants and a snow-white coat. Elegant and poised, just as she was yesterday.

She looks around at the rooftop and sighs.

"I don't think I've been here in over a decade," she admits. "Certainly not up here."

"Has it changed?" I ask.

"Not even a little bit."

"It's… not quite what I expected," I say with a harsh laugh. "Cillian made it seem like heaven on earth."

She smiles sadly. "I never did understand why the boy loved this place so much."

"I think it was more about the experience than the place."

"Perhaps," she says with a shrug.

I try and read her expression, but there's nothing there. I wonder if she learned her poker face from her husband—or if it was actually the other way around.

"You have an answer for me, don't you?" I ask.

"I do."

"And I'm not going to like it."

She nods. She's not apologetic or regretful. Nor is she spiteful.

Just matter-of-fact. Straightforward. Honest.

"We won't be helping you, Artem. Not with money or with men. It's not our place to concern ourselves with the matters of the Bratva." She fixes me with a level gaze. "This is your fight, not ours."

I look her in the eye and I know instinctively that nothing I can say will make a difference.

I nod. "Very well."

I expect her to get up and leave. But she stays seated. Cranes her neck around to survey the view I admired last night.

"I keep thinking of him as a child," she muses. "All those little memories I've suppressed for so long. He was such a beautiful child. Everything was funny to him."

"That never changed."

"I'm glad," she says. "I was always so worried about him… out in L.A., on his own."

"He wasn't on his own," I correct. "He had me. We had each other."

She smiles, a sad smile that makes her powder blue eyes swim for a moment. "That helps to know," she says. Her eyes scanning over me like she's searching for clues. What kind of man was with her son at the end, perhaps. "You're married."

I had thought about removing my ring months ago after Esme had left, but I never followed through. Apparently, my hurt pride wasn't strong enough to withstand the desire to keep a small part of Esme with me, no matter how hollow the gesture was.

"Yes."

"Do you love her?"

I look at her, immediately uncomfortable with the conversation. The only person I had ever discussed this kind of shit with was Cillian.

Without him around, I just bury it deep.

"Love has no place in my life," I answer.

She sighs with exasperation. "Why?" she demands. "Because the Bratva always comes first?"

"Yes."

"Then you are a weak man."

I look at her with amusement. "Excuse me?"

"Are you not strong enough to have both? To protect both? To balance both?" she asks. "Why is it always either-or with you men?"

"She wants me to give up the Bratva," I say with a scowl. "It wasn't my idea to choose. It was hers."

"I see," Sinead says. "And you chose your legacy."

"It's not a choice," I snap. "It's what I *have* to do. I have to avenge my father's death. I have to avenge Cillian's death."

"Even if that's not what he would have wanted you to do?"

"My conscience won't rest until I get back what was stolen from me," I say. "It doesn't matter what Cillian would have wanted. He's not here to tell me otherwise."

She taps her fingernails on her thigh. "You know, Artem, I used to tell my husband something when we were newly married and his ambitions were greater than his capabilities," she says. "*'Get out of your own way.'*"

"Am I meant to apply that advice to my own life?"

"All men should," she replies. Then she unfolds herself to her full height once again and settles her sunglasses back on her face.

She turns to go back to the ladder, but pauses before she gets far. "I wish I had more to offer you," she says. "But all I have is my thanks."

"For what?" I ask.

"For taking in Cillian," she replies. "For being there for him when I wasn't."

"He didn't blame you."

"He should have," Sinead says bluntly. "I should have fought for him harder than I did. Family is the one thing you never regret fighting for. It's also the one thing that leaves you with regret when you haven't done enough."

I sit there, turning her words around in my head. "Take care, Artem," she says. "I hope you get what you want."

Then she disappears over the edge.

Leaving me stewing in indecision.

Questioning every choice that's brought me here.

25

ESME

THE WOMEN'S SHELTER—SOUTH OF CARLSBAD, CALIFORNIA

"Jesus, does the little brat ever stop crying?" Tonya complains as she soaks her bread in the bowl of potato soup in front of her.

"He's only four days old."

I follow her lead and dip my bread in my own soup. It's stale, so it soaks up the broth pretty well and softens the roll up considerably. I'm not complaining, though. My belly has been satisfied the last three days and I'm never taking that for granted again.

"Still, can't you do something about the noise?" she groans.

I look down at Phoenix, who's strapped to my chest as usual. Gabby's blanket has been a godsend. It's stitched so long that I can wrap it around my body to secure him in place.

"What do you want me to do?" I ask. "I've changed him and I've fed him. He's just sleepy."

"So why isn't he sleeping then?"

"Jesus," I sigh. "It's not that damn simple. Clearly, you've never been around a baby before."

Tonya's eyes go dark for a moment, but then she pushes the anger back and shrugs it off.

"Yeah well, I never got to keep my baby," she says callously.

"What?" I gasp, looking at her with shock.

I can see the way her slight shoulders tense immediately, but she's trying hard to act as though it doesn't affect her.

She runs her hand over her shaved head self-consciously and twists her spoon around in her bowl. "Yeah," she mumbles. "Had a baby a while back. Girl. Didn't keep her."

I raise my eyebrows and choose my words carefully. I know the moment I meet Tonya with anything close to sentiment or pity, she'll pull back and completely ignore me.

"That must have been hard."

Tonya shrugs. "It wasn't like I could keep her," she tells me. "I didn't know what the fuck to do with her. I could barely keep myself alive at that point. I'm still trying to figure out how to do that."

"How old were you?" I ask.

"Fifteen."

"Fuck."

She smiles. "I love it when you swear."

I frown. "Why?"

"Because you're like a little Pollyanna princess," she tells me. "It's funny."

I roll my eyes. "I'm no Pollyanna."

"Yeah, no one buys that shit," Tonya says.

I feel eyes on me suddenly and I turn slightly to catch Nancy enter the dining area. She's scratching her arms wildly, her eyes skitter over the crowded tables, looking for a spot to fill.

"Cracko's here," Tonya warns me. "Thank fuck our table's full."

A part of me feels sorry for Nancy. She looks at Phoenix with a longing that's impossible to deny.

But I'm also frightened of her.

She's high through most of the day and prone to bouts of manic emotional highs and lows.

Yesterday, she'd gotten into a fight with someone in an adjoining room.

She went back to cut the woman's hair off in the night.

She shuffles down the food line and then settles into a table on the far corner of the room. I'm not upset about that in the least.

I'm almost too exhausted to care, though. I haven't been sleeping very well. Each night, I hear every creak, noise, snore, and nightmare from the other women in the shared room. Sleep is elusive.

Quite apart from them, I have to wake up every three hours to feed Phoenix. I'm so worried that his crying will wake them up and piss them off that I spend most nights tip-toeing along the line between sleep and consciousness, jumping to attention at Phoenix's slightest stir.

The lack of sleep is really starting to weigh on me. This will be my fourth night at the shelter and it's still pretty early, but already my eyelids are heavy with exhaustion.

Phoenix lets out a sharp cry and Tonya winces as though someone's just knifed her.

"Stop being dramatic," I tell her.

We've fallen into an easy and unexpected friendship, though I knew better than to categorize it as that to Tonya.

"That sound makes me want to pull my ears right off," she says.

I roll my eyes again and force the pacifier into Phoenix's mouth. He's been rejecting it for the last hour, but now, he finally accepts it and quiets down a little.

"Jesus, finally," Tonya says. "Why the fuck didn't you do that before?"

"I *tried*."

"All right, all right," she says, holding her hands up as though I'm brandishing a gun in her direction. "Don't bite my head off."

I take another mouthful of soup-soaked bread and sway a little from side to side in the hopes of coaxing Phoenix to sleep.

His eyes are tired but he just keeps staring up at me stubbornly.

"Suit yourself," I whisper to him, running my finger across his cheek.

"Tonya?" I ask cautiously. "What happened with your daughter?"

She looks down at her now-empty soup bowl. "Gave her up for adoption," she says. "The closed kind. Nice couple. Fucking picture perfect. That's the whole reason I picked them. Apparently, they'd been trying for ages to have a baby and it never happened for them. Fucked up."

"What was?"

"Dunno," Tonya says with a shrug. "The whole fucking situation. People like them who have their shit together and can't have a baby. And then there's people like you and me. Lives are shot to shit. Can't hardly take care of our own damn selves, much less a little rugrat. And we still end up knocked up. Don't have two pennies to rub together, but we got babies. *That's* what's fucked up."

The ring I've hidden in my bra pricks me right on cue. The diamond is worth hundreds of thousands of dollars, if not more.

And yet, I can't bring myself to sell it.

I can't bring myself to let go of the one last thread that ties me to the past.

"I used to have my shit together," I say.

"Oh yeah?" Tonya asks. "Had yourself a man?"

I see Artem's six-foot-three frame in my mind's eye so clearly that for a second it's as if he's just walked through the door.

Then I blink and his image fades, leaving me feeling cold and lonely.

"Yeah," I reply shortly.

"He left you?"

I shook my head. "I left him."

Tonya frowns. "Did he beat you?" she asks.

"No."

"Cheat?"

"No."

She stares at me as though she can't quite comprehend any other reason why a woman would leave a man who was still interested in sticking around.

"Then why?" she demands, as though she's owed an explanation and I'm obligated to give her one.

"…It's complicated."

She rolls her eyes. Hard.

"That's such a fucking crock of an excuse," she says, practically snarling at me. "You know what my man did when he found out I was pregnant? He told everyone that I was a slut who fucked so many guys that he was definitely not the father."

"Oh, Tonya—"

"Wipe that fucking look off your face," Tonya says as she glares at me. "It's fucking ancient history. I'm over it."

"What did you do?" I ask.

She shrugs. "I considered an abortion," she admits. "Made the appointment and everything. But... then I couldn't go through with it. So I dropped out of school, had the baby, and handed her over to a woman who was ready to be a mom."

"I'm sorry."

"Who are you sorry for?" Tonya seethes. "My baby got two great parents and I... well, I got to live my life."

"Right," I say. I don't bother pointing out that she isn't living much of a life at all.

For the first time, I see Tonya's eyes land on Phoenix's pink cheek and linger there a moment. Almost... tenderly.

But then she notices me watching her and she turns her face away instantly.

"You still haven't answered my question," she reminds me.

But now I know that she's just trying to distract me.

I shrug and she cuts me off before I can even open my mouth. "And don't tell me it's complicated again."

"But it is."

"Fuck you."

I sigh. "He was... is a dangerous man," I tell her.

Tonya raises her eyebrows. "Dangerous?" she repeats.

I nod.

"So he *did* beat you?" she asks with confusion.

"No, no it wasn't like that," I try and explain. "He was just... he was involved in... something that I didn't want in my life."

"Like drugs and shit?"

"Something like that," I say. That's the easiest way to explain it.

"So he was an addict?"

"No."

"A pusher?"

"Jesus, Tonya, how many times are we gonna do this?" I say, getting a little testy myself. "Does it even matter at this point?"

"Yes, it does," she insists, with such passion that it takes me by surprise. "Don't you get it? You had a man that wanted to stick around, wanted to provide for you and protect you. You say he's dangerous—well, fuck, all the better to protect you, don't you think?"

When she puts it like that, it all sounds so straightforward.

"He's only one man," I say softly. "At the end of the day, no matter how powerful, he's only one man."

Tonya shakes her head in disgust. "You really are a fucking princess."

That pisses me off. "You don't know me."

"I know enough," she snaps back.

"Yeah, just like I know you would have kept your baby if your man hadn't turned his back on you," I shoot back at her.

I regret my words immediately. It was a cheap shot, a low blow, spoken in anger.

She winces, confirming the truth of my assessment, but I still feel like the worst person alive. It's the lack of sleep and the fear and the fact that maybe Tonya knows more about me than I know about myself right now.

It's all getting to me.

"Sorry," I mumble immediately. "That was—"

"Fair," Tonya mutters. "I hit you, so you hit back. Maybe you're not such a Pollyanna after all."

I smile. "High praise, coming from you."

"Don't get used to it."

I laugh and after a minute, Tonya starts to laugh, too. The tension dissipates immediately. Tonya's hunched shoulders relax.

We fade into a soft silence. Tonya is still scraping with her spoon at her empty bowl as though she can refill it with just the force of her imagination.

"Here," I say, handing her my last piece of bread. "I'm full."

"Like hell you are."

"I'm serious," I insist. "I've had my fill. Just take it."

"I don't take charity."

"Tonya, you live in a fucking shelter," I point out.

The woman glares at me for a moment like a feral animal.

And then laughter snorts out through her nose.

"Jesus, bitch has claws!" she says admiringly. But she takes the piece of bread I'm holding out to her.

She chews and contemplates for a while. I keep Phoenix close to me. He's finally fallen asleep, thank the Lord.

"She's still staring at you," Tonya says after a minute. I don't even have to look to know who she's talking about.

"What's her story?" I ask, resisting the urge to look in Nancy's direction.

"Fuck if I know," she replies. "She's been in and out of this shelter for a couple of years now. The story changes every time. She definitely served time though."

"Served time?" I echo in alarm. "For what?"

Tonya glances at me. "I dunno. There are rumors though."

"Yeah?"

Tonya's eyes dip down to Phoenix and then back to me. "One rumor is that she did it for killing her kid."

My body goes cold. "Are you serious?"

"But that's just a rumor," Tonya says quickly. "It's more likely that she was caught in possession of drugs or some shit. Woman's an addict, after all."

I take a deep breath and wrap an arm around Phoenix, securing him to my chest. "She seems a little… unhinged."

"Yeah, well, drugs will do that to you," Tonya says with a shrug.

"How does she even get her hands on it?" I ask.

"Fucks for money," she says matter-of-factly. "Woman's gotta do what she's gotta do, I suppose."

I shudder, trying desperately not to judge, but the fear for my son has grown. I never liked the way she looked at Phoenix.

Now, I have legitimate reason not to.

"She asked to hold Phoenix again yesterday," I admit to Tonya.

"Did you tell her to go fuck herself?"

"I told her I needed to feed him," I reply. "She disappeared after that."

"Don't worry. She's not gonna steal your baby."

But suddenly, I'm not so certain.

I can still feel Nancy's eyes on my back. It's making me increasingly uncomfortable.

"Don't you wish you'd stayed with your man now?" Tonya asks.

I glare at her. "Shut up."

I haven't been idle the last few days. I've been planning my next move.

I have decided to head for the ocean. There's a little beach town that I've looked into called Loral Beach. A bus route runs periodically from here to there.

I'm hoping I'll be able to find work once I arrive. What I'm going to do with Phoenix, I still don't know, but one step at a time.

The only other question is when to leave. I've given myself another week at the shelter because I need to heal up a little more and recuperate.

Once I get to Loral Beach, I'll need to start working immediately. That's the only way I'll be able to rent out a place for Phoenix and me.

It's not the greatest plan I've ever had, but it's my only option. I don't want to stay in this shelter any longer than I need to.

I'm already pushing my luck by staying this long.

"Hey, where'd you go?" Tonya asks, waving a hand in my face.

"Nowhere," I say with a shake of my head.

"You're always thinking," she observes. "About your man?"

"About my future," I correct.

She smirks. "Right." She folds her arms and leans over the table. "You don't plan on staying here long, do you, Princess Pollyanna?"

I purse my lips together and gesture to the piece of bread that's still in her hands. "Just eat," I sigh.

26

ESME

After we're done with dinner, Tonya heads over to one of the common areas to play cards with some of the other women.

I head to my dorm. I change Phoenix, feed him again, and settle into my lower bunk. Just before I sleep, I count out the money I've hidden in my bra.

I've got four hundred and sixty-seven dollars. I've also got my wedding ring, but I have no intention of selling it if I can avoid it.

I put the small bundle of cash, as well as the ring, back into my bra and secure everything so that they'll be protected in case I start lactating. Then, unable to keep my eyes open any longer, I fall asleep with my arm wrapped protectively around Phoenix.

I'm so tired that it's the first time my sleep isn't disturbed. It's a hard sleep, totally dreamless, just black and deep and so fucking welcome.

At least, it is—until I stir in the early hours of the morning and notice something.

Or rather, the lack of something. A glaring absence.

My sleep-addled brain tries to figure out what's wrong.

What am I missing?

The answer comes at the same time the panic sets in.

Where is my son?

I can't feel his little form beside me. I can't feel his warmth against my cheek. It's dark, so I gently pat the space next to me trying to determine if he's rolled away from me somehow.

But he hasn't.

He's not in bed with me at all.

Panic so acute stabs through me like a spear. I get up so fast I knock my head against the top bunk.

I hear a low grunt that I recognize as Tonya rustling above me, but she murmurs in sleep and doesn't wake.

I stumble out of bed and look around in desperation—when I hear humming.

I freeze as I catch sight of Nancy's wild hair. She's sitting by the window, thin dredges of moonlight creating a weird crisscross pattern against her face.

I glance down at the small bundle in her arms.

Phoenix.

My first instinct is to rush over there and rip Phoenix from her arms, but I hesitate, terrified of how she might react and what she might do to my baby if I don't succeed in taking him from her on the first try.

I walk over slowly but she doesn't look up at me. Her eyes are fixed on Phoenix.

He's awake, I realize. His big, beautiful eyes are fixed on her with mild interest.

He's playing with one of her long curls with his small fist. He pulls at it, but Nancy doesn't seem to mind.

"There's my handsome boy," she coos at him.

"Nancy," I say, but my voice trembles just a little. "Nancy, can you give Phoenix back to me, please?"

The moonlight is throwing all the scars on her arms into high relief. The effect is alarming and somehow threatening at the same time.

"Pretty baby," Nancy coos without addressing me.

She hasn't even acknowledged my presence yet.

"Nancy, please," I say. "He might be hungry."

"He's not," she snaps impatiently. "Look how happy he is with me."

Goosebumps prickle at my skin. I move closer slowly.

"There, there, pretty boy," she says, running her fingers along his cheek the way she's seen me do countless times.

I want to grab her head and bash it into the wall and the urge is so strong that it takes me by surprise.

I don't shy away from the violence.

Instead, my body welcomes it. Craves it, even.

Is this what Artem feels when he fights?

Maybe that is the difference.

You just need to find the right reason to commit to a fight.

"I had a baby once, just like this one," Nancy muses.

Her voice carries in the silence. I inch a little closer. I glance at my baby, and I'm relieved to see that Phoenix looks fine. It doesn't look like he's been hurt in any way.

I don't encourage Nancy to continue with her story, but she does anyway.

"He was a beautiful baby, my boy," Nancy says, still looking down longingly at Phoenix. "Smart fella, too. I used to lock my room door, but he knew where I kept my keys."

A step closer. I try not to breathe too loud. To jar her from this awful memory. My skin crawls with every inch of distance I close.

"He got in one day and found my stash," she goes on, and with every word, I get more scared, more desperate to get Phoenix out of her arms. "He was blue when I found him but I tried to save him anyway."

"Negligence," Nancy says. "'Criminal negligence,' they accused me of. But how...? I locked my fucking door. It was locked! He was just... he was too smart. He was such a beautiful boy. So smart."

Phoenix senses the shift in the air. The growing tension. The approaching violence.

He gives a sharp cry and raises one hand in a small fist. My heart jumps erratically.

"Nancy," I say quietly. "He needs to be fed."

For the first time, she looks up at me. "You were fast asleep and he was whining," she reprimands. "You didn't even notice! He could have rolled off the bed and fallen. He could have been kidnapped. That would be negligence, too... right? And then you'd lose *your* baby."

My heart is thundering so hard that I almost don't hear that last part, the accusation she flings at me with wide eyes that are desperate to be absolved.

"Nancy," I say, feeling tears well up. "Please just hand him over."

She stands slowly.

I freeze.

Time stands still.

But then she hands Phoenix to me and I snatch him away as relief swarms my body and calms my thumping heart.

She walks dreamily back to her bunk on the other side of the room while I check to make sure Phoenix really is okay. He gurgles in my arms and I feel my tears slip free.

It's still dark outside, so I get back into my bunk.

But I don't sleep.

I know that as long as I'm in this shelter, I will never sleep again.

I'm done waiting. Next week is too far off and I can't wait that long.

My body will deal. What I can't deal with is having Phoenix anywhere near Nancy.

Phoenix coos against me. I wrap him up in my arms and pull him close. He settles his cheek against my breast and I feel my warmth intermingle with his.

"It's okay, little bird," I whisper to him. "I'm getting you out of here. We're getting out."

The moment I see sunlight, we're gone.

27

ARTEM

TWO WEEKS LATER—A SAFEHOUSE NEAR LOS ANGELES, CALIFORNIA

"I hope you get what you want."

Sinead's parting words to me still stick like a thorn in my head, needling in so deep that the only way to remove it, is to… find an answer.

I've been back in LA for almost two weeks now. I've gotten back in contact with all the men still loyal to me. We've established a safehouse on the very outskirts of the city.

It's not as large a contingent as I would have liked. But it'll have to do. I'm hoping my ranks will swell in the coming days.

Either way, the new safe house is secure and I'm able to operate under Budimir's radar.

For now.

I've got eyes on my uncle, but he's well-protected. So well-protected in fact, that it makes me wonder just what he's so fucking scared of.

If he believes I'm really dead, what else does he fear?

The answer is an easy one: *everybody.*

He's unsure of the alliances he's built.

He's uneasy about his current position, his stolen power.

You better be scared, motherfucker. You're standing on quicksand. Living on stolen time.

And sooner or later, it will all come to a very sudden end.

Adrik walks into the room that functions as my office space.

"Don," he says formally. "Got some new reports for you."

"Any news from Alexei?"

"Not yet," Adrik replies. "He's established a contact with the Ratmir gang though."

"Good." I shake my head. Lately, I've had to focus really fucking hard to get anything done. My head is swimming with so much shit that it's tough to concentrate on the task at hand.

"I hope you get what you want."

I'm on the cusp of getting what I want. I'm actively working towards it, anyway.

And yet… it isn't as fulfilling as I would have thought.

Because it's not the only thing you want.

Fuck.

"Boss?"

I raise my eyebrows and look at Adrik. "Sorry," I say. "Repeat that last bit."

"We had eyes on Budimir coming out of the Four Seasons this morning," he tells me. "He didn't look happy."

"Another alliance gone south," I infer. "We can't get complacent, though."

"No, sir. And also, Svetlana is here," he tells me.

"Perfect," I say. "Send her in."

Adrik backs out of the room, but he keeps the door open wide enough for a tall, curvy brunette to walk in.

The last time I saw Svetlana was probably about two years ago, at her father's funeral. A funeral that Budimir had not attended, if I remember correctly.

But my father and I had gone.

She is just as beautiful as I remember. A striking woman, full of pride. Her eyes are large and winged with black liner that accentuates their upward tilt and brings the bright green of her irises into full focus.

Her dark hair is a mess of subtle waves that falls over her shoulders. Her makeup is subtle, only nude lipstick and the faintest hint of blush finishes off her look.

She's wearing a black silk, wrap-around dress that hugs her shapely figure and shows just the right amount of cleavage.

Bombshell. That was how Cillian had described her.

"Artem," she says, giving me a seductive smile that I know not to trust.

That was how she had been trained to look at all men.

At least, the ones who can do something for her.

If she is interested in me, it's not for my good looks.

"Or do I need to address you as 'don' now?" she adds teasingly.

"Artem works for me," I reply. "Drink?"

"Mojito," she replies.

I raise my eyebrows. "I'm not one of your marks, 'Lana," I remind her.

She smiles and relaxes into her seat a little. "Beer, then" she replies.

"Still a beer drinker."

"Always."

I get up and move to the tiny makeshift bar in the corner. I grab a beer for her and a bottle of water for myself.

"What happened to Artem Kovalyov the whiskey drinker?" she asks in surprise.

"Things change," I answer simply. I leave it at that and change the subject. "How have you been, Svetlana?"

She hesitates, still eyeing my water, before shrugging and meeting my gaze. "Busy."

"So I've heard." I fold my hands and lean back. "I was impressed with your resume."

"You have plenty of spies," she points out. "Why call me?"

"None like you," I say.

She bats her eyelashes. "Stop it. You'll make me blush."

"And if you do, I'll know you're playing a part."

Her smile drops at once. "Meaning what?"

"Meaning there are women who blush and women who don't," I say. "And you most definitely fall into the latter category."

"I don't know if I should be offended by that or not," she smiles.

I laugh. "It was definitely a compliment for someone in your line of work."

"You didn't extend me an invitation here to flatter me, Artem," she says. "Why am I here?"

"You know why."

"You want me to seduce someone."

"Budimir Kovalyov," I fill in. "My uncle."

Her eyes betray a hint of fear. "I see."

"I'm not going to lie to you," I say. "It's not an easy job. Budimir enjoys his women, but they've only ever been expendable to him. No woman has ever managed to hold his interest longer than a few months. But that's exactly what I'm hiring you to do. Hold his interest. Earn his trust. Make yourself a part of his entourage and eventually, he'll let his guard down."

She doesn't move, but I can see the fear blossoming in her. She knows full well how dangerous Budimir's temper can be, and how fickle his affections.

"Even if he doesn't open up to you directly," I go on, "you might be able to pick up on little things. Plans that might be useful to me, alliances that I haven't anticipated, fractures within his ranks that I can exploit."

Svetlana considers my words carefully. "I've seen your uncle on a few occasions," she admits. "But I was a young girl then. It was back in the early days of my father's career with the Bratva."

I nod and motion for her to continue.

"Aren't you concerned that he'll know who I am?"

"If you accept the job, I will have a new identity ready for you by tomorrow, as well as a binder detailing your fabricated past life."

"Homework," she drawls. "How wonderful."

I smirk. "I think you can handle it."

"But do I *want* to?" she asks. "That's the question."

I lean in and my expression turns serious. "Svetlana, your father was one of the most loyal bodyguards my father ever had at his side. It may not have shown, but Stanislav took his death hard."

"It showed," Svetlana says quietly. "He set up a monthly allowance for Mama after Papa's death. For as long as she lives, she'll be provided for."

"I didn't know that."

"I thought the payments might stop after Don Stanislav died, but they didn't," she tells me.

I nod. "Nor would I want them to."

"I know why you called me, Artem," she blurts. "It's not just because I'm good at what I do. It's because you value loyalty, like your father did. You wouldn't have called me at all if you felt you couldn't trust me."

"That's true. Budimir never valued loyalty like Stanislav did. He never attended the funerals of his men, never bothered to learn about their families, never saw that they were taken care of. It was always one-sided for him, which is why he will never last as don."

Svetlana nods. "This job is more dangerous than I'm used to."

"I'm aware of that," I nod. "And your pay will reflect the risk."

"Money is not what I'm worried about," she says. "If he finds out who I am and who I'm working for, he'll kill me."

I don't mince words. "Without a doubt."

I'm not going to lie to her. Trust goes both ways.

She takes a deep breath, and that her breathing quickens as she weighs her options. I can see the conflict behind her dizzying green eyes.

There's a part of her that likes the danger of the assignment.

There's another part of her that wants to run from me and never look back.

"You have to be sure, 'Lana," I tell her. "There will be no going back."

She bites her lip. "How long do I have to decide?"

"Twenty-four hours," I say succinctly.

She nods. "Okay, I'll have my answer to you by then."

She takes her beer and glugs it down with all the vigor of a truck driver. When she sets down the bottle, it's empty.

"What if he doesn't like me?" she asks. "What if I'm not his type?"

I snort. "You're every man's type."

She starts to pick at the wrapper on the beer bottle with her lacquered nails.

"And once you've killed the motherfucker and taken control of the Bratva again," she muses softly, "where does that leave me?"

"You'll be part of the team," I say. "You'll be Bratva."

She raises her eyebrows as if that's the first real carrot I've dangled in front of her. "You're serious?" she asks.

"I am."

"Women aren't traditionally part of the Bratva."

"Well then, it's about time to drag us into the twenty-first century, don't you think?"

She smiles down into her lap. Then she looks up at me, stone-faced but with a blaze in her eyes.

"I don't need twenty-four hours," she says, with confidence. "I've made my decision."

"Glad to have you on board." I stand and shake her hand across the desk.

I walk her to the door. Before she leaves, she turns back to me and rests a friendly hand on my forearm. Her smile is soft, but it turns sad suddenly.

"I heard about Cillian," she whispers. "I'm sorry."

My jaw clenches. "Another thing Budimir will answer for."

"He has a lot to answer for," Svetlana replies. "And if I can do something to help bring him to his knees, then I will."

Then she's gone.

I watch her get into her car and drive away.

Gaining Svetlana's allegiance is not something I counted on, but it's something I hoped for. She has her mother's grace and beauty, but she has her father's courage. She's smart, skilled and subtle in the art of deception and seduction.

Getting her on my team is an undeniable victory. Another piece on the board working to topple Budimir.

I should be fucking thrilled.

And yet…

Why do I still feel so fucking empty inside?

The answer is so obvious that I miss it at first. Then it hits me between the eyes and I retreat to my desk and sit down.

"Esme," I say, uttering her name out loud for the first time in weeks. Months, even.

I pick up my phone and call Stefan. He's my tracker. If I need something found, he will find it, no matter where it's hidden.

"Yes, boss?" he answers on the second ring.

"Remember the license plate number I gave you a few days ago?" I ask.

"Yes, sir."

"Did you locate the car?"

"Of course, boss," he replies. "But you told me you didn't want to pursue that lead."

"I've changed my mind," I tell him. "Send me the location where the car was found."

"Yes, sir."

I hang up and head out of my office. Adrik and Maxim are in the main common area with some of the other boys. I signal the two of them over and they converge around me instantly.

"I'll expect daily reports from both of you," I tell him. "Mornings and nights."

"You going somewhere, boss?" Maxim asks in concern.

I hesitate for a second, realizing that this is it.

This was when I make the choice once and for all.

"I hope you get what you want."

"Yeah," I nod. "I'm going somewhere. And I don't know how long I'll be."

Maxim and Adrik exchange a glance. I can see the reservation in their eyes, but I've made the decision now.

And I can feel it in my gut—it's the right fucking decision.

"Keep me updated," I say again. "Got it?"

"Got it, boss," Adrik affirms.

Then I turn and head up to my room to pack.

"I hope you get what you want."

What I want means nothing without Esme.

Without my child.

And it's about fucking time I get them back.

28

ARTEM

ONE WEEK LATER—A SMALL TOWN NEAR TIJUANA, MEXICO

The trail's going cold.

"Fuck," I mutter under my breath, as I head into some random shitty diner to get some food.

I'm starving. I'm so obsessed with finding Esme that everything comes second. Everything else feels like a fucking afterthought.

Food. Sleep. Shelter.

I don't give a damn about any of it.

I just want what I'm hunting for.

My wife. My child. My future.

But I've been hunting for Esme for a week now, and my frustration keeps growing relentlessly.

I slump down at the breakfast counter. A middle-aged waitress materializes in front of me.

"Can I get you something, señor?"

"Food."

"Uh… anything in particular?" she asks sarcastically. "Menu's right there. You do know how a restaurant works, sí?"

I fix her with a cold glare. "I don't give a shit. Whatever's good. And coffee. Strong."

Then I plop my head down against the back of my hands.

Just then, an older man with grey whiskers takes the stool beside me.

"Hey, Francesca," he greets the waitress.

"The usual?" she asks him.

"Yes, ma'am. Heart attack on a plate. No better way to start the day, am I right?"

He's got a whimsical Southern drawl that's way out of place down here outside of Tijuana, Mexico.

I hear her chuckle, but I'm rolling my eyes. *Fuck, he's the chatty type.*

I wouldn't have stopped here if I had the choice. But I haven't slept in almost three days and I was starting to hallucinate on the drive from the next town over. I had to pull over somewhere or crash.

Right now, I think I'd choose crashing over a conversation with the jovial gent on the stool to my right.

"You doing all right there, son?" he asks. The man goes so far as to pat me on the back reassuringly. "Not lookin' so hot, if you'll permit me to say so."

I just grunt.

"You a local or you passing through?" he asks. "'Course, that's a bit of a loaded question, 'cause this here is a small town and I myself am a local, but you are unfamiliar to me. So I'm guessing you're just passing through."

I peel myself upright with a weary sigh. Francesca sets a plate of bacon, tortillas, and scrambled eggs in front of me, then slides a full mug of extremely black coffee along with it.

I take a sip of the coffee first. *Fuck, that's good.* The caffeine hits my system and brings me back to life, at least a little bit.

I realize I've been looking at this all wrong. Colonel Sanders here isn't an irritant.

He's a potential source of information.

I give him a friendly nod. "Just passing through. Looking for someone, actually."

"Oh, yeah?"

I pull out the picture of Esme I've been carrying around in my pocket and show it to him.

"Have you seen this girl?"

He frowns, but he doesn't look like he doesn't recognize her. "Hmm. Sure looks a lot like Emily."

"Emily?" I'm wondering if Esme had the forethought to use an alias.

"This waitress who worked in the diner across the street," he tells me. "Pretty young thing. Disappeared without a trace after something went down with a customer."

"Do you remember anything else about her?" I demand. "Anything at all?" My voice is growing louder and other customers are looking over in mild alarm.

"She was pregnant," he says, all nonchalant.

I shove off the stool immediately. The Southern man flinches away from me as though I'd just tried to take a punch at him.

"Which diner?" I ask. "What's the name of the fucking diner?"

He recoils in fear. "That one over there," he says with a point out the window. "La Paloma."

I throw a fistful of crumpled pesos on the counter and charge out the door without another word.

～

La Paloma is hopping when I walk in. Almost every table is full. I look around as a young waitress hustles past me carrying a tray that's far too big for her.

I head to the counter but there's no one behind it. I do see a little bell next to the cash register though and I ring it hard a few times.

A minute later, a woman exits the kitchen. She's wearing dark lipstick and a pinched expression that clearly betrays her annoyance.

She stops short when she sees me, her eyes skittering over my tattoos and the look of annoyance on her face turns to one of suspicion.

"Is there something I can help you with?" she asks.

I produce the picture of Esme. "Did this girl work for you at any point?"

Her eyes glance at the picture and I can tell immediately.

Esme was here.

The woman looks up at me. "No."

My face falls. "Excuse me?" I demand.

"Never seen that girl before in my life." She starts to turn away.

I round the corner of the counter and she almost runs right into me. Her eyes go wide with alarm as she registers my height and build.

"I don't want any trouble," she says.

"Then answer my fucking questions," I snarl.

Her eyes skitter past me, and she sighs deeply. "Mira, I don't know where she is, okay? She disappeared after that... incident with your jefe. She hasn't come back or contacted me or any of my staff. I don't know what else to tell you."

I frown.

Clearly, she thinks I'm someone I'm not.

The question is... who?

"I don't have a boss," I tell her. "I'm new in town."

She looks at me again. "How do you know Emily?" she asks cautiously.

"I'm her husband," I reply.

"You are?" an incredulous voice bleats from behind me. I turn and find myself staring down at the petite waitress who'd passed me a minute ago with the overloaded tray.

"Yeah."

"Can I have five minutes, Ruby?" she asks, the woman standing at my shoulder.

The woman sighs. "Fine, but be quick about it. We're understaffed as it is."

The waitress gestures for me to follow her, and we move into a corridor with a door to the right that leads to the kitchen. She hurries past the kitchen and further down into the corridor until the noise lessens.

We're standing right outside the staff bathrooms when she turns to me.

"I'm Sara," she says. "Are you really her husband?"

"Yes."

"What do you want with her?" she demands.

Her voice is strong for such a small person. I know she's nervous of me, but there's a determination in her eyes that impresses me at the same time.

"I want to make sure she's safe." It's an honest answer.

She studies my expression for a long time. "What's her name?" she asks.

"What?"

"You say you're her husband," Sara says in a measured tone. "Then you'll know her real name. It wasn't Emily."

"You're right," I say. "It's Esme."

I see the flash of recognition in her eyes. She seems to relax a little.

"She saved my life," Sara whispers. "Right here."

I don't like the sound of that. "What happened?" I ask.

"There was a group here for dinner. A bunch of mafia guys with tattoos and bad attitudes. Kinda like you—no offense. One of the men followed me back here and… he was going… he was going to…"

"I get it," I cut in. "You don't have to relive that." My stomach is curdling in anger already.

It's bad enough that they—whoever "they" are—touched this sweet, innocent young woman.

But if they laid a hand on my wife…

"Yes," Sara gulps. "I thought I was alone, but Esme was in the bathroom. She came up behind him and bashed his head in. She was so pregnant. Ready to pop. But she risked herself for me."

"What happened after that?" I ask urgently.

"She told me to go back inside," Sara admits. "She told me she needed to leave town."

"Did she tell you where she was headed?"

"No," Sara says, shaking her head. "I'm sorry—she didn't tell me a thing. And honestly... I don't think she knew herself."

Disappointment sours through me. Another dead end.

So close and yet so far away.

How much longer will I be chasing a ghost?

And then I remember something.

"She didn't have a car, did she?"

Sara frowns and thinks about it. "No, she didn't," she remembers. "I guess she took the bus out of town."

I nod. "Thank you," I tell the girl as I move past her towards the exit.

"Wait!" Sara calls out after me.

I glance behind me.

"If you find her, tell her..." She swallows hard, straightens up tall as if to psyche herself up, and then finishes, "Tell her I think of her every day."

I nod solemnly. "So do I."

Then I head for the bus station.

29

ARTEM

A stoop-shouldered African American man sits inside the ticket booth.

"Excuse me."

He looks up and his eyebrows rise as he takes me in.

"You don't look like the type of person who takes the bus," he comments.

"I'm not here for a bus," I tell him. "I'm here for information."

"Route map is right over there," he says, pointing at the stand of brochures behind me.

"Not that kind of information. I need to know if you sold a ticket to a woman in the last few weeks. She would have been dark-haired, exotic features, very beautiful. Heavily pregnant."

"What's it to you?"

I grip the edge of the counter hard between my fingers. This man knows something. The trail isn't dead after all.

"I need you to help me find her," I say. "I'll pay you whatever you need."

He scrutinizes me up and down. Then, seeing something in me—fuck if I know what—he sighs.

"Yeah, I know that girl," the man says. "Except she wasn't pregnant when she left town. She'd had her baby."

My body goes cold with stillness.

Esme had given birth.

In this shithole of a town.

"Beautiful little fella, too," the man continues. "Didn't look much like her, though. But he had her eyes."

"He?" I say, feeling my heart swell with an emotion I can't quite name.

Is it joy? Pain? Hurt? Loss? Regret?

Maybe it's all the above, and my mind simply can't process it.

I have a son.

Fuck.

I have a son.

"Phoenix."

"Excuse me?"

"His name. The baby's," he tells me. "She named him Phoenix."

Phoenix?

"I'm guessing you're the father, am I right?" he asks directly.

"Yeah," I mutter. I'm still lost in thought, testing the name in my head again and again.

I have a son.

His name is Phoenix.

I have a son.

His name is Phoenix…

I wrench my eyes back down to meet the man's.

"I'm going to get her," I announce. Like I'm trying to reassure him. Like I'm trying to reassure myself, too.

"You should never have let her go in the first place."

Well, I guess I deserve that.

"You sold her a bus ticket, didn't you?" I ask.

"I did," he says. "I can give you the name of the town. Better yet, I can tell you where she'll be."

I pump my fist in pure joy.

At last, a fucking break.

I have a son. His name is Phoenix.

I have a wife. Her name is Esme.

And I'm coming to save them both.

~

The shelter looks like a ravaged shell, a skeleton masquerading as a refuge. I don't focus on any of the women who pass by me.

But I feel their eyes following me down the hall.

"She stayed here," Maisie Blackwell tells me as she gestures to the large dorm room that holds at least a dozen chaotically organized bunk beds. "In that bed over there. Bottom bunk."

There's a woman lying on the bed now, with her back to us.

"How long did she stay?" I ask.

"Not long," she answers. "A week."

Fuck, I curse inwardly. So close yet again.

And yet here I am, grasping at air once more. Still chasing a ghost who doesn't want to be found.

"You don't know why she left?"

"She disappeared one morning before breakfast," Maisie replies. "Maybe it was hard for her dealing with the other women. Not all of them took kindly to having a screaming infant around."

I twitch instinctively at the mention of my son.

My son.

I have a son and nothing about that feels real. I know it won't until I see him. Until I see her.

I think back to the moment I first found out.

Suffice it to say, it was nothing like I imagined it would be.

"Unfortunately, I don't have any more information to give you," Maisie Blackwell tells me. "Like I said, she disappeared weeks ago. Didn't leave a note or anything."

I look around and my eyes land on a slight woman loitering in the corner of the room. She's got a shaved head and scars that line her scalp.

She looks young, but she has the worn-down expression of someone much older. She's looking at me with narrowed eyes, but it's not suspicious.

More like she's trying to figure out who I am.

Maisie notices who I'm staring at. "That's Tonya," she says. "She and Emily used to eat their meals together sometimes. Maybe Emily told her something before she left."

Someone calls for Maisie's attention. "If you'll excuse me, Officer," she says. "I'll be up front if you need me."

I wince at her use of the title. I didn't have much of a choice besides lying.

It's a battered women's shelter—she wasn't about to give up information about a former tenant to a tattooed mob boss who came charging through her door with a vengeance.

A fake badge and an air of authority opened the door, though.

I nod at her. "I appreciate your cooperation, madam."

Then I turn my attention back to Tonya.

She stares back at me, matching my intensity for a little while. But soon she starts to squirm with self-consciousness.

"What?" she asks. All bold challenge with nothing to back it up.

I move into the room. She backs up against the wall. "I don't think you're supposed to be in here," she says. "You sure as hell don't look like a cop, neither."

I take another step closer. A few women perk up, wondering what's happening.

I ignore them all and keep my attention fixed on Tonya.

"What do you want from me?" she asks.

"You knew Es... Emily?" I ask, correcting myself at the last moment.

Her eyes go wide. "You're her man," she says.

My silence is confirmation.

"Fuck," she breathes, but her expression changes instantly. "You came for her."

"Where is she?"

Her brow furrows and she looks angry—really angry. "Fuck if I know. Bitch didn't exactly tell me before she fled the coop. Didn't even say goodbye."

"When did she leave?"

She shrugs. "Few weeks ago, I guess," she replies. "Can't have gone far, with the little brat in tow."

Goddammit. Another dead end. I'm sick of this. Sick of coming so close and missing again and again and again.

I need to get out of this shithole now. Before I lose my temper.

I turn and start walking out of the shelter.

"Hey, where are you going?" Tonya asks.

"To find my woman."

"Tell your woman that the decent thing to do before you leave is to say thanks to the person who sacrificed her bunk for you!"

I suppress my smile. "I'll tell her."

Tonya opens her mouth, then lets it fall closed again.

I wait patiently. Silence opens more doors than force, sometimes.

Then she mumbles something, but it's too low for me to catch.

"What was that?" I ask. "Speak up."

She pauses, considers repeating herself. Then she changes her mind.

"Nothing," she says quickly. "Never mind."

I leave Tonya to her lone bunk and make my way back outside. I'm frustrated enough to punch a hole in a wall.

But that won't get me anywhere. I need to focus. Find a new way forward.

I'm driving aimlessly through town, trying to blow off steam, when I pass a bus terminal.

That's as good a lead as any, I suppose.

I park, hop out, and check the schedule, wondering where the fuck Esme had decided to go next.

Tonya was right about one thing: with a newborn in tow, she can't have gone far.

And then something catches my eye as I'm staring at the maps detailing all the different routes.

I see the ocean.

Months Earlier

"That's one thing I miss about the compound," Esme tells me as she places her head against my shoulder. "The ocean. It was so close, I used to go for midnight runs when I needed an escape."

"The ocean, huh?"

"Cesar loved it, too. We always used to joke that we'd get a little hut on the ocean one day. No one else around for miles. Just us. I've always wanted to live by the ocean."

"It's been so long since I've been near the sea," she muses. "I miss it."

"I'll get you to an ocean soon," I promise her.

"Yeah?"

I nod and kiss the top of her head. "Yeah. We can take long walks on the beach and our child can splash around in the water."

She smiles—a bright, open smile that leaves me with a fierce sense of pride and possession. "That sounds perfect," she nods. "That's exactly what I want."

"You know what I want?" I ask.

"What?"

"I want to recreate that day on the beach on our honeymoon..."

Esme's cheeks blush scarlet as she remembers the longing that unleashed between us on the beach that afternoon. The day we broke through together.

"One day," she murmurs through the blush. "One day."

The beach. She went to the fucking beach.

I leap in my car and rev the engine as I head towards the beach town that's only an hour from where I am.

The map has indicated that it's a small little backwater place. If she's still there, it shouldn't be a problem to track her down.

I have a gut feeling that this is it. This is where I find her.

The question is, once I do find her... then what?

I don't allow myself any time to focus on that right now.

First, I'll reclaim my wife and my child.

The rest—I'll worry about later.

30

ARTEM

Three hours.

In the end, that's all it took. That's how long I needed to close the final distance.

It was surprisingly easy.

Once I'd gotten to the surprisingly pretty beach side town, I'd made some inquiries and checked in at local pubs and cafes.

The fourth time I'd thrown the lure into the water, I'd gotten a bite. The owner of a café had pointed me in the direction of a day care center in the heart of the town.

I'd walked in at seven in the evening and asked to speak to someone in charge. A short conversation later and the blonde behind the receptionist's desk had given me an address.

That address belonged to a small, subsidized apartment complex not too far away.

I park my car on the street, just in case Esme is watching through the window.

Even from a distance, it looks shabby at best. It turns my stomach to know that my wife and son are living here.

Apartment three-fourteen. That's what the girl told me.

There are no elevators, so I take the stairs up to the third floor and I walk down until I hit the right place. The whole place smells like disinfectant, cigarette smoke, and the salt of the ocean.

There is a window set right next to the door, but the curtains are drawn so I can't see inside. I cover the peephole with one hand.

Then I take a deep breath and knock twice. I knock softly, calmly, even though every nerve ending in my body is screaming to kick the door in and drag her out of here at once.

No response.

I wait, but I can't hear a thing from inside.

Is she here?

The woman at the day care told me that Esme's hours were nine to six, which means she would have left at least two hours ago.

I knock again, this time a little louder than before.

The wait is killing me. I feel like I'm going to choke through the silence.

Just when I'm contemplating knocking down the door and forcing my way in, I hear soft footsteps. I keep my palm pressed firmly against the peephole.

"Who is it?"

I feel my body go still with recognition at that soft lilt.

Esme.

I'd finally found her.

"Who is it?" she calls again. I can hear the reluctance to answer in her tone.

I don't answer but I knock again. I hear the bolt being undone and a second later, the door opens a crack, chain rattling.

Two large hazel-gold eyes look right at me.

Then she gasps.

She slams the door shut at once. I freeze for a moment at the sheer fucking audacity. As if a door will keep me away from my wife and son.

But then I hear the chain clank. The doorknob turns once more.

And then the door swings inward.

Esme just stands there, staring at me as though she's confronting a ghost.

"Artem?" she says at last. Her voice trembles like she's not sure whether to cry or scream.

"Can I come in?" I ask. It's taking all of my willpower to stay cool.

She drops her hand and moves back, letting me in without a word.

I'm not fooling myself into thinking that she wants me in her space, though. I've taken advantage of her shock to get this far.

I have a feeling that shock is about to fade very, very quickly.

"You found me," she whispers.

"It took me some time, too."

I scan around the apartment—if you could even call it that.

It's comically tiny. The kitchen and living room are basically one space, but there are two doors in the left-hand wall.

One is open—the bathroom.

The second door is closed. Which makes it a bedroom.

And if the living area is empty…

The bedroom is where my son lies.

"He's sleeping," she says quickly, noticing where my gaze is focused. "I just got him to go down."

I turn to her, my gaze is sharp, angry… accusing.

"Phoenix," I murmur.

I have the satisfaction of seeing her flinch back with shock.

"How did you know?" she asks.

"You left quite the trail behind you."

"Who did you speak to?"

"Who didn't I speak to?" I counter. "There was Sara, Geoffrey, Maisie, Tonya… Did I leave anyone out?"

Her eyes glaze over at my tone. She pivots away from me and hugs her arms across her chest.

I wince at her obvious fear.

I had planned on holding back, taking it easy on her.

These past few months can't have been easy. I can see the truth of that in her excessively thin frame, her hollowed-in cheek bones and the dark circles under her eyes.

She's still as beautiful as ever. Nothing can destroy that.

But her beauty is more haunting than glowing now.

"You can't even look at me," I spit.

At that, she turns on me, angry as hell.

I see the spark in her eyes, that old fire that used to infuriate and attract me in equal measure.

"What do you want from me?" she demands. "I did what I had to do!"

She's upset and clearly rattled to see me, but I can see the underlying emotion hiding just underneath indignation.

She wants me to understand.

She wants me to absolve her of her guilt.

She glances towards the closed bedroom door before her eyes flicker back to me.

"You could have stayed," I say quietly.

"You told me we could be a family," she throws back at me. "You promised me a different life. You told me you would leave the Bratva behind."

"Esme—"

I move forward, my hand reaching out to her.

But she flinches back, a sob escaping her lips. She looks so… worn out, almost defeated.

"Is this life better?" I ask.

Her eyes flash. "Fuck you."

I'm angry, too, but my anger is quickly fading as I face those startling hazel eyes of hers.

What does our son look like? Is he more Moreno or Kovalyov?

I won't care either way. I'm just curious, desperate for more.

Of him.

Of her.

Of us.

"Esme..." I try again, moving closer.

Another step back and she's going to hit the wall behind her. There's nowhere else for her to go. This shoe box of an apartment doesn't leave her very many opportunities for escape.

She shakes her head. "No, Artem," she says. "It's not that easy. What do you want?"

"I want you," I answer. "I want my son."

She keeps shaking her head, but she looks as if she's trying to convince herself of something.

I can see the need in her eyes. She's missed me.

"Did you really think I'd just let you go?" I ask quietly.

"I thought you did," she says, and her voice hikes up with emotion.

Hurt. That's what I'm hearing.

For a while there, she really believed I'd given up on her.

Shame fills me as I realize, that for a few grief-stricken months... I had.

"I thought it was what was best for you," I admit.

"And now?" she asks.

"Now I'm thinking straight for the first time in months. And I know beyond a shadow of a doubt, that what's best for you... is me."

Her nostrils flare for a moment, whether from fear or anger, I can't quite tell. Maybe it's both.

"Are you still with the Bratva?" she asks.

"I'm standing here in front of you, aren't I?" I say, choosing my words carefully. "I came for you."

She stills for a moment, as a blind, desperate hope floods her face. I know how my words come across. I know how she's interpreting them.

And miserable bastard that I am, I don't correct her.

Because correcting her might be risking the opportunity I have in front of me right now.

The opportunity for her to hear me, listen to me, give me a chance to show her what life could be if we were together.

"You did?"

"Yes," I rasp. "The Bratva means nothing if I don't have you, Esme."

Her eyes are filled with tears. The gold of her irises are like beacons and I can't stop myself any longer.

I grab her neck, running my fingers over her jaw for a moment.

Her hand settles on my chest as her eyes lock onto mine.

I see the desire flare on her face just before I slam my mouth down on hers.

She releases a moan that reverberates inside me, setting off a long-suppressed urge that I've been fighting these many months.

Her lips part easily underneath mine and I feel her tongue wrestling back as I push her up against her shitty apartment wall.

She feels tiny against me. As lean and lithe as ever. Like she didn't just give birth.

But I move carefully anyways. Her body gave us a son. As much as I want to ravage her, break her just to build her back together—I also want to respect the miracle.

It's the same struggle as always for us.

Violent love can't run unchecked.

But fires need sparks to come to life.

I pick her up and her legs wrap around my waist. I'm already hard, painfully hard, but I ignore the strain in my pants as I pull the white cotton dress off Esme's shoulders.

The dress comes apart in my hands and I toss it to the side. She's not wearing a bra, and only a pair of tiny black panties.

She gasps as my head dips down towards her breasts. They're the only part of her that has gotten bigger. I cradle the beautiful round globes in my hands, exploring them greedily.

"Don't squeeze too hard," she warns me, mid-moan. "I'll start lactating."

Fuck.

I didn't think that was the kind of thing that would turn me on, but apparently, it does. My cock jumps impatiently and I know I need to get my pants off immediately.

I gently run my tongue over her nipples without putting much pressure on them. She groans with pleasure as I slip my hand into her panties and start running my fingers between her lips.

She's nice and wet already. I reach up for the swollen nub of her clit.

"Oh, Artem," she groans.

I can tell from her breathless moans that she's been craving me as much as I've been craving her.

Unable to take it anymore, I fumble with the buckle of my pants, but Esme's hands reach out and push my hands away.

She takes over and undoes my buckle and zipper. I don't think she even notices the gun strapped to the waistband as she pushes down my pants, then my boxers.

As they pool around my ankles, I step out of them and kick them both away. But before I grab hold of her, Esme has ducked down until she's on her knees in front of me.

She looks up at me with hungry eyes as her hand circles around my shaft. She keeps her eyes on me as she strokes my cock. Then I watch as her tongue slips out and starts stroking against me.

"Fuck," I growl. My eyes close involuntarily.

I'm not prepared for when she takes the entire length of me into her mouth, shoving me so far deep inside her that I hit the back of her throat.

"Fuck," I groan again. I lean forward to grip the wall with both hands.

She doesn't stop or slow down. She sucks me off, harder and harder until my hand lands on the top of her head.

I want to come right in her mouth, but I stop the urge and pull her back to her feet. It's been months since I've touched her.

I want to be able to look my wife in the eye when I explode.

I scoop Esme up and carry her to the low sofa that's pushed to one corner of the apartment.

Before her back even hits the cushions, I've pushed my cock deep inside her.

She clings to me as I thrust into her. I want to take it slow, but I don't have the restraint to manage that right now.

This is a desperate fuck. A fuck months in the making.

There'll be time for lovemaking later.

This is something far more primal.

Her full breasts bounce in my face and I feel her body tighten as the orgasm rolls over her.

Her nails dig into my back. I welcome the little darts of pain she's sending through my body.

"Fuck... Artem... yeah..."

Then her walls tighten around my cock and they pulse violently as she comes. Her eyes roll back in her head. Waves rip through her.

And the moment I see her face relaxed into the ebb of satisfaction, I let myself go, too.

I erupt inside her. She rides the shock waves as we both pant deeply.

Slowly, it recedes, though it feels like we're coming together for an hour.

Then her body relaxes underneath mine, and when I lift my face off her neck, I see the contentment draped across her features.

She meets my gaze and gives me a dazed smile. I kiss her lips softly and push myself off her. I'm pretty damn sure the sofa is gonna collapse under our combined weight.

She makes no attempt to move or cover herself up. I slump on the floor beside the sofa with my arm still draped over her breasts.

My eyes rake over her naked body. She's as beautiful as I remember, but there are small changes.

She's clearly lost a lot of weight since the baby.

Her bones are much more prominent now. They cut sharp angles in her soft figure.

But the most obvious change is the large Caesarean scar that adorns her lower belly.

I trace the scar in the same way she used to trace the tattoos on my chest. She watches me quietly, but she doesn't stop me.

"You'll need to tell me about it one day," I tell her. "When you're ready."

She sighs. "I don't remember much of it to be honest," she says in a detached voice. "I was unconscious for most of it."

My eyes meet hers, and I feel the weight of every single moment I've missed in the last several months.

"Was anyone with you?" I ask.

"Geoffrey is the one who took me to the hospital," she tells me. "You mentioned him earlier. The man from the bus station. But after that, I was on my own."

A growl rumbles deep in my chest. Anger and regret all mixed up in one. "I wish you didn't have to do it on your own."

She turns her eyes up to the ceiling, and I know she's blinking away her tears.

"I made a choice," she replies.

I nod, but say nothing.

Then I hear a sound that sends me shooting up to my feet. A long, drawn-out cry that punctures the silence like a lightning bolt across a clear sky.

My son.

Esme gets off the sofa and turns to me.

"Do you want to meet him?"

I just nod, feeling the enormity of the moment rushing to meet me.

Once I see him, it'll be real. It will change everything.

It already has.

Esme takes my hand and leads me to the room. The door swings open.

As I expect, the room is a matchbox. There's a low single bed, threadbare blankets, colorless pillows.

And right next to all that sits a baby bassinet.

I hear a string of gargling noises, punctured by a sharp cry every now and again.

Then I see a little fist rise from the bassinet before disappearing from view.

I freeze instinctively, but Esme moves forward. I watch as she stands over the bassinet and looks down with a transformative smile on her face.

"Hola, little bird," she coos, her tone thick with love. "Did you sleep well?"

I see his hand reach for her. He grabs one of her fingers tightly. Esme leans in and kisses his brow.

"I have someone special I want you to meet," she whispers.

Then she plucks the baby from the bassinet.

I feel my heart churn in a way I've never actually experienced before. Time feels slower. All sound drops away.

Esme steps back around, and for the first time, I'm given an uninterrupted view of my son.

He's small, but he fits perfectly in the crook of Esme's arm.

His face is turned up to her. Then she angles him in my direction and I see his face.

My own features reflected back at me. The jaw, the nose, the brow—it's Kovalyov through and through.

All except the eyes.

He's got his mother's eyes, soft and molten and as yet unmarred by the evils of the world.

"*O bozhe moy,*" I breathe in Russian as Phoenix looks at me with something close to confusion.

"He's beautiful, isn't he?" Esme asks.

I nod and swallow. "He's perfect."

"Here," she says, moving closer.

"What are you doing?"

She smiles patiently. "I thought you might like to hold him."

Have I ever held a baby before?

No, I'm sure I have.

And even if had, this... this is different.

I offer up my arms and Esme gently places the squirming baby into them.

"Just relax," Esme tells me as he fusses a little.

I pull him closer to my chest and place an arm right underneath him, securing him in place. He seems to like that position better.

After a moment, he settles a little.

"You're a natural," Esme says.

"Phoenix," I whisper, testing how his name feels on my lips. I look up at Esme. "It suits him."

"That's what I thought," she agrees. "I know it's not one of the names we discussed..."

"It's perfect," I tell her with finality.

She nods, and we just look at our son together for a few moments.

"This is what I always wanted," Esme says, putting her hand on my arm. "You, me, and Phoenix. Just the three of us."

I glance up at her, hating myself for having lied to her before.

I know I need to clear things up, but I find myself looking back down at my son.

I let myself get distracted.

I let myself off the hook.

But for one moment...

One blissful, perfect moment...

None of that matters.

I have what I need right here.

31

ESME

I wake from a restless sleep that leaves me with the vague feeling that I've been dreaming, even though I can't remember what about.

I'm settled in one corner of my small bed. Artem is taking up the rest of it. I don't mind, though, especially because Phoenix looks so comfortable nestled against his Papa's broad chest.

He sleeps with his butt sticking up in the air and I smile to see Artem's hand cupping it gently, holding him securely in place.

They look so damn perfect.

I can't help but stare.

I won't lie: Artem's appearance had taken me completely by surprise. I hadn't been prepared for it in the slightest, and it had brought up a whole host of emotions.

Emotions that I'd been avoiding for so long.

Emotions I never thought I'd feel again.

I slip out of the bed and head to the kitchen. I make myself a cup of plain tea, a taste I had developed after Phoenix's birth, and sip it slowly.

It's nice to turn my brain off. Even if it's only for five minutes, the silence does me some good. Helps me reset, recharge, recalibrate.

After I've finished my cup of tea, I put it in the sink and take a deep breath. The peace I found while drinking it vanishes as quickly as it had come.

And my nerves are as unsettled as ever.

My fingers twitch. I know then what I need, though it's been so long that I wonder if I've lost the touch. I don't know where I'd get that solution anyway, so I just put it out of mind.

Maybe a walk might help clear my head instead.

As I grab my coat, it strikes me that I have never been apart from Phoenix for even a single moment since his birth.

I've never had the option of taking some time for myself because there was no one I trusted enough to leave Phoenix with.

I peer through to the room and see that Artem and Phoenix are still fast asleep. Phoenix's last feeding was an hour ago and he had nursed well, which means he shouldn't get hungry for another two hours at least.

I shrug my coat on and slip out of the apartment. I feel a fierce sense of independence as I walk down the stairs.

It's alarming how amazing it feels to be out on my own, no baby strapped to my chest or my boob.

For the first time in months, I feel like a real human being. And every time a tiny pang of guilt arises, I just close my eyes and picture my son nestled against his father.

Right where they both belong.

I walk down the lonely street that leads to the apartment and take a sharp right towards the main drag of town.

People are just filing out of their homes on their way to work. I find myself smiling at strangers. It's ridiculous how happy I am right now.

Because Artem's back.

Because I feel like myself again.

Because it seems like maybe—just maybe—the world isn't as cruel as I was starting to believe it was.

I haven't really made a conscious decision about where to go, but when I turn the corner and see the music store down the road, I feel the tug of fate.

Like I had a destination in mind all along. Or that the universe had a destination in mind for me.

I'm not sure which of those options I like better.

I cross the street, slip inside the store, and I'm hit at once with the sensual sounds of classical music and a romantic, floral scent that complements it perfectly.

I close my eyes and stand there for a second. It's been how long since I've had an instrument underneath my fingers?

Too long. Way too long.

I remember Tamara lying in the sun on the beach during one of her trips down to Mexico. "Isn't this amazing?" she'd murmured to me. "To just lie in the sun and soak it all up?"

That's how I feel in this store. Like I'm soaking up life, nature, beauty.

It's incredible.

I don't open my eyes until I start to sense that I'm being watched. When I do, I see a little girl crouched behind the grand piano and staring at me with that open, child-like curiosity.

I've seen her before. She's here most mornings and evenings with her parents, who own the store. Whenever I walk past this shop, she's here.

"I know you," she mumbles to me.

"Do you?" I ask with a warm smile.

She has mousy brown hair that's been braided into pigtails and tied together with neon pink scrunchies. Bright, observant eyes. A generous double helping of freckles.

"You walk by here all the time," she says, as if she's informing me of that fact.

"I do," I chuckle. "I really like this store. It smells nice."

She smiles shyly. "I'm Katie."

"I'm Esme."

"Do you play any instruments?" Katie asks.

"Yes," I tell her. "Piano."

"Really?" she asks. Her eyes go wide with renewed interest. "I just started to learn, but it's really hard."

"It can be," I concede. "Why don't you show me what you've learned?"

She twists back and forth, hands tucked behind her.

"I bet you're really good," I coax. "Come here. Pop up on the bench and teach me something."

She can't resist that. With a smile, she scurries around the piano. We settle down on the bench together.

But Katie loses her nerve suddenly. She glances up at me, chin wobbling like she might cry.

"Tell you what," I reassure her, "I'll go first. Okay?"

She nods, a little appeased by that.

I glance up and notice the man standing in the opposite corner of the store. He's got the same mousy brown hair as Katie, though it's wispier than his daughter's.

He meets my eye, and gives me a small nod of encouragement. so I assume it's okay for me to play his piano.

I turn my attention back to the instrument.

It feels so good to have my hands poised over piano keys again. I didn't realize I'd missed it this much. It's like I can breathe again for the first time in a long time.

I stroke the first key and it's like I'm floating away.

Everything nonessential fades.

There's only me and the music.

I play the Nocturnes from Chopin and I let each note take me deeper and deeper, farther and farther, higher and higher.

Taking me away to a time when I was still naïve enough to believe that one day, life might be as simple as the next chord.

I remember a time when I could sit in front of my piano and play every day, when I still dreamed of playing piano in concerts all over the world.

I remember a time when my brother was still my hero, my biggest motivator, and my biggest fan…

Many Years Ago

The keys clang. Wrong note. I yell in frustration.

"What's the matter, little bird?"

I scowl and turn to face him. Cesar is standing by the window, looking at me with amusement.

"I can't get it right."

"You will," he tells me confidently. "You just need to practice."

"It's too hard."

"I don't doubt it," he replies. "Which will make it all the more impressive when you master it."

I sigh and kick into thin air. My legs don't quite reach the ground. That in and of itself is frustrating.

"Papa wants me to play for his guests next week," I admit.

"Ah."

"I'm not good enough," I say sheepishly. "If I make a mistake, Papa will be angry."

"Papa will deal with it."

Cesar walks forward and nudges at my shoulder. I move down a little so he can sit next to me.

I don't feel as frustrated when Cesar is here. He makes me less scared of Papa.

"I don't like when you go away," I tell him. "Why can't I go to your school, too?"

"It's only for boys."

"I want to be a boy."

"No, you don't," Cesar rebuffs quickly. "Trust me. You're better off being a girl."

"Why?"

"Because you'll fly under Papa's radar," he mumbles.

I frown. That doesn't quite make sense to me. But I'm only seven. Cesar says there's a lot I won't understand until I'm older.

"What?"

"Nothing," *Cesar says, shaking his head and smiling quickly.* "Trust me, it's better that you're a girl."

"Fine. Okay."

He smiles and bumps his arm against mine. "One day, little bird, you're going to be a fantastic pianist. You're going to be a beautiful, strong woman and you're going to choose the life you want to live. Not because you're allowed to, but because you fought for it."

I sigh. "I don't know what you mean when you talk like that."

He laughs. "Sorry, I'm ranting now. Will you play me something?"

"I'm not very good."

"So keep playing until you are," *he encourages.* "Either way, I'll listen."

I smile and start playing. This time, I get it right.

∽

"Are you crying?"

Katie's question jolts me back to the present and I try hastily to blink back my tears. "Sorry," I say, smiling down at her. "I get emotional when I play."

"Why?" she asks, sounding dumbfounded.

"The music helps me remember things about my childhood," I admit to her. "From when I was your age."

"Like what?"

"Memories of my older brother," I tell her.

"Oh," Katie nods. "Where is he?"

She's a perceptive little thing and I don't want to lie to her. "He's… not around anymore," I say simply.

Katie nods so solemnly I almost laugh. "Do you miss him?"

My answer is swift: "All the time."

And it's true. I do still miss my brother, but my feelings go further than that.

I hate him for leaving me with such a mangled, fucked-up image of who he was.

In fact, I hate him for leaving me at all.

"You play really good," Katie tells me. "Like really, really good."

I smile. "Thank you," I tell her. "That means a lot to me."

"I wish I could play like you."

"You will one day," I tell her. "You just need to keep practicing."

"I don't like my teacher," she admits, leaning in a little and lowering her voice down to a whisper.

I fight the urge to laugh as I lean in too. "I didn't like my teacher, either."

"Really?"

I nod. "He was awful. He was really boring and really mean and he never smiled."

"Mine, too!" she chirps. "Maybe we have the same teacher."

That makes me laugh. "Maybe."

Her father comes over. "I hate to interrupt. But Katie, we've got to go to school."

"Yes, Daddy."

Katie hops off the bench and scurries into the back to get her things. We watch her go, then I turn to the man and he gives me a kindly smile.

"You play beautifully," he tells me.

"Thank you," I say with a blush. "It's been a while since I've played."

"You can't tell," he assures me, before gesturing to the piano. "But if you ever need to practice, feel free."

"Be careful: I might take you up on that offer."

We both chuckle. Katie scurries right back out with a pink backpack looped over her shoulders. I say goodbye to the two of them and start the walk back to the apartment.

32

ESME

I feel good. Unburdened. Hopeful.

For a little bit.

Just like with the tea, though, the peace of the piano leaves me as soon as the moment ends. All my old anxieties rush back in.

And the closer I get to home, the more I realize I don't know what Artem's return means for us.

I'm fairly certain he isn't planning on staying in this town forever. And I'm starting to realize that I won't be able to bear being parted from him again.

The first time was different. I was reeling from the shock and trauma of bloodshed and violence.

I had just killed another man—in self-defense, obviously but it had still shaken me.

I was terrified of bringing my child into a world marred by such tragedy, and I was thinking a lot about Cesar, too.

He had hated being the son of a don. I could see that now. He had slowly wilted under the unforgiving pressure of what he was supposed to be.

Papa expected so much from him at such a young age. It turned Cesar, from the kind, sensitive man he was, into someone colder, harder… more ruthless.

And in the process, it broke him.

I didn't quite know how much was an act and how much was really him.

I still don't.

And honestly, I'm not sure I want to.

But like Artem has told me countless times before, life is not black or white. It's grey.

There are no heroes. There are no villains.

There are just people who make choices.

When I slip back into the apartment, I hear Phoenix's familiar gurgling sounds and I know he's up. My breasts are feeling a little heavy and I know I'll have to feed him soon.

But I slow as I approach the bedroom door. I hang back and peek inside.

Artem is sitting up on the bed, his back resting against the wall. He has Phoenix hoisted up against his legs that form a backrest of sorts.

Phoenix reaches to graze Artem's nose. Artem laughs and lets him pull at it to his heart's content. Something inside me twists into a thick knot and I move into the room.

"There you are, beautiful," Artem says, turning his dark, sexy eyes on me.

It hasn't been that long a span of time that we've been apart.

But his body has changed considerably.

I didn't think it could be improved upon, but somehow, he has found a way. He is all hard muscle now, not an ounce of fat. Honestly, there are moments he looks like he is carved out of marble.

His abs are defined, creating sharp ridges in his abdomen, adding a new row to his six pack. There are a few new scars on his body, one I identify as the stab wound that had almost killed him, and the other as the bullet wound near his shoulder.

His jaw has a healthy layer of stubble, longer than what I'm used to, but it still suits him. He looks sexy in a feral, animalistic way that makes my clit throb.

And his eyes… his goddamn eyes. Those haven't changed a bit.

They are just like I remember them. Intense, strong, powerful and staring at me with a possessiveness that I am just now realizing I have been craving since the moment I saw him last.

"Come here," he tells me.

I go to him without hesitation. Truthfully, I think I'd do anything he says as long as he looks at me like that when he says it.

I plunk down on the bed next to him. He wraps his arm around me and pulls me close. His smell breezes over me, musky and masculine. I missed that, too.

Phoenix smiles and reaches a hand out for me. I wind my fingers through his and lean in to kiss his cheek.

"My sweet boy," I say softly to him.

"Where'd you go?" Artem asks.

"For a walk," I tell him. "I needed to… think."

He nods at that, but I can't really read his expression.

"Sara told me to give you a message," he says suddenly.

I turn to him. "Yeah?"

"She told me to tell you that she thinks about you every day."

I smile, feeling my eyes cloud a little. As horrific as the last few months have been, the people I've met along the way has made it bearable. Sara is a gem in an ugly world.

"How did she seem to you?"

"It looked like she was doing her best to cope."

I nod. I get that. I get that so much.

"You saved her from being raped," Artem says gently, as though waiting for me to confirm it.

I glance at him, and he's looking at me with a soft expression.

But he also looks... proud?

"I couldn't let him do that to her," I say. "Not after... I know what it's like to have a man you don't want touching you, touching you."

Artem stiffens. He remembers that. The night we met, a lifetime ago, in that dark club bathroom...

"It's a violation no human being should ever have to suffer," I go on. "I was heavily pregnant. I was so scared. But I just couldn't stand by and do nothing."

"Of course not," Artem says. "That's not who you are."

"I think I killed him."

"You didn't," Artem replies.

"Really?"

"Really," Artem nods. "I asked. You injured him. Badly. But you didn't kill him."

I sigh. "I don't know how to feel about that."

"If you had killed him, he would have deserved it," he points out.

"True. More than most."

He leans in and kisses my lips gently. "It seems you leave quite an impression wherever you go."

I smirk. "Is that a crack?"

"It's a compliment," he says innocently.

"At least I got to say goodbye to Sara," I sigh. "I left Tonya without a word."

"Yeah…"

I frown at Artem's reaction and study his expression. "You mentioned you met her, too, right?"

He nods. "You may have hurt her feelings, leaving the way you did."

"Fuck," I sigh. "I knew I would. But I was just so panicked when I made the decision to go, and I didn't think I could deal with another goodbye. I had to leave that place."

"I'm not blaming you," he reassures me. "My only question is why didn't you leave sooner. That place was depressing as fuck."

I nod, remembering just how awful it felt. To be surrounded by so much grief and heartache was… overwhelming, to say the least.

"I'd just given birth to Phoenix, my body needed time to recover, and I couldn't afford to rent out a place of my own, especially considering I had no money coming in. The shelter was my best option to recuperate."

I look at Artem, and realize how much he still doesn't know.

But his eyes are looking at me and they're soft and gentle and they're saying, *Tell me.*

So I tell him.

I tell him about Sara and Ruby and the third trimester of my pregnancy.

I tell him about cramps and sporadic doctor's appointments whenever I could find the money for them.

I tell him about the time I woke up believing I'd lost the baby because I had bled into my underwear.

I tell him about going to the bus station late at night, only to have Geoffrey drive me to the hospital as I went into labor and subsequently lost consciousness.

I tell him about waking up to meet my son, only to flee the hospital hours later.

I tell him about my time at the shelter and the unexpected friendship I'd found with Tonya.

I tell him about Nancy and the moment when I realized I wasn't about to endanger my son's life by staying at the shelter any longer.

I tell him about accepting an under the counter job at the day care, because it meant I would get to earn money as well as be with Phoenix.

I tell him about sleepless nights and busy mornings.

I tell him about leaking breasts and bouts of incessant crying.

I tell him about walking by the ocean in the evenings with Phoenix.

I talk so much that, by the time I've run out of things to tell him, I'm parched and my throat is dry and I feel emotionally drained.

I hadn't even realized how much I needed to tell my story.

Artem, to his credit, doesn't say a word the entire time. He just listens to me, holding my hand or stroking my back while I let it all spill out of me.

And when I finally fall silently, he takes a deep breath and shakes his head.

"Esme," he says softly. "I'm sorry."

I frown. "You're sorry…?"

He nods. "For everything that you had to go through," he explains. "I should have been there with you the entire time. I should have given you the life you deserve. You should never have had to take a job that's beneath you or sleep in a shelter or…"

"I'm the one who chose to leave," I point out. "I never apologized for that."

Artem falls silent at that, his expression flickering with conflict, and I realize something.

He's angry at me for leaving.

I take his hand. He meets my gaze. He knows what I'm thinking. He knows I can see that these months haven't been easy for him, either.

"You should have said goodbye," he grits finally. It looks like it hurts him to admit that he was wounded by that.

"If I had, I would never have left."

"Exactly."

We look at each other for a long, tense moment. So many unspoken things flying back and forth between us.

Love and hate and hardship and the desperate fire that's kept us coming back for more and more and more of each other from the start.

It's overwhelming. I can't look away but I can't keep staring into his eyes and feeling like my soul is completely bared.

So I whisper, "Artem…"

He silences me with his lips.

I gasp against his mouth. I feel Phoenix's little fingers cling to my hair but I let that go as I kiss my husband.

His tongue slides between my lips, hot and insistent. I let him come in. Claim my mouth. Taste me tasting him.

Until I'm forced to break the kiss because of the growing discomfort in my chest. I wince as Phoenix tugs on my hair harder.

"Sorry," I apologize. "I need to feed him."

Artem smiles. "Go ahead, *kukolka*."

"We still have a lot to talk about," I remind him.

"I know. But for right now… let's just be together."

And really, there's no way I can resist that.

33

ARTEM

Fuck.

Four missed calls from Maxim and two from Adrik.

"You okay?" Esme asks as she comes out of the bedroom, holding Phoenix.

"Of course," I say. "I just noticed that you don't have any food."

Esme bites her lower lip. "Yeah, well… I kinda live day-to-day."

"Don't worry," I reply. "I'll go out now and get a couple of things."

"Okay," Esme says without argument. "I'll see you in the evening then?"

"Evening?" I repeat, turning to her.

"I have to go in to work today," she tells me like it's unavoidable.

My eyes narrow. I step forward. "You're not going to work today. Or any day."

Esme raises her eyebrows. "Excuse me?"

"Esme, that job is beneath you. It's not what you want to do," I tell her. "And you don't have to anymore."

"But—"

"Tell me you like going in to work every day, and I won't say another word," I challenge.

She hesitates. I can see her contemplating a proud lie.

Then she sighs. "Fine. I don't like the job."

"Then don't do it," I tell her. "You're not on your own anymore. I'm here."

I see the light spark in her eyes. Hope kindling.

Again, I feel the guilt resurface. We still haven't discussed our plans for the future.

Esme still has no idea that I'm poised to take over control of the Bratva.

I have to tell her—I know that. But I'm selfish enough to cling to the moments before then.

One more morning. One more day. One more hour.

Then I'll tell her.

Then I'll explain.

"Are you sure?" she asks.

I'm not even sure what that questions means.

Am I sure about what?

Her?

Us?

"I'm sure," I answer firmly.

"Okay," she says with a smile. "But I think I'll go in anyway and explain it to them."

"If that's what you want." I pull out my wallet and pull out a couple of hundred-dollar bills. "In case you see anything you want on your walk."

"You don't have to do that," she says, eyeing the money almost suspiciously.

"I haven't been around for a while. Just take it. To make me feel better if nothing else."

She laughs and accepts the money. I snag her wrist and pull her close to me so I can kiss her hard, my lips pressing up hungrily against hers.

If we'd been alone, we'd probably be fucking on the floor right now.

But we have a son now.

Things are different.

And I'm all right with that.

Esme leaves a few minutes later. The minute she's out of the apartment, I grab my phone and call Maxim back. He picks up almost immediately.

"Boss."

"What do you have for me?" I ask, jumping straight into it.

"Anton Yahontov," Maxim says immediately. "He's a brigadier working for Budimir. Too low ranking for us to consider a real threat, but he's only a few miles away from you right now."

I freeze. "What?"

"I thought he was tailing you for a while," Maxim replies. "But not the case. He has a home in town."

"That's good to know."

"It might be worth paying him a visit."

"And why's that?" I ask.

"Because my sources tell me he's been in a few meetings with Budimir's goons," Maxim tells me. "He may not have sensitive information for us, but he might have something."

I clench my fist. Finally, a fucking break in this brewing guerilla war. "Then I'll stop by and say hello," I reply darkly.

"Got it, boss," Maxim replies. "And congrats on finding her, by the way."

"How the fuck do you know that?" I demand.

He chuckles low. "It's in your voice. You don't sound half dead anymore."

Cheeky motherfucker.

"Keep me posted," I growl, fighting to keep a smirk off my face.

"Will do, boss," Maxim answers. "I'll drop you his location."

The line goes dead and a couple of seconds later, my phone pings with a location alert.

I leave the apartment, jump in my car, and drive straight to the house.

It's nestled in the deep suburbs of the town, but I'm not worried. I can be in and out with no one being the wiser.

The house is run down, obviously neglected, but it's clear that someone's inside. There's a car parked in the driveway and the blinds have been drawn.

I stake the place out for an hour but it seems he's the only one inside.

Considerate of him to make this so easy for me.

Once I'm confident we're not going to be interrupted, I turn off my engine and decide to get this over with quickly. As I hide away my gun, I feel a stab of uncertainty.

When Esme finds out, she's going to be devastated.

But embracing this life is the only way to protect her and Phoenix.

Once Budimir knows I'm alive, he'll come for me.

I have to get him first.

I already know he hasn't stopped searching for Esme. Maxim uncovered one of his plots to find her. But he's got his men searching in the wrong place.

He thinks she's gone back to Mexico. He's assumed—incorrectly, of course—that she's found refuge with one of her father's former allies.

It's a good thing he doesn't know Esme like I do.

I set my jaw with determination and get out of the car.

I've always known who I was. This has nothing to do with my father. It doesn't even have anything to do with Cillian.

This is about me.

I am what my father made me.

And there is no life for me outside of the Bratva.

I make my way around the narrow fence that leads to the back of the house. The garden is small and unkempt. Weeds have overrun the grassy area and the brick walkway has been uprooted.

I step over and move to one of the windows. I scan the area, thankful that the other houses give me coverage. There's only one window facing me, but the blinds have been drawn.

It's not a guarantee I won't be noticed, but I'm far enough away that my features should be obscured.

Then I hear movement. I duck sideways behind the door.

I glance through the window, and see the man I assume is Anton Yahontov. He's of medium build and height, nothing particularly notable. I can see large, ugly tattoos peeking out from his sleeveless muscle tee.

I roll my eyes, then return to the front of the house. I keep my gun in hand and knock casually.

A few seconds later, I hear him coming. Like an idiot, he doesn't ask who's at the door before he opens it.

But he sure as fuck knows who I am when he sees me.

He goes deathly pale, his unnaturally red cheeks going even redder beneath his grisly beard.

"Make one move and I'll blow your intestines right out," I growl, keeping the gun pointed directly at him.

He nods slowly.

"Good man. Now, let's step inside so none of the neighbors will be disturbed."

He backs into the house. I follow and slam the door shut behind me. A quick scan reveals he's unarmed and unprepared.

Fucking fool.

"Sorry to drop by unannounced," I say politely. "Just had a couple of quick questions for you."

"You're supposed to be dead," he rasps.

He looks more awed than anything else at the moment.

"I know," I agree. "And I'm keen to stay dead. At least in my uncle's eyes."

"I had no choice," he tells me, even though I have no idea what the fuck he's talking about. "I had to swear fealty to him or risk my wife, my daughter."

I pause for a moment, studying his expression. He's not lying to me. That's what my intuition is telling me.

Still, trusting him would be a mistake too.

"Isn't that convenient?"

"I swear to you," he pleads. "That's how he convinced so many to back his claim to the Bratva. He had files on their families, their parents, siblings, their wives, their kids."

"You expect me to believe that?" I snap. It's all a front, though. I just want him to keep talking. To give me more information. There's no telling what will be useful in the end.

"Half the men that follow Budimir follow him because they want to," Anton admits. "Probably more than half, in fact. But there's still a large number that were forced into the whole shit. It's a fucking mess."

I stay quiet. Sometimes, silence is the best interrogator.

"Oblonsky," he goes on, as though desperate to make me understand. "You know the man? He served your father for twenty-three years."

"Alexander Oblonsky?" I ask.

I know the name, though my interactions with the man have been few and far between. He was a part of Stanislav's security team for decades.

Anton nods fervently. "He had a wife," he tells me. "A son and a pregnant daughter. When Oblonsky opposed your uncle's claim to the Bratva, Budimir had his family brought in."

I tighten my grip on the gun. I have a nasty feeling that I'm not going to like what Anton says next.

He swallows and continues. "We stood there and watched as he killed Oblonsky's wife first. Then his son. And lastly, the daughter. She… she was at least seven months into her pregnancy…"

He shudders a little, as though the memory is a poison he was trying to shake off.

It doesn't take a genius to know why it affected him so much.

He's substituting the victim's faces with his own loved ones.

"And Oblonsky?" I prod.

"He had to be held back, restrained. Budimir wanted him to see what his defiance cost," Anton replies. "Make an example out of him, you know? The man was screaming, *Kill me now, you bastard!* But Budimir wanted to keep him alive. So that he could live with the pain of knowing that he had caused the death of his family."

I clench my jaw so hard I'm afraid my teeth may shatter. That son of a bitch. That murderous, traitorous son of a bitch.

Anton shakes his head, still engrossed in the memory. "Oblonsky had a knife on him."

"He tried to kill Budimir?"

"No," Anton sighs. "No, not Budimir. He killed himself. Slit his own fucking throat before anyone could stop him. Budimir was furious."

Of course. Of course he was. Sick, sadistic motherfucker.

He loved the suffering. Reveled in it. Hadn't he left me to bleed out in the woods on my own?

Hadn't he dragged Cillian away to finish the job on my best friend?

Budimir Kovalyov doesn't like quick, clean deaths.

When the time comes, I'll make sure he's repaid in kind.

I focus back on Anton, who's staring at me with wide eyes.

He is scared of death, like any reasonable man. But he's more scared of Budimir. Of the immediate threat to his family.

"I am not my uncle," I tell him quietly. "I do not plan on earning loyalty with fear."

"I may not have wanted to follow your uncle," Anton says. "But I still cannot help you."

I pause and look the man in the eye. He's frightened, of course, but still proud. Still strong. He is not yet a lost cause.

So I take a chance.

I make a decision.

I lower my gun and put it away.

Somewhere in the afterlife, my father smiles proudly.

Put away the gun and use your brain, he once told me. I thought that was dumb advice then. And yet here I am.

"Listen to me, Anton," I tell him. "Once I take back the Bratva, I will look after my men. That protection extends to their families."

Anton tilts his head. Still cautious, but curious. Starting to sway, I think.

"I am no angel," I continue. "When a man betrays me, he will pay for it. But I will not exact revenge on his family. On the innocent. That is not how I intend to lead."

Anton closes his eyes for a moment. Weighing what I'm saying and what it means for him and his family.

"Fuck," he says as he opens them.

That's all it takes to tell me he's made his choice. He's chosen to follow the true don.

He's chosen to follow me.

"I am not a part of the big meetings, the important ones," Anton sighs, confirming what Maxim has already told me. "But I do know one thing that might be useful to you."

"Go on."

"He's planning on initiating a don's council meeting soon," Anton tells me. "He wants to legitimize his claim, and to do that—"

"He needs to be recognized by the other dons as a don in his own right," I finish.

Anton nods.

"When is this meeting?" I ask.

"A week from tomorrow," he replies. "I don't know when or where."

"No, but I might." I nod and tuck my gun away. "Thank you for this information."

I turn to leave. My back is exposed and if there was ever a time to strike me down and rid himself of the anxiety of picking sides, it's now.

But I have a feeling that his decision is firm.

Anton says nothing as I stride away. My hand is on the doorknob when I hear him call after me.

"You're just going to leave?"

I turn to him, smirking. "Do you want to offer me tea?"

"I... You don't know what I'll do after you leave," he points out in disbelief. "What if I call Budimir and tell him that you're alive? That you're coming after him?"

I shrug. "Sometimes to gain trust, you have to give it," I tell him. I look directly at him and our eyes meet. "Time to choose a side, Anton."

Then I walk out of his house and leave him to his decision. I know I've just taken a huge risk, but I feel good about it.

Even if Anton betrays me to Budimir, they don't know where I am or where I'm operating from. My men are careful and all are on high alert.

I've got my spies in well-placed positions. I'm confident in the risk I've taken.

I did what a don must do.

Stanislav would be proud.

∽

Once I've driven back into the main town, I make another call. It takes a while before I hear a silky voice on the other line.

"Well, well, look who it is."

"Svetlana," I reply. "How are things?"

She chuckles. "I think you'll be pleased," she says. "Budimir has engaged my services for tonight. It'll be the third time this week."

I try to control my excitement. "Fucking perfect," I growl. "Has he given anything away?"

"Not a thing," Svetlana says. "He's still tight-lipped around me. All I know is that he has an important meeting coming up next week. He gets hard every time he talks about it."

"With you?"

"He gets hard with me all the time. Most men do."

I can't help but chuckle at that. "I meant who does he talk about the meeting with, 'Lana."

"With his men," she replies. "But I'm around."

Hell fucking yes. Things are coming together.

"Any info on this meeting he's so excited about?" I press.

"Not yet, but tonight I'm accompanying him to a business event."

"A business event?" I repeat.

"That's what he called it," she says. "I imagine I'll have more information for you tomorrow."

I clench my fist, thrilled by a day of positive progress. "Good job, Svetlana. I knew I made the right decision with you."

"You bet your ass you did," she says. I notice the new confidence in her tone. "Oh, and Artem?"

"Yes?"

"I want a raise."

I raise my eyebrows. "The amount I've offered you is pretty fucking generous."

"The last time we were together, I sucked Budimir's cock twice," she says matter-of-factly.

I cringe. "Jesus. Fine. You'll get what you want."

I can practically see the smile of triumph on her face. "Thanks, boss," she says sweetly.

Then the line goes silent.

Whatever. It was fucking worth it. Clearly, Budimir has no idea that Svetlana is a plant. But he will soon enough.

If the information I've been given pans out, the don's council meeting is only a week away.

The perfect fucking time to make my move.

34

ESME

AT THE BEACH, LATER THAT AFTERNOON

"Wow, it's nice out here," Artem says, looking out at the ocean, sprawled out before us like a meadow made of blues and greens.

"Nice?" I exclaim in astonishment. "It's much more than nice, you Neanderthal."

He laughs. "I forget how much you love the sea."

I breathe in the fresh ocean air. I can taste the salt on my tongue.

"It makes you feel like you're in another world," I explain. "Like, for as long as you're standing in the sand with water at your feet, you're free."

"Do you feel so trapped?" he asks.

I take his hand. "Not anymore."

He leans in and presses his lips against mine. So soft that, for a moment, I can barely feel him.

Then the kiss deepens and my only desire is to press myself against him.

But Phoenix gurgles between us, strapped to my chest with the yellow blanket that is so sentimental to me now.

I break away and look down at our son. Artem runs his hand through Phoenix's dark hair. It's starting to curl at the edges a little and neither of us can stop touching the tiny ringlets.

"There's no one around," Artem says, looking around the abandoned beach.

"There are bigger ocean towns that attract the tourists," I explain. "The locals are used to the ocean. They're only out here when it's warm enough to swim in."

"I'm not complaining," he says. "I like having this place all to ourselves."

"Me too. Just the three of us."

We hold hands as we continue on down the beach. We walk a few feet away from the shoreline, but I can feel the chill of the Pacific soaking into the soft sand.

As we walk further, we lose sight of the boardwalk, and the buildings gives way to trees. Once we've cleared the town, it really does feel like the ocean belongs to us.

"You could swim by the beach every day if we lived here," I tell him with a nudge.

Artem doesn't react to that at all. I know enough to know that that means he doesn't want me to know what he's feeling.

We fall into silence. I try to picture him living in this town with me.

And I can't see it.

The picture is hazy at best. None of it feels natural.

Because Artem is not meant for a quiet life by the ocean.

Because you're trying to make him something he's not.

The thoughts are uncomfortable. I shove them away.

"How's the little *solnishka*?" Artem asks after a while. He gazes fondly at Phoenix's dark head of hair.

"Fast asleep," I tell him.

"Good," he says. "I've been waiting for that."

I laugh. "Why?"

"Because," Artem says, with a very familiar glint in his eye, "his mother looks so fucking sexy right now, and I need a little one-on-one time with her."

I can't help the blush that flushes onto my cheeks. "Here?" I ask.

"What are you worried about?" Artem pokes. "All the people that might see us?"

I laugh. "Fair point."

"It's not the first time I've taken you on the beach either."

His words trigger the memory, as well as the heat between my legs.

Within seconds, I'm wet, and the idea of having Artem inside me is titillating as hell.

"Get the blanket," I tell him in a deep, husky voice.

We find a shady spot under an abandoned pier and pull out the large beach blanket that Artem's been carrying around in the basket I packed for our beach outing.

Then I ease Phoenix into the portable bassinet. He doesn't even twitch, still deeply asleep.

Before I can even turn around, I feel Artem's hands on my hips.

I turn into him and his lips are on my neck, his hand cupping my breast and massaging gently. I push him down onto the beach blanket and unzip his pants.

I pull them off him, followed by his shirt, until he's stretched out before me, naked and magnificent. He looks so fucking sexy that it just makes me wetter.

I sit up next to him, my hands exploring his defined pecs and his steel abs. He plays with my hair as I continue staring at him with longing.

As my fingers drift over his body, Artem's hand pulls up the flimsy white dress I'm wearing. He slips his fingers in sideways under my panties and starts exploring my wetness.

I feel his finger slide inside me as I bend down and kiss his neck, my hand stroking his cock slowly.

"Mmm... I've missed this," I whisper to him.

"I've missed you," he answers, his tone thick with lust.

I keep stroking his cock, while he fingers me with increasing speed. Once my body is rolling with waves of desire and I can't stand it anymore, I hike my dress up around my waist and get on top of him.

I straddle him, my thighs tightening around his waist and my hands on his chest. His tattoos peer back at me, dark and glinting slightly in the lattice of shade and sun.

"How many of these do you have?" I ask as I slowly trace the outline of his chest ink, grinding my hips against him slowly.

His cock is pressed up between my legs, teasing my pussy lips without yet entering me. I graze him with one hand as my other hand continues to caress his chest.

"I've lost count," he groans.

"Are you done?"

He smiles. "No, I've got at least two more to get."

"Oh?"

He nods, his hands squeezing my thighs as his cock twitches with need. "Yeah," he says. "One for you. One for Phoenix."

For such a simple gesture, I'm surprised by how warm it makes me. "I like that idea," I say. "Maybe I'll get one, too. Maybe right… here?"

I trace a teasing fingertip around the outline of my hardened nipple. Artem's groan deepens, expands.

"How about, first, you fuck me," he growls. His hand closes over mine and together, we squeeze my breast and send sensation surging through me.

But as he tries to sit up, I put both hands back on his chest and push him down to the earth again.

"Patience," I whisper to him. He laughs—probably because he knows the truth as well as I do.

That neither of us can wait a single fucking second longer.

I bend down and kiss him hard, entwining my tongue in his. His hands open and close on my thighs, but he doesn't force me down on him. Not yet.

He lets me make the final move.

I lift my hips and line up the head of his cock with my pussy. Then I inch down on top of him.

An instant later, he fills me up.

"Oh God," I gasp involuntarily.

I wind up and down on his length. Hips meeting hips. The friction, pure and beautiful and so fucking intense that I feel it from head to toe.

He holds me tightly in place, but he lets me take the lead. He doesn't push into me. He just lies there, allowing me to take this at the pace I want.

I move on top of him slowly, taking the time to kiss his lips, his neck, and his chest.

My breasts spill out into his face and his tongue laps at my nipples for a few moments before I put my hands on his chest and start riding him a little faster. Then he throws his head back and groans, a masculine sound that rumbles from him and through me and just takes everything one notch higher.

I press deep onto him. Rise up and slide down again. There's so much of him to ride on. So much cock parting me, splitting me. And as the first orgasm starts to build up deep in my core, my muscles tremble and give way.

That's when Artem takes the reins.

He grips my hips and forces me to balance on my knees. Then he starts ramming into me from below. I can feel his balls slap against my ass and I moan, my breasts bouncing wildly.

I don't care, though. There's something intensely animalistic about being taken out in the open, under the sky, surrounded by the elements.

But then, there's something intensely animalistic about just having sex with Artem.

His cock is a fucking weapon and he impales me over and over again, until my cheeks are flushed from exertion and my body is shivering with jolts of my coming orgasm.

I'm moaning so wildly that Phoenix starts to stir in his bassinet.

He smiles indulgently at me. "You might have to be a little quieter, *kukolka*," he tells me.

But I can tell he loves what he does to me. How he makes me shred all my inhibitions to pieces.

"I don't know if I can," I answer breathlessly. "Not when you're fucking me like that."

I say it partly because it's true.

And partly because I know what it will do to him when I say something like that.

With a hungry glint in his eye, Artem grabs hold of me suddenly and twists me around so that I'm lying on my back and he's on top of me.

It's so quick and sudden that it takes my breath away. But I love feeling tiny in his arms. I love him throwing me around and the flex of his muscles under my fingertips.

He hikes my legs up high around his waist and starts pummeling into me with greater and greater force. And of course I start moaning again, louder than before, and I have even less control over them than I ever do.

Artem's hand clamps down over my mouth.

I squirm against him and try to seize my moans in my throat.

But that only makes the orgasm come faster.

I tighten my walls around his cock, basically choking him as I come, my screams muffled against his hand.

But he doesn't stop fucking me. He keeps going, speeding up the tempo of his thrusts until I'm clawing at his back and sucking on his fingers.

I can feel him bruising me, but I don't fucking care.

I want his cock, and I want it hard.

I throw my head back as my back arches with a second orgasm in as many minutes.

I open my eyes. Artem's face comes into view. It's the only thing I see, the only image that fills my world. Him and our son—that's all that matters. That *is* my world.

His jaw is clenched with exertion, his irises dark with desire, and little beads of sweat dot his forehead.

I can see his own orgasm coming in his eyes, so I don't turn my gaze. I want to watch it.

I keep the eye contact and grip him hard with my legs as he fucks me to within an inch of my life.

Give me more, I'm saying with my body. *Give me all of you and I'll give you all of me.*

My second orgasm is more violent, more all-consuming than the first, and for a moment, it feels as though my heart is going to beat right out of my chest.

I'm riding high on all the new sensations coursing through my body that I barely even notice Artem coming inside me seconds later.

He stays on top of me propped up on his elbows. He kisses my neck and my breasts, rubbing his face in between them.

I run my hands over his hair and wait patiently for my heartbeat to calm down a little.

"Wow," I breathe when it's all said and done. I search for words to describe what just happened between us and come up empty. "I mean… wow."

He turns to me and smiles, before slowly shifting off me.

"How's the little man?" he asks.

I pull myself up enough to look into Phoenix's bassinet. He's still sleeping contentedly, his little lips moving gently in a suckling motion that's so precious it gives me no choice other than to lean down and kiss his nose.

"Sleeping like the angel he is," I reply.

"I'm glad his mama's screaming didn't wake him up," Artem teases.

I hit his arm and settle into the crook of his embrace. "That was your fault, not mine."

He laughs. "Well, I'm happy to take the blame for that one."

We lie like that for another half an hour before Phoenix wakes up and demands milk. I feed him as Artem swims in the ocean. He's glistening and beautiful, a mirage flashing between the waves.

This is what I always wanted.

This is what I need.

Ocean. Artem. Phoenix.

My pulse quickens as I watch Artem run out of the ocean. Ice-blue drops of water glint off his muscular body like diamonds.

When he joins me back on our large beach blanket, I pull out the picnic lunch I'd made for our day at the beach and we pig out on ham and cheese sandwiches, salt and vinegar potato chips, sweet cherry tarts.

Artem drinks beer. I drink lemonade. Everything feels kind of magical.

Careful now, Esme. Nothing lasts forever.

I swat away the unwelcome thought, but it lingers at the back of my head stubbornly. I'm aware that Artem and I still need to have a discussion about our future.

But I'm putting it off.

I can sense he is, too.

We both just want to cling to the illusion of perfection that we're currently engulfed in.

Is that so wrong?

After we finish eating, we pack up. Artem slings our bag over his shoulder and takes Phoenix from my arms.

"I'll carry the little one back," he tells me.

Phoenix stays awake the whole way back into town. Even when we cross the boardwalk and get into the car, he coos happily in Artem's arms, running his tiny fingers through the curls of Artem's beard.

I end up driving back because I don't want to intrude on their bonding moment.

Though that's also dangerous, because I can't stop looking over at them and having my heart melt and ooze out through my eyeballs.

We get back to the apartment just after the sun has set. Phoenix yawns hugely against Artem's chest and starts the heavy blink that means bedtime is imminent.

Once he's changed and bathed, I feed him again and settle him back into his bassinet for the night. He's asleep from the moment I set him down.

Artem and I end up in the shower together so that we can wash the sand off our bodies.

Of course, that inevitably ends with shower sex.

But this time, it's slow and tender. It soothes the ache between my legs and when we fall into bed, naked and immensely satisfied, I go to sleep every bit as fast as my son did.

∽

I sleep soundly for a while. But my body clock has me blinking awake when it's still dark outside.

I glance over at the bassinet. Phoenix is still where I placed him earlier.

But Artem is not by my side like I expect him to be.

It's funny—the bed is so small, and yet it still feels empty without him.

"Artem?"

No answer. He must be in the bathroom or something.

I turn to Phoenix. My breasts are heavy, so I feed him. Then I put him back in his bassinet. Still no sign of my husband.

"Artem?" I call out again.

No answer.

I pad out of the bedroom and into the tiny excuse for a living room.

Artem is sitting on the low sofa in the darkness. Gazing at the far wall as if there's something there.

But there's nothing. Nothing at all. His gaze is miles away from here.

He looks at me then, but he still feels so far away.

It scares me all over again. It tells me what I've known deep in my heart since right after he showed up at my door: that the bubble is about to break.

I temper my emotion and sit beside him.

The fairy tale is about to end.

You wanted to know how long this would last, didn't you?

Well... here's your answer.

"Tell me whatever you need to," I begin.

He sighs deeply. It's a sound I've never heard from him before. "I'm sorry," he says.

"Don't tell me you're sorry," I snap. "Just tell me what you have to."

He nods, but it's still several more seconds before he finally breaks the silence.

"Esme, you and Phoenix, you mean the world to me," he says.

I squeeze the armrest and brace myself for what's coming.

"But I never should have made you believe I was leaving the Bratva behind."

The hairs on my arm rise.

But nothing else changes.

And I know why instantly.

Because I've been expecting this all long.

Deep down, I've always known where Artem's choice lay.

"The last several weeks, I've been consolidating power," Artem continues. "I've been preparing to take on my uncle and fight for what's mine."

I nod slowly, as though I understand. Part of me doesn't. Part of me does.

"I thought I could let you go," he confesses. "I thought I could give you the freedom you crave so much. But… I'm a selfish fucker. I want you in my life, Esme. You and Phoenix. We're a family and we need to stick together."

I look down at my trembling hands, trying to process everything he is telling me.

"Hate me if you must. Get angry with me if you have to," he says. "But come back to Los Angeles with me."

I look up at his intense eyes, pooled in shadow. Despite their darkness, they're so clear. They make me feel like I can fall into them.

"What if I say no?" I ask.

His body tenses instantly.

"I… I don't know if I can accept that," he admits. It's a vulnerable answer. An honest one.

"Meaning what?" I ask. "You'll force me back? Lock me in a room? Visit me at night to demand I perform my wifely duties?"

A ripple of hurt flashes across his eyes but his jaw doesn't unclench. He's still determined. Still hopeful.

"I will never force myself on you," he says icily. "I just want you to understand why I can't walk away from the Bratva, Esme."

"Okay," I say. "Tell me."

"You may think it's just about getting revenge. Avenging Cillian and Stanislav. And it is about that, I won't deny it. But it's more."

He grips my hand and continues.

"The Bratva is my family. I owe it to the men who are trapped there under Budimir to free them. I owe it to the men who died for my father to come back and fight on their behalf. I owe a lot of things to a lot of people."

He hasn't blinked or wavered once. His voice is strong and unyielding.

It's the voice of a don.

"I've realized what I want now, Esme," he tells me. "Maybe if I'd been born to a different family, things might have been different. But this is the only life I know. I can't be anything else but what I am. This is it for me, Esme. This is my life. And I want you in it. I want to leave Phoenix with something and this is all I have to offer. My legacy. My father's legacy. The Bratva."

I stare at him.

My heart is pained, but I know what my decision is without having to think about it.

I've known it for a while.

But it had only cemented itself in my consciousness earlier today when we were at the beach.

All I really need is my husband and my son.

"This is not the life I want," I tell him straight. "But…"

I look up and Artem is waiting patiently for my answer. He looks calm, but I know he must be nervous about my answer.

"But if it's the only way I can keep you in my life, and in Phoenix's… I suppose I'll have to accept it."

There's three seconds of silence and then Artem smiles.

"You'll come back to L.A. with me?"

I nod.

A part of me always knew this was an inevitability. I'd known it from the moment Artem showed up at my doorstep.

For so long, I've been terrified of reliving the nightmare I lived in the Moreno compound under my father's oppressive presence.

But I'm a stronger woman now.

And Artem is not Papa. He is a stronger man. A better man.

And I know beyond a shadow of a doubt that he will protect me with his dying breath.

In the end, all I had to do was ask myself one simple question:

Do I love him?

And every time I ask myself that, no matter the circumstances, the answer stays the same. Every single fucking time.

Yes.

Yes.

Yes.

35

ARTEM

A FEW DAYS LATER—LOS ANGELES, CALIFORNIA

Esme is singing.

It's a soft sound and I don't even think she knows she's doing it. Music just comes out of her when she's happy, as easy as breathing.

I stand silently in the new apartment for a moment and listen. I can't help the smile that spreads across my face.

It's been a few days since I found her again. Since we found each other again, really.

Having her and our son under one roof has been a blessing I don't deserve. But I cherish every second like it's priceless. Like I'll never have it again.

The apartment is modest, settled in a good neighborhood that's not overly flashy. I want Esme to be safe as well as comfortable, and that means flying under the radar for a little while.

When all this is over, I will buy her a proper home. I will give her the lifestyle she deserves.

But until then, I need to play it safe and not draw unwanted attention to ourselves.

Of course, Esme was thrilled with the place. It's a spacious two-bedroom filled with natural light. Bright, clean, simple. Maxim made sure the kitchen and nursery were stocked prior to our arrival.

Esme's singsong murmurs move from the kitchen to the second bedroom to check on Phoenix.

I'm about to go join her—to touch her bare hip and lean over her shoulder while she sings, to breathe in her scent, to feel her warmth against me; all those things I love—when my phone rings.

I pick it up despite the unidentifiable contact number.

"Yes?"

"Hey, *sladkiy*."

"Svetlana," I say. "Do you have any news for me?"

"I do indeed," she says, enthusiasm shining through in her tone. "The dons' council meeting is set for Wednesday. Over dinner and drinks, of course, rich old men being the fat pigs that they are. Eight o'clock is the designated time. At the Regency."

"Excellent," I say with a triumphant clench of the fist. "Do you have a guest list for me?"

"Not exactly," Svetlana replies. "But I have a few names. Maggadino. Ambrosino. Guzik. Juarez."

The name "Maggadino" makes my chest ache. One of the last conversations I ever had with my father was about that Italian asshole. I paid it little mind that day. Too angry to realize that my time with Stanislav was hurtling towards its end.

I don't have time for those feelings right now, though.

I have a war to win.

Svetlana continues, "I happen to know that none of them have yet recognized Budimir as don yet. Your uncle thinks this meeting will be a step in the right direction."

That makes me scowl. The thought of Budimir taking what's rightfully mine is downright fucking nauseating.

Fucker doesn't know what he's in for.

"Did you manage to wrangle an invite to join him at the meeting?"

It's a long shot. Even my horny uncle probably wouldn't be dumb enough to bring a piece of ass to a business affair. But worth asking nonetheless.

"Unfortunately not," Svetlana says wistfully.

I can tell that she's disappointed by the exclusion. Apparently, not even her many talents can get Budimir to bend that far.

"He's booked out the suite for the night, though," she adds. "He wants me to wait there until after the council meeting is over."

"He's anticipating that this meeting will be successful," I realize. "Wants you there to celebrate."

"Or to punish, if things go badly," Svetlana suggests darkly.

I grimace. That's certainly not out of the question. But it won't happen on my watch.

"I'll have men stationed around the Regency," I assure her. "I've assigned one to you specifically. In case things go south."

"Really?"

"Of course," I say. "Like I said, you're a part of the team. And I protect my men... and women."

"Thanks, darling," she murmurs.

I hang up and turn to see Esme standing at the threshold of Phoenix's room. She's watching me carefully, clearly having heard some of my conversation.

"Who was that?" Esme asks.

"Her name's Svetlana," I reply. "She's working undercover for me."

Esme's eyebrows rise. "Undercover?" she repeats. "Where?"

"I've positioned her… within Budimir's inner circle."

I keep it vague. No reason to stain her with the more unsavory aspects of what I'm doing to reclaim the Bratva.

Not because I don't trust Esme, but because I want to spare her from the darker side of the world.

But she steps forward, her eyes trained on me, her expression curious, even interested.

"I know how mafia entourages work," she tells me. "They comprise of the underbosses, security detail and… women, most of them prostitutes."

I nod. "Svetlana is more than just a prostitute. She's Bratva now."

Esme's eyes go wide for a moment. "She must be incredibly brave."

She's damn right about that. Svetlana is putting herself directly in the line of fire for my sake. "Her father spent his whole life in the mafia," I tell her.

"So did mine," she reminds me. "But I couldn't do what she's doing. It takes a special kind of woman to do a job like that."

"True," I reply. "But there are so many different ways for a woman to be special."

I take her hand and bring it to my lips. She smiles knowingly at me.

"Do you think my ego is so fragile that I'd begrudge another woman a compliment?" she asks with a wink.

"Um… there's only one right answer here, right?"

She laughs and slaps my hand away just as Adrik enters the living room.

"Hey, boss," he says as nods to me. "Mrs. Kovalyov."

Instantly, Esme's lips screw up with distaste. "Seriously, Adrik," she admonishes, "I've asked you to drop the 'Mrs.' a hundred times."

He smiles. "Habit."

"Well, drop it," she snaps.

"Yes, ma'am."

"*Ma'am?*" she repeats in horror. "I changed my mind. I think I preferred 'Mrs.'"

Adrik chuckles under his breath, but his smile drops as he turns to me. "I got the location."

"Perfect," I say. "Let's get going."

"Wait," Esme says. "Where exactly are you going?"

Adrik and I exchange a glance. "*Kukolka…*" I start to say.

But she raises a hand and cuts me off.

"Don't you '*kukolka*' me, pendejo!" she snaps with fire in her eyes. "I agreed to come back to L.A. I even agreed to accept the fact that you are don of the Bratva. But I need to be kept informed. Comprende?"

Part of me wants to chuckle. No one could ever accuse my wife of lacking passion or steel.

But I value my testicles being attached to my body, so I know better than to laugh in her face.

Besides, the real reason for her outburst is her nerves. She's worried about me. Paranoid, panicky.

The best way to soothe her concerns is to tell her what she wants to know.

She's earned that right in spades.

"Polish mafia headquarters," I tell her.

"And how many men are you taking with you?" she demands.

I suppress a smile. If something happened to me, I'm fairly certain that Esme could take control of the Bratva and lead it capably until my son comes of age.

Whether she sees it or not, she has the strength and the intelligence for it.

"A dozen," Adrik answers for me.

"That's it?" she says.

I smile. "Babe," I say. "I've got this."

"You have to be careful," she lectures sternly. "What if Budimir has got to the Polish gang already? What if you walk into a trap?"

"We've weighed the risks—"

"That doesn't mean you've eliminated them," she counters.

I walk forward and take both her hands in mine, forcing her to look me in the eye. "I know you're worried," I say. "But you don't have to be. I know what I'm doing. I've done this a few times before."

"You had the might of the Bratva behind you at the time," she points out. "Now, that force backs your uncle."

"All true," I agree. "But every one of my men are worth ten of Budimir's."

She shakes her head and mumbles something that sounds a lot like "Ugh, *men*."

"Trust me, Esme," I tell her. "I'm not taking any unnecessary risks. Not when I have you and Phoenix to think of."

She sighs deeply and pulls her hands out of mine.

"You better come back without a scratch tonight, Artem Kovalyov," she says. "Or else I'll kill you."

I smile. "I might make a mafia wife out of you yet, Esme Moreno."

"The name is Esme Kovalyov," she says instantly.

I shiver at the way she says that. My cock stiffens, too.

Yes, my wife has fire aplenty.

"How could I forget?" I say, unable to keep from grinning ear-to-ear.

She's about to lean in and kiss me when a piercing cry carries through to us.

"Phoenix," Esme says hurriedly. She darts into his room to check on him.

When she's gone, Adrik looks at me with raised eyebrows, waiting for orders.

"Go round up our men," I tell him. "We're leaving in five."

He nods and leaves the apartment, while I hang back. The moment the door shuts behind him, I move to the half open door and watch as Esme picks Phoenix up and rocks him gently from side to side.

"You're okay, little bird," she says. "You're okay."

"Esme?"

She turns to me.

"I'll see you tonight."

She nods solemnly. "You better."

I give her a wink and head out the door.

The car's waiting for me downstairs. The rest of my men will meet us on the road about a mile out from the Polish facilities.

And then, the games will begin.

∽

Twenty minutes later, I see three black SUV's fall into line behind us. My entourage is complete, and yet, something is missing. I realize with a painful jolt that something will always be missing.

Cillian.

He should be here, driving the car while I coordinate with the rest of the team.

I glance towards Adrik. He's a loyal man and a strong fighter. So is Maxim. So are all the men who have pledged their loyalty to me.

But it doesn't matter.

My history with them is surface deep when I compare it with the friendship I had with Cillian.

I wonder if that loss will ever stop hurting.

We park right in front of the safehouse, a surprisingly unimpressive building for a mafia faction that has been active and influential for a few decades now.

I'm the first person out of the car, but the rest of my crew quickly follows. We're all packing heat—a show of strength is necessary—but

I've purposefully limited the number of men I've brought with me to avoid the appearance of a direct assault.

But some fear may be necessary.

I just need to toe the line.

I've come here for a conversation, a possible alliance, not a fight. If I'd brought any more men, that's the way our presence might be construed.

My men stand back, waiting for me to take the lead or issue an order. I don't say a word. I just stride towards the headquarters gates as my men fall in line behind me.

There are four men at the gates. They get to their feet as we approach, their expressions wary, but I keep my body language casual.

"Excuse me, boys," I say. "I have an appointment with your boss."

They nod humorlessly and open the gates. We flow inside.

There are more men in the courtyard who glance up as we enter, but I breeze right past them and into the building.

I walk into a large living room setup, where yet another bunch of men are milling around.

The hierarchy is obvious. The underbosses are reclined on the couches, drinking whiskey and smoking cigars.

The men hovering around the periphery of the room are soldiers, runners, grunts.

But every single one of them turns to look at me when I enter.

"Is Kaminski in?" I ask.

No one answers for a moment.

"Are you all fucking deaf? I asked if Kaminski is in."

Finally, someone speaks up. My gaze swivels over to track the speaker.

It's one of the smug idiots on the couch. He's tall, broad, muscular, with a distinct and massive tattoo of an eagle sprawling across the front of his throat. Apart from that, his features are forgettable.

"Who's asking?" he says.

"Artem Kovalyov."

I hear someone swear to the side, but I don't even glance in his direction.

"Send a message up," Eagle Tattoo snaps at an aide.

I stand there silently and wait. The atmosphere is tense at best, but I keep my expression calm, unbothered.

I don't have to fake that. I *am* calm. I *am* unbothered.

I'm in my element.

Then I hear footsteps. A few seconds later, three men stomp down the stairs into the middle of the space.

The last one I recognize immediately as the Polish mafia don, Kaminski. I've seen him in passing before when I was a boy.

He hasn't changed much. Maybe a few kilos heavier and a few more grays in his hair and beard.

"*Kurwa!*" he exclaims in Polish as his eyes settle on me with disbelief. "It is you."

"Surprise," I chuckle, raising my hands with a smile.

"You must have some kind of death wish coming back to this city."

I shrug. "I have a slightly different perspective."

"Which is what?" Kaminski asks, taking a few steps forward as his underlings converge around him.

"This is my home," I reply. "And I'm taking it back."

Kaminski smiles, his eyes taking stock of the men behind me. Then he turns to his.

"Out," he orders. "All of you."

Of course, he doesn't actually mean all his men. A few of his underbosses stay behind, including the guy with the eagle tattoo.

I count quickly and silently as the room empties. In the end, there's fifteen of them and twelve of us.

I don't want it to come down to bloodshed. But if that becomes necessary, I like our odds.

Kaminski plops down on a couch and gestures for me to sit as well. I move forward and take the sofa directly opposite him.

My men spread slightly to occupy more of the room, but none of them sit. I can feel them at my back, scanning the area, staying vigilant.

"My sources tell me you haven't picked a side yet," I begin cautiously.

He grunts, "Didn't see the point of getting involved in a fight that's not mine."

"Fair," I agree. "But I'm guessing you want to cash in where you can."

He smiles, showing yellowed teeth. "For that, all I need to do is present your uncle with your head," he says. "Budimir put out a standing contract on your life. Of course, that was before he announced that you were dead. Which means your head is probably worth a lot more now."

"Probably," I say. "But Budimir will just give you money. Maybe after that, he'll throw you a bone every now and again. I can do more for you. Far more."

"If I ally with you, of course," Kaminski amends.

"Of course. So the only question now is… are you interested?"

"That depends," Kaminski muses. "On your offer."

So far, this has gone exactly as expected. I reach into a pocket and pull out the list of concessions that Adrik and I hashed out last night. Territories, shares of various trades and businesses, some rights of passage through Bratva-controlled parts of the city.

It's a lot. More than I would've wanted to give up.

But as much as I hate it, we need Kaminski's cooperation.

He scans the handwritten list. I watch his face for signs of approval or distaste, but he gives nothing away.

"Well?" I ask when he sighs and leans back.

"Those are generous terms," Kaminski says.

"It's a one-time offer. Expires very soon."

"And if I say no?" he asks.

I glance around at the rest of the silent men in the room. "We'll leave."

He smiles again, baring those sharp, yellow teeth. "And you think I'll just let you walk out of here…?"

"Perhaps not," I acknowledge. "I hope you will, though. For your sake."

Kaminski raises his eyebrows. "For *my* sake?"

I nod. "You don't want to sacrifice your men unnecessarily, do you?" I ask.

He frowns and makes a big show of counting out how many Bratva soldiers have come with me. "*Jeden, dwa, trzy… jedenaście, dwanaście.* Twelve. Twelve men. You really think you can take on all of us with only twelve men?" he guffaws.

He's playing like he's unconcerned, but this man is don for a reason. I know that beneath the bravado, he's assessing the situation. Trying to figure out if I'm just naïve or if I know something he doesn't.

"I know I can," I answer smoothly. "But I brought in reinforcements, just in case."

Kaminski's laughter dies instantly. "*Pierdolić,*" he growls. "You're talking bullshit."

"Did you really think I would risk coming here with only a dozen men?" I ask conversationally.

"Liar."

I shrug. "It's your risk to take."

I see a muscle in his jaw twitch, but otherwise he stays calm and unflustered. Finally, he leans forward.

Behind him, I see his men tense. They're waiting for his answer as much as we were.

"I like your style," he tells me. "If I had to bet on a Kovalyov man, it'll be you."

He extends his hand out to me.

I clasp it with mine.

"You have yourself a deal."

I nod and get to my feet. "I'll be in touch."

Then I turn and walk out of there with my men close behind. Adrik falls into step beside me as we go back out through the courtyard and the gates.

He doesn't say a word until we're back in the car. "If he had ordered his men to attack, we would have been outnumbered ten to one."

I nod. I knew the math as well as he did.

But Kaminski hadn't called my bluff. He bought it.

And we just bought ourselves an ally.

36

ESME

THE NEXT MORNING

I take him deep, his cock filling my mouth as his tongue pushes through the folds of my pussy. I have to jerk back just to gasp so that I don't choke on him.

I love giving Artem head. It's such an erotic experience, and one I never thought I'd enjoy. But apparently, when you find the right man, it can be a huge turn-on.

Usually, I like to concentrate on him.

But today, he insisted on eating me out while I suck his cock.

I've never actually tried the sixty-nine position with anyone before, and I'm finding it overwhelming.

I can feel my juices coat the bedsheets beneath me, but Artem seems oblivious as he tongue-fucks me relentlessly.

I lick his balls as my hand strokes his massive shaft, but the moment his tongue circles my clit, I know there's no way I can concentrate on what I'm doing.

He eats me out passionately and I come right on his face, gasping and moaning and clinging to the sides of the bed as though I'm scared to float away.

Before I can even catch my breath, Artem climbs on top of me and I feel his cock slide inside me easily.

He starts to fuck me hard, anchoring me in place with his massive chest.

We come together seconds later and I sigh with contentment, thankful that Phoenix has his own room and has started sleeping soundly.

Artem dips his head down to my breasts and sucks on my nipples for a moment before pulling away and getting out of bed.

I sit up, drawing the sheets around my breasts as I watch him reach for his boxers.

"Where are you off to?" I demand playfully.

"I have a meeting," he sighs. "Several, actually, and I'm late to them all."

I smile guiltily. "Is that my fault? Did I delay you?"

"Delay?" he asks with amusement. "Is that what you call attacking me when I was practically out the door?"

I laugh. "I didn't attack you!"

"You threw your naked body on me and dragged me by my cock into bed," he reminds me as my cheeks blush scarlet. "What do you call that?"

"Um... love?" I offer.

Artem laughs but his eyes soften.

"Fair enough," he says, pulling on his boots. "Love it is."

Once he's fully dressed, he walks over to me and gives me one last kiss.

"Alik and Gennadi will be with you today in case you want to go out."

I sigh. "Artem, I don't need two bodyguards."

"Yes," he says firmly, "you do."

"The whole point is that I'm meant to be traveling under the radar, right?" I ask. "I'm going to stick out like a sore thumb if I'm accompanied by two bodyguards the whole time."

"Which is why they're dressed in plainclothes," he tells me. "They'll blend into the crowd, don't worry."

"Still really unnecessary."

"I'm not taking any risks where you and Phoenix are concerned."

Right on cue, I hear a piercing cry from the next room. I smile and Artem shakes his head.

"Speak of the little devil," he says. "At least he didn't cock-block me today."

I laugh and get out of bed, letting the sheet fall away from my body. I feel Artem's eyes on me and my skin heats up instantly.

As though we didn't just finish getting *extremely* filthy with each other.

He reaches out and slaps my ass gently. I dodge his second swipe and wrap my robe around me.

"Hey, now! *No tocas*," I reprimand. "Hands to yourself, mister."

"I'm only human, woman," he growls. "Put your clothes back on or come over here."

I smile as I knot the rope of my bathrobe. "I thought you were late, eh?"

"Fuck."

I follow him out of the bedroom. Artem stomps into the living room, but I make a small detour to get Phoenix.

He throws his tiny fists in the air when he sees me. I pick him up and take him back out to where Artem is.

"Hey, little man," he says, placing a kiss on Phoenix's head. "I'll see you later tonight."

"You'll be here for dinner?" I check.

"Yes."

"Okay, then," I reply. "Have a good day."

As if he's a normal husband headed off to a normal job, and I'm a normal housewife about to embark on a normal day of tending a home and raising a child.

None of this is normal.

But I'm starting to realize… maybe I like it that way.

"You, too," he says. "And please don't ditch Alik and Gennadi."

I smirk. "Fine. But only because you asked so sweetly."

He rolls his eyes but kisses me once more. "Thank you," he says when he pulls away. "Now, I really have to go."

He kisses Phoenix again and whisks out the door.

I'm left standing in the kitchen, holding our baby and buzzing head to toe with the aftershocks of Artem's tongue between my legs and his kiss on my lips.

It's a scene of such domesticity that it takes me by surprise and makes me realize that my dreams are closer to reality than I've realized.

Yes, I'm still very much a part of the world I vowed to leave, but it feels like a small price to pay for a man like Artem.

My last few months alone had put things in perspective. I know now that it was wrong of me to have deprived Phoenix of his father.

My reasons were valid, of course. But just seeing how my baby's eyes light up when Artem whirls him around the room is enough to make my heart hurt for ever having separated them in the first place.

"Let's have a good day, yes, my little angel?" I whisper to Phoenix, tweaking his button nose. He gurgles and squeezes my fingertip.

Artem had floated the idea of hiring a nanny, but I'd nixed it immediately. I just don't know if I can trust anyone at this time.

Maybe once the threat of Budimir is gone, I could get on board with hiring some help. But not until then.

I set Phoenix in his crib to play while I take a quick shower. When I'm clean, I go to my new wardrobe and throw open its doors.

The day after we'd moved in here, Artem had brought a selection of clothes for me.

I knew it was probably superficial of me, but I was thrilled. I'd spent so many months living in the same two items that it felt amazing to be able to swap out my old clothes for new, stylish ones.

I choose dark jeans that fit me perfectly and I pair them with a teal silk blouse and a beige cashmere sweater that's so soft I could sleep in it. I leave my hair loose around my shoulders and then I change Phoenix. Artem brought in a selection of clothes for him too, but only a few.

He'd understood that I might want to do most of his shopping on my own.

And that's precisely what I planned on doing today.

I put a fresh diaper on Phoenix and then I help him into light blue overalls and white booties with little sailboats on the sides.

He looks so gorgeous that I can't help myself—I take a bunch of pictures on my phone and send them to Artem.

Then I grab Phoenix's diaper bag and head downstairs with the little one in tow.

The moment I enter the building's entryway, I spy my bodyguards. Alik has ash-blonde hair, dark eyes, and the palest skin I've ever seen.

Gennadi is dark-haired, with light blue eyes and a grisly beard that hides how pretty his face is underneath.

I wave to them and they both approach me immediately.

They're dressed in plainclothes just like Artem told me they would be, but nothing about them says "civilian." They look like military men going home for the summer.

"Madam Kovalyov," Gennadi greets me.

I raise my eyebrows at him. "Call me that one more time and we're gonna have problems," I warn. "My name is Esme."

"Would you prefer Ms. Esme?" Alik asks respectfully.

"No, I wouldn't," I reply, before steering towards the exit. "Come on, boys."

∽

There's a dark blue jeep parked in one of the designated resident parking spots outside the building. Alik gets into the driver's seat, Gennadi takes the passenger seat, and I get into the back with Phoenix to buckle him into his car seat.

"Where to?" Gennadi asks, purposefully avoiding addressing me.

I suppress a smile at his decorum. "Um, how about Citadel Outlets?" I suggest. "They'll have lots of different stores for you, right, *cielito*?"

It's an easy drive there. I alternate between gazing out at the azure California sky and tickling Phoenix just so I can hear his musical laugh.

When we get to the Citadel, I get out the moment the car is parked.

"Which one of you boys are gonna carry Phoenix's diaper bag for me?" I ask cheerfully, waggling the pink-and-purple duffle between them.

Alik and Gennadi exchange a look, but they both offer their arms out to me. I hand it to Gennadi. Lucky man.

Alik helps me load Phoenix into the stroller. Then, with everybody situated, we walk into the nearest store, a huge Osh Kosh, while the two of them stay constantly roving around me, scanning for threats.

An hour and three bulging shopping bags later, we exit. Thankfully, the car is parked close enough that the boys are able to drop off my bags before moving on down the street.

Phoenix makes a gurgling noise, and I stop to stoop over and check on him.

"Are you hungry?" I murmur. "Should we stop for lunch?"

Standing again, I'm doing a slow pirouette, trying to decide which café to choose, when I see something bizarrely familiar. Or someone, rather.

Our gazes lock.

And I damn near scream.

Oh my God.

It's Tamara.

37

ESME

It's definitely my cousin, even though she's taken pains to change up her look a lot since I last saw her.

Her hair is now a platinum blonde that clashes slightly with her darker complexion. Her makeup is heavier, too, and I realize it's been daubed on to make her nose appear thinner and her lips appear fuller.

She's wearing a tiny yellow mini skirt, with black knee highs and a faux fur jacket. She looks like a girl I'd walk across to the other side of the street to avoid.

Which is exactly what I plan on doing.

"Esme!" she exclaims, then claps a hand over her mouth like she shouldn't be saying my name at all.

We maintain eye contact for maybe three full seconds before I spin around on my heel and try and march away from her.

"No," she calls after me. "Wait! Esme, please!"

And the pleading tone is what makes me stop short. I turn hesitantly, and Tamara runs towards me, her eyes filled with regret.

"Esme," she says again. "I thought you were... I thought you were dead."

I'm burning up with anger, but I choke that down for now. "Almost. But not quite."

She flinches back as though I'd slapped her. "I'm sorry," she says in a quiet voice. "Please forgive me."

I clench my jaw. This is the last thing I expected or wanted today, but now that I'm confronted with Tamara, it's hard to turn my back on her.

Despite how she betrayed me.

"You—"

"I haven't had any contact with Budimir since that day in my apartment," she interrupts, putting her hand over her heart. "Cross my heart and hope to die."

"You *will* die if you ever lie to me again," I snap.

I surprise everyone with those words. Alik, Gennadi, Tamara—and most of all, myself.

Who do I sound like?

The wife of a mafia don.

I don't have time to worry about that, though, not as both my bodyguards step up behind me. I hold up my hand and they stop reluctantly.

Tamara's eyes go wide as she realizes that I've got muscle at my back.

"So Artem's alive then?" she says, glancing back to me.

"Why? Are you going run and make a call to his uncle?" I demand.

I see the hurt and defeat pass across her eyes. She shakes her head slowly.

"You have every right to believe I would do that," she says. "But I wasn't lying when I said I've had no contact with him. I served my purpose and he had no further use for me."

"He's not a man who rewards the people who've helped him," I tell her. "You chose the wrong man."

"I didn't *choose* anything," Tamara retorts, her tone sparking alive for the first time. "He threatened my life. He threatened the lives of all the people I loved. What was I supposed to do?"

I stare at her, at the desperation in her eyes. She wants me to absolve her of her guilt.

I truly believe she hated betraying me to Budimir.

But I don't know if I have the capacity to let that go.

I sigh. "I don't know," I admit. "I don't know what you should have done. I wouldn't have known what to do, either."

"Can we talk?" Tamara begs. "I just want to know that you're okay."

I take a moment and glance back at Alik and Gennadi. They don't look happy with this little run-in, but they don't interrupt either.

"Okay," I concede. "I was just gonna go get something to eat. Why don't you join me?"

A relieved smile spreads across Tamara's face. "That sounds good."

﹋

We find our way to a Parisian-style café and sit at a table in the middle of the restaurant that faces the windows overlooking the street. Alik and Gennadi seat themselves at the table opposite us.

Only once Tamara and I have ordered, does she glance towards the stroller that I've propped pulled up next to me. Phoenix is gazing around happily.

"He looks like Artem," she observes.

"Yes."

"But he's got your eyes."

I smile. "That's the only thing he's got from me," I say. "But otherwise, he's the spitting image of his father."

"Were you pregnant? When you came to me that day?"

I nod, unable to speak.

Tamara closes her eyes for a moment like she's holding back tears. "You didn't tell me," she says finally. Her voice is strained, hoarse.

"I was processing everything at the time," I say. "I was alone and scared and I came to you because you were the only family I had left."

I don't mean to make her feel guilty—though she certainly deserves it—but I can see by the flush on her cheeks that that's exactly how I've made her feel.

And my hard heart unclenches just a little more.

She's Tam-Tam. She's family. The only family I have left.

I've learned the hard way in the last few months how important it is to keep my loved ones close.

"Tamara," I say, reaching out and putting my hand on hers, "it's okay. I'm not angry about it anymore."

"You're not?"

"Well… I'm trying not to be," I admit. "It hurt like hell to know you outed me to Budimir. But I guess I can appreciate the situation you were in. You were just trying to survive."

"I hated myself for doing it all the same," Tamara says to me.

And honestly, I believe her.

That's enough—for now. Enough to figure out what happens next with our friendship.

"You changed your hair," I point out, trying to turn the conversation in a lighter direction.

She smiles, but there's a sigh in her tone when she speaks. "I was trying to re-invent myself after what happened. I got a new apartment. Even got myself a new job."

"And did that help?" I ask. She's not as bubbly as I remember. Not as carefree.

She got a taste of what my life was like, and it changed her forever.

"Not really," she confesses. "I think I needed closure for that to happen."

"You mean you needed to talk to me."

Tamara nods. "I know I've probably given up my right to ask, Esme," she says sadly. "But how have you been? Like, *really*?"

I chuckle at the thought of catching her up on everything. I don't even know where to start with that story. Nor do I want to.

"It's been a wild ride," I say in the end. That'll have to suffice for now.

I do believe that Tamara is sorry. I do believe she no longer has contact with Budimir.

But I have a son to look out for. I don't want to take any chances.

Our relationship can survive in some form, maybe.

But it cannot be what it was.

Neither one of us are naïve enough to hope for that.

"Apparently," Tamara agrees. "It gave you a baby."

I smile. "That's a long story…"

"Do you wanna tell me about it?" she asks cautiously.

"Maybe one day."

She nods, but doesn't press me. "He is beautiful, Esme," she sighs. I can hear the sincerity in her voice. "The cutest baby I've seen in a long time."

"I think so too. But then, I'm biased."

"You're not," Tamara assures me. "Not in this case, anyway. What's his name?"

"Phoenix," I say.

"Phoenix," she echoes with a dreamy lilt to her voice. "I like it." She glances back up at me. "You look happy."

I play with the cutlery on the table. "I am. I really am. As happy as it's possible to be."

"So he's good to you?" Tamara asks.

"He is," I say. "Better than I could have imagined, given how we got married. Given *why* we got married."

Tamara smiles. It seems genuine, as far as I can tell. Though I'm still suspicious of all of this.

"I'm so glad," she tells me. "You have no idea how happy it makes me to see you like this, Esme. It suits you."

"Happiness?" I laugh.

"Motherhood," she clarifies.

"Ah," I smile, looking towards Phoenix's downy black mop. "Motherhood surprised me too. In more ways than one."

"Oh, yeah?"

I shrug. "I never thought about kids ever," I say. "And when I did, it was only as this vague, faraway concept. It never felt like it applied to me."

"That's definitely how I feel about kids," Tamara agrees. "It's probably how I'll feel even in ten years."

"You don't know that."

Tamara sighs. "I can't see myself as a mother," she says. "I can't see myself as anything, really."

I frown. "What do you mean?"

"I mean…"

She sighs again, deeper, and it makes me feel strangely sad somehow. She looks lost. Just like I was a few weeks ago.

"I don't know," she admits. "I just don't see myself in traditional roles. A wife, a mother. But you make it all look so easy."

"I've barely begun being a wife and a mother," I point out. "I might suck at it."

"You won't," Tamara says, with so much confidence that it makes me curious.

"How can you be so sure?"

Tamara looks at me with a measured expression. "You just have that maternal vibe," she tells me. "You used to look after me a lot. Every time I freaked about something—mostly boys— you used to talk me down off the ledge. You were always so calm and comforting. It made me feel better."

"That was Cesar, not me."

She shakes her head. "No, it was *you*, Esme. You helped me. And you helped him, too. He leaned on you."

I frown at that. "He never leaned on me," I tell her. "I was always the one running to him. The one leaning on him."

Tamara shrugs like I don't know what I'm talking about. "I dunno. There was just an air about the two of you," she says. "It's like he used to come to you when he was most broken, and you'd just fix him right up again. Even if you didn't know that's what you were doing at the time."

I try and think back to old memories, something that might ring true with what Tamara is telling me.

But I don't seem to come up with anything.

"I think you're wrong."

"I'm not," she says, shaking her head. "He told me so himself."

That jolts me. "Um… what?" I ask, wondering if I'd misheard her.

I can't ever remember the two of them talking. Cesar tended to avoid the house when Tamara was visiting. He'd never been a huge fan. She was too loud and too excitable for him—at least, that's what he used to tell me.

"Yeah," she says. "I was spending the weekend one time and I ran into him in the garden."

"Where was I?"

"If memory serves, you were sleeping off a hangover," she chuckles. "I'd convinced you to get drunk the night before."

Plausible enough. That had happened a few times, so it wasn't like I could pinpoint when exactly this memory occurred. I could have been anywhere between fourteen and sixteen.

Close to the end of Cesar's life.

"Anyway, I always bounced back much quicker than you did and I got bored in the room," she continues. "So I went down to explore the gardens and I ran into Cesar."

"And he... he talked to you?"

"Trust me: he tried hard to avoid me," she laughs. "Broke my heart, too. I always had a little crush on him."

"Ew, Tamara!" I say. "He was your cousin, too."

"I know, I know," she giggles. "But I was a stupid teenager and it wasn't like he and I were ever very close."

I shake my head in dismay. "So..."

"So, he asked me where you were and I told him you were sleeping," Tamara continues. I find myself clinging to every word. "It was small talk for the first few minutes and then I noticed how—I dunno, how *sad* he looked."

"Sad."

"Very sad," she confirms. "So I asked him what was wrong and he told me he'd had a rough couple of days. I asked him what he did to cope and he said—and I quote—'I talk to Esme.'"

I talk to Esme.

Those words do something to my heart that I can't quite explain.

"He really said that?" I ask quietly.

Tamara nods with a small smile. "He really said that," she repeats.

"Did he... did he say anything else?" I ask. I'm greedy for more information. For the brother I loved. For any scrap of him I can cling to and feel like he's still with me—some way, somehow.

Tamara gives me a sad smile and I feel my heart drop with disappointment.

"Sorry, hon," she says gently. "He wasn't in a very chatty mood. At least, not with me."

I nod as an image of Cesar floats across my eyes. I see him, not as the man he turned out to be, but the boy he was. All easy smiles and silly anecdotes that he made up just to amuse me.

I used to think he was larger than life. But I realize now that that probably wasn't very fair to him.

He already had so much pressure from Papa.

He didn't need more from me.

"You still miss him, don't you?" Tamara asks, reading my expression.

"Of course," I say in a choked voice. "I miss him every day. Even…"

I trail off, leaving my sentence unfinished. Thankfully, Tamara doesn't press me to continue. I sigh and fuss with Phoenix's little overalls for a few seconds.

"I always envied your connection with him," Tamara says.

"Because you had a crush on him?" I tease.

She laughs. "No, I mean, just the sibling connection the two of you had. It must have been nice to have someone to rely on no matter what."

No matter what.

The phrase falls dully against my chest and it makes me feel lonely for a moment.

And then something else hits me suddenly, a realization that I might never have come to if it hadn't been for Tamara.

He used to come to you when he was most broken, and you'd just fix him right up again.

Maybe subconsciously, those were the moments I lived for, because it made me feel like Cesar needed me.

It made me feel strong, important... special.

And when he died, I felt like I'd failed him.

Because a part of me had always known he was suffering.

And I hadn't known how to fix him. I tried my best to figure it out, but before I could, I lost him.

"I haven't had anyone to rely on since Cesar's death," I admit, keeping my hand on Phoenix and patting him gently every now and again. It's almost time for his next feeding.

"Your papa protected you," Tamara points out.

"No," I reply, shaking my head. "Papa protected himself and his business. I was only ever a commodity to be sold and bartered when it suited him. Not a person. Just another Moreno cartel asset."

"Is it strange for you now that he's gone?" Tamara asks.

"Sometimes," I say. "But it's a good kind of strange."

She smiles. "I figured as much."

"I was alone for a very long time. I got too good at it. But then..."

"Artem came along," Tamara finishes.

"Artem came along," I echo. "And it was the saving grace of my life, although I didn't know it at the time."

Phoenix lets out a long, annoyed cry and I know it's time to feed him. So I take him out of the baby carrier and hold him to my chest before I get my cover-up.

I drape it over my shoulders and make sure it's secure before I feed him underneath it.

"Does it hurt?" Tamara asks once I'm settled into place.

"Breastfeeding? It was a little uncomfortable at first," I admit. "But I got used to it."

"You think you'll have more?" she asks.

"I really haven't thought about it," I answer honestly. "I mean, I'm still getting used to having this one. But... maybe one day, in the future."

Tamara shakes her head, looking at me with something close to awe. "I'm glad I got to see you like this, Esme," she says in a hushed tone. "It makes me feel like it's possible for me to find my happy ending, too."

"You'll definitely find your happy ending, Tamara," I tell her. "And I want that for you."

"Do you mean that?" Tamara asks. "After everything I put you through?"

I nod. It's the truth. A hard truth, a thorny truth—but a truth nonetheless.

"You were put in an impossible situation. I know what it's like to have to make hard decisions."

"See?" Tamara says. "There you go: taking care of people."

All I can do is smile.

After that, we fall into easy conversation, nothing too heavy.

And it helps. It helps remind me of a simpler time, when we were young and hopeful and life hadn't beaten the naivete out of us yet.

Once I burp Phoenix, I put my cover-up away and I catch Tamara looking at him with a tender expression on her face.

"I still can't quite believe you have a baby," she mumbles.

I laugh. "Sometimes, I can't believe it either."

She looks hesitant as she asks, "Esme… would you mind if… if I held him?"

I grin. "Of course! Here."

Phoenix's little legs churn in the air as I hold him over the table. Tamara's hands are reaching out to grab him from me.

Her fingers touch his torso.

And then the unmistakable bang of a gunshot tears my world to pieces.

38

ARTEM

ARTEM'S TEMPORARY HEADDQUARTERS

"What did you say?" I demand.

"The council meeting," Maxim repeats quickly. "It's been moved up. Svetlana just called and gave me the intel."

"Moved up?" I say furiously. "To when?"

"Now." He stops short, but I can see that he's just as tense as I am. "Budimir just left the compound for the hotel. The meeting will start in less than an hour."

"Fuck," I curse under my breath. "Fuck! We're not prepared for this today."

"We have to yank the plan," Maxim says. "Just stake out the hotel and—"

"No," I deny firmly, practically spitting out the word with venom. "We're not yanking anything. We don't change a fucking thing. We're still in play."

"But…"

I turn around so fast that Maxim almost plows right into me. "I'm not letting that slippery motherfucker get away from me again. Not this time."

"Then what's the plan?" he asks immediately.

Immediate and unquestioning loyalty. Ready for battle. He's a good man.

"We know where the meeting is and we know where it's being held," I say. "We're going."

Maxim doesn't flinch. He nods and turns towards the door.

"I'll let the men know."

I move into my office space and go through my collection of guns. I choose my favorites and then head outside where the vehicles are already being brought around.

"Maxim, Adrik, Vasyl, Zion," I call.

The four of them move forward, and I can see they're all kitted up and armed. "I want each of you commanding your own unit. You'll have ten men apiece."

"That only leaves you with three," Adrik points out.

"I only need three," I reply.

"Boss—"

"Drop it," I say firmly. "This is how we're doing it. We don't have the numbers and if we wait until we do, we'll miss our opportunity."

Adrik sighs and steps back.

"Budimir has been consolidating power this whole time," I continue. "He's being tolerated by the other dons, but he's also brought in other allies, ones that are more likely to be loyal to him than the normal power players."

I holster another gun and lock eyes with my men.

"We can't afford to play it safe anymore," I finish.

The moment the words are out of my mouth, I think about my wife, my son. Am I betraying them right now by walking into a dons' council meeting led by Budimir?

It's reckless. It's foolhardy. It's fucking suicide.

But the best plans usually are.

"Do we have eyes on the Regency?" I ask Zion.

"Yes," he informs me. "But there'll be ten different dons present, including their entourages. We're talking about more than a hundred armed and trained men in one building. If they all turn their sights on us…"

He trails off, leaving the rest unsaid.

But he doesn't need to continue.

We all know what will happen if I fail.

"Not everyone is happy about Budimir's take over," I say. "Not everyone is happy about the bastards he's invited into the inner circle."

"We're betting a lot on that being true," Maxim acknowledges grimly.

He's right. But we don't have a choice.

Strength is the only language that the underworld understands, and I need to walk in there, guns blazing.

"What about Svetlana?" I ask, turning to Vasyl.

"She's on the thirty-first floor," he answers right away. "The King's Suite."

"Who do we have on her?"

"Luka."

I nod. "Tell him he's not to abandon his position," I order. "No matter what. And if shit goes south, he's to get Svetlana the fuck out of the building."

"We might need him," Maxim interjects. "We'll need every man."

"Svetlana is part of the team," I say. "But she doesn't have to die today. I'm not going to leave her unprotected. She put her neck on the line for several weeks up until this point. I won't forget that."

Maxim nods, stone faced. "I'll tell Luka."

"Good," I say. "That's it. Let's get going."

I jump into the closest SUV, and we head into the heart of the city, towards the Regency. The whole time, my fingers twitch towards my phone.

I desperately want to hear Esme's voice before I go in there. But I resist the desire.

This isn't a goodbye.

I *will* see her again. I *will* hear her voice again.

I don't need to hear it now.

Today is just business as usual.

∽

The moment we get within a block of the hotel, I notice that security has been ramped up. Of course, the general public will assume that a politician or some high-profile celebrity is in town.

But I know better. I see the guns in the jackets of the suited men swirling around the entrances. I see the reinforced armoring of the cars.

This is all the city's richest criminals here to do their dirt.

And I'm getting ready to crash the party.

We park the cars in the hotel's parking lot, but I make no move to get out.

"Hold back," I tell my men. "We need to wait until everyone is inside."

So we wait, watching as more cars line up outside the hotel. They deposit a group of men and drive off. Some of them park in the lot. Most don't.

I look up at the towering building, knowing that Budimir is in one of the topmost floors, probably already congratulating himself on his coronation as the newly legitimized don of the Kovalyov Bratva.

Not for long, you son of a bitch.

"Maxim is approaching," one of my men lets me know.

I roll down my window as Maxim approaches. He's dressed subtly, but I can see the thick outline of the bullet proof vest he's wearing underneath.

"What is it?" I ask.

Maxim's face is grim. "Kovar is here."

I stare at him in shock for a moment. "Say that name again."

He grimaces. "Kovar. I recognized him immediately."

"Budimir invited *that* motherfucker to the don's council meeting?" I say, mostly to myself.

Maxim nods.

"Fuck," I grumble. "The old bastard is more off the rails than I thought."

Throughout my whole childhood, Kovar was more of a ghost than a person. Like the boogeyman—a myth about a terrible creature lurking in the shadows.

It wasn't until I got older that I understood he was real.

And he wasn't a ghost. He was a man. A cruel man. A bloodthirsty man. A man with no code, no morals, no philosophy.

He just lived for spilling blood.

I had never come face to face with him, nor was that ever a realistic possibility. Not since Stanislav and the other dons exiled him from the council table.

Several Years Earlier: "Exiled?" I ask. "Can you do that?"

Stanislav looks at me with careful eyes that give nothing away. But I can tell from the set of his jaw that he's pissed off.

"I can do whatever the fuck I want," he tells me. "I am the fucking don. And he is nothing but a sewer rat that needs to be squashed."

"A sewer rat that made a hundred million last year."

"By selling children into prostitution," Stanislav snarls, and I realize suddenly that he's not pissed with this Kovar scum. He's pissed with Budimir for forcing this conversation to happen in the first place. "By selling children for parts."

"We haven't exactly picked a moral business to deal in, brother," Budimir says calmly. He seems completely unruffled by Stanislav's obvious annoyance.

"Selling guns and drugs is one thing," Stanislav points out. "We don't deal in children. And we don't let anyone else deal in children on our turf."

"He's prepared to give us a cut."

Stanislav slams his hand down on the table. The sound seems to reverberate around us. I see the color drain from Budimir's face.

But it's not fear I'm sensing from him.

"When did you start turning from opportunity, brother?" Budimir demands furiously.

"It is my prerogative to do as I please," Stanislav replies. "This is my fucking legacy."

Budimir seems to retreat within himself. He says nothing.

"What about the other dons?" I fill in. "What will they have to say?"

"They have all agreed to the exile," Stanislav replies. "None of them want their brand tarnished with this mudak."

"He will not just slink away and disappear."

"No," Stanislav agrees. "He will continue to operate, certainly. But not in my fucking city. Not on my fucking turf. If he comes back to Los Angeles, he knows what's waiting for him."

I can see my uncle's teeth grinding together, but just as swiftly as his anger had come, it's dissipated. "You are right, brother. Forgive me. We do not need zasranec like that staining our territory."

Stanislav nods and leans back, satisfied.

I pick up the file that's sitting on my father's massive table. When I open it, I see the images of all the children who'd landed in Kovar's net.

I see ten-year-old girls in red lipstick and silky negligees. I see their wide, shocked eyes staring into the camera with a hopelessness that's chilling.

I turn the page and see more children. Dead children, stripped and sliced and mutilated so their organs can be resold for a profit.

It's fucking sickening. Even that word doesn't do it justice.

"We don't need his fucking money," I growl.

Budimir's eyes turn to mine. Dark, hooded, searching. His expression is hard to read at first.

And then he nods slowly. He smiles.

"Indeed," he says. "You are your father's son, Artem. His son, through and through."

∽

Had that been the moment—the one when Budimir made his choice?

The memory makes my blood run hot.

Fuck Kovar. Fuck Budimir.

They'll both pay for everything they've done.

And unfortunately for them, "exile" is no longer a word in my vocabulary.

I said it on that mountaintop months ago, when my body was broken and my world shattered:

My name is death now. And death is what I have to offer.

"The other dons might not have been warned about this invite," Maxim suggests. "They won't like it."

"It won't matter," I reply. "The Bratva still controls the entire Western coast. No matter how powerful they may be, their combined strength doesn't come close to the Bratva's."

Maxim nods, acknowledging that I'm right about that.

"Budimir is going to make a show of power," I continue. "He's going to force them to stay silent and fall into line. They may not like it, but they won't directly oppose him."

"Well, then," Maxim says, "it's up to you to give them a choice."

At that, the adrenaline starts to course through my body.

It's gametime.

39

ARTEM

Two quick shots with a silencer takes out the man patrolling the back entrance.

My soldiers catch him before his body even hits the ground. They drag him to a vehicle and throw him into the trunk. A Bratva man takes his place so no one is the wiser.

Just like that, we're in.

I slip into the hotel through the back entrance with my men behind me. I can hear Maxim coordinating with his contingent of soldiers as we find our way to the lobby.

Adrik walks towards me, having already entered the hotel from a separate entrance to avoid unnecessary scrutiny.

"I have the list," Adrik says, passing it over to me.

I scan through it, seeing the names of all the men who were in the Presidential meeting suite on the penthouse floor.

The names include every don who'd been invited, as well as their men.

Per tradition, each don has only two men present. It's an old rule meant to keep anyone from launching a surprise attack against the other dons.

But today, it's their Achilles heel.

Fucking perfect.

I scan further down the list and come across five additional names. I glance at Adrik with a frown. "What's this?"

"The waitstaff," he explains. "Those five have been cleared to be in the room before the meeting officially starts. To serve the wine and food. They'll be cleared out once the meeting gets going."

"That's our in," I say. "Have they gone up yet?"

Adrik smiles. "All five are currently tied up in the staff quarters," he says with obvious satisfaction. "Follow me."

The room Adrik leads us into is secured by two of my men. I walk inside to find the waiters, lying on the floor. They're unconscious, but they've been bound and gagged all the same. Stripped to their underwear, too.

Meaning there are uniforms laid out for five men.

"I want to be in that room with you," Maxim says, stepping forward.

"As do I," Adrik requests immediately.

I nod. "The two of you are with me," I say, before looking around at the rest of my men. "Alexei. Vasyl. You two as well. Get your uniforms on."

We get dressed quickly. When we're all suited up, my men grab the food trolleys and we take the main elevator up to the penthouse floor.

Security is mostly stationed inside the Presidential meeting room. Only two men standing outside the door.

"Move fast," I whisper as we stride down the hall. "We can't make a sound."

Adrik and Maxim walk forward with their heads down. One of the security guards raises his hand.

"Hold on," he barks. "We need to check ID. Make sure you're cleared for entrance."

The moment he looks down at his piece of paper, Adrik and Maxim have both struck. Their dagger-wielding hands swipe across their victim's throats with expert skill, and before either guard can hit the ground, Adrik and Maxim grab them and pull them to the side closet where they deposit the bodies.

I step forward, Vasyl and Alexei flanking me.

"Nicely done," I say. "From here on out, heads down. And don't interact unless you have to. We're free-balling it to the end now."

We enter the room, making sure to let the doors swing closed quickly so that no one notices the sudden lack of security just outside the door.

I slip in behind my four men and dart to the side of the room.

I stay at the very back of the pack, making sure not to make eye contact with anyone as my men move forward, pushing their food trolleys.

The dons are all seated around a table in the center of the suite. I count each one, ticking their names off the list in my head.

Maggadino.

Ambrosino.

Guzik.

Juarez.

Ruwindu.

Bufalino.

That sadistic motherfucker, Kovar.

And lastly, Budimir.

My men circle the room, but no one pays them any attention. That is the beauty of posing as the staff—you become virtually invisible.

Even my uncle's eyes slide right off my face as if he's never seen me before.

I can see a visible fault line between the dons. Budimir sits in the center of the lavish meeting hall, his feeble attempt to conquer the room off to a poor start by the look of things.

On his right sit Maggadino, Ambrosino, Guzik, Juarez and Ruwindu. The legitimate dons. Battle-tested, diplomatic, wise. They look displeased.

On his left sit Bufalino and Kovar. The sewer rats of the underworld. Grinning like rats in a slaughterhouse.

The tension is palpable, but Budimir is projecting an air of calm. I know him well enough to know that it's all a fucking façade.

He's treading on thin ice. He may control the Western coast, but his hold is tenuous at best. He's one turf war away from extinction.

It isn't enough to have power.

You need to hold it, too.

I notice Ruwindu's gaze flicker to Kovar with distaste. He is the youngest of the reigning dons, only a few years older than I am.

The snake tattoo snaking up his arm disappears into his sleeve and reappears at the nape of his neck.

It appears to move as he adjusts in his seat. Like it too is pissed at Kovar's unwelcome presence at a council meeting.

"I'll have some of that champagne," Kovar says, clicking his fingers towards Maxim, completely unaware of who he is.

I've only ever seen pictures of the asshole, but he's bigger and more disgusting in real life. His tattoos are just as ugly, a multitude of unintelligible etchings, heavy on the blood-red.

Maxim comes forward, eyes downcast, and offers him a tray of champagne. Kovar snatches one with a flourish and downs half the glass in seconds.

"What a party!" he crows, clearly aware of the open hostility in the room that's directed at him. "I hated to miss it these last several years."

"You were exiled for a fucking reason," Maggadino intones harshly.

"Not a good reason," Budimir interjects, before Kovar can get a word in. "Kovar should have been included in the council meetings from the beginning."

"Stanislav was threatened by my presence," Kovar replies. "Which is the only reason he convinced you all that I was a menace. Why, I wouldn't hurt a butterfly!"

I grit my teeth, trying to control the rage that roils through me at his words.

"My brothers," Budimir says, standing up. "I invited you all here today to usher in a new era. My brother was a good don, but he was short-sighted. His ambitions were painfully... limited."

Motherfucker.

As Budimir continues to parrot his agenda for a bigger and brighter future, I notice Guzik scanning the room.

He's the most still of all the dons, and yet, his eyes are never stationary. They land on Adrik—and I see recognition pass across his face.

Then his eyes dart to Maxim, and the same thing happens.

Again with Alexei, and with Vasily, until they've crossed over all the waiters. All my men.

Then he looks at me.

Fuck. He knows something is up.

The question now is: what will he do about it?

My next move will depend on his.

"I have bigger aspirations—"

"Budimir," Guzik interrupts, raising his hand slightly. He has at least four jeweled rings adorning his fingers.

My heart is pounding.

If he gives us away, it could all end here, as quickly as it started. I'll be tortured and dumped in the Pacific. Esme will never know what happened to me. My son will never know his father.

All I can do is wait.

"Yes, Guzik?" Budimir says, frowning with annoyance. Clearly, he's not happy about being interrupted.

"Your nephew..." he croons.

I tense. Every muscle on high alert. Watching, watching, watching...

"What about him?"

"You claimed he was dead," Guzik continues. "But we never saw a body."

"Is my word not enough?" Budimir asks.

Guzik shrugs. "I think it's an important symbol," he says. "There are still many among your faction that are loyal to him, no doubt."

Budimir's eyes narrow. "There are none who would follow him over me," he claims. "He's only a boy."

"Some would argue he's the rightful don of the Bratva," Maggadino chimes in.

"I am the rightful fucking don of the Bratva," Budimir roars, raising his voice with venom. "You know why: because I took what I wanted, the way all great dons do. As for Artem... my nephew is dead. And if he isn't, then I will hunt him down and put a bullet in his brain myself."

"So he's not actually dead then?" Guzik presses.

Budimir grits his teeth, realizing he's slipped. "There are reports that claim he might still be at large," he admits. "But it's a small problem. He doesn't have the men or the strength to come against me. The Bratva made a choice after my brother's death. They chose me."

"Did they, though?" I ask loudly.

I step out from the shadows.

A ripple of shock runs through the room, though no one actually speaks. My men part like the Red Sea and I walk between them, approaching the small circle of dons.

Some of them are staring at me with dumbfounded expressions on their faces.

Others look mildly impressed.

But only Budimir looks furious.

"Hello, uncle," I say. "Congratulations on your first dons' council meeting. But you forgot one very important invitation."

He scowls. "I should have made sure you were dead in that forest."

I grin. "But you wanted to make me suffer, remember?" I remind him.

"It's not a mistake I'll make again."

"You won't get the chance to correct it."

Budimir stares at me for a moment and then he laughs coldly. "You think you can take on the might of the Bratva alone?"

"The might of the Bratva?" I echo.

I don't glance at my men—I don't want to risk it—but I can see from my peripheral vision that they're converging around Budimir, positioning themselves so that they can take him down if they have to.

"The Bratva has splintered, whether you realize it or not," I tell him. "You stole their loyalty; you never earned it."

Budimir glares at me, the loathing evident in his filmy eyes. "You sound like your father."

"My father valued his men," I tell him. "He protected them. What he didn't do was threaten them."

I see the flicker of uncertainty pass across his eyes. He's wondering where I've gotten my information and how. He's wondering who he needs to kill.

"I am the rightful don of the Bratva," I announce to the whole room. "And I am claiming what is mine."

"You are a fool," Budimir barks. "Every man in this room answers to me!"

He practically screams the last word and I can start to see my uncle unravel. This is not how he had imagined this meeting going. The disappointment is making him sloppy.

"Each man here is an ally, not a lackey," I reply. "And each man who gives you their loyalty will expect loyalty in return."

"Don't preach to me, you little shit," Budimir snarls. "I command more men than every other man in this room combined, and if asking nicely won't do it, then sheer force will have to suffice."

Maggadino rises ponderously to his feet. He glances towards Budimir and then towards me.

Slowly, one by one, every other don does the same.

"This is not our fight," Maggadino says. "I will not concern myself with this."

He turns and makes for the door. The two guards he had with him follow behind.

The remaining dons seem to realize that they have a decision to make, too.

"Maggadino is right," Ruwindu booms. "This is not my fight."

He makes his exit. Behind him follow Juarez, Guzik, and Ambrosino, and each take their men with them.

Budimir glances towards the two underworld mob bosses to his left.

Kovar and Bufalino.

I know instantly what the two of them will choose. They know that I will be the death of their ambitions, whereas Budimir will grant them free rein and a third of the profits.

They're with him.

That leaves ten men remaining against the five of us. Two against one.

Every man in the room is doing the math in his head. Calculating angles and odds, figuring out which narrow path leads to survival—and to victory.

But not me.

I did all that months ago, up on that frigid mountaintop. Every time I ran until my lungs bled or heaved boulders until I couldn't lift a finger more, I was practicing for this. Preparing for this.

And the answer has not changed.

Everyone moves at once. My men hurl the trolley carts towards the remaining bodyguards and unsheathe their weapons.

Gunfire blasts through the air as Budimir's guards, as well as Kovar's and Bufalino's, jump into the fray.

I hear someone grunt in pain and then I hear a yell, but I don't take my eyes off my uncle, who is standing behind his largest bodyguard.

The fucker hasn't been in a real fight for a long while now. He always shied away from the actual battles. Considered himself above them, like the king who sends his army in while he sits comfortably up in his castle watching the whole thing unfold.

I can sense his panic from here.

Fucking coward.

My only goal is to get as close to him as possible. I want to see the life drain from his fucking face when I do what I came here to do.

I feel the screaming brush of wind next to my ear. I've narrowly missed a bullet aimed at my head, but I don't feel panic or fear.

I never have.

This is what I was born to do.

And if I die, it will be a glorious fucking death.

Except the moment the thought enters my head, I chase it right back out again. This isn't like any other fight I've ever been in.

I can't die. Not this time.

Esme needs me. My son does, too.

So it's not fear that I feel.

It's duty.

I duck low and vault over the sofa that stands between me and the towering bodyguard protecting Budimir.

I fire at him, but he's pushes Budimir to the side and jumps in the opposite direction.

My path towards my uncle is clear, but the bodyguard decides to be a fucking hero. He starts firing, forcing me to take cover.

I'm aware of the sounds of gunfire and fighting behind me, but I can't concentrate on anything other than finishing Budimir once and for all.

If I lose now, my men will certainly die. But if I can just get my hands around his throat, that will end it for everyone. Kovar and Bufalino will scatter to the wind. The Bratva will be back where it belongs.

All I have to do is…

"Fuck!"

I turn around to see Maxim collapse to the ground, blood spurting out of his stomach.

"No!" I yell. I abandon my position and run towards him.

I shoot at the fucker who's standing over him, and he drops before he can finish the job.

The moment I see Maxim, however, I know that it's too late. He's bleeding out too fast, the color already draining from his face.

I get down on my knees beside him anyway. Above us, the gunfire continues in every direction.

"Hold on, brother," I say. "Help's on the way."

He smiles hopelessly, and blood drips from his mouth. "I thought you could lie better than that…"

"Surround them!" I hear Budimir order.

When I look up, I realize that my distraction has given Budimir and his men the upper hand. They've got us surrounded now, and I realize that Alexei is being held at gunpoint and both Adrik and Vasyl are injured, though their injuries look only surface-deep.

When I turn back, Maxim is staring unseeing up at the ceiling.

Rage curdles in my chest like poison.

But it has nowhere to go.

We're pinned. Surrounded. Outgunned, outnumbered, outmaneuvered.

I lose.

Budimir steps out from behind his bodyguard, a cold sneer on his face. His two lackeys, Kovar and Bufalino, flank him.

"Did you really think you could storm the meeting with four men and live to tell the tale?" he demands. "I'm going to make an ornament of your fucking—"

The rest of his threat is drowned by the sound of the main entrance being blown into smithereens.

Everyone ducks down, including Budimir, who seems as stunned as I am at the sudden intrusion.

"Who the—"

Within seconds, the huge space is filled with armed men pouring in, their guns pointing towards all of us.

"Guns down!" the masked man at the head of the pack barks.

Is that a fucking Irish accent?

"Artem Kovalyov," the masked man continues. "Ronan O'Sullivan sends his greetings."

40

ESME

THE PARISIAN CAFÉ AT THE CITADEL OUTLETS

Oh, God.

I can survive anything.

But my baby... someone please protect my baby.

Fear has me paralyzed. My body is hunched over Phoenix as he screams in my ear. Chaos breaks all around me, but the only thing I can hear, apart from my son's panicked screams, is my own heartbeat.

Is my body trembling? It feels that way. But I don't feel connected to my physical self any longer. I feel as though I'm floating.

Floating away from my body.

Away from my son.

"Phoenix," I whisper to him, but my own voice is drowned out by his wailing.

I know that Tamara is close by, but I can't bring myself to look up. I can't bring myself to look up and see the men storming the café.

Once I see them, I'll no longer be able to convince myself that this is just a horrible nightmare.

"Esme...!"

I hear my name. I think Tamara is the one calling to me. I can hear her fear, her uncertainty, but I don't look up. I don't answer back.

Phoenix.

That's the only thought running through my head.

Even if they let me live, they will never spare my son.

He is the heir to the Bratva after Artem. He is as much a threat as his father.

The old uncertainties come roaring back.

Oh, God—why didn't I just stay away?

Why did I come back to L.A.?

My thoughts falter for a moment. And suddenly, a memory comes into high relief.

It's the moment, almost a year ago when I first saw Artem.

Did I know then that he was going to be an important part of my life?

Sometimes, it feels like I did know.

I remember that strange sensation in your gut that stirs anytime you meet someone who leaves a lasting impression.

It was more than just the fact that he was beautiful, handsome, dangerous.

It was the way he looked at me, claiming me with his eyes in a way that made me want to give him everything I had.

I came back to L.A. for him.

For Artem.

Because I love him.

And that's when it hits me. I always assumed freedom and independence was what I craved most in the world.

But I was wrong.

I wanted family.

I wanted a real family, after all those years of living in a broken one.

I came back to L.A. because Artem is my family. Phoenix, Artem and I were a real family. Nothing like the broken shell Cesar and I had been born into.

I have the chance to break the cycle that made me and I took it, knowing all the risks.

There is no turning back now.

"Esme!"

Tamara's anguished scream forces me upright.

She has her hand on my arm, and she's squeezing so hard that I can already feel her fingerprints bruise my skin.

Phoenix is still crying in my arms. We're both speckled with tiny cuts from the explosion of the window.

But we got off easy.

The seats closer to the window took the brunt of the damage. At least a dozen people are slumped over, sliced to ribbons and very much dead.

The men stepping into the café through the glass window they'd just blown apart don't seem the least bit bothered, though.

I clutch my son close to my chest as the soldiers approach, trying desperately to calm him.

"Shut the kid up," someone barks at me.

"He's not a kid," I growl back, surprisingly even myself with my tone. "He's a baby!"

"I know one way to shut him up," someone else suggests acidly.

I feel my body go cold. "Don't you dare come near my son," I snarl.

I look around, trying to catch sight of Gennadi or Alik. They were sitting in the table right next to us... weren't they?

"I suppose you're wondering where your bodyguards are?" one masked man asks, stepping forward.

He's decked out in full blown riot gear, and I can only see his eyes through the black mask that obscures his features.

An uncomfortable itching feeling stirs in my head and I wonder why it's making me feel so... uneasy. More uneasy than I currently was at least.

Why does his voice feel familiar to me?

Like I've heard it before... a lifetime ago?

"Boys," the man calls out mockingly. "Where are the bodyguards?"

The men behind him part to reveal two bodies, stacked one on top of the other. Lifeless limbs thrown carelessly as though they were cargo and nothing more.

The tears that prick at my eyes are immediate. I hadn't known either man long, but they'd been protecting me. They didn't deserve to die this way.

"There's no one left to protect you," the man informs me.

I look around the café. There are still people who are alive, but they're cowering under the tables silently, hoping to escape notice.

I see a few of the waitstaff huddled behind the counter of the restaurant's bar. Surely someone will call the cops. If the police get here, maybe we have a chance.

"No one's coming," the man says, as though he's reading my mind. "We have friends in law enforcement that are happy to look the other way for a little while."

"Bullshit," I snap.

"Oh, don't get me wrong—the cops will get here eventually," he agrees. "But they'll be too late to stop me taking you… and throwing your brat off a fucking bridge."

I won't let him see my fear. I won't let him see my fear. I won't let him see my fear.

I repeat the mantra in my head until it's true. Until I have control of my body, my emotions.

My days of cowering in corners while violent men do their worst to me? Those days are over.

I'm a don's wife now.

"Last time I saw you, that little shit was in your belly," he remarks.

I stare at him, trying to recognize the eyes, but I'm coming up blank.

"Who are you?" I demand.

"Wow! I'm hurt," he gasps sarcastically. "I would have thought you'd remember trying to knock my lights out in that shithole of a diner."

"Sara," I breathe.

"Was that her name?" he asks. "Yeah, she was a sweet piece of ass. Not that I got to taste it."

He shifts, and I see a tiny glimpse of the ink on his throat.

The man with the eagle tattoo.

I shake my head uncomprehendingly. "Why are you here?" I ask. "What do you want with me?"

"Oh, I know exactly what *I* want," he tells me. His tone makes his ideas in that department disgustingly clear. "But unfortunately, my needs will have to wait until after Budimir is done with you."

I knew it.

I had known it all along, and yet the revelation still cuts me like the sharp edge of a dagger.

"You work for him?"

He nods slowly. "He recruited me and my men months back," he tells me. "Of course, your man tried to do the same not long ago. But we'd already chosen our side."

"Then you chose wrong," I tell him with a strength I don't feel.

Tamara's fingers tighten around my arm and only then do I realize that she's still holding on to me.

"Did I now?" he asks, sounding mildly amused.

"We have to go," another masked man says urgently, as he comes up behind Eagle Tattoo.

He ignores his partner completely and keeps his eyes set on me.

"Your man is dead," he says plainly. "And if he's not, he soon will be. Budimir controls all the gangs on the Western coast."

"You don't know my man," I hiss. "Artem Kovalyov will take back what's his. And when he does, he's going to crush every fool who moved against him."

"Is that right?" he chuckles.

"That's a fucking promise."

I can see the deadly smile he's giving me from the crinkle in his eyes. He steps forward so that he's only a foot away from me.

I cringe away from him, holding Phoenix even closer to my chest.

"Here's my promise," he whispers. "Once Budimir is done with you, I'm going to fuck you so hard that you're gonna split right down the middle. And afterwards, you're going to thank me and beg for more."

I spit in his face, "Fuck you."

"Good! I like a little spirit in the sack," he chuckles. "I like a woman who fights back. It makes breaking her all the more entertaining."

My blood is boiling with equal parts fear and anger, but I don't have any means to strike back. Tamara is clutching my arm and Phoenix is still crying loudly against my chest.

Eagle Tattoo straightens up. "Now, let's get the fuck out of here."

He signals to his men. Two of them converge in towards us. I back away immediately, holding on to both Tamara and Phoenix.

"Don't be fucking stupid now," Eagle Tattoo groans. Then he looks towards Tamara. "You can scram. We only want her and the brat. Step aside now."

Tamara does start to move, but she doesn't step aside like she's just been ordered to. She steps forward, putting herself between him and me.

"No," she says.

My heart clenches.

I know how much it takes her to do this. She's terrified, and even if I hadn't heard that fear in her voice, I see it in her trembling body as she stands directly in front of me and Phoenix.

She's standing up for me.

Doing what she should have done months ago.

Atoning for her sins—with bravery and heart and loyalty and love.

Eagle Tattoo glares at her for a moment and sighs deeply.

"Fucking idiot," he growls.

He raises his gun, but before I can so much as scream, he's fired.

Tamara drops to the floor—a gasp forever trapped in her throat.

"No!" I scream, but before I can take a step forward towards her, two men have grabbed me.

They start pulling me towards the door and all I can do is scream and plead and curse at all of them as I clutch my baby and cry for one more innocent life stripped away—because of me.

Just before they push me out the door, I glance behind at Tamara's lifeless body. I see blood pooling around her, but her face is turned down and invisible to me.

"Tamara..." I whisper as I'm forced into a car waiting outside.

I'm sorry.

I don't even know who I'm apologizing to as I look down at my infant son, whose dark eyes are fixed on me with uncertainty.

I'm so, so sorry.

41

ARTEM

THE PRESIDENTIAL SUITE OF THE REGENCY HOTEL

For two seconds, I think we've won.

The Irish came. Ronan and Sinead sent their men to fight on my behalf. They honored their son's sacrifice.

It's over. It's over. We've won.

But Budimir is one second faster than me.

And that's what makes all the difference.

In one motion, he grabs a gun from his bodyguard's holster and pumps two rounds into the huge man's back. Blood erupts and the falling corpse forces the Irishmen to scatter.

Budimir uses the distraction to burst through the doors right behind me.

For the first time in my life, I'm frozen in fear.

He's getting away.

The bastard is getting away.

The fight resumes around me, loud and chaotic and deadly. The Irish are firing at Kovar and Bufalino and their men, who are returning fire even as they drop one by one.

It ends quickly—the Irish far outnumber the rat-faced fucks that Budimir just abandoned.

The last gunshot sounds distinctly ominous, even as it ends the life of that smug bastard, Kovar.

But I don't wait for the satisfaction of seeing the lights fade out from his eyes.

I have to chase down my uncle.

I get to my feet, blood staining my clothes, my hands, and probably my face, too. I can feel the dry crust of battle settle over me like a second skin.

I look around for my men. Maxim is sprawled out next to me, skin pale and cold. The loss weighs heavily on me.

But I have no time to mourn.

I turn and sprint towards the back entrance of the room that Budimir just escaped through.

"Boss!" Adrik's voice is hoarse from exertion. "Where are you going?"

I don't bother replying. I just grab a loose gun from the floor and run faster.

I hear them shouting my name—Adrik, Vasyl and Alexei—but I ignore them all and keep going. Adrenaline is pumping, giving me second wind.

If I let the slippery motherfucker go, I'm not sure I'll get another opportunity.

Little drops of blood mark the path Budimir took. I follow them into the fire escape and start jumping down the stairs, leaping over three, four steps at a time.

I see a fast-moving figure down below and when I lean over the railing, I see Budimir's shadow nearing the ground floor.

He looks up and catches sight of me, his eyes going dark with loathing.

I duck back as he starts shooting up towards me, but the angle doesn't allow for accurate aim.

The bullets cease, just in time for me to hear the fire escape slam shut and I know they're out of the building.

I continue down, rushing as fast as I can until I reach the ground floor myself. A few passing tourists gasp as I burst out into the open.

I know what I probably look like, but I don't fucking care. The only thing I care about now is finding Budimir and pulling the bastard's black heart right out of his chest.

I scan the area for my uncle.

Looking, looking… *there*.

I dart across the street, and I raise my gun to the shrieks and screams of the people walking past. They alert Budimir to my presence, and he darts behind a cement pillar that takes the bullet meant for him.

"Fuck!" I roar.

Budimir jumps into his armored vehicle.

I race forward, ignoring the terrified people fleeing the scene, but I know that I won't be able to get Budimir now.

The car roars out into the street. I jump back, narrowly avoiding being struck.

Then I hear Budimir's voice carry towards me from the open sunroof of the car.

"I'll take good care of your wife and son," he bellows.

Then he's gone.

I stand there as Budimir's words hit me square in the face. It feels as though he's struck me, and suddenly, the pain of my physical wounds disappears underneath the acute fear of what I have yet to lose.

"Fuck!" I yell furiously.

I double back and head back to the Regency's lot, where Adrik and the rest of my men are pulling out, along with the men the O'Sullivans deployed.

I jump into the first car with Adrik.

"Safehouse," I reply. "Now."

I turn in my seat and spy Maxim's body in the back. He would almost look peaceful if it weren't for the sheen of blood that almost completely obscures his features.

I grimace yet again.

Cillian. Maxim. Stanislav.

Too many good men dead because of my uncle. Far, far too many.

"What's his wife's name?" I ask.

"Lena," Adrik answers softly. "He's got two girls."

I catch sight of Luka then. "What the fuck are you doing here?" I demand. "Where the hell is Svetlana?"

"She insisted on staying in the field," Luka tells me. "She told me to tell you that her position hasn't been compromised yet. Budimir had two men assigned to her, and they took her away as soon as the fighting started."

"She went with them?" I ask.

"She did," Luka says. "Don't worry; they didn't see me."

I know this information should leave me feeling like I have the upper hand again, but it doesn't.

He has my wife.

He has my son.

The grim reality of those facts repeat in my head, over and over again, a mantra that has me unravelling.

"Boss—"

"They have Esme," I snap, cutting Adrik off. "They have my son."

Adrik stares at me for a moment and grabs his phone. I know who he's trying to contact, and I also know that no one will pick up.

"Don't bother," I tell him. "Alik and Gennadi are gone."

"It's not too late," Adrik says quickly. "Budimir wouldn't have captured them just to kill them. He's using them as bait."

"I know," I reply, and the tone of my voice silences any further discussion.

The moment we get to the safehouse, I head inside. My weary men follow behind me. They all look tired and uncertain, but my determination has just reached new heights.

I turn, just as Ronan's men file into the safehouse behind us.

"I appreciate the help," I tell the main soldier. "What's your name?"

"Kian," he replies, extending his hand out to me.

"How many men were you sent with?"

"A hundred."

It's impressive, but not even close to the number we'd need to take on the entire Bratva.

Still—it's a hundred more men than we started with.

"What made your boss change his mind?" I ask.

Kian shrugs. "You'll have to ask him that," he says. "I just follow orders."

"What were your orders, exactly?"

"Come here and help you take the Bratva back from your uncle."

I raise my eyebrows. "I haven't done that yet."

"Well, then, I guess we can't go back home until you do," he says with a grin.

I don't let the surprise show on my face, but in essence, Ronan has transferred command of a hundred of his men to me. It's a gesture that tells me a lot.

He never forgot about you, Cillian.

He never stopped thinking of you as his son.

I don't believe in an afterlife or an after-anything. But in this one moment, I actually hope that I'm wrong. That there is such a thing.

If only so that Cillian could know that his family hadn't abandoned him as completely as he'd always believed.

I nod and turn around, so that it's clear I'm speaking to all my men. "We have to move fast," I announce. "And this time, we're pulling no punches. We're going to attack in full force. All our men. We're going to take back my father's compound."

"We're still going to be out numbered," Adrik points out.

"Yes, we are," I agree.

I stand my ground and wait for someone to tell me that I'm insane.

That this plan of mine basically amounts to a suicide mission.

But no one does. Every man in there stays silent.

Some look nervous. Some look resigned. Some look eager.

They all look loyal.

"I know this house," I tell them. "So do many of you. We're going to spend the next two hours planning our method of attack. Then we storm the compound."

I turn towards my office, but halfway there, I glance back over my shoulder.

"Oh, and one more thing," I say. "When we do manage to take the compound, the men who declared loyalty to Budimir are to be given a choice."

"What?" Adrik asks in shock.

I don't hesitate, though. I head into my office and close the door. The door stays closed for maybe five seconds tops, and then it flies open and Adrik enters, along with a handful of my unofficial underbosses.

The last to enter is Kian, but no one asks him to leave, and the door closes behind him.

"You want us to give Budimir's men a choice?" Adrik demands, jumping right into it.

"Yes."

"They fucking betrayed you!" he practically yells.

I stare him down until I see him swallow. "I... I just mean... there should be consequences."

"And there will be," I say. "But the consequence doesn't have to be their lives. I have it on good authority that many of them were threatened into choosing Budimir. Their families' lives were on the line."

"And you believe the source?" Vasyl asks.

I nod.

I can tell Adrik is not happy. A few others don't look convinced of my decision either, but I don't take back my words.

I plan on being a leader who listens to everyone's opinions. Like my father raised me to be, even if I couldn't see the wisdom of that back then.

But there are some issues I cannot and will not compromise on.

Every man deserves a chance to right his path.

"Get the men organized into groups," I say. "I want teams targeting the compound's exterior. Once we get inside, those teams need to turn their firepower outward. We don't want Budimir's allies and reinforcements trapping us on the inside."

"That might happen regardless," Adrik points out.

"We'll see," I reply, confidence bolstering my tone and brooking no argument.

My eyes twitch to the small makeshift bar in the corner of the room. Once upon a time, I would have craved the whiskey. The reassurance of it.

Now, all I see there is weakness in a bottle.

My wife.

My son.

That's where my strength lies now.

"We'll need an extraction team," Luka says. "For…"

"No," I say, cutting him off. "I will extract my wife and son myself. Budimir is going to rue the day he ever thought of taking what was mine."

We spend the next hour making our plans.

I try to not upend the table I'm sitting at. The rage never subsides. I feel like I'm a raw bundle of nerves waiting to explode.

And then my phone rings.

"Fuck," I growl. "Everyone. Out. Now!"

I pick up just as the last few guys clear out and leave me to an empty room.

"Hello?" I answer carefully.

"Artem?"

Svetlana's voice is shaky and slightly nervous. She's speaking low, urgent, her normal hint of flirtation completely gone.

"Where are you?" I ask.

"I'm in the compound," she tells me. "In one of the rooms on the top floor. Don't worry—I'm safe."

"Have you seen Budimir yet?"

"No," Svetlana replies. "I was brought here from the hotel and told to stay in this room. But the place is chaos. Everyone is running around like chickens with their heads cut off."

"Have you heard anything?"

"They have your wife, Artem," she whispers. "And I heard a baby cry, too."

My heart drums so hard that it fucking hurts. The rage galvanizes into purpose.

But there's hope there, too.

Esme is still alive.

Phoenix is still alive.

And as long as they both still draw breath, I have a fucking purpose.

I have a reason to continue fighting.

"I'll do what I can, Artem," she says.

And before I can say another word, the line goes dead.

42

ARTEM

I stride out of the room, and look towards the assembled men.

"Come on," I tell them. We're moving out."

No one says a word. They take one look at my face and start rallying to follow my orders.

Kian approaches me as everyone gears up, his eyes flitting between my men and his.

"How confident are you of taking this compound?" he asks me.

"A hundred percent," I answer.

He raises his eyebrows. "Any chance that math is wrong, mate?" he says with a grim chuckle.

I clap my hand on his shoulder. "You've done more than enough, Kian. You're not under obligation to come with us. I won't lie—I'd gladly take your assistance. But you don't have to be here."

The Irishman meets my gaze calmly. "Our don sent us here to follow you, Artem. And that is what we'll do. Until you've killed that motherfucker who killed Cillian."

I pause, looking at his face with new awareness. He has stark blue eyes and sandy brown hair. The cut of his face is similar to Ronan's but it's not an obvious characteristic.

"Kian," I repeat. "Kian… O'Sullivan?"

He nods grimly. "Cillian's younger brother," he replies. "I was only a boy when he was… when he left."

That means he must be in his early twenties now, but he looks older.

"Your father sent his heir down here for a mission that has a good chance of ending badly?" I ask.

Kian snorts. "He didn't want me coming. I insisted."

I clap my hand against his shoulder again. "Well, I appreciate you coming," I tell him. "I know Cillian would have, too."

Kian nods. I can tell he's ready to get going.

So am I.

"Move out!" I yell.

My men and I head out towards the line of cars that are driving up now to collect the various teams.

The drive to the compound is laced with an underlying tension, but there's also a certain muted fervor. I look around at my men, knowing that I have their loyalty and they have mine.

It's the strongest weapon we have against Budimir.

When we approach the compound, I see a lone guard on the lookout post. He looks sweaty and unprepared and I realize that Svetlana's intel was sound.

I've thrown a spanner in the works and Budimir is scrambling to get his shit together.

I don't intend to give him much time to rally his men.

This is the perfect time to strike.

"Drive through the gate," I order Adrik.

Adrik smiles and relays the command into his walkie-talkie. I see a second armored jeep drive up next to us.

A second later, both vehicles accelerate simultaneously and we race towards the black gate that closes off Stanislav's compound.

The man at the post starts shooting useless rounds that bounce off of the reinforced windshield.

"Brace!" I command my men.

The combined force of both jeeps crash into the black gate. It thunders apart.

And we're in.

A handful of Budimir's men wait out on the lawn, guns in hand. They scatter as we plow forward, attempting to take cover.

My men roll down their windows and start firing.

We mow them down ruthlessly.

But I can see more troops amassing in the distance, near the garage where all my father's prized vehicles were once housed.

We screech to a halt in the main front courtyard.

The moment we're at the steps that lead up to the massive mansion, I signal to my men to get down.

I'm the first one out of the jeep.

I scale the steps three at a time until I'm the front door. Just before I reach them, the doors fly open and I'm faced with four armed soldiers.

Four against one—truly unfair odds.

For them.

I feint to the side and shoot twice. I hit both my targets and they drop to the floor instantly with new holes in their foreheads.

I stab the third in the throat and shove him into the fourth, then fire another pair of rounds into each of them.

The whole thing takes less than ten seconds.

I lead the charge into the mansion. My men fill in behind me, their weapons drawn and their faces alert.

"Fan out," I signal to them.

I know that more men will soon be coming from every direction of the mansion, but I'm calm. Calmer than I've been since this day started.

Adrik roars and points up. More men on the balcony overhead.

"Take cover," I yell, just as they open fire.

The soldier in front of me takes the brunt of the opening salvo and goes limp against me. I drag him to the side and jump for cover behind a large pillar. Two more of my men go down, and I catch a glimpse of Kian take deadly aim at one of the shooters.

He's got talent, I realize in seeing him fight that he moves like Cillian.

"Hold your fire!" someone roars.

Frowning, I reload and glance out from the pillar.

The voice that's silenced the shooting appears on the staircase.

He has a gun in hand, but both hands are raised up in surrender.

It's Anton Yahontov.

I step out from behind the pillar, only a little so that my body still has coverage but I can be seen.

"Yahontov," I breathe.

"Coming back to L.A. was a mistake," he tells me. "He has spies everywhere. Until then, he thought you were dead."

"I wasn't planning on staying dead forever."

"Yahontov," one of the armed soldiers snarls, coming forward. "What the fuck are you doing?"

"Warning him," he replies. "And now he's been warned. We have you surrounded, Artem. It's time to put your guns down."

But as he talks, I notice some of the soldiers at his back move imperceptibly. They slip behind their own men.

I sense in my gut what's about to happen.

Fuck, I hope I'm right.

I don't turn my eyes away. Just wait patiently. There's a signal coming—I just don't know what it is.

"It's time to give up," Yahontov intones.

And apparently, that's the sign.

Half of Budimir's men turn on the other half.

And they fire.

It's brutal and sudden and quick.

It's not a fight. It's an execution.

Just like that, probably two dozen of Budimir's men drop to the ground.

"Fuck," I hear Adrik say. "What the fuck was that?"

I smile, stepping over a body as I walk towards Yahontov. I offer him my arm and he takes it.

"There is a contingent of men upstairs with Budimir," Yahontov says. "About twenty, I'd say."

"He's here?" I say, my jaw setting with new excitement.

"He's here and hiding," Yahontov nods. "But he also has—"

"Your *wife*," a sickeningly familiar voice snarls from the top of the staircase.

Before anyone can react, more gunfire lets loose. This time, it's not good for us.

Yahontov's men on the balcony go down in a hail of bullets.

The odds tilt back in Budimir's favor.

And suddenly, our position starts looking a little grimmer.

43

ESME

THE KOVALYOV FAMILY COMPOUND—LOS ANGELES, CALIFORNIA

"Stop fucking struggling, you little bitch!" the guard snarls at me. His hand is wrapped around my forearm in a vise-grip that I can't shake.

Phoenix is struggling in my arms. He's been crying for so long that I'm starting to get worried by the color in his cheeks.

All through the chaos at the café, the car ride here, the rough drag up the steps and into this mansion, he's been crying.

I don't blame him.

I feel like crying, too.

"My baby!" I say desperately. "He's scared."

"He's a baby," the idiot replies. "He doesn't know shit."

Then he shoves me into a large room off the hallway, follows me in, and slams the door behind me.

Phoenix throws his little fists in the air and screams with indignation as I stumble through into the room. I collapse into the first chair I see and press my son against my chest, trying to shush him, calm him, soothe him.

As I do, I glance around at the windows. They're all either out of reach or barred outside with iron. No chance of escaping through there.

"Why am I being held here?" I demand.

I'm a lot more confident now that Eagle Tattoo is not here. He disappeared right after we arrived on the compound.

It's a sprawling estate that reminds me of Papa's in terms of size, if nothing else. Papa's was white and linen and beachy—this place is dark, stone, foreboding.

Well, actually, they're similar in another way—both places are impenetrable fortresses.

But Artem knows this place.

He'll find us.

He'll save us.

I say that to myself again and again. I whisper it to Phoenix, too, and it seems to help somehow.

But doubt has planted itself inside my chest and made it difficult for me to breathe.

I glance at the guard who's ushered me in here.

Maybe I can take him.

It's just me and him…

If I hit him with something hard…

I may have a chance to escape.

But the idea of putting Phoenix down to take such a reckless gamble makes me want to gag.

And, seconds later, the choice is removed from my hands when the door opens and three more guards stride into the room.

They surround me. More men trying to intimidate me into silent submission. It's been that way my whole life.

I'm fucking sick of it.

I ignore all of them and look down at my son.

I'm trying to be as calm as possible, because Phoenix is clearly reacting to the panic that's wafting off of me.

But the fear of what the next few hours might hold is overwhelming.

"Well, gotta say, I heard she was pretty," one guard says. "But didn't realize how pretty."

"Put your dick back in your pants, Cena," another guy retorts. "She's off limits."

"Says who?"

"Someone has to say so? Budimir will cut off our fucking cocks if we touch her."

"Yeah, sure, he will—if we touch her *before* he does. He won't have a problem with what we do to her after."

I sit there, and for the first time since I've left my father's compound, I feel truly and completely invisible.

I am reduced back down to an object.

A thing to be used and discarded as it suits the whims of the men I'm surrounded by.

Even in the darkest days of our relationship, Artem had never treated me like an object or an ornament.

"Bet she has a nice, tight pussy."

"Are you kidding me? Look at that little shit in her arms. He's probably stretched her the fuck out."

"Yeah, I hear pussy bounces back fast."

"Fuck you all." The words leave my mouth before I can think twice about them.

But even after they're out, I realize I don't regret saying them. Not even a bit.

I've taken enough shit from the cruel and ugly men in this underworld. I won't do it anymore.

I look up and meet the gaze of all four men that surround me. Defiant. Proud. If I'm going to die here today, that's how I want to do it.

"What did you say, bitch?" one of the men rasps in shock and anger.

I frown, realizing that he's probably only a year or two older than I am. He's so fucking young and it makes me sad.

So young, and yet he's already twisted. Already broken. Already stained.

"I said, *Fuck. You*," I enunciate. My words come out with jagged edges.

And fuck, it feels good to fight back.

Phoenix starts crying right on cue, and all four men wince away as though the sounds is actually hurting their ears.

"Shut him up."

"He's a *baby*." I glare back at them. "All he knows is what he can feel and he feels unsafe. Please, just… find your humanity and let me go."

They look at each other in disbelief, like the concept of "humanity" was utterly foreign.

One guy turns to me. He's got blonde hair and dark eyes and a face that might have been beautiful if it hadn't been so filled with contempt.

"And what do you think will happen to us if we do that?" he asks in complete sincerity. "You think Budimir will let us live?"

"He's just a baby," I say, feeling my anguish clog up my throat. "What has he got planned for my baby?"

"I wouldn't worry about the kid," he replies. "I'd worry about yourself."

"I don't care what happens to me."

"You will when his cock is jammed down your throat."

I set my jaw and look him right in the eye. "I hope he does. Because I bite."

A twinkle sparks in his eyes and he smiles at me as though I've just won his respect.

"Now that's something I'd pay to see," he chuckles.

"Let me go," I plead. "Please."

"Maybe I will," he says, leaning in closer.

There's an encouraging spark in his eyes. Like, maybe "finding his humanity" isn't such a reach after all…

Then he finishes, "If you blow me right now and promise not to bite."

Any hope I had dies instantly.

He won't let me go, no matter what I do for him.

None of them will risk their necks to save mine, or my son's.

We're on our own.

Except for Artem.

His name reverberates around inside my head like a prayer, but I can't bring myself to really think about him.

What if I never see him again?

The thought scares me more than anything else has. Next to the fear I have for my son and what will happen to him.

"Well…" the blonde soldier says, leaning in and running his nose along my cheek. "What do you say? I promise I have a delicious cock. You'll love sucking it."

I slap his hand away as I stare daggers at him. Phoenix has just quieted down, but I can hear him start to whimper again, as though sensing that something is wrong.

"In your fucking dreams."

"Bitch!" he snarls at me. "I'm gonna teach you some respect."

He grabs a fistful of my hair and I gasp with pain as he twists my head back, forcing me to look up at his face.

Phoenix squirms and grasps at my shirt with shuddering cries as he prepares to scream.

"Please," I say, even though the word hurts as it exits my mouth. "Please don't."

I cannot allow him to hurt me with my son in my arms. Holding onto my pride could cost my son everything. He is so helpless, so dependent on me for his safety.

So even though I hate myself for doing it—I have to beg for mercy.

"Say you're sorry," he orders.

I just stare at him, wondering if there's any chance of me getting out of this unscathed.

It strikes me all of a sudden: I can leave with physical scars or with emotional ones.

I can leave with my son or without.

That's the choice.

The answer seems simple when I think of it that way.

"I'm sorry," I whimper immediately, and the words don't hurt so much because the reason why I concede and say them at all is in my arms right now.

"I can't hear you," he seethes in my face.

He's still holding my hair tight and I cringe against the pain. It feels like, if he pulls a little harder, he'll tear off my scalp right along with my hair.

"I'm sorry," I repeat. Tears of pain blossom in the corners of my eyes.

But he's not done.

"Do you like my face?" he muses, taking advantage of my new meekness.

I can barely hear him over Phoenix's screaming.

"Shush, little bird," I say to my son, rocking back and forth in the chair. "Cálmate. It's okay, it's okay…"

"Shut him the fuck up!" the blonde guard screams at me.

A tear falls down my cheek and lands right on Phoenix's. He hiccups suddenly and looks at me with wide eyes as though shocked about the sensation of water on his cheek.

"I'm sorry, little bird," I say to him. "I'm so sorry…"

I rock him back and forth even as the blonde soldier releases my hair for a moment.

I cringe down, but I don't look at him.

I know what's coming.

He grabs my hair again, but this time, he just wants clear access to my face. When he has it, he backhands me hard across the cheek.

Knuckle cracks against jaw.

My vision dissolves into flecks of white light like falling snow.

He rears back to swing again—when the door opens.

And the violence in the air suddenly shifts. The guard freezes, releases me. My vision starts to piece itself back together bit by bit.

I hear a voice. "What the fuck do you think you're doing?"

Oh, no.

Oh, no.

Oh, no.

I thought I was saved.

I was so, so wrong.

When my sight finally resolves, I find myself looking at Eagle Tattoo's broad, mashed-up face.

He's not looking back at me, though. His fury is directed at the blonde man standing between us.

"I… I was teaching the bitch a lesson," the guard tries to explain, but his tone falters.

"She's not your bitch to teach," Eagle Tattoo rumbles. "Now get out. The lot of you."

The men hesitate and Eagle Tattoo glowers furiously at them.

"Get the fuck out of here before I blow your brains out!" he bellows. "My orders have come from Budimir himself."

There's only a moment's hesitation before all four men exit the room. When the door snaps closed, Eagle Tattoo walks over to me, his eyes roving from my face to my breasts.

"Did he touch you?" he asks. He almost sounds concerned.

"He slapped me."

"Did he try to rape you?" he asks.

I still, feeling a sense of dread overtake me. This is not an innocent line of questioning. Not by any means.

"Answer me."

"He tried to convince me to have sex with him," I say softly.

"Well, who can blame him?" Eagle Tattoo smiles, and for a moment it actually feels like he's trying to flirt with me. "Artem's a lucky motherfucker. No wonder he got you pregnant so fast."

I look down at Phoenix, who's whimpering a little in my arms, but he's stopped crying. It's almost as though he realizes that crying won't help us now.

"Please," I say. "Please, just let me and my son go."

He laughs. "I thought you were smarter than that."

"He's only a baby."

"Exactly," he agrees. "He's only been in your life a short time."

Those words send my mind into new echelons of panic. I grip Phoenix a little tighter.

"My husband—"

"Your husband is dead," he snaps. "There's no one left to rescue you. It's just you and the boss. But before that… it's just you and me."

I can sense where he's leading me. My body seems to resign itself to the inevitability to what's about to happen.

I can feel it giving way—giving up hope, giving up the fight.

I have escaped this horror countless times now. Artem saved me once.

Will he be here to save me again?

I can't believe he's dead. But even so, it feels like there's no way out.

And a part of me no longer cares. Because I know now that I will endure anything—if it means my son will be safe.

"I'll do whatever you want," I say suddenly. "And I'll do it willingly. Just please... don't hurt my son."

Do I believe my own words? In the moment, they feel sincere, but I'm not sure anymore.

I don't feel like myself. I feel like a trapped and desperate woman who will try anything to save her son.

That is exactly what I am.

That is all I am.

"Oh?" Eagle Tattoo asks. "Is that right?"

"Yes."

"You'll do whatever I want?" he asks again.

"Yes."

"You'll get naked and suck my cock?"

"If that's what you want," I whisper, my voice as deadpan as my face.

"You'll spread your legs for me?"

"If that's what you want."

"You'll take it in the ass?"

"If that's what you want."

He stares at my expressionless face. I can tell he's annoyed, but I cannot give him any more concessions. If he's expecting me make a show of enjoying my own rape, then that's one line too far.

"But you can't hurt my son."

"Put him down over there," Eagle Tattoo tells me. "I'm not fucking you with that brat in your arms."

I stand up immediately and walk over to the largest sofa in the room. It's soft and cushy and I settle Phoenix into the ample cushion. Then I put a cushion on the open side of the sofa just to secure him.

I know I don't have to worry—he's still too young to roll—but I do it anyway.

I feel numb. That feeling scares me more than anything else. Am I really going to lie down and let him rape me?

Yes.

Yes you are, if it means you can protect Phoenix.

There's pride in this. There's dignity in this, even if it seems like both are long gone.

Save your son. Save your little bird.

I draw in a deep, shuddering breath and steel myself against the horrors that await me.

And I make a promise to myself, to Artem, to Phoenix: no matter what happens, I won't cry. I refuse to shed a single tear here.

"Hurry the fuck up," Eagle Tattoo orders me.

The sound of his voice has my skin crawling with disgust and new rage.

And the reality of my situation settles over me like a cold shower.

"You're strong Esme," Cesar says, his voice clear as a bell in my head. "You were always so much stronger than me. Don't take this sitting down."

"I'm alone, Cesar."

"No, you're not. You have me."

"You left me a long time ago."

"Then who are you talking to right now?"

"Myself. Just myself."

"Yeah? Then maybe you should listen to yourself. You are a fucking warrior, and it's about time you owned it. If you want to be a don's wife, you have to act like a don's wife."

"Come here."

The monster grabs my arm and pulls me to him. My body slams against his chest and I realize just how big he is, just how strong he is.

I can also feel his erection against my thigh and I have to bite down on my tongue to keep from gagging right in his fucking face.

No matter how determined I am to fight back, there's no getting around the fact that he's bigger than me. Stronger than me. More trained, more capable than me.

The one thing he's not is more desperate.

I glance around as he slides his tongue along the curve of my neck.

There are several objects I can use as weapons, but I need to get my hands on them first.

"The table," I say.

"What?" he asks distractedly.

"Let's go to the table over there. I don't want Phoenix seeing this."

He rolls his eyes but he wrenches me towards the table so hard it feels as though he's trying to pull my hand right out of the socket.

My eyes stay fixed on the giant candlestand in the center of the table.

Eagle Tattoo pushes me back against the table in the same way and starts undoing the zip on my jeans. He's so absorbed with his task that he doesn't see me reach for the candlestand.

He doesn't see me cock it back.

He doesn't see me grit my teeth, summon all the strength in my body, and bring it crashing down over his head.

Or at least, that's what I planned.

But he looks up at the very last second, sees what's happening, and pivots enough.

Just enough.

Instead of cracking open his skull like I did in that little diner in Mexico, this time, all I do is catch him on the shoulder.

He grunts in pain.

His face turns dark.

And he wrenches the candlestand out of my hands and flings it across the room.

In the same motion, he pins my wrist against the tabletop and leans all his weight on it so hard I cry out.

"You fucking bitch!" he roars in my face, his skin tuning an ugly hue of red. "You fucking whore! I was gonna be gentle with you, but now I'm going to rip you in half."

He slaps me across the face.

But I keep struggling. I keep fighting.

Because I understand something about myself in this moment.

I am not the type of person who will just lie down and take it.

I am not the type of person who will accept their fate and concede to it.

I will fight so long as there is breath left in my body.

I fend off his hold just enough to release my left hand from his grip. Then I claw at his face, and my nails dig into his flesh.

He growls in pain. When he looks at me again, I can see that I've left my mark.

It looks like a feral animal has clawed him, leaving fresh red streaks of blood along his face.

Then my eyes find his and I know that I've crossed the line and pushed him over the edge.

I can see murder in his eyes.

Oh, God... he's going to kill me in front of my son.

The scream is tunneling its way out of my throat when I see something move just behind the massive man. He seems to notice we're not alone at the same time.

But he's too slow. Too preoccupied.

So I see the shiny dagger's blade, but he doesn't.

He doesn't even see the knife before it slashes across his throat. It cuts through his flesh like butter, drenching me in a spray of blood.

And then he slumps to the ground, gurgling his way to death.

I blink away the droplets of blood and push myself off the table.

The person holding the knife killed the man who came to hurt me.

But what does she want?

44

ESME

The woman standing in front of me looks like an apparition for a moment. She's tall, brunette, and beautiful.

"Are you okay?" the woman asks, glancing back at Phoenix, who coos softly on the sofa.

I stumble forward to make sure he's okay, but I don't make a move to touch him yet. I don't want that beast's blood anywhere near my son.

"Esme?"

I turn when she says my name. "I... are you real?" I ask stupidly.

Her expression flushes with concern and she moves closer to me, pulling off the soft overcoat she's wearing. Underneath, she has on a figure-hugging black dress that emphasizes her hourglass shape.

She moves forward and puts the coat over my shoulders.

"You're shivering," she tells me. "My name is Svetlana."

Svetlana...

Why does that name sound so familiar?

Then it hits me all at once.

"You're with Artem," I say. "You... you're helping to bring down Budimir?"

"Yes," she says, looking relieved that she doesn't have to explain it to me. "I am."

"What are you doing here?"

"I was at the hotel when the fighting started," she tells me. "Artem attacked Budimir's council meeting."

I shake my head. "What... I thought that wasn't until later?"

"Budimir moved it up and Artem decided to act fast," she tells me. "I was brought here from the Regency and I heard the guards talking about you..."

"Where are they now?" I ask, terrified that someone would walk in and kill us both.

"Artem has just stormed the compound with his men," Svetlana tells me. "It's chaos out there. Budimir has barricaded himself in one of the rooms downstairs."

Relief floods through me immediately, but Svetlana notices my expression and shakes her head. "Esme, we don't know who will win this fight."

"But—"

"Artem is still outnumbered," she tells me. "And Budimir fights dirty. Not to mention the fact that he has you."

"But... we can leave now," I say desperately. "We can get out—"

"We can't just walk out of here, Esme," Svetlana tells me, grabbing my hand. "Budimir's men are still all over the place."

I close my eyes for a moment and try to breathe. "What do we do?"

"I was only able to get in here because the soldiers guarding this room were called away to protect the entrance," she tells me. "But now we have a dead man in here with you and me. It won't take a rocket scientist to figure out what's happened."

"Who saw you come in here?" I ask urgently.

"No one," she replies. "I'm not watched like you are."

"Okay," I say. "Well—"

Before I can finish my sentence, I hear the sound of gunfire and I freeze. It doesn't sound like it's right around the corner, but it doesn't sound very far either.

Svetlana turns her gaze to the door as well and I can sense her nerves as well. Still, her expression remains calm, almost impassive, as she turns to me.

"Wait here," she instructs.

"W... where are you going?" I ask, grabbing her without meaning to.

She doesn't flinch. Instead, she puts her hand on mine and squeezes it with reassurance. "Don't worry. I just want to see what the situation is like out there."

"What if someone sees you?"

"This isn't my first day on the job," she says with a wink.

Then she walks towards the door and slips out of it. I stand there in the room, feeling my heart thud against my chest so hard that my ribcage actually hurts.

It's all in my head.

It's all in my head.

I try and calm myself down as I get to my knees in front of my son. There's flecks of blood on my hands, but I wipe it away on the cushions of the sofa and focus on Phoenix.

He looks a little calmer, but his eyes are wide open, staring this way and that, as if waiting for something to happen.

"It's okay, little bird," I say. "I've got you. It's all gonna be okay."

I hear the door open a moment later, and Svetlana slips back into the room. Her expression is carefully orchestrated, but I can tell that she's worried.

"What's going on?" I ask.

"Artem is in the building," she tells me. "Budimir's men have him surrounded."

"A standoff?"

"It looks like it, but from my point of view, it looked evenly matched," Svetlana says. "I… I think you're going to be the bargaining chip."

Of course I am.

Svetlana comes forward. "Esme, I think they're going to come and get you soon."

"No!" I gasp. "I have to get Phoenix out of here."

Svetlana glances towards my son and I see her eyes soften with worry. "All the men are out at the front of the house. Every man is involved in the fight against Artem's men. There might be a chance to get you out of here without being seen. But we'll have to move fast."

"No."

"No?" Svetlana looks at me as though I've gone mad.

"I can't leave," I explain. "Artem is here. My husband is here. I can't leave him. They're coming for me, Svetlana. I can do something. I don't know what yet, but I can do *something*."

"But your son…" Svetlana objects, looking between him and me.

"Will you take him for me?" I ask. "There's enough confusion in the house. You can take him and get out. Or barricade yourself in a room somewhere. Just keep him safe for me."

"Esme—"

"Please," I say. "I don't want him near the violence. And if he's with me when they come for me, they'll take him, too. They'll use him as bait."

I see Svetlana's jaw twitch uncomfortably as she looks at my son. Then she nods slowly.

"Okay," she says. "First thing's first, we can't let them see you like this. You've got blood on your face."

She takes her coat off my shoulders and wipes me down with it. The soft cashmere grazes over my skin and removes the blood that marks me.

"There," she says. "There's still some on your clothes but not enough to be immediately noticeable."

I'm aware that I still feel very numb, but the feeling is slowly itching back into my extremities, filling me with a new sense of urgency.

"You'll have to help me move him," Svetlana says, glancing at eagle tattoo, who's sprawling across the floor, face down.

I nod, steeling myself, as I reach down to grab his ankles while Svetlana takes his arms. Even with our combined strength, his dead weight almost has my knees buckling. But I draw strength from my son and I keep going.

We push him behind the sofa and Svetlana makes sure he can't be seen from the front of the room. She takes the dagger that she used to kill Eagle Tattoo and wipes it off on his shirt.

Then she walks around the sofa and hands it to me, hilt pointed towards me.

"Make sure it's concealed," she says. "And if you get an opportunity to strike—"

"I'll take it," I say without hesitation.

For the first time since she's walked into the room, she smiles. "All right then," she says. "I'm going to leave before they find me in here with you."

I grab her hands before she turns away from me.

"Thank you."

And again, I think about the mantra that has followed me through the last few months of our lives.

I have survived on the kindness of strangers.

Svetlana nods slowly. "Do me a favor," she says, "and survive."

"Do *me* a favor," I echo, "and protect my son."

She nods solemnly. I turn and pick Phoenix up off the sofa. I hold him for a moment, but I don't let myself linger.

I can't prolong this. I don't have the luxury of a goodbye right now.

Nor do I really want one.

This is not the end.

I lean in and whisper in his ear, "Be safe, little bird."

Then I hand him over to Svetlana, who takes him gently, hooking one arm under his small body to secure him against her chest.

"Good luck, Esme," she says.

Then she walks out the door with my child.

The moment the door closes behind her, I feel loneliness engulf me. I feel my fear more acutely than ever before.

But I don't give in to the shivers clawing through my body.

I can't falter.

I start pacing and I make it only three steps before I hear the sound of approaching footsteps… running footsteps.

I conceal the dagger in my jeans and stand to face the door just as it bursts open.

I'm hoping to see Artem, but I see two armed guards instead. Their faces are tinged with sweat and panic.

One guard gestures to me. "Come with us."

They don't have control of the situation, and I can see that immediately. Neither one even seems to notice that I'm apparently in this room alone and unguarded.

They just nudge me forward with their guns. These cruel men are worried. Terrified, really. Fearful of their lives.

And that makes me hopeful about mine.

45

ARTEM

There's a second in which everything moves in slow motion.

I see Budimir standing in the shadows, well out of the range of fire.

I see his men move forward, decked out in full riot gear, looking like black beasts ready to feast on the dead.

I see his proud sneer as his loyalists shoot down the men who have just betrayed him.

Someone tries to shoot at Yahontov, or maybe they're aiming for me, but I manage to push him out of the way.

The two of us duck for cover, but it takes only a moment before my men are firing back with equal vigor.

"Enough!" Budimir screams, and I can hear the suppressed rage in his voice. "Artem Kovalyov!"

Budimir's voice pierces through even the gunfire, but my men don't stop shooting. I know they won't until I give the command.

"Get your men to stand down," Budimir yells loudly, realizing the same thing. "Or your wife will die."

The rage is thick in my veins, but I give the order immediately. "Hold!"

The moment the shooting stops, the silence feels resounding. Ominous.

I step out from behind the pillar and watch as Budimir descends the staircase, behind at least ten of his armored soldiers.

It doesn't exactly project an image of strength, but I know Budimir well enough to know that he would never risk his own safety for a symbolic gesture.

I move to the center of the room.

Budimir halts in front of me, several feet away. My men slowly converge around me, but their guns are still cocked and ready.

"If any of your men open fire," Budimir says darkly, "I will slit your son's throat and rip your wife open from throat to pussy. You understand me?"

I don't reply. I just stare at the motherfucker, until Budimir bares his teeth.

"You fool," he snarls, shaking his head. "Why didn't you just stay dead?"

"How could I?" I ask. "After you stole my father's legacy and his life?"

"*Now* you care about Stanislav?" Budimir asks. "You were never interested in his legacy, Artem. You were never interested in anything but yourself."

"That's true of the man I used to be," I acknowledge. "I've made a lot of mistakes in the past. I'm looking to correct that now."

"By taking back what you think is yours?" Budimir asks.

I know what the bastard is doing. He's stalling for time, trying to draw out the inevitable with this pointless fucking conversation.

And I'm forced to go along with it because he has the upper hand right now.

He has my wife.

He has my son.

"The Bratva *is* mine," I growl at him. "And yes, I will take it back. When I do, you will be the first to die."

"It's between you and me now, nephew," he says. "You really think my men will follow you?"

"Some will," I reply confidently. "Some won't. Everyone has a choice."

"You do, too," Budimir offers. "And it's a simple one. Walk away or stay and fight."

I grin. "You really expect me to believe that if I choose to walk away now, you'll just let me go?"

He shrugs. "I won't let you go. You already know that," he says. "But I might be convinced to spare your wife. Your son."

I stiffen imperceptibly. "How fucking stupid do you think I am?" I demand. "The moment I'm dead, you'll kill my son."

"On the contrary," Budimir says. "I will give him the Bratva."

I frown. "What?"

"I have no children of my own," he tells me. "Nor will I. Someone has to take the Bratva one day, and even I can't live forever."

I clench and re-clench my gun. I don't like where this is going.

"I will raise your son, and when the time comes, I will hand over the reins to him. So you see, Artem—I am not an unreasonable man. Nor am I a petty man. Your son will one day be the next don," Budimir concludes. "*If* you choose correctly."

I find myself pausing, taking a moment to weight the pros and cons of his offer.

I believe that he's serious. Budimir doesn't have children, and he needs a successor. There's a certain fucked-up logic to it all.

"Well, Artem?" Budimir says. I can see the smirk playing on his lips.

He knows that I have to consider the option. Maybe he even believes I will take him up on it.

I glance around at my men, but their faces are impassive, unreadable.

If I'm dead, they will be forced to pledge their fealty to Budimir.

"Are you really considering this?"

Kian is the one who spoke. I look towards him as he steps forward, his gun raised in anger.

I hold up my hand, and he stops, but he's not pleased about it. I see the same stubbornness in his face that I saw in Cillian's for so many years. It hardens my resolve.

I know what I came here to do.

"You bought yourself mercenaries, Artem?" Budimir asks, mild surprise coloring his tone. "I never would have believed it."

"Fuck you," Kian spits. "We're not fucking mercenaries."

Budimir's expression sours. "Hmm, I suppose not," he replies. "No one would willingly choose Ireland for fighting men."

"You murdered my brother."

"I've murdered a lot of men," Budimir replies without a shred of remorse.

Then he stops for a moment. His eyes search Kian's face.

"Wait. Can this be... Cillian's brother?" Budimir turns to me. "Well, well... You really did go groveling to the Irish," he infers, clearly amused. "Nothing is beneath you, it seems."

I snap my jaw shut, realizing in this moment that I can't possibly take Budimir's offer, no matter how good of an offer it might be.

My son's life is worth everything to me.

But what Budimir is offering Phoenix is not survival. It's a living hell.

My uncle is nothing more than a bully and a monster. He will mold my son in his image and keep Esme and Phoenix apart.

It is not the life Esme wants for herself or for our child.

It's not the life I intend for us to have.

"I did what I had to do," I reply. "For my family."

Budimir's eyes narrow at me but he holds his tongue just as one of his men appears at the balcony. He steps aside to let two armed guards walk forward. And between them...

"Esme."

Her eyes find mine and it's as if she's heard my whisper. She looks scared. But there's also a certain conviction in her posture, in her gold eyes that helps calm me.

My queen is okay.

But where's Phoenix?

That's the first thought that pops into my head after I've reassured myself that Esme looks fine. Physically, at least.

I meet her eyes again, but she looks away this time, as though she's scared to give something away.

"Bring her down," Budimir commands. "I'm sure Artem wants a better last look at his wife."

Esme strides down the staircase with both of Budimir's men flanking her. She walks stiffly, her back arched straight, her hands barely moving.

The closer she gets, the more I can see the signs of struggle in her appearance. Her clothes have been torn in places, and there's a smattering of blood splayed across her blouse.

Worst of all, there's a trapped look in her eyes that I hate seeing.

Like she's back in a cage she thought she'd left for good.

I step forward instinctively.

"Nuh-uh," Budimir reprimands, shaking a finger at me. "You can look, but you can't touch."

"Fuck you!" I practically yell, my rage bursting free through clenched teeth.

"Careful now," my uncle warns me. "Or I might stop being so nice. Do you really want to watch the life drain from your wife's face while you stand there and watch?"

The guards come to a stop a few feet away from Budimir. There's about four long strides between my uncle and Esme.

Too fucking close for my liking.

I turn my gaze towards Budimir. "You're the one who should be careful," I tell him. "Because I'm going to make you pay for what you've done."

He cocks his head to the side. "Does that mean you're rejecting my offer?"

I glance towards Kian, and then towards Esme.

"You can take your offer and shove it up your ass, traitor."

Budimir clenches his jaw for a moment. His eyes churn, calculating his next move.

He's nervous about a full-blown battle. He doesn't want to risk losing. Nor does he want to risk his own life in the process.

That's always what mattered most to him.

"Maybe we should ask your pretty little wife for her opinion," Budimir suggests. "Considering we're discussing the future of her son, too."

Esme looks towards me with confusion, but I already know what she's going to say.

I know my wife. This is just another one of Budimir's mind games.

"Go ahead," I say with a shrug. "Ask her."

"Are you so sure of her response?"

"I don't have a single doubt."

Budimir's smile is less convincing this time. He looks towards Esme. She freezes instinctively, her body cringing back as she's forced to meet his eye.

"I've given your husband two choices," he tells her amicably. "He's overpowered, in men and in strength, but I've decided to be generous."

She doesn't move a muscle.

Budimir continues, "His choice is simple: give up his claim to the Bratva and surrender his son to my custody. I will raise the boy myself, give him all the perks and luxuries of a don's son and when the time comes, he will take over the mantel of don."

It strikes me that Esme listens to all of this without much of a reaction. Her eyes widen for only a moment before she seems to get a hold of herself.

"What will happen to me?" Esme asks, after a moment's pause.

I hadn't expected her to ask questions, but I wonder if she's trying to buy time, too.

"You will have a choice just the same," Budimir says with a sickly-sweet smile that I don't trust at all. "You can stay with your son on this compound as my concubine."

"And Artem?" she asks without blinking.

Budimir raises his eyebrows. "Artem cannot be allowed to live," he says calmly. "But you already know that."

Esme doesn't even look at me. I see her fingers twitch.

"What's my other choice?" she asks.

"Well, then, you will die," Budimir says matter-of-factly. "Just like your husband will die and your son will die."

She glances in my direction but she's still not looking me in the eye. It's starting to make me feel strange.

Why the fuck is she not looking at me?

"Artem," Esme says to me. But she's still looking square at Budimir. "Phoenix is my son, too. I should get to decide."

Fear wraps itself around my chest. "You can't trust him. Fighting him is our only way out of this."

"If he wins, we all die," Esme says. "Including Phoenix."

"See, Artem?" Budimir smiles at me. "Even your woman can see that's there's only one viable path here. Sometimes fighting is not the smart choice."

"Esme…"

"I can't risk my son, Artem," Esme says, her eyes meeting mine for the first time.

She looks terrified, but determined. She looks like she's made up her mind and she's not going to back out now.

"I'm sorry," she whispers, moving forward.

But she doesn't move towards me—she moves toward Budimir.

"Try and understand. I'll lose you both. But this way... I can save my son."

"You're making a mistake, Esme," I say, my voice carrying across the room to her.

I see a tear slip down her cheek. It catches the light of the chandelier and looks golden from where I stand.

A single gilded tear.

She shakes her head at me.

"Let me do this, Artem," she says. "Tell your men to put down their weapons."

"Esme—"

But my words are drowned out by Budimir's laugh. "It seems you overestimated her affection for you, dear nephew."

Then he glances at Esme and extends his hand out to her.

"You're a smart girl," he murmurs. "And you've made a wise decision."

I stare in shock.

Esme steps forward and puts her hand in Budimir's.

What the fuck is happening right now?

I know Esme.

The Esme I know would never choose Budimir over me.

I meet her eyes, those beautiful honey-gold eyes that lit a flame in my chest so long ago. A flame I've never let die. It feels like the ending of a chapter.

My heart aches.

Then she moves so fast, that it takes everyone—including me—a moment to catch up.

The hidden blade in her hand slashes through the air and into Budimir's throat. He doesn't see it coming until the blade has buried itself to the hilt.

His eyes go wide in horror and shock as he realizes the mistake he's made.

He let Esme get too close.

He let his guard down.

And it cost him his life.

That's the price of underestimating Esme Kovalyov.

46

ARTEM

My men take advantage of the moment and move on Budimir's soldiers. With their boss dead, most of them give up immediately.

The few who struggle or attempt to run are cut down immediately.

But I'm not concerned with anyone but Esme.

I rush towards her just as she turns to me, her gold eyes meeting mine freely now.

"Artem," she gasps as my arms engulf her.

I hold her tightly for a long time. Eventually, I lean back so I can look down at her face. She's got tears swimming in her eyes, but they don't fall.

"Are you okay?" I ask, aware of the way her body is shaking.

"I... I think so," she replies. "It's... it's a lot."

I nod. "You're okay now," I tell her. "You were amazing."

She smiles against the tears. "Did you believe me?"

I shake my head. "Deep down, I didn't."

She looks at me with a dazed expression and I know she's still processing everything that's happened. It'll be years before she truly gets a grip on things.

But we have that time now.

"Esme," I say gently. "Where's Phoenix?"

"Svetlana," Esme answers, to my surprise.

"What?"

"Svetlana found me in the room I was being held," she explains. "She's the one who killed Eagle Tattoo and gave me the knife. I told her to take Phoenix and keep him safe."

She's talking fast and erratically, but I don't press her for more information. I'm content with the knowledge that Phoenix is safe.

For the first time, I glance down at Budimir's lifeless body. I feel a snarl ignite on my face at the sight of his pale, bloodless face.

In death, he has been stripped of the power and strength he seemed to possess. He just looks like a sad old man now.

"His death was too quick and too kind," I whisper, mostly to myself.

Then I feel Esme's hand against my cheek. She forces my eyes from Budimir and back to her.

"He's dead," she says. "Isn't that enough?"

"I wanted him to suffer."

She flinches a little, but before she can say another word, someone clears his throat behind us.

I turn to see Adrik.

"Yes?"

"We've got Budimir's men rounded up," he tells me.

"How many?"

"Thirty-three," Adrik replies. "A few fled while we were standing off against each other."

I nod. "Take them outside," I tell him. "You know what to do."

"Wait."

I turn to Esme, who's looking at me with mild horror. "What is he going to do?" she asks.

I hesitate for only a moment. But I don't want to lie to her, either.

"They are traitors, Esme," I tell her. "They had a choice. They could have chosen me but they stuck to Budimir. There is a cost for that."

"You're going to kill thirty-three men?" she gasps.

"I have to send a message."

"Yes, you do," she agrees. "But don't let that be your message."

I frown.

"You see that man over there?" I ask, pointing to Yahontov. "He was Budimir's man before now. But he and a few others chose to pledge their fealty to me instead. Those men will be spared. Those men will not face consequences for having chosen Budimir in the first place. But the others… there is a price that must be paid."

"You can't do it, Artem."

"Esme—"

"No," she interrupts fiercely. Her eyes blaze.

Then her face softens and she takes both my hands in hers. She glances over at the line of men that have been rounded up.

Their faces are somber. Some are resigned to their fate. Most have been a part of this world long enough to know what they're facing.

"I understand now that violence is always going to be a part of this world," she tells me softly. "I understand that sometimes… it's necessary. I've accepted that. But I can't accept unnecessary violence. Unnecessary death."

I say nothing. She takes a deep breath and continues.

"Exile these men if you have to. Banish them, punish them. But don't kill them. There's no need for it anymore. Their leader is gone, killing them now would just be cruel and pointless. It's a cruel and pointless world, Artem. You don't need to make it more that way. That's what my father did. That's what your uncle did. You're better than both of them."

I stare down at her earnest face, surprised by how much her words are resonating with me.

I am the don now.

I have the power to change my world as I see fit.

To be a better leader than the men who came before me.

And I owe that to the world. To my men. To my family.

I turn to Adrik, who's looking at me with raised eyebrows, waiting for my command.

I let go of Esme's hands and walk over to the marked men who were short-sighted enough to have chosen my uncle.

"My wife has just pleaded for your lives," I announce. "It makes me wonder: does that make her naïve or wise?"

I see hope blaze on a few faces, but the rest remain black with hopelessness.

"I'm inclined to believe the latter," I finish.

I feel a collective sigh rise into the air, but the atmosphere is still tense and expectant.

"There will be consequences," I tell them all. "But you have your lives at the very least, and you have my wife to thank for that."

I turn to Adrik. "Take them to the garage," I instruct him. "Make sure they're contained there until I decide what to do."

"Got it, boss."

I turn back to Esme and she walks into my arms.

"Thank you," she says into my chest.

"No," I say. "Thank you. You're stronger than you look, my love. Isn't that right?"

She laughs, and when she does, the laughter seems to break open her face and melt away the fissures of worry and fear.

She looks like my wife again. Strong, brave, beautiful.

And I feel my heart expand.

I can breathe again.

EPILOGUE: ARTEM

THE REGENCY HOTEL—SIX MONTHS LATER

"We're glad to have you back, Don Kovalyov," Maggadino says. He clasps my hand just before he walks out of the hotel suite.

I watch the elevator doors close on him.

When he's gone, I breathe a sigh of relief.

Well, that's done. Order has been restored. Alliances have been re-established.

I'd purposefully postponed a don's council meeting until I had the Bratva fully back in hand. It took me almost six months to get everything in order, but I wasn't about to rush it.

Budimir had done a lot of damage in the short time he'd been in charge. It cost me endless time, effort, and money to undo his stunted, brutal legacy.

Choosing underbosses and reorganizing the Bratva hierarchy.

Distributing businesses and assigning territories.

The never-ending work of the don. All the things I once despised doing. The things I told my father I didn't give a flying fuck about.

That's what makes up my days now.

I couldn't be more grateful.

I've had help, of course.

The O'Sullivan clan's assistance in the takeover had not only shifted the balance of power back to me, but it had also taken out two underworld mob bosses whose men had been scattered to the wind after their deaths.

I don't have to worry about Kovar or Bufalino anymore. Neither does anyone else in the city.

Thank fucking God.

True to my word, I haven't brought down the hammer on the remaining rats quite as brutally as I would've expected.

They have Esme to thank for that.

Most chose exile. Some reneged on their betrayal and were reassigned to low ranks. They'll never hold true power in my Bratva again. But they have their lives and a chance to remake their legacies.

We all deserve that kind of mercy.

I know that better than anyone.

The only other project that occupies some of my time—but mostly Esme's—is the renovation of my father's mansion.

Once all the damages sustained in the fight had been dealt with, Esme threw herself into re-decorating it. Most of the rooms were transformed within weeks, so much so that sometimes I walk into rooms and fail to recognize a single thing in there.

"Do you hate it?" Esme had asked me when I'd looked around at my father's old office that she had converted into a family sitting room.

"No, I don't hate it at all," I'd told her. "It's just so different."

"I wanted the space to be warmer," she explained. "It was so... austere."

I'd laughed at that. If only she knew how right she was. "My father was austere, so that would explain it."

"You're sure you don't mind all the changes I'm making here?"

"I'm sure. This is your home now. I just want you to be comfortable here."

We'd ended up having sex on the wide sofa that occupied the space where my father's desk once sat.

Pure fucking bliss.

That is probably the best part of my new reality.

Esme.

Phoenix.

Our family.

Being don wouldn't be so sweet if I didn't have the two of them with me.

"The cars are out front, boss," Adrik says, snapping me out of my idle thoughts.

I nod. "Before we leave, sit down for a moment," I say, looking towards Vasyl and Alexei. "You two as well."

The three of them sit down, forming a lose circle around me. I open a fresh bottle of whiskey and pour out four glasses.

It's the first drink I've had in months. These days, my drinking has become sporadic. It's something I engage in on special occasions.

The last time I was drunk was when I'd been in the mountains. Almost a year ago now, drinking away my losses, drowning my demons.

I don't need to do that anymore.

"We've got our shit together," I tell my underbosses. I pick up my glass of whiskey. "We've solidified control of the West Coast and we've eliminated threats to the Bratva. But we've got more to accomplish. I have plans for all of us."

Adrik smiles and raises his glass. "To the future of the Bratva."

We raise our glasses and I take a sip of the rich, bitter whiskey.

"Our future would not have been possible without the sacrifices of others," I say. "So I propose another toast. To Stanislav," I say, raising my glass.

My men murmur and toast to Stanislav.

"To Maxim," I continue.

"To Maxim!"

"To Cillian."

"To Cillian!"

"You're really going to toast to me without me?" comes a familiar voice from the doorway. "Pretty damn rude, I'd say."

I turn.

And the whiskey glass falls from my hand.

It hits the ground and shatters, but I don't notice. Don't give a damn.

Because there's a ghost in the room.

Or at least, I thought it was a ghost.

But Cillian O'Sullivan looks very, very real.

He's flesh and bone. Warm. Living.

He's got a cane in his hand and he leans on it a bit as he crosses the distance between us.

He's got scars I don't recognize.

Those blue eyes, though—stubborn, laughing, alive—those haven't changed one bit.

And when he takes the final step forward and embraces me, I realize just how damn much I missed my best friend.

"You're not getting all soft and sentimental on me, are ya?" he mumbles in my ear.

I release him from the hug and step away.

"You look like shit," I comment wryly.

"Still better looking than you'll ever be," he fires right back.

I laugh, he laughs, and the men looking on from the table laugh. It's a soul-cleansing laugh, the kind that only happens a few times in a man's life. When something truly takes him by surprise.

"Now," Cillian says, eyes sparkling, "can we finish that toast? I'm fucking dying for a drink."

I find a pair of fresh glasses and pour us each one. Adrik, Alexei, and Vasyl all stand to join us. We clink glasses and drink deeply.

It tastes like salvation.

It tastes like redemption.

It tastes like the future I've shed blood, sweat and tears for.

It tastes really fucking good.

Once we've all drained our glasses, my lieutenants make mumbled excuses and slip out of the room.

It's just Cillian and me.

I feel like a fool—I keep looking at him, wondering if he's real or if I maybe just sustained a traumatic brain injury and this is all a sick hallucination.

But he's real. He's here.

"So?" I say after a minute of silence.

He glances back at me curiously. "So what?"

Jesus—all these months later and it takes him no time at all to infuriate me again.

I slam my hand on the table and roar, "So are you going to tell me how the fuck you got here?!"

He laughs again at that. That infuriating Irishman's laugh that drives me up the wall the same way it always has.

He reaches out for the whiskey bottle and refills our glasses.

"Yeah, I'll tell you," he says mirthfully. "And boy, I promise you this—it's one hell of a story."

∽

A few hours later, Cillian and I head downstairs. He promises me that he'll be at the club opening tonight—he just has to go take care of a few things first.

We hug again and then he limps away, still leaning on that silver-tipped cane.

I can't believe the story he told me. But it makes sense, in the end.

And something tells me there's more of it yet to be written.

I make my way to the curb out front, where my Jeep is waiting for me. Adrik is constantly suggesting I use a driver, like Stanislav and Budimir had done, but I refuse every time.

I may be the don now.

But I'm going to do it my way.

It takes me only fifteen minutes to drive from the hotel to my new investment and business venture. It's a huge plot of land that I bought only four and a half months ago.

The building that stood on the plot was dilapidated to say the least, but with money and manpower, I have transformed it into the night club it is now.

The façade is sleek and simple, almost understated. Then you walk inside and realize just how huge it is. The dancefloor is the central focus, but there's a separate area for the DJ and a whole section devoted to the bar.

The private rooms are spacious, luxurious, and they're hidden behind the VIP section.

I hand my car over to the valet and head inside.

The place is quiet when I walk in. Only the staff is present, bustling around as they prepare for opening night.

"Hello, handsome."

I turn and see Svetlana walking towards me. She looks the part in her figure-hugging gold sheath dress and four-inch heels. The perfect hostess.

"'Lana," I greet with a courteous smile.

She kisses me politely on the cheek. "I didn't expect you here so early."

"I wanted to make sure everything was ready for the big night."

"Of course you did," Svetlana says, rolling her eyes. "The two of you are made for each other."

I frown. "Is Esme here?"

Svetlana smiles and nods. "She's in your private rooms right now, changing that little Casanova you have for a son," she confirms. "She came early to make sure everything was ready for the big night. Sound familiar?."

My smile gets wider. "If you'll excuse me."

Svetlana just winks.

I leave her and walk through the VIP section towards the private rooms, but I veer right from there and keep walking. I hit a black wall that looks like a dead end, but I make a sharp right and find a black door that blends into the wall.

I walk inside and lock the door behind me.

My quarters are meant to function as a meeting area as well as a lounge area. I enter into the office space, and then walk through the trellis partitions to the lounge that I had constructed with Esme and Phoenix in mind.

There are large sofas and recliners in the spacious room. I've even had a play space set up for Phoenix. That's where I find Esme.

She's got her back to me, as she leans over the cot in the corner, her fingers entwining with Phoenix's as the two of them coo back and forth at each other.

I stand there silently, admiring the two of them together. Esme looks like a modern-day Aphrodite with her dark hair in smooth waves that fall down to her middle back.

The dress she's wearing is made of champagne silk, fitted at the bust and held together by a halter neckline that ends in a dramatic side bow. It fans out at the waist, flowing down her soft curves with ease.

"Wow," I breathe.

She gasps and turns to me with a start. The moment she sees me, her face relaxes and she smiles widely, lifting her skirt a little and twirling around for me.

"You like it?"

The dress's bodice is worked in the front with tiny seed pearls, and I notice the pearl earrings I'd bought her earlier that month dangling from her ears.

"You look breathtaking."

She beams at me before walking right into my arms. "You look handsome."

"I try."

"How did the meeting go?" she asks cautiously.

"It went well," I say. "I've reforged a few old alliances and new oaths of fealty have been pledged to the Bratva."

"My peacemaker. I never thought I'd see the day."

I roll my eyes and grumble, "Don't think I won't get a little handsy with anyone who tests my limits. You most of all."

Phoenix gurgles a little as he turns on his chest and catches sight of me. He's not sounding out words yet, but he has just started recognizing faces. Another reason why he's always attached to Esme.

"Hey little bird," I say, adopting the moniker that Esme uses on him all the time. Half the time, I don't even realize I'm doing it.

I pick my son up and plant a kiss on his forehead. He smells like baby powder and fresh soap. He's also wearing a long-sleeved shirt with little black suspenders.

"Someone just had a bath," I observe.

Esme laughs. "I gave him one just now."

"Why the fuck am I paying Talia if you're the one doing all the work?" I ask.

Esme laughs. "Because Talia's his nanny, but *I'm* his mother," she says. "I'm still the one in charge of taking care of him and raising him."

"And I have no problems with that," I say. "But it's not necessary for you to be washing him when you're all decked out like this."

She smiles patiently at me, as she runs her hand over Phoenix's downy hair. "I got dressed after I washed him."

"Not the point."

She laughs. "Will you stop being so grumpy?" she demands, patting my arm. "It's the grand opening tonight. You should be excited."

"And I am," I say. "In more ways than one."

I paw at her ass. She yelps and ducks away from me laughing. "No tocas! Keep those filthy hands to yourself, Mr. Kovalyov," she exclaims. "Talia could walk in at any moment."

"Let her walk in. We'll show her a thing or two."

She narrows her eyes at me. "We've had this conversation before—you cannot grope me in front of the nanny. It took her a week to look me in the eye the last time she walked in on you pawing at me like a horny teenager."

"That was her fault," I point out. "She was the one who just pranced into our private quarters."

"If I recall, it was the main sitting room."

"Still my house."

Esme laughs and shakes her head at me. "Some things never change."

She turns her attention to our son in my arms. He's playing with my lapel, little fingers grasping and tugging.

"Doesn't he look amazing?" she asks.

"He always does," I reply. "As do you, my beauty."

"Ah-hem!"

I turn to see Talia standing awkwardly by the trellis partition.

"Sorry, I didn't mean to disturb you," she says with a blush.

"You didn't, Talia," Esme stammers quickly. "Why don't you take Phoenix for a walk…? Once the party gets going, I'd prefer him to stay in here."

"Of course, Mrs. Kovalyov," she says.

I see Esme's nose scrunch up. She makes the same expression every time anyone addresses her in a remotely formal way.

Svetlana is the only one who's comfortable addressing Esme by name, and that's mostly because the two of them have formed a close friendship in the last few months.

Talia's wearing nicer clothes today. She's dressed in black pants and a white blouse. She's even put her hair up in a tasteful chignon.

She still looks uncomfortable as hell though, but that probably has more to do with me than what she's wearing.

She's in her early twenties and came highly recommended. But the deciding factor was the fact that Esme warmed to her immediately.

"I can trust her with my son."

That's what Esme had said after our second interview with her. I felt the same.

I watch as Talia scoops Phoenix up in her arms and exits the room quickly. The moment we're alone, I grab my wife and press my lips down on hers.

"Boy," she gasps, when I pull back, "you don't waste any time, do you?"

"You dress like that and expect me to keep my hands to myself?" I ask. "Keep dreaming, woman."

I find her mouth again, and her lips part for me immediately. I push her up against the nearest wall and my hand starts sliding up her dress—just as I hear the click of the door on the other side of the room.

"Fuck," I growl, just as Esme pushes me away from her and adjusts the skirt of her dress. "Why didn't I lock the fucking door?"

Esme suppresses a smile just as Svetlana appears between the trellis partition. "Sorry to disturb you two," she says, a knowing twinkle in her eyes. "But we need you out there, boss. A line is starting to form already."

"Today is invited guests only," I say impatiently. "Tell the rest to fuck off and come back tomorrow."

"He's a real people person, isn't he?" Esme teases.

"Such a charmer," Svetlana chimes in.

I roll my eyes as the two of them laugh at my expense. Maybe I'm not such a fan of this friendship after all. Two against one is unfair odds.

"Shall we, husband?" Esme asks, extending her hand out to me.

I take her hand, a swell of pride rising inside me.

I've accomplished a lot in the last six months. I've taken back the Bratva, saved my father's legacy, and established my own at the same time.

But none of that accounts for the pride I'm feeling right now.

That's all about the woman standing next to me.

∼

"We came a long way to get here, Artem," Kian says, his gaze constantly flickering around the club like he's still sizing it up. "But I'm impressed with how you've handled things."

I just smile impassively. "When do you intend to return to Ireland?" I ask.

"In three days," he replies. "So I'll be back here at least one more time before my flight."

"You are welcome anytime, my friend."

Kian looks around at the wide range of different crime families that fill the lounges in the VIP section.

He's stuck around for longer than I ever could have asked. He and his men have been invaluable in cleaning up Budimir's many messes.

"And apparently I'm not the only one," he chuckles.

"Being the don is not just about throwing your weight and watching the ants scatter to the wind. Diplomacy is needed. Intelligence is needed. Brute force is never enough to hold power. In short—I like having friends."

Echoing my father's words does strange things to my heart in my chest. It feels like not so long ago that he was saying them to me himself.

But they feel right on my lips. His crown feels right on my head.

I'm where I belong.

"Wise words," Kian says with an inclination of his head.

His blue eyes are alert as he gives the room another once over. He'll be don one day, whenever Ronan decides to step aside.

That doesn't look like it was going to happen anytime soon. Ronan might be getting along in years, but the man is made of steel.

I'm sure he'll live well into his nineties and until then, he will hold on to power.

But that's fine with me.

Kian's time will come. And for now, we are friends, allies, equals. It's a good relationship between my Bratva and his.

One that I intend to maintain.

His parents couldn't make it tonight, but they sent a bouquet of flowers to congratulate me on the opening of the club.

The note in the arrangement said, "To a friend—With love, the O'Sullivans."

It was written in a looping female handwriting.

Sinead, no doubt.

Kian sees one of his lieutenants enter and excuses himself to greet the man. I take the opportunity to walk out of the VIP area towards my personal quarters.

It's past one, but the night has only just begun for many still here. The only thing I want, however, is my wife.

"Esme," I say softly.

All is quiet, so I move deeper into the room, but Phoenix's cot is empty. I hear movement in the adjoining bathroom and I open the door and walk inside without knocking.

Esme is standing in front of the mirror. Her eyes catch mine instantly.

"Hola," she greets with a mischievous gleam in her eyes.

I walk up behind her and put my arms around her waist, pulling her against me. I'm already half-hard, and the moment her ass meets my crotch, I'm fully erect.

"Where's our boy?" I ask.

"I had Talia take him home," she says. "Adrik and Alexei went with them."

"Good," I say, spinning her around so that she's facing me. "Did I tell you how fucking beautiful you look in that dress?"

She smiles, running her hand down the front of my shirt. "Hmm, I can't recall," she says playfully. "But you're welcome to say it again."

I laugh. "More beautiful than a brute like me has words for. But honestly, you look the most beautiful when you've got nothing on."

"Well, then," she says, pushing me back, forcing about a foot of space between us, "there's no point in this dress staying on."

She undoes her halter neckline and lets the fabric slip off her beautiful breasts. She shimmies out of her dress and kicks it to the side on the terrazzo floor.

She's wearing a white lace bra that barely covers her nipples and a matching white thong that has me salivating instantly.

She removes her bra slowly, while I watch with hungry eyes. The moment her panties are off, I pull her to me again and hitch her legs up and around my waist.

I set her on the marble counter and she gasps slightly as her skin makes contact with the cool surface.

Then she starts ripping away at my clothes, her nails grating over my skin.

When I'm as naked as she is, I slip my finger inside her as her hand wraps around my cock.

She's so fucking wet. I groan with want. I feel her shiver against me as she grinds against my cock impatiently.

I've explored her body in every single fucking position, in every single fucking way known to man in the last several months.

But it's not enough.

It's never enough.

My desire for her seems to go on endlessly. No matter how many times I have her, I always want more.

And the feeling seems to be mutual.

"I want your cock inside me now," she whispers as her tongue plays with my ear.

I push her thighs apart and slide my cock inside her. She moans loudly, wordlessly, until her lips form the shape of my name.

"Fuck me hard, Artem," she groans.

I breathe her in as I fuck her, watching as the waves of her hair toss wildly in the air with each thrust.

I still remember the first time we'd fucked. Just like this. Hot and heavy and desperate in a club bathroom. Clinging to each other like we were the only things on earth that mattered anymore.

That's where it all began.

And we've ended up right back here.

I grab Esme's face as I push into her, our lips are separated by half an inch. Her breath, hot and wild, mixes with mine.

"Artem," she whispers.

"Esme," I whisper right back.

I press my lips to her neck, letting my tongue tease the sensitive skin at her nape. I feel her nails dig into my back, I feel her pussy clench around my cock and I feel her orgasm rear up to meet my own.

And it feels like this moment has been a fucking lifetime in coming.

It was worth the wait.

EXTENDED EPILOGUE

Thanks for reading GILDED TEARS—but don't stop now! Click the link below to get your hands on the exclusive Extended Epilogue to see Artem's special surprise for Esme!

DOWNLOAD THE EXTENDED EPILOGUE TO GILDED TEARS

SNEAK PREVIEW OF CORRUPTED ANGEL: A DARK MAFIA ROMANCE

I found my angel.
Then I broke her wings.

Alexis should've never set foot in my world.

Men like me stain girls like her. We take their innocence and tear it to shreds.

She thinks she's tough. She thinks she can handle me.

But she doesn't know just how deep my darkness goes.

It was for the best that I claimed her for a night and left her behind.

Anything more than that would have been cruel.

I thought I'd seen the last of Alexis Wright.

So imagine my surprise two years later when the door to my office opens...

And *she* walks in.

The girl I ravaged. The girl I devoured.

Now that's she's in front of me again, I have just two questions for her:

First—what is she doing here?

And second…

What does she mean, "our baby"?

⁓

Alexis

It is getting dark outside.

I flick on the lamp at my desk and stretch up in my chair, trying to avoid the inevitable end-of-the-day hunch. My stomach grumbles and I slide open the bottom drawer of my desk, eyeing the goodies inside. Ah, yes, the good ol' secret snack drawer. It's a secret not because I'm ashamed of how much I snack, but because Vicky Oberman in the cubicle across from me will pop over the divider like a meerkat if she hears the tell-tale crinkle of a bag of chips.

I pull out a packet of Twizzlers and slide the drawer shut. I stare at the blinking cursor on my computer screen while I gnaw on the end of a stick of strawberry licorice. I told my fiancé, Grant, that I would be home late tonight because I wanted to finish up this story, but I'm not sure I can be bothered.

It's just a fluff piece—the unlikely story of how a community center caretaker found the exact skates he used to wear when he visited the center as a child. Mr. Finkel spent half of the interview reminiscing about how much everything used to cost in those days (a can of soda—a nickel; a hot dog—a quarter; two scoops of ice cream—ten cents), and the rest of the time talking about how kids these days have no appreciation for the luxury of having a community center to go to.

Now, it is my job as the dedicated local news journalist to turn that pile of boring jelly into a thought-provoking article examining the role of community centers in empowering the youth of tomorrow.

Or at least, that's how I've decided to spin it. My editor, Debbie Harris, just wants me to write the story. In fact, her exact words were, "Nobody's going to read it but that caretaker, so just make sure you don't misspell the guy's name."

Debbie makes no bones about how she doesn't expend time or energy on the puff pieces when there are bigger stories to tell. I just wish she would give me one of those bigger stories. My work at the *New York Union* so far has involved precious little in the way of substance.

"Wright!" comes a clipped voice from the entrance to my cubicle.

Oh, boy. Speak of the devil.

I spin to face Debbie, a Twizzler still hanging out of my mouth. She is a stern-looking Scottish woman with perfectly coiffed blonde hair, black-lined eyes, and lipstick that is never out of place. She has a commendably infinite selection of bold-colored pantsuits. Today's number is a fuchsia blazer and slacks with a bright white top underneath. She looks about forty-five, but in my two years of working for the paper, I have never heard her discuss her age. I heard a rumor that someone in the office tried to throw her a birthday party once and the person was never heard from again.

"How's the story going?" she asks in her thick Glaswegian accent.

"Good." I bite off the end of the Twizzler. "I was just—"

She waves a hand. "Nope, all I need to know. I'm just here to give you your assignment for tomorrow." She grins. "You'll like this one."

My heart picks up. Debbie's finally going to give me something meaty to sink my teeth into.

"It's a dog show!" she announces.

"Oh."

"Don't look so disappointed." She leans against my cubicle wall. "You haven't heard the best part."

I cock a brow, waiting.

Debbie leans in a little. "All the dogs are celebrity impersonators."

"Debbie!" I groan, letting my head fall back in frustration. "That's just more of the same crap I always get. Why would you get me all excited?"

She kicks the bottom of my chair, startling me upright, then folds her arms and glowers at me.

"You and your lack of patience again," she scolds. "Do you know how lucky you are to even have this job? I've got a dozen résumés in the drawer who would love to write a story about a parade of dogs in wee outfits."

"Yes," I sigh. "You're right. I'm sorry. Thank you."

She smiles and leaves.

I know Debbie's right, but I can't help my frustration. As cute as the dog show does actually sound, I want to write stories that make a difference.

The clock hits five-thirty and I start to pack up. I don't feel like staying late today. I just want to curl up on the sofa with Grant and a big glass of red wine and watch some mindless TV. In fact, that sounds exactly like what the doctor ordered.

It takes nearly forty minutes to get from the newspaper offices in Manhattan to our loft in Brooklyn. Grant is lucky—he was just made junior partner at a commercial law firm in downtown Brooklyn and his walk to work is less than ten minutes.

It's an unseasonably warm evening for November, but there's still a bite in the air that makes me draw my coat closer around myself as I walk from the subway to our apartment building. I walk up the front steps and into the waiting elevator, dreaming of a full-bodied pinot noir.

The apartment door is unlocked, which is surprising. As close as his office is, Manhattan law is no joke, and Grant works tough hours. He'd said he wouldn't be too late tonight, though, so I wonder where he's gotten off to. I drop my keys in the bowl and walk into the living room, expecting to find him there, but he is nowhere to be seen.

"Grant?" I call. The aged floorboards whine under my feet as I walk toward the bedroom, dropping my bag on the sofa on the way.

Squeak. Squeak.

I've been arguing with Grant since we first moved in together about the mattress in our bedroom. He loves it, but I can't stand the creaky springs. The thing is, though, that the springs only make noise whenever he and I get down to some adult business. Seeing as how I'm standing out in the hallway, I start to realize with growing horror that that means...

Oh, Jesus.

When I push open the bedroom door with fingers that suddenly feel pale and trembly, I'm greeted with something I never, ever wanted to see.

The first thing I see is Grant's pale ass, clenching as he thrusts.

The second thing I see is the horrified face of the woman beneath him, who has just locked eyes with me and realized—way, way too late—that she's made a big mistake.

My jaw hits the floor.

The woman tries to push Grant off of her and cover up with the comforter, but it takes the big oaf a second to realize what's happening. When he finally does and looks up to see me standing in the doorframe, his face falls.

"It's not what it looks like!" he yells. He's leaping out of bed, pulling on a pair of boxers—the ones I got him for his birthday last year, I notice—and gesticulating wildly.

Looking at him makes me feel nauseous, so I look at the girl instead. She's huddled beneath the comforter. Her bottle-blonde hair is in wild disarray and her eyes are wide with shock.

"It's not what it looks like!" Grant repeats, like I hadn't heard him the first time.

For a second, I want to believe him. It would be so much easier to drink down his lies than to accept that my fiancé, the man I've spent every Sunday cuddled on the couch with for the past two years, has betrayed me in the worst way.

But there's no denying that it is exactly what it looks like.

Anger fills my veins like kerosene. All I need now is a match.

"Then what is it?" I demand, eyes widening. "Were you inspecting each other for lice? Did she lose an earring down your pants?"

Grant rushes over. His sandy hair is standing up in wild tufts and there is lipstick smudged around his mouth. "Baby, let me explain!"

The sight of those lips—the lips that I thought were mine alone to kiss—sets fire to my blood, singing my skin from the inside.

He's got big, soulful eyes. I remember falling for them, for him. They looked good in the candlelight at the Italian place he took me for our first serious date. Even now, part of me wants to soak up the emotion there and forgive him.

I put that part of me in a box, lock it, and throw away the key.

"Get out," I demand coldly, jabbing a finger toward the front door. "Both of you need to get out right now."

My heart is trying to climb up my throat. I feel like I'm going to throw up. How could he do this to me? I am two seconds from completely breaking down, and like hell am I going to let Grant be here to witness that.

Grant frowns. "But it's my apartment."

"I said get the fuck out before I throw you out!" My raised voice does the trick. With a yelp, the woman runs past me toward the front door.

Grant turns and reaches for a pair of pants. I must not've been clear; maybe he needs me to repeat myself one last time.

"Did I stutter? I said, *Get. The. Fuck. Out!*"

Hearing the venom in my voice, Grant abandons the pants and bolts out the door. Two seconds later, I hear the front door slam closed.

I collapse in the hallway, like a puppet whose strings have been mercilessly snipped.

The room seems to ring with the echo of my pounding heart. I am still and silent for a long time, my mind blissfully blank. I just stare at the wall, listening to my ragged pulse.

I remember picking out the paint for the hallway. The color is called Gray Steel. After I moved in, I wanted to make it feel more like our home, rather than just his, but Grant liked everything the way it was. He wouldn't let me move furniture around, or redecorate the living room, or reorganize the closet. He eventually relented and allowed me to paint this one hallway, where the walls had been scuffed in a few places already. I was given a few square feet to make my own. At the time, I was grateful for it.

How could I not see back then that Grant wasn't willing to make room in his life for me?

My eyes sting with tears. I throw my head back against the wall. We were supposed to get *married*. After all the sacrifices I made for him, all the times I put him first, and now I find out that our life together meant fuck-all to him?

I break out into wretched sobs. Fat tears roll down my cheeks, shoulders shaking, chest heaving as I struggle to breathe. I'm not sure whether I'm mourning the loss of my fiancé or the loss of the life I'd planned with him—marriage, babies, a family of my own.

Whatever it is, I lost something today. And goddamn it, it hurts.

～

I have not the faintest desire to get out of bed in the morning, but I know that work is the only thing that will remove the image of Grant's lipstick-stained grimace from my mind. So I slog my way to the office and finish up the community center piece. Then it's time to check out the dog show.

It feels good to do nothing. For a change, I'm actually grateful that Debbie loves handing me the nonsense assignments. I don't have the brain capacity for legal drama or deep investigative reporting. A dog show of celebrity impersonators is about the most I can process right now.

As predicted, it is very twee. My favorite is a greyhound dressed like Ziggy Stardust, who howls into a microphone on command. He doesn't end up winning anything, which is disappointing. The winner of the best costume category is a poodle with a laconic grin who goes by "Pawl Newman." Second place goes to a weiner dog in a sparkly jumpsuit and a ginger wig who the owner would have us believe is Elton John. I leave thinking that Ziggy was robbed.

I head back to the office to start writing up the piece, wondering if this is it for me. Am I doomed to spend the rest of my days writing articles that nobody will read until I eventually retire to become a childless, angry cat lady? There has to be more than this.

During the day, I text my best friend, Clara Fitzgerald, to update her on the latest in my love life. She tries to call me several times during the day, but I don't answer. When I finish work at five-thirty on the dot, I call her back.

"Finally!" she groans. "I was beginning to worry about you."

"Sorry. It's just been a busy day." I fish a chocolate bar out of my purse and start munching on it on my way to the subway.

"I can't believe Grant. What an absolute pig."

"I know." I sigh. "Look, I'm going to lose you in the subway soon. Can I call you later?"

"No need!" Clara says brightly. "I'm on my way over to your place now."

"Clara ..."

I really don't feel like company tonight. It's Friday, which means there will be a movie on TV and I can be as hungover as I want in the morning. There's a bottle of wine on the rack that Grant's boss got us for our engagement that we were supposed to wait until the wedding to drink. That bad boy's getting cracked. I've also got a pint of Ben and Jerry's in the freezer. My evening is set.

"Oh—I'm losing you," Clara hisses into the phone. "Can't—cutting out."

"Clara!"

"See—soon!"

She hangs up and I curse under my breath. Clara is very kind, and wise, and unbelievably forgiving, but she's also the pushiest person I've ever met. She seeks to control everything in her environment, which I know is something that has come out of two hard years of sobriety but still frustrates me sometimes.

Still, I guess it will be nice to spend some quality time with my best friend. I'll need to move out of Grant's apartment soon, so it could be fun to do a little damage to it.

Clara is waiting in front of my building when I get home. She is holding two big shopping bags and bounds up to me, throwing her arms around my shoulders. One of the bags smacks against my spine.

"Ouch," I complain. "What is that? A bag of bricks?"

Clara chuckles. "Just you wait."

We head up to the apartment and Clara sets the bags on the kitchen island, then throws herself across the sofa. Her mass of golden curls spills over the armrest and she tilts her head back to look at me.

"How are you feeling?" she asks.

I sigh and slump into the armchair opposite. "Weird."

"Maybe a little free?"

"Nope. Just weird." My head lolls to the side and I meet her gaze. "We had a plan, Clara. Grant and I had a plan. After we got married, we were going to travel, and then we were going to start our family. Grant wanted a girl first, but I wanted a boy, a little fella I could dress up as a sailor and teach to always be polite. He'd be the kind of kid that would call adults 'ma'am' and 'mister,' and everyone would fawn over how cute he was."

"Were you planning to have a child in the 1950s?" she asks skeptically.

I frown. "Well, it doesn't really matter now, does it?"

"You can still have all that," Clara says. "You're only twenty-six. You've got your whole life ahead of you, and it's better to start fresh now than spend the rest of your life tied to a man who was never going to put you first."

"You're right." I look back to the ceiling. "I'm just scared to start over."

"If life didn't scare you, it wouldn't be worth living."

"I'm sure that will be comforting in a couple of weeks, but at the moment, I just ..." I look over at her. "I don't know. I'm hurt."

Clara sits up, green eyes twinkling with something I can only describe as mischief. "You know what I hear when you say that?"

"What?"

"That you need a distraction," she says. "Let's go out tonight."

My eyebrow raises skeptically. "Out?"

"Yeah. Like to a club." She folds her legs under her, looking every bit the yoga instructor she is. "Yes, let's go dancing! I'll tell you the same thing I told my students today: if all else fails, feed your soul with deep stretches and heavy bass."

"You did not say that to your class."

"I did, too."

I chuckle. "Okay, sensei. All the same, I think I'll nama-stay home."

"Please come out with me?" She pouts her pink lips. "It'll be good for you. Now that you've kicked Grant to the curb, you can actually have a little excitement in your life."

Clara always thought of Grant as boring, with his long monologues and predictable patterns. He was the sort who adhered to a weekly schedule like his life depended on it—CrossFit three times a week, his favorite cop drama on Tuesday nights, fish for dinner every Friday. It's ironic that after years of being able to tell the time based on his movements, he would throw me a curveball so unexpected that it would knock me on my ass.

"Grant was boring, wasn't he?" I realize out loud.

Clara nods. "An absolute snoozefest. A pretty face, but very little going on upstairs."

"Very little going on downstairs either," I remark. "I can't imagine that floozy was with him because of his commendable ability to fall asleep almost immediately after ejaculating."

She snickers. "That's the spirit!"

"Ugh. Why was I even with him?" I scrub a hand over my face. "I think on some level I always knew I was settling. I'm just annoyed that it took this happening for me to realize it."

Admittedly, I was always curious about the concept of having a spark in a relationship. It was something I never felt that Grant and I had. I presumed that what we did have—comfort and security—was better. Stronger. More stable.

Clearly, Grant didn't think so. With my blinders off, I realize I shouldn't have thought so, either.

"Your dad likes him," Clara points out. "I think you've always been a little blind where your dad is concerned."

"Dad only likes him because he's also a lawyer," I reply. "He just likes having someone around he can talk torts to."

I haven't even told my dad the news yet. In fact, I've hardly spoken to him lately. He's been busy defending the innocent, and I've been busy looking for new ways to describe canine outfits. I always worry that my dad judges me for not living up to my potential. I hate the thought of disappointing him.

Clara shoots to her feet and goes to the island, grabbing the bags she brought before setting them down on the coffee table. "Let's do something fun. You remember fun, right?"

"I just don't know if I'm in the mood, Clara ..." I eye the bags suspiciously. "Plus, don't you think a club will just be a den of temptation to you?"

She waves dismissively. "Please. I am so Zen these days that the thought of alcohol doesn't even faze me. I just want to dance with my best friend and help dig her out of the misery spiral she's about to sink into."

"Who said anything about a misery spiral?"

"I see you glancing over at the freezer." She flattens her lips. "If I don't get you out of here, you'll end up watching terrible romcoms until you pass out in a puddle of melted ice cream."

I am annoyed that she has anticipated my evening plans so astutely.

"Fine," I sigh. "Let's go dance."

She squeals and perches on the coffee table, pulling items out of the bags. She has brought her entire makeup kit, as well as enough hair-styling tools to supply a pageant.

"What's all this?" I ask suspiciously.

"This is your future." She pulls a sparkly dress out of one of the bags with a flourish. "Gaze upon it with glee, for I am going to give you a makeover."

I eye the dress. "That's not going to fit me."

Clara is petite, with toned everything and an ass that defies gravity. I run on the curvier side, with a flat stomach but flaring hips, thick thighs, and generous cleavage. I have the kind of body that looks great in pencil skirts and form-hugging jeans, but I'm dubious about the slinky number that Clara has picked out for me.

"It absolutely will fit," she replies. "You can trust me. I'm enlightened."

"You're ridiculous."

"Ridiculously wise." She fans out a selection of makeup brushes. "Now... Where to begin?"

Clara pokes and prods at me for the next hour. By the end of it, my face is so caked with makeup and my hair so full of spray that I question whether I will be able to keep my head upright. Clara announces in a singsong voice that she is finished and somehow goads me into the sparkly dress. Then she guides me to the mirror, and the first thing I see is her hopeful expression.

And then... Wow.

Clara has coaxed my normally curly hair into silky waves that cascade over the tops of my breasts. My blue eyes pop under thick black false lashes, with gold and purple eyeshadow and thick black liner on the upper lids. My lips are light pink and shiny, and my skin is flawless, like creamy marble.

And the dress... Damn, the dress. It clings to me in all the right places, with a deep V accentuating my cleavage and a fringe at the bottom that tickles the tops of my thighs when I move.

"I don't even look like me," I comment, turning my face from side to side, entranced by my own reflection.

"That's not so bad, is it?" Clara brings the makeup to the mirror and bumps me out of the way while she starts on her own face. "Tonight you can be anyone you want to be."

She's right, I realize. I am transformed.

Maybe going out is a good idea after all.

∽

Clara and I hit up a few bars on the Lower East Side before making our way to what she claims is the best club in all of New York City—Fiamma. Once we get inside, it is a veritable buffet of sights and sounds. Loud dance music pulses through the speakers and ultra-glam revelers pack the dance floor and wave their arms above them as neon lights slash through the crowd.

I had a couple drinks in the earlier bars, but I never drink to excess when I'm around Clara. She says it doesn't bother her, but it doesn't seem fair. I'm working with a bit of a buzz, so Clara and I skip the bar and head straight for the dance floor.

I don't know the song playing but let the beat flow through me as I start to dance, winding my hands toward the ceiling and rolling my hips. It feels good to dance. I lose myself in it, swaying and twisting and tossing my hair. Clara and I make eye contact and break into giggles. It is the first time all day that I have felt truly alive.

I look over my shoulder to see how crowded the bar is, and my eye lands on a man cutting through the crowd a few feet behind me. My breath catches.

I'm just drunk enough to have one crystal-clear thought amidst the chaos: *That is one fine specimen.*

He must be around 6'5" as he towers above the crowd of high-heeled glamazons. His dark hair feathers around his face and the nape of his neck. It's the kind of hair that looks silky to the touch, and my fingers twitch at the thought of running my hands through it. His full lips are set in a hard line, as though annoyed at having to swim through the sea of bodies. He glances over, and for a second, our eyes meet.

My heart skips a beat and I go still, like a deer in the headlights. His eyes are dark pools that draw me in until I feel as though I'm drowning. He looks away, and I snap back into the present, realizing that for the past few seconds, I've forgotten to breathe.

The man disappears without so much as a backward glance. Maybe he wasn't looking at me at all.

Clara pokes my shoulder. "You okay?"

I nod and go back to dancing. "Sorry. Got distracted."

"By that hunk of man meat?" She licks her lips. "I don't blame you."

I dance until my feet ache, and sweat shimmers on my chest. I even indulge in a little bump-and-grind with a few guys who come my way, but the second any of them start asking too many questions, I grab Clara and we scoot into another part of the crowd. I just want to have fun, and at the moment, the idea of chatting up any guy is the opposite of that.

Clara and I hit the bar and I order drinks. She starts to drift off in the direction of a sexy guy with a very impressive afro and I have to wrangle her back to my side as she has my wallet and phone in her purse.

We hit the dance floor again and the guy comes over, performing silly dance moves like some sort of mating ritual for Clara's approval. It works. One second I'm shimmying with my best friend, the next I'm sipping a drink next to her while she and the hot rando paw at each other like teenagers.

I scan the club, my vodka cran tasting increasingly bitter with every sip. I don't even realize what I'm looking for until I see him—the hot guy I maybe made eye contact with earlier. He's leaning against the wall near the VIP area, scrolling through his phone.

I don't get him. He doesn't seem to belong here. He's too serious, and he looks too bored. He's wearing a slim-fitting black suit, with a black shirt and a red tie. It's bold, but he's not peacocking. He's just... being.

As though he can feel my gaze, the man looks up from his phone. His gaze skewers through me from across the room. A blue light splashes across my face, and I have no doubt that this time he is looking at me. Everything seems to slow down around me and my pulse races. His mouth lifts ever-so-slightly in a smirk. My mouth is dry, and I down the rest of my drink in one gulp. When I look back up, he is already walking up the stairs into the VIP area.

I turn back to Clara and grimace. She and her new friend look as though they're trying to eat each other, but at least she's having fun, I suppose.

Clara breaks away and whispers something in the guy's ear, then comes to talk to me.

"Hunter and I are going to get out of here," she says. "You'll be okay to get home, right?"

I nod, forcing a smile. "Sure."

She smooches my cheek and grabs Hunter's hand. The two of them disappear within seconds. It's almost impressive, or rather, it would be if it weren't so annoying.

I heft a sigh and glance down at my empty drink. I'll grab one more for the road. There's a bottle of wine waiting for me at home, and if I'm remembering correctly, I've got a big bag of Doritos in one of the cupboards.

I squeeze my way to the bar and order another drink, swaying to the music. The bartender, a gorgeous redhead covered in tattoos, hands me my drink, and I take a sip absently as she keys it into the till.

Only then do I realize that my wallet disappeared from the club at the same time that Clara did.

∼

Gabriel

The bass vibrates through the floor, but it's a lot quieter up here than it is in the club below. I am sitting in my usual booth at Fiamma, my favorite club out of all the bars my family owns in the city. It's a good place to conduct business. There's little chance of being overheard, and my father would never set foot here, preferring to keep to the old drinking holes he and his friends spent their youths in, shrouded in a cloud of cigar smoke.

To my left sits Vito Gambaro, my best friend since grade school. He will be my consigliere, my right-hand man, once I take control of the syndicate. For now, he's my most trusted confidant, and the only person in the organization who I know without a doubt expresses loyalty to me and me alone.

Across from us sit Dom Rozzi and Diego Berdini. Dom is a good capo but takes his pleasures in the simple things in life, not caring much for politics or strategy. He thinks with his muscles and his dick, and doesn't like any problem he can't fix with his fists. True to form, Dom is staring lecherously at a pair of long legs that saunter past. Diego chuckles.

I lean toward Vito. "Is the meeting set?"

Vito glances at Diego, but the older man is too distracted by Dom's drooling to notice our sidebar. "Yeah. They'll meet with us at the docks tomorrow."

I sip my whiskey. "Good."

"Are you sure this is a good idea?" Vito asks.

I send him a dark look.

Vito is immune to the power of my glares and leans closer, lowering his voice. "Your father will be livid if he finds out."

My father is the don of the Belluci crime family and Vito is right—he will be downright furious if he learns that I am making plays behind his back. Unfortunately, it is a necessary evil. If my father has his way, he will bring ruin to the family and end a generations-long dynasty of power. He has always been a greedy man, but as of late, his greed has begun to consume him. I intend to prevent that from destroying us all.

"He will come around to see that it is the best move for the business," I state. "He may act like one, but my father is not a fool."

I hope that is the truth. Lately, his actions have shown otherwise.

We Bellucis command the majority of the docks, a vital piece of real estate for any criminal organization. The Irish mafia, run by the Walsh family, controls a small chunk for themselves. My father has been gearing up to wrest control of the docks from them entirely but cannot see why that is a bad idea. The Walshes are strong, and I suspect that they have another power backing them as they have had a recent surge in resources and capabilities. The don is blind to this.

He refuses to think of the Walshes as anything other than the tick on our back that they have been for the past couple of decades.

"What are you two whispering about?" Diego interjects.

I look over at the older man. His dyed black hair is slicked back from his forehead, and fine lines furrow his face. Beneath his suit, his arms and chest are covered in faded tattoos, a map of the tumultuous life he has led for so many years.

Diego is like an uncle to me, and I wish I could trust him as he'd be a valuable ally to have. Unfortunately, he has been a close friend of my father's since they were teenagers.

"Vito was just reminding me of the time that he and I snuck in here when we were kids," I reply.

Diego laughs, exposing teeth yellowed by decades of smoking. "I remember that. I had to come down and throw you both out on your asses because the bouncers were too afraid to deal with you."

"Everyone was," Vito chimes in. "Nobody wanted to be the one to give the twelve-year-olds beer, but Gabe knew how to throw his weight around, even then."

"You two were always getting into trouble." Diego leans back, grinning. He nods to me. "You were the king of the castle before anyone even handed you the keys."

I chuckle. I guess nothing has changed.

The waitress comes by with our next round of drinks, and the conversation soon moves onto the upcoming boxing match. This divides the table as Vito backs the more experienced Russian powerhouse, whereas Diego and Dom maintain that the Bronx-bred newcomer will easily unseat Vito's champion.

I don't care much for boxing or sports in general. They are just distractions. A distracted man is an easy one to fool.

I glance over the balcony at the throbbing dance floor below. My gaze catches on a brunette in a sparkly silver dress that splinters the flashing strobe lights. I saw her face in the crowd earlier as I cut through the dance floor, and I remember thinking she was stunning.

I watch as she dances with wild abandon, occasionally swishing her long wavy hair into the faces of the other clubgoers, but she doesn't seem to notice or care. Even from this distance, I can see that her body is built for sin, and my cock stirs as I watch her hands glide over her cleavage and hips.

Diego's voice cuts through my leer. "Gabriel, did you hear me?"

I look back to him, blinking. Who is the distracted one now?

"No," I answer. "What did you say?"

He leans closer, glancing out of the booth to make sure nobody is close enough to overhear. "Your father wanted me to check that you know your role in the upcoming merger."

We always speak in veiled terms when in public, and I understand his meaning.

I nod. "It is not complicated."

My father's plans never are. He lacks the elegance of strategy that my grandfather employed while consolidating our power decades prior. The don's plan to harness control of the docks involves mostly muscle and firepower, the only strategy being to kill the Irish before they can kill us. I am meant to conduct this strategy from the north, while our other forces push in from the east and west.

"I know you have your misgivings, but this acquisition will weaken our competitors enough to push them out of business," he says. "You'll see."

The only thing I will see if this plan goes ahead is a long and costly mob war. One is already brewing due to my father's machinations, and attacking the docks will pour gasoline on the smoldering embers.

Luckily, before that can happen, I intend to meet with the Irish leader's youngest son, Damien Walsh. We will strike a tentative peace while the Bellucis still have the upper hand that will hopefully bring a little order back to our streets. My father has wasted enough men and money on this already, and when I bring news of the arrangement to him, I am hoping he will have enough sense to see it is the best solution.

The trick will be in arranging this truce without drawing Damien's suspicion. If he thinks an attack is imminent, it could spook him and make him unpredictable. I need him to be calm and malleable.

Before I can answer Diego, my phone begins to ring. I check the screen and my jaw tightens. It's the big man himself.

"Excuse me," I say, exiting the booth.

I make my way to the back alley, where it is quieter. I lean against the bricks and look at my phone, considering whether it would be worth it not to answer. No, I decide, I need to be on his good side.

"Hello, Father," I answer.

"Where the fuck are you?" he growls.

"Fiamma."

"Of course. Where else would you be? It's not as if we have a war to plan, is it?"

I grit my teeth. "Do you need me?"

"I need you to remove your head from your ass and start acting like the leader you're going to be one day," he bites out. I can just picture his face turning purple, as it always does when he gets wound up. "I'm beginning to think that maybe Felicity is right. Maybe you're not going to be ready to take over when the time comes."

Felicity Harrow, that scheming witch. My father has been absolutely obsessed with the woman for the past two years, and you can pinpoint the decline in his senses from the second she walked through the door. My father has always let his dick do more of his thinking than any man should—Felicity was just the first woman to capitalize on it. She quickly moved from mistress to advisor, spreading her influence like a virus.

"I'm with Diego," I reply, trying to keep my voice calm when all I want to do is scream at him. "We are going over the plans for the merger."

That takes some of the wind from his sails. "Why didn't you say that?" he grumbles. "I swear to God you take pleasure in pissing me off."

I ignore his question. "Do you need me to come to your office?"

"No. Just wanted to check to make sure you weren't fucking around."

In other words, he was hoping I would be so he could flex his authority a little. We play this game often.

"Great. Tell Felicity I say hi."

I hang up the phone and head back into the club, consciously trying to relax my jaw. How I am even related to that man is beyond me. He is shameless in his arrogance.

It will be his downfall.

Back inside, I stop next to the wall before heading back to the VIP section to quickly check my emails. With everything happening, it can be easy to forget that I have a lot of responsibilities besides keeping my father in check. He largely leaves the running of our legitimate businesses to me, claiming that he finds the work tedious and beneath him. In truth, he just doesn't have the head for it. If he can't shoot it or fuck it, he's not interested.

My spine tingles and I glance up from my phone. My gaze connects with the girl I watched dance earlier, and her eyes widen as she realizes she has been caught staring.

I hold her gaze, heat flooding my bones. Her lips are a bold, juicy red. She is heavily made up, like all of the women in here, but she seems less comfortable in it somehow. Other women would smile at me, flutter their lashes, and try to lure me in to dance with them. She is just still, as though she hopes by not moving, I will not be able to see her.

Any other time, I would love to stalk that prey, to melt away her hesitance until she was putty in my hands. But not now. Now, there is business to attend to. She will have to remain a fantasy and nothing more.

I turn and climb the stairs for the VIP area, returning to my booth. I will ask Diego to reiterate the details of my father's plan even though I know them already. That way, when the don asks Diego about our meeting later, he will corroborate my story.

The men and I talk for a little longer, but even Diego's attention begins to stray towards the delights of the club. I have achieved my objective, however, so I dismiss them for the evening, and I decide that the best thing to do would be to go home and do some work. I could do work every hour of every day and still not get enough done.

Then I look down from the balcony and see *her* again. It's the girl in the glimmering dress, but she's not dancing anymore. She is at the bar, and it looks as though she is arguing with the bartender.

Interesting. I didn't peg her as the fiery type, but from her irritated gestures it looks as though I was mistaken.

Perhaps what I need tonight is not more work, but a little distraction. And I know exactly how I am going to get it.

Click here to keep reading CORRUPTED ANGEL!

MAILING LIST

Sign up to my mailing list!
New subscribers receive a FREE steamy bad boy romance novel.

Click the link below to join.
https://sendfox.com/nicolefox

ALSO BY NICOLE FOX

Kovalyov Bratva Duet

Gilded Cage (Book 1)

Gilded Tears (Book 2)

Princes of Ravenlake Academy (Bully Romance)

Can be read as standalones!

Cruel Prep

Cruel Academy

Cruel Elite

Bratva Crime Syndicate

Can be read in any order!

Lies He Told Me

Scars He Gave Me

Sins He Taught Me

Belluci Mafia Trilogy

Corrupted Angel (Book 1)

Corrupted Queen (Book 2)

Corrupted Empire (Book 3)

De Maggio Mafia Duet

Devil in a Suit (Book 1)

Devil at the Altar (Book 2)

Kornilov Bratva Duet

Married to the Don (Book 1)

Til Death Do Us Part (Book 2)

Heirs to the Bratva Empire

Can be read in any order!

Kostya

Maksim

Andrei

Tsezar Bratva

Nightfall (Book 1)

Daybreak (Book 2)

Russian Crime Brotherhood

Can be read in any order!

Owned by the Mob Boss

Unprotected with the Mob Boss

Knocked Up by the Mob Boss

Sold to the Mob Boss

Stolen by the Mob Boss

Trapped with the Mob Boss

Volkov Bratva

Broken Vows (Book 1)

Broken Hope (Book 2)

Broken Sins *(standalone)*

Other Standalones

Vin: A Mafia Romance

Box Sets

Bratva Mob Bosses (Russian Crime Brotherhood Books 1-6)

Tsezar Bratva (Tsezar Bratva Duet Books 1-2)

Heirs to the Bratva Empire

The Mafia Dons Collection

The Don's Corruption